DARIEN:
GUARDIAN ANGEL
OF JESUS

DARIEN: GUARDIAN ANGEL OF JESUS

ROGER ELWOOD

WORD PUBLISHING
DALLAS LONDON VANCOUVER MELBOURNE

PUBLISHED BY WORD PUBLISHING,
DALLAS, TEXAS

Book design by Mark McGarry
Set in Minion

LIBRARY OF CONGRESS CATALOGING-IN-PUBLICATION DATA

Elwood, Roger
Darien: Guardian Angel of Jesus / Roger Elwood
p. cm.
Includes bibliographical references.
ISBN 0-8499-1174-5
1. Jesus Christ—Fiction.
2. Bible. N.T.—History of Biblical events—Fiction.
3. Guardian Angels—Fiction. I. Title.
PS3555.L85D36 1994
813'.54—dc20
94-3582 CIP

PRINTED IN THE UNITED STATES OF AMERICA

4 5 6 7 8 9 BVG 9 8 7 6 5 4 3 2 1

To Tom Williams,
for giving my books
the best of all covers.

We not only live among men, but there are airy hosts, blessed spectators, sympathetic lookers-on, that see and know and appreciate our thoughts and feelings and acts.

HENRY WARD BEECHER
Royal Truths

ACKNOWLEDGEMENTS

When all of us realized the striking potential scope that existed with *Darien: Guardian Angel of Jesus,* we knew it would not prove achievable in any reasonable respect without the Lord's ever-constant impetus and encouragement as the manuscript progressed.

Accordingly, we praise the Lord for what He gave us along the way, which was that wonderful peace that truly does passeth all understanding, peace He was merciful enough to bestow upon everyone involved with *Darien: Guardian Angel of Jesus,* from yours truly, the author, even when certain forces would try to derail my determination; to Joey Paul, who is without question the most intuitive of all editors; to brilliant and dedicated Tom Williams, the very best of art directors in Christian publishing; and to a number of others who similarly caught the vision of what we wanted to accomplish with this particular book, including my warmest appreciation to Laura Kendall, a very special friend and associate at Word Publishing who understands me as an author and a human being.

At least two others at Word deserve recognition: Pat Bianco, one of God's most shining gifts to my sometimes chaotic life, with its manifold, often self-inflicted wounds; and Lyn Wheeler, who must be described similarly. These two are the truest of dear friends as well as the best possible business associates, to whom I have been related by the shed blood of Jesus the Christ, our Savior and Lord.

A large number of other individuals provided encouragement and insight as I wrote the manuscript, relative to the details of the story itself, and to my particular state of spirituality at the time: Dr. Harold Lindsell is certainly chief among them; my long-time pal Marjorie Holmes, whose *Two from Galilee* and subsequent books have been an inspiration, to be sure, and who has the most genuinely sunny personality of anyone I have ever met in my fifty-one years of living; Dot and Bill Conover of Friends to Israel Mission; and Rick Pritikin of Thomas Nelson Publishing.

Though not directly involved in this latest book, Warren Wiersbe nevertheless has been a pivotal influence. Without him, Darien probably would never be reappearing as a character. Joan Winmill Brown was very helpful as well in this regard. So was Paul Schumacher, a truly fine gospel singer and one of my closest friends, who died in 1993 of colon cancer.

One could say that there are no new real truths on the map of human experience but, rather, just those existing truths that are waiting to be discovered or rediscovered. I hope that *Darien: Guardian Angel of Jesus* succeeds in presenting some fresh and stimulating ideas that have more than a measure of inerrant biblical truth in them, and in such a way as to challenge your mind, your heart, and your very soul. If any of this proves to be the case, then the long hours, days, weeks, and months spent at my computer as I wrote this book will have been worth more than words can portray.

One of the special joys of writing novels set in the New Testament period is the blessed opportunity to travel back, mentally, and perhaps even spiritually, to those most remarkable days, and trod, in that manner, some of the very steps that Jesus Christ took throughout His earthly ministry.

All of us who have become involved with this book have been able to share that precious privilege with which the angel named Darien has been singularly blessed . . . to be at the side of Jesus.

PREFACE

My original novel entitled *Angelwalk,* which introduced the character of Darien, an unfallen angel, frequently has been compared to *The Screwtape Letters* by C. S. Lewis. It was actually written as something of a modern *Pilgrim's Progress,* which might be called the fictional autobiography of Darien, an unfallen angel who was among the majority of angels refusing to join Lucifer's rebellion and who chose, along with countless thousands like him, to remain true to his Creator.

True to his Creator?

Yes, that he was, and that he is, but *Angelwalk* also showed that Darien was assailed by doubts about whether Satan's prophesied fate in the lake of fire could be deserved, in view of its severity. In the colloquial vernacular, Darien wondered, *Was Satan really such a bad guy?* Throughout *Angelwalk,* Darien's journey brings him in contact with various demonic entities, such as those in charge of countless millions of abortions around the world, including the greed of many of those involved in this bloody and dehumanizing industry, as well as demons behind numerous other corrupt acts and morally bankrupt philosophies. But *Angelwalk* is ultimately a novel of triumph because Darien is able to conquer his doubts when presented with the ghastly truth about an angel with whom he once had been close. In time, Darien comes to realize the truth in a climactic encounter in the midst of hell itself.

This latest book brings Darien back to the narrative and shows us his most memorable assignment of all, given to him specifically by Almighty God . . . *being at the side of Jesus as His guardian.* Darien is there every step of the way for the purpose of seeing that nothing—human or demonic—harms the Lord's flesh-and-blood body until that body must be sacrificed for the sins of the human race.

This proves to be a time of enormous triumph as well as edification for Darien. He is going to experience the greatest joy imaginable . . . until he is brought face to face with the death of that earthly body, for it is at this point that he is to discover how powerless he is, and yet somehow he has to avoid questioning the wisdom of his Creator. At the scene of the crucifixion atop the hill of Golgotha, this angel must survive a personal crisis every bit as severe as what he endured in *Angelwalk.*

Finally, while I unreservedly accept the Bible as God's inspired Word, inerrant and infallible, I do have to acknowledge that different interpretations are possible when you are dealing with certain passages, not in terms of moral issues such as delineated in the first chapter of Romans or with the Ten Commandments, as another example, or in Leviticus; but the fact is that, in matters of prophecy, it has been otherwise for centuries. Which certainly makes writing a novel somewhat perplexing from time to time, forcing the novelist to make choices for plot-oriented origins. One instance that I can point to is certainly Matthew 27:52–53: "And the graves were opened: and many bodies of the saints who had fallen asleep were raised; and coming out of the graves after His resurrection, they went into the holy city and appeared to many." Some Bible commentaries pass over this altogether, while others, such as *Clark's Commentary,* explain away any basis for the supernatural manifestation of divine intervention and, instead, make this passage metaphorical.

In *Darien: Guardian Angel of Jesus,* the supernatural premise is upheld. Most commentaries squarely support the miraculous interpretation as opposed to the rationalistic and metaphorical.

My own rendering is based on how the following works look at the verses indicated: *The Life Application Bible* (commentary portions); *Oxford New International Standard Scofield Study Bible* (commentary portions); *Matthew Henry's Commentary for Today's Reader*; *Ellicott's Bible Commentary*; and *Jamieson, Fausset and Brown's Commentary.* Various versions of the Bible handle these verses without ambiguity: *The Living Bible,* the *New International Version,* the *New King James Version,* the *Master Study Bible,* the *New American Standard,* and so on.

Other instances required much prayer and research in order to remain faithful to Scripture or, where it is silent, to interpolate scenes not inconsistent with the rest. Consider this: Did Jesus have, as a Child, the ability to perform miracles? Did His divine intelligence manifest itself prior to His appearance, at the age of twelve, before the religious leaders in the temple, where He impressed them greatly?

After consultation with Warren Wiersbe, Harold Lindsell, and others, I concluded that Jesus had the ability to do miracles but did not exercise it before turning the water into wine at the marriage feast at Cana.

Second, I recall a conversation with professor Walter Elwell at Wheaton College; he said that Jesus' intelligence would not have suddenly manifested itself at the temple. That may have been the first *public* display, but there surely were others, of a more private nature, with family members and friends as well as one-on-one encounters with strangers He would meet. If, today, some very young children can excel at the use of computers, enter college before most of their peers are out of grade school, and become prodigies in other ways, it should not be surprising that the Son of God would manifest an even more extraordinary capacity to understand, to analyze, and to speak on a level unmatched by any of His earthly contemporaries.

CAST OF CHARACTERS

Aaron A dedicated, long-time scribe who is able to uncover at least a portion of the truth about Jesus and issues a warning that few, if any, actually heed.

Abiathar A merchant who befriends Benaiah.

Adultery The fallen angel who was charged by Satan with the task of breaking up marriages as well as entire families and also with helping to spread a variety of sexually transmitted diseases.

Andrew One of the twelve apostles.

Baktar An extremely wealthy Egyptian who befriends Jesus, Mary, and Joseph and helps them return to their homeland.

Balthasar One of the three Magi from the land of ancient Persia who is directed by God to visit the two-year-old Jesus.

Benaiah A blind eighteen-year-old boy.

Benjamin Another scribe, one who rejects Jesus as the Messiah.

Caiaphas The Sanhedrin's high priest and the most vocal antagonist-critic of Jesus; his anger is founded in personal jealousy and apprehension that masquerades instead as religious indignation.

Darien An unfallen angel given a new assignment by almighty God.

Despair A fallen angel, at times a regretful one, dedicated to spreading melancholy and depression.

Durong Another fallen angel, with various duties meted out by Satan.

ELIAS	An insurrectionist sympathizer looking to Jesus to help overthrow the rule of Rome over the Holy Lands.
ESTHER	A wealthy woman listening to Jesus during the Sermon on the Mount who comes to a saving knowledge of Jesus as her Redeemer.
GABRIEL	Another unfallen angel.
GASPAR	Another of the three Magi, roughly the equivalent of Thomas, intellectual and sometimes cynical.
HAKKI	An Egyptian who meets the angel Darien as he lies dying from injuries sustained during an earthquake.
HEROD THE GREATER	The influential but increasingly dictatorial ruler whose decree sends Jesus and His parents fleeing to Egypt; a man once great but ultimately destroyed by his passion for corruption.
JOHN THE APOSTLE	The youngest of the twelve, and the only one attuned to the presence of Darien and other angels.
JOHN THE BAPTIST	The great prophet, quite unlike those who preceded him; he insistently announces the coming of the long-awaited Messiah, and then baptizes Him in the Jordan River.
JOSEPH	The earthly stepfather of Jesus, a kindly man who lived until shortly before the crucifixion of Jesus.
JOSEPH OF ARIMATHEA	An influential member of the community who sides with Nicodaemus to try and get Jesus released instead of Barabbas.
JUDAS	The apostle who betrays Jesus.
LEGION	The most powerful of the many thousands of fallen angels, second only to Satan himself.
MARY	The earthly mother of Jesus, who knows that her beloved Son is extraordinary but, for many years, looks at Him as through a glass darkly, not quite perceiving the full truth of His incarnation.
MATTHEW	The former tax-gatherer, who must overcome the stigma attached to men who make their living in the way he used to do.
MELCHIOR	The third Magi.
MICHAEL	Unfallen archangel, the successor to Lucifer.

MILFULT The fallen angel in charge of propagating abortions worldwide, but with particular emphasis on the United States.

NATHANIEL The brother of Mary, once bitterly ashamed of her pregnancy because it clearly happened before her marriage to Joseph.

NICODAEMUS A wealthy, respected member of the Sanhedrin who becomes an early acquaintance of Jesus and later desperately attempts to stop the blood-lust and jealousy that seem to be motivating Caiaphas and a majority of the other religious leaders, blinding them to the reality of a Man whom they should be worshiping instead of so callously condemning to the most torturous death.

OBSERVER The tragically misguided fallen angel who became Satan's personal journalist, recording history from the devil's perspective, often an unwilling participant in evil and sin, but one chained to his master in much the same way as a drug addict is to cocaine, heroin, and other substances.

PONTIUS PILATUS Roman proconsul-governor of Israel, whose decision to wash his hands of the blood of Jesus the Christ is to haunt him for the rest of his life and change his relationship with his wife until finally, he has to impose a sentence on her that is harder than sending brave soldiers to their deaths.

PROCULA PILATUS Wife of the proconsul-governor, and the dreamer of a dream that seems to foretell her punishment and her husband's if they support the venomous demand of the mob that Jesus be crucified.

REBEKKAH Midwife to the mother of Jesus, a streetwalker who has deceived herself into thinking that her way of life is not sinful.

PETER One of the apostles, by far the most headstrong.

STEDFAST A guardian unfallen angel.

THADDAEUS One of the twelve apostles.

THOMAS The intellectual apostle to whom everything must be

proven, later to become one of the most effective witnesses for Jesus.

TORMENT The fallen angel behind much of the world's pain and suffering, whether on battlefields everywhere or, two thousand years later, in abortion clinics and through the gay liberation movement.

VIRTUE An unfallen angel.

PROLOGUE

And there are also many other things that Jesus did, which if they were written one by one, I suppose that even the world itself could not contain the books that would be written . . .

JOHN THE APOSTLE
John 21:25

THE MIND of God.

In the beginning was God, and then all that came to be. The galaxies throughout creation issued from Him.

Without Him there would be nothing. He spoke, and it was. He thought, and it came to be.

He conceived of angels, and they were. Before everything else except Father, Son, and Holy Spirit, they lived.

Before a single bird flew, before even one plant grew on earth, before there were oceans and forests and air to breathe, before the sun rose by day and the moon reflected its light by night, angels added their magnificence to the heavenly home of a triune Creator.

Oh, the songs they sang! The music they played! The joy they gave to the Three-in-One who took them from holy mind into the realm of iridescent being!

Their process of birth changed the history of what was to be for all of eternity. First, one angel, then ten thousand upon ten thousand.

Ah, that original creature, so perfect it seemed but another extension of deity, so sublime in purity, so loving in adoration, so total in devotion.

The son of the morning . . .

It was as though the Trinity had added another member. Each took part in the forming of this shimmering, glorious new entity.

The Holy Spirit gave him a will, a separate will with a touch of holiness, a will of loyalty that should have been unencumbered, unquestioning, standing in the presence of the Trinity, ready at that very early moment to do what each of its members wished.

The Son gave this son surpassing intelligence, a mind capable of acts second only to that of which Father God Himself was capable.

And the Father, forming the last detail in His mind, took a mental paintbrush and sketched in something else . . . beauty.

A will, a mind, great beauty.

All that was necessary for the son of the morning, created in the mental recesses of holiness, was for the Father to speak, to cause him to be, to take him from thought to a sweeping majesty capable of soaring from one end of heaven to another.

And so he was born, this highest of all, this Lucifer—in no more than an instant—a single speck of sand on the beach of forever . . . launched from *inside* God! The mind of God became the womb of God, and His Word was mother of this creature's being.

I declare that you are! the Father spoke.

Thus it began, the formation of a heavenly chorus, one angel at a time.

God thought, and they were, the others dazzling, like Lucifer, but not the *magnificus* that he was.

God spoke, and they came forth into the serene splendor of that immutable place.

They knew few bounds.

There was little of which they were not capable. They could not create, as did the Trinity. And they had no degree of omnipotence, omniscience, or other such qualities as Father, Son, and Holy Spirit possessed.

But they were eternal.

They could not die.

They never knew illness or age.

From the first instant of being, they would always be.

Then God created more life, life intended to be eternal as all else in His holy realm . . . The beginning of earth and all other planets.

Life breathed.

Life walked, and flew, and swam.

Life lifted up its orchestra of adulation to its beneficent Creator, in harmony with Him and every other created form.

Yet, emerging from the shared joy of the Trinity, Lucifer, unlike so many others of his kind, brought to heaven the very first tears.

He who had shone so brightly in the mind of almighty God, his Creator, eventually caused only spiritual darkness . . . and searing punishment where once bountiful reward was dispensed.

Sorrow came in on the resplendent wings of Lucifer; then it followed him from heaven with a third of the angels chained to a will that was corrupted by his majesty, and the remainder of the shining hosts of glory watched their fellow beings begin a long and terrible journey that was destined to end in misery for them all at the dreaded end of times, plunging the insurrectionists into the flames without end.

In rebellion's wake stood an angel named Darien, watching, awaiting whatever the future held, whatever command his holy and loving Creator gave, questions beginning within him, answers that would take this unfallen one through epochs of history.

And finally, it would be at the side of Jesus the Christ, God's only begotten Son, serving as His angelic guardian, that the last fragment of what Darien sought would be provided in a sudden and glorious revelation reaching beyond the vastness of time and space to the very gates of heaven itself . . .

PART I

While shepherds watched their flocks by night,
All seated on the ground,
The angel of the Lord came down,
And glory shone around.

NAHUM TATE
While Shepherds Watched

As Darien left heaven on his journey to earth, he knew that, behind him, others of his kind were ready to sing in exultation, ready for that most singular of all moments when the Christ Child would be born of a virgin after the Holy Spirit had come upon her in the middle of the night and Deity miraculously became an embryo in her womb.

The long-prophesied Messiah was at last born to the people of Israel who, though expecting Him because of the foretellings of their great prophets, would largely remain blind to the reality of His presence among them!

Darien could scarce contain the joy that was flooding through him. His whole being shimmered with it. The beginning of a new covenant . . .

A well-nigh unfathomable fusion between the infinite and eternal, and that which was finite and temporal!

Darien knew that much and just a little more. He knew that the Son had taken on human flesh in His mother's womb and would soon come forth as a baby.

Looking back at heaven, Darien saw, for a moment in eternity, that his home would not be the same while the Son of God was on earth, one member of the Godhead now transplanted to a rebellious and sinful world. Mortality was to be wrapped like a finely stitched leather glove around what had been His transcendent glory.

Human, yet divine!

Yes, the Son would seem every bit as human as any man, and He would be that . . . human truly. But the very core of Him remained absolute divinity, which was now co-existing with humanness. He was a man, and He was God in the same form.

What others of flesh and blood would see was a reflection of what they themselves were, frail men and women; at least that is what Jesus would seem to vast numbers of them. What heaven saw, however, was a changeless member of the triune Godhead, beyond the touch of the many moral and spiritual afflictions that sin had brought en masse, *a member who, having participated in the creation of everything that existed, now became, in a strange and beautiful way, one of His own little ones.*

The greatest of mysteries, the most wonderful of truths!

The majesty of this, the complexity of it, was not lost on Darien, an angel who seemed to have been questing all his life. This angel paused for a millisecond in the midst of his journey as he pondered the profound nature of what was taking place.His omnipotent Father becoming a helpless infant!The very God who smashed the army of a powerful pharaoh of mighty Egypt was soon to be born incarnate in a manger, on a humble bed of damp straw, joined by horses and donkeys and a few chickens because there was no place for Him elsewhere. And yet King Herod had a palace; the emperor of Rome lived in one as well. The servants of both had finer accommodations than that very basic manger. And yet One who, with a single spoken judgment, could have swept away all of whatever it was that these earthly rulers possessed, became but a simple Child inside His mother as she waited for Him to come forth . . .

CHAPTER 1

No room for the Son of God! Darien exclaimed to himself with astonishment as he arrived in Bethlehem, where the Father had told him the glorious birth was to take place. *No room for the Creator of the human race! How blind human beings have been since sin entered the Garden of Eden.*

The angel decided to head without delay for the lowly stable to which God had directed him.

"*How can it be so, Father?*" he had asked just before leaving. "*They should be surrounding Him with what He deserves.*"

"*For the parents, Jesus is special,*" God reminded Darien. "*They may not as yet fully comprehend the great mysteries embodied in His birth, but they know enough to realize how extraordinary their baby's very existence is. However, it is nothing either of them can talk about, for none would believe what they say.*

"*To many others around Mary and Joseph, now and for years into the future, Jesus will remain a mere man, possessed of a brilliance that sets Him apart but still of mortal flesh and only that. A very few, including His chosen apostles, will perceive something else about Him, but that is all.*"

Darien saw how dusty the little village of Bethlehem was, how loud and crowded, especially at the *agora,* the marketplace that was the hub of many of the villages and towns of that region. Various craftsmen sold their handcrafted wares: Makers of farm and other tools, potters and weavers of baskets, silversmiths, and others were present, most of them but the latest in a long flow of generations of families whose male members had continued with the same trade that had been taught for many centuries.

Small children were taken to the *agora* by one or both of their parents, this again owing more to tradition than any other motivation but also to practicality, for the sooner sons and daughters became accustomed to the routine of everyday life, the more effective they would be later in their lives.

Beggars also were much in evidence; the blind, the lame, the elderly who had come from poor families. They were hoping for acts of charity from some of those merchants and customers crowding the marketplace.

The angel saw something else that fascinated him.

A woman had run into the marketplace, screaming, "*Adon, Adon,* my husband! I did not do as you suspect."

She was calling her husband "Master, Master," or she might have said, "*Baal, Baal*" instead of *Adon, Adon,* which was a similar term.

Darien stood still, fascinated while observing a vignette revealing the culture of that region; it was one of many he would encounter.

Adultery . . .

The woman was suspected of adultery, and she would be made to submit to a trial of sorts in front of everyone in Bethlehem.

Yet no jury gathered to judge her, no one but the local Hebrew priest who solemnly handed her a cup containing a bitter-tasting drink. If, after drinking the liquid in it, she became ill, she would be pronounced guilty and stoned. However, in the event that there were no measurable aftereffects, her innocence was assumed.

The woman trembled as she held the earthen cup to her lips.

No one spoke. It seemed that no one breathed, either, especially her husband, who prayed that he was wrong, for he loved her deeply.

She downed every drop of whatever the liquid was and tossed the cup on the ground, where it broke in half.

Seconds passed.

Any time now, she would start to choke and bend over in pain if she was the adulteress her husband reluctantly had claimed.

A minute went by.

Followed by another. And another after that.

The woman smiled triumphantly and turned toward her husband, who was now walking triumphantly up to her, his arms outstretched. The two embraced and began to kiss passionately, and everyone in the marketplace cheered.

A short while later, merchants approached the couple and, in jubilation, offered them free items from their shops.

Then, toward evening, a celebration began in which everyone participated, partly out of relief but also due to the guilt many of them felt for believing the story of adultery in the first place.

The woman survived, the marriage grew stronger, and an injustice was avoided by the direct providence of almighty God.

"*Father, it was good this poor woman was saved,*" Darien observed in communion with the Creator.

"*It should not have been otherwise. She did nothing wrong. Only gossip and rumor caused her plight. The truth was needed here, and the truth was what came out.*"

"*Will the husband and wife become closer than ever now?*" the angel asked hopefully.

"*Oh, they will, Darien, for you have just touched upon the transcendent good that will come out of all this. Those two will have a strong marriage for many years, and many children and grandchildren will give joy to their lives.*"

CHAPTER 2

As Darien continued through Bethlehem, he noticed a few pleasant-looking whitewashed homes—mostly flat-roofed, single-story structures, some of which were made at least partially of sun-baked brick. Typical middle-class families were living in them, a majority with animals in their sideyards, goats and sheep and chickens primarily, some of these the pets of their children but most serving as sources of sustenance—meat, eggs, or milk.

The angel also glimpsed occasional larger residences set some distance back from the rest, these belonging to the few wealthy Jews who had decided to settle in Bethlehem to escape the frenetic activity of the cities.

As for the poor, with no housing whatsoever, they were generally to be found on the outskirts of tiny Bethlehem, usually sprawled in ditches or under trees or just collapsed in the middle of the road.

The family of the Son of Man being treated not much better than the commonest of Bethlehem's street beggars, Darien thought, still stunned by the reality that was unfolding in spite of his having been warned about it in advance by almighty God Himself, *and into this ragtag environment was born . . .*

He stopped himself, trying to obviate a combination of anger and sorrow that was threatening to explode inside him.

Mary and Joseph had had to go from place to place and were turned away unfeelingly from all but one, Darien told himself. *May that one hospitable, kindly man, so different from others in this same community, be given a chance for redemption so he can spend eternity in one of the Father's many mansions!*

As the angel was passing through those narrow streets, he noticed two women at a hand mill. The one on the left was married and wore a headdress decorated with coins, an outer garment with long sleeves which she had rolled partway up her arm, and beneath it a quilted jacket. On the right was an unmarried woman wearing a white veil over her cap, which had a chain of coins hanging from it.

Grinding was traditionally a woman's job—virtually all men of that time considered it humiliating—in preparation for baking and cooking. Since all cooking was done in the morning, the grinding was accomplished at night, when the woman worked long enough to make enough flour for a full day's use.

Darien was fascinated by the sight of both women working together with a single handle, each having placed one hand above the other. For a few minutes they stopped, resting their arms, and then continued an obligation of family life that had been going on for thousands of years.

At last, the angel came upon the destination he had sought since leaving heaven; he stood outside for a moment, surveying the meager accommodations the young family had been forced to accept.

This particular stable, more than others he had glimpsed earlier, was the lowliest of structures in that tiny village, not on a par with even the ramshackle caravansaries that served the needs of numerous weary travelers passing through that region. These were essentially rambling buildings with inn-like quarters on the second floor over musky stables where camels and asses and goats spent the night, along with anyone else who could somehow ignore the odors.

Wealthy visitors were the ones who commanded just about all the rooms situated above the stables, rooms which, despite their tiny size, at least were intrinsically more private than the stables below, where groups of people shared space with the beasts inside and on the courtyard. Privacy was an instant casualty for most of the impoverished travelers who utilized any of the caravansaries. It simply did not exist except for the rich, quartered above the stables, and even theirs was achieved only by hanging blankets over the otherwise open doorways. In this way, those blessed with money, livestock, and land could keep out the noise and odors of a dirty courtyard, to whatever extent was possible.

The Son of God should be resting in the finest of earthly quarters, Darien thought, *for He has stepped down from heaven to the earth itself, not for His benefit or glory but for the redemption of sinners.*

Amazed at the near-poverty-stricken circumstances, Darien walked slowly inside, having no idea what to expect.

Peace and love.

The interior of that one little stable seemed an oasis of blessed human warmth, contrary to so much else in the immediate area with its surfeit of noises and general and usually frenetic activity.

The angel found Mary and Joseph stretched out in the hay, waiting for the birth of a son, a miracle.

Dear people, when you both come to realize just who it is that most blessed Mary will bring into a sin-ravaged world, the angel thought to himself, *nothing will ever be the same for either of you two again!*

Darien smiled as he thought of the blessed truth embodied in that tiny, pinkish form of young flesh about to appear. Not even the mothers of Abraham, Isaac, Jacob, Daniel, David, and Solomon were as privileged as Mary was.

You have the Son of God in your womb! he wanted to shout to her. You were entered by the Holy Spirit one evening, and a new life was created, a life beyond anything you could possibly realize right now.

Darien shivered briefly, awe filling him.

He could feel Jesus *moving* as though God's blessed Son were instead inside himself and not in the midst of His mother's gentle warmth.

Weeping!

Like no human being could imagine the act! The angel sensed the tears that were being shed.

The incarnate Deity wept.

"*But why, Jesus?*" the angel asked.

"*I know what you do not,*" the reply came. "*I see what is ahead. The joy of this blessed birth will last for a season and no more.*"

. . . *for a season and no more.*

Darien fought the sense of sorrow carried by those few words. In a moment of great joy they seemed so out of place, and he loathed their implications.

"*Tell me, please,*" he begged, hoping he had misunderstood their weightiness. "*Prepare me.*"

"*If you knew, you would not be able to contain what you would feel. It is My love for you that makes Me withhold what the Father, Son and Holy Spirit have realized since the beginning of time.*"

"*But I could, Jesus, oh, I truly could,*" Darien insisted. "*I am of much stronger will now than during that earlier period.*"

There had been a time when he could not have uttered such words, for any like this would have been untrue—but no longer.

"*I know what Satan is like,*" the angel added quite seriously. "*I no longer harbor any of the slightest illusions about him. For I have trod that path called Angelwalk, and I have seen what You wanted me to see, and I cannot doubt the truth ever again."*

Darien was concerned that Jesus not misunderstand him as he was then, not as he had been before.

"I no longer have any doubts," he said, *"doubts that Satan truly deserves the punishment that is his . . . preordained by a just Creator."*

The tears stopped.

The baby Jesus moved.

The moment of birth was nigh as His flesh-and-blood mother cried out.

Darien could not move, mesmerized by the glorious miracle that was about to take place in such an unlikely spot.

Divinity was, in an instant, entering the world as a blood-smeared body, just like any other child.

"Listen to your Father, anxious angel . . ." Jesus the Christ told him lovingly. *"Listen well, My guardian."*

Darien could scarcely cope with that thought.

"How can I be the guardian of Someone divine?" he persisted. *"Surely I am not worthy of being what You say."*

He thought of Stedfast, who had been devoted to comforting men, women, and children on the verge of death but also to helping them at other times.

Ordinary flesh-and-blood people . . .

But not the Son of the living God!

I am to do that, Darien told himself, *not Stedfast or Virtue or Kindness or any of my brethren.*

Jehovah, God Himself, interceded then, speaking from heaven to stem this angel's anguished entreaties.

"I, who created you, must have your trust, which only you can give, for I cannot force it upon you."

Darien knelt before the bulging womb of a virgin.

"You have it, Father," he said with great emotion.

"Take the hand of My Son, faithful Darien," God asked of him. *"It is truly time now for what will come about this day."*

Darien reached out, touching the eternal spirit of Jesus with his own, gasping as a surge of pure and unsoiled emotion swept through him when he grasped the utter majesty of what was happening.

"Are you with this Child whatever happens?" God demanded in love. *"Will you stay by His side from this moment on?"*

Darien did not hesitate, his entire spirit filling with the sublimest ecstasy, far more satisfying than anything physical could have been for any human being.

"Yea, Lord!" he shouted. *"I shall be at His side without fail. Not even the legions of hell itself will ever part us."*

"Well said, good and faithful Darien," God spoke. *"One part of your journey has ended. The other is just now starting."*

The baby Jesus emerged fully then.

Through His human mother, the incarnated divine Son of God, separated from the holy Trinity, at last entered into full space-time history as He let out His first hearty flesh-and-blood cry.

"My son, my son!" His mother, Mary, cried in joy at the sight of this immaculately conceived Child.

And so said the Father as well.

CHAPTER 3

FAT-TAILED SHEEP.

This breed was easily recognized by the animals' fat, fleshy tails.

By nature, they were even more docile than other kinds. Their meat proved better tasting, and the wool was of a decidedly superior quality.

There were many such sheep in that one particular herd that one particular night. When they were brought to market a week or so later, the revenue gained from selling them at auction would be among the most substantial ever earned at one time in that entire region, providing food and clothes and other necessities for more than one family. Until then, the safety of scores of sheep, fat-tailed and otherwise, remained in the hands of just four men.

Simple shepherds kept watch over all of those fluffy, white-wooled bodies. Such men made the most basic of livings in those days, and hardly an easy one at that. They were forced to spend virtually all of their time out in the open, facing the ghastly Israeli heat of summer and the freezing temperatures of winter. Long hours dominated their lives, and a certain loneliness that was only partially alleviated by their work with the sheep.

Shepherds carried with them a club and a staff. The club, made of long-lasting oak, was about two feet long with a spiked knob at the end about the size of a large orange, very useful in defense against predators, animal or human; it hung from a strap, or girdle, around the shepherd's waist. The staff was much larger, four to six feet long, and fashioned from a peeled vine branch. Its chief value was in aiding the shepherd when he was climbing; he also used it for slashing twigs or leaves or simply for leaning on when surveying his sheep or looking over the countryside for possible danger.

Some shepherds, particularly the younger ones, also took along a sling made of twined wool, its large center portion specially reinforced to hold stones, generally small, smooth ones found in the summer in dry river beds.

Shepherds generally wore little more than a thick camel-hair cloak over their shoulders and a thin veil around their faces to protect them from wind and rain as well as the baking heat of the desert, which covered most of Judea. With the need to travel often over rocky terrain and cover substantial distances, these men, or boys as sometimes was the case, carried with them as little as could be managed, especially in terms of food, which seldom consisted of more than bread, cheese, some olives and figs, a few dates, and perhaps a small portion of raisins.

Danger was always present in the form of fierce predators that roamed the land, seeking prey they could devour; bears, jackals, and leopards as well as hyenas participated in the slaughter of other creatures, often even carrying human babies off into the dark.

In addition to such weapons as they had, shepherds often erected a sheepfold, an enclosure of stones piled high to keep out the hungry predators. Strung around the top of the enclosure were branches of thorns. There was no gate to open or close. The shepherd himself stayed in any opening, blocking any sheep from leaving.

In other instances, these dedicated men used the many caves embedded in the limestone hills that stretched from Galilee to Sinai. These were truly fine natural chambers adaptable to sheltering smaller herds from wind, rain, and freezing temperatures, as well as the predators of that region.

Violent death could come for human or animal at any time. And if the shepherd died, the sheep would be left defenseless. That barren land was periodically littered with the remains of human and animal alike.

Nevertheless, it was a living that the dedicated shepherds treasured, for these were the ones who truly loved the sheep placed in their care. Though "dumb" creatures, the sheep sensed what had happened, the danger in which their master had put himself for their welfare, and the already-present bond deepened. Each shepherd could call to a certain member of the flock by name, and that lamb would come running, usually without delay.

"*Father?*" the angel asked.

"*Yes?*" Almighty God replied.

"*If only men would follow You the way trusting sheep follow a man . . .*"

"*That would be wonderful.*"

"*If Lucifer had never—*" Darien started to say, his voice trailing off.

"The one leads to the other. I agree with you that this is an eternal tragedy. But remember this, not all sheep are obedient either. There are some who give even their loving, protective shepherd the deepest grief."

And some of the sheep were inclined to do this, which was how the term "black sheep" came into being.

Early in the history of Israel, any errant sheep happened to be black, though this was surely nothing more than a matter of coincidence. Later, other such rebellious ones proved to be as white as the rest of the flock, but that label continued to be applied to them.

Come . . .

The sheep knew that word.

They would awaken immediately or stop eating or interrupt whatever activity they happened to be doing. Just the sound of their master's familiar voice was all that was necessary. They knew nothing else but obedience.

Then they would wait, their ears cocked, their bodies scarcely breathing. The one who took care of them from the moment of their birth had spoken. Some or perhaps all of them would be called. They could only stand ready to obey, for he loved them and they loved him and would do whatever he asked.

Come, my sheep. Come to me . . .

If he spoke not a single name or two, the entire flock knew it was to respond *en masse*, not out of panic but simply because he called.

The shepherd speaks with authority but also kindness, and they follow, *Darien reminded himself. If only people did the same . . .*

He wondered for a moment if true intelligence, the kind possessed by human beings, was always the blessing it should have been. Mere lambs were more attuned to their shepherd than members of the human race were to their Creator.

Darien heard the sounds below of one of the shepherds speaking out, apparently in some momentary concern that a lamb had wandered off.

What was being said came through a language that was not heard anywhere else throughout all of Judea, a language passed down from generation to generation, not spoken between the members of a given family or the residents of a particular town or village or even between two nationalities, but was reserved, it seemed, *only* for use between shepherd and flock.

So beautiful, Darien thought. *So very beautiful . . .*

It was not entirely as though words were being used at all, but a song sung in melody only, without lyrics, a kind of urgent lullaby, extorting the lost lamb to return to the protection of its master.

The shepherd was saying he loved that little one, even as the scores of others remained present and were not in any kind of trouble or danger; yet his heart went out to this single lamb that he had noticed was missing, and this was the case without the man ever having to count, knowing the truth instead from something *inside* him, a sense of connection in some deep and abiding manner.

As You loved me, O Father, Darien thought. *You were calling my name throughout my own wanderings, assuring me that you would never leave nor forsake me. I heard Your voice often, saying, "There is a place for you, My child, after you find out what you must."*

For Darien, the shepherds he would soon encounter represented not just some hard-working individuals in the midst of what they had been doing for all of their adult lives, but something of greater profundity, the beginning of a new mission.

He would have a glorious announcement to give to that group of shepherds, words uttered by almighty God and given to him as the words' messenger, carrying them with him as though they were the essence of life itself, for when the Creator had spoken in the past, life had begun, and so it was that He was born.

The Almighty speaks, and what never was now is, Darien thought. *From His mouth I take with me in my mind that which heralds a miracle.*

This angel, blessed of God with such a mission, saw them now, feeding the peaceful flock of sheep.

Oh, what glory you will see at its very beginning! Darien whispered silently. *If you only knew how wonderful it will be.*

The four shepherds were suddenly surrounded by the brightest light any of them had ever known. They were terrified, yet the sheep, usually skittish, remained calm.

"How can they be so quiet?" one of the men said. "They seem peaceful, almost unaware of what is going on. What is happening here?"

Though their masters were upset, the sheep were not, attuned as they were to another Master altogether, for it could be said they were able to know somehow that ultimately it would not be necessary for any more of their kind to be sacrificed for the sins of mankind.

As he saw the innocent creatures below, Darien recalled what God had told him about a turning point in the future when sin at last would be no more.

"The lion shall lie down with the lamb," the Creator had said.

"What a glorious day!" Darien had exclaimed, his very being exultant in expectation.

The angels could only pulsate with joy at the anticipation of that future. They knew the leopards of Judea and the lions of Africa slay lambs such as those Darien glimpsed, if given the opportunity. But they rejoiced to know that at the end of the ages of time, the large cats would cuddle with their once-victims.

Praise Your name, O Father God, Darien prayed with much fervor. *Praise it throughout eternity.*

He smiled so warmly that the brightness of his presence seemed all the more beautiful to those below.

"Do not be afraid, for behold, I bring you good tidings of great joy, which will be to all people." Darien spoke with a stirring majesty that came through him directly from his heavenly Father.

The shepherds glanced at one another, thinking themselves perhaps on the edge of madness.

"For there is born to you this day in the city of David a Savior, who is Christ the Lord," the voice from above continued.

The men fell to their knees in fear and trembling before the sudden visitation.

"And this will be a sign to you: You shall find a Babe wrapped in swaddling cloths, lying in a manger."

One of the shepherds said, "We are the simplest of men. None of us can grasp what you say."

"You will now see a greater Shepherd than any you have ever known," Darien told them, his voice resonant in the night. *"A babe . . . in yonder Bethlehem, come from His virgin mother's womb into a world beset with sin. He will provide a path of salvation for all who fall down before Him in acceptance and adoration."*

The four men began to shout as one, *"The Messiah!"*

They were now prostrate before the shimmering being who had confronted them so unexpectedly.

"It is He of whom you speak," Darien acknowledged, aglow with the glory

of that place from which he had come. Go thence, and behold this Child. See what the Holy Spirit has wrought, for no man was the father but He.

Suddenly, joining him in that moment were a multitude of the rest of the angels come from heaven to be by his side, and singing a sublime chorus unlike any music the shepherds had ever before heard, their words rang out like ten thousand chimes, "Glory to God in the highest and on earth, peace, good will toward men."

This continued for several minutes, overwhelming these men not accustomed to anything but the nitty-gritty of hard, everyday life.

Finally, Darien and the other angels gone, the shepherds puzzled out loud among themselves.

"What is it we have seen?" the younger one asked.

"Was it a devil?" the oldest of the four speculated foolishly.

The third rubbed his chin, then said, "I felt such joy as I have never before experienced in my life. Can that come from anything evil? I felt it in my very soul. And we were told of only the Messiah."

The other two mumbled agreement since they knew that their long-time comrade spoke the truth.

"I was worried before this happened, you know," the fourth shepherd admitted to his friends, "worried about what was to befall us with that sadistic King Herod still on the throne. He is but a human monster, and yet it is true that God's chosen people must remain in subjection to *him!*"

"You said you were worried *before* this happened," another said. "Does that mean you are not so now?"

The fourth shepherd smiled.

"Along with that joy," he said, "there was a peace truly beyond any understanding."

This shepherd tried to steady himself, not wanting to be judged by the others as unstable or weak.

"'How can it be?' I ask myself," he went on. "Nothing has changed. We are still dominated by a madman. And yet I feel . . ."

"No fear . . ." the other shepherds said at virtually the same time as their comrade.

Peace, a strange peace, a peace that passeth all understanding!

And it was something they all shared . . .

"You, too, experienced what I am describing?" he asked, incredulous.

They nodded, frowns disappearing, eyes opening wide, as understanding came.

"I could not admit it to myself at first nor to either of you," the younger shepherd confessed. "I reasoned that you might have thought me mad, under the circumstances."

"It was as you say with me also," the veteran of the four agreed with similar candor. "If we feel as we do and have been rightly told of the birth of the long-awaited Messiah, then it must be that that messenger who brought us these tidings right out of the very air above us surely was sent by God Himself."

He paused for emphasis, hoping the full impact would be felt by his comrades as much as he was experiencing it.

"Do you realize what that means? Do you realize what the four of us have seen and spoken with this night?"

Bewildered, but with a sense of growing expectation, they looked at one another without saying anything else, stunned as they were into mutual silence.

Instead of further conversation, they gathered together the compliant animals and headed toward Bethlehem.

CHAPTER 4

As the four men entered the stable, they thought not of the bare surroundings, nor did they wonder how it could be that the Messiah would begin His life in such a place.

They had one propelling desire, that of seeing Him, and when they did, they would agree, during the years to follow, that they each heard yet more angels singing hallelujahs to the King of Glory . . .

Seven days had passed.

Jesus was so appealing as an infant that word about Him spread within a period of twenty-four hours throughout Bethlehem and other communities. Many mothers came to see this baby, so like every little one ever born and yet, at the same time, different from all others.

"May I touch him?" woman after woman asked, aware that they were being presumptuous but unable to contain their emotions.

Mary never refused, for the mother of Jesus sensed that He was under special protection in those early days, and, as a result, no one would be able to harm Him even accidentally; nor would He be allowed to injure Himself.

Again and again, both parents were complimented.

"You should be very proud," commented one mother. "I have midwifed many, many babies over these years, and none have been like your son Jesus. But it is more than just something about His physical appearance."

This mother was having difficulty conveying an impression that was as deeply personal as anything in her life.

"I peer into those little eyes," she continued, "and I can see something that I cannot describe, but I know it is there just the same, something serene, something wonderful."

The midwife for Jesus' delivery had seemed to suffer the same perplexed confusion.

When Joseph had tried to pay her what she had earned she sheepishly mumbled, "Thank you, sir . . . ," avoiding his eyes but managing to cast a furtive glance at the baby before running from the stable without saying anything else to either of the parents.

He noticed that the woman had dropped the coin he had just placed in her hand.

"Wait!" Joseph had shouted after her. "Your money is here. You deserve it! Please take it. Please—"

Paying him no heed, the midwife had disappeared into the darkness of that Middle Eastern night.

Joseph turned to Mary.

"So strange . . ." he muttered. "She is not a wealthy woman. Surely the money must mean something to her. And yet she—"

His words trailed off as he saw again the perfect little body of his son in his beloved Mary's arms.

A day or two later Joseph noticed the woman in the marketplace as she stood at a stall to buy some freshly made bread.

I must try to find out what was wrong, he thought.

So Joseph approached her and asked what had been the trouble with her that night that would make her act as she did.

"Did we offend you in any way?" he inquired. "You were gone so quickly. I hope that we did not—"

"I felt so ashamed after seeing the purity of your son," she interrupted, her gaze not meeting his own.

"Why?" Joseph asked, genuinely puzzled and not as perceptive about Jesus just then as the woman herself.

The woman tried to avoid Joseph's gaze as she replied, "Oh, sir, I have been living in sin for so long, and this has been bothering me. When I was holding your dear son and He looked up into my eyes, I began to . . . to feel so very dirty . . . I . . . I . . . knew I could not stay in that Child's blessed presence any longer."

"He is just an infant," Joseph replied, not grasping the significance of what she had said. "Our son has no such power as you are implying. You imagine the things you tell me, woman!"

The woman wiped away some tears.

"You will find out someday, and you will remember what I have said," she added cryptically. "I wish you and His mother much happiness."

And then she left.

Joseph never saw her again.

Her name was Rebekkah.

After fleeing from Joseph that afternoon, she went without delay to the familiar refuge of her rather spartan quarters located above a leather craftsman's shop, the presence of hanging aged skins making her stop for a moment, as she did most days, and inhale, enjoying the distinctive odor.

Rebekkah had been born into a typically lower-middle-class family, one that was only a notch or two above poverty. In those ancient times, it was often difficult to tell the difference between those who were poor and those and who were not.

Perhaps the best guideline was the housing—or lack of it. The truly poor were continually on the move through city streets and country roads while others had marginal rooms in which to sleep but little else. Their clothes were the same as what wandering poor possessed, and they lacked regular meals and found little or no work. Whatever money they could earn was put in securing that very lodging which they deemed as essential as food due to the harsh weather throughout Israel in the winter months. They would joke among themselves that they had a choice in life: starve to death or freeze to death.

Rebekkah, though, had managed to keep herself relatively well groomed. Her parents oversaw this, fussing around their daughter daily as she grew up. The act of denying themselves for their daughter's health and appearance was a routine matter.

Neither Rebekkah's mother or her father really gave thought to any other course of action since both of them were determined to live through Rebekkah, happy when she was happy, sad when she was sad, hungry when she was full because they had given to her from their own portion of any food that became available, even if this meant theft from open-air markets, or begging.

And so she stood out, often looking better than the children of parents who were markedly better off, her long brunette hair well combed, her face scrubbed and smooth, feet that would have been bare covered by durable scandals, clothes hardly fashionable but at least not worn thin and littered with holes.

But Rebekkah hoped for more. Above all, she wanted to be able to pay back her mother and her father who had sacrificed so much for her.

Women in biblical times did not have the flexibility of various lifestyle choices that would come in future generations. Within nearly every household throughout Israel, they engaged in certain limited activities such as carding wool and preparing flax for linen; they were the ones, never their husbands, who spun thread and yarn using hand spindles with stone or clay whorls. Women also dyed basic materials used in daily apparel and wove the cloth on vertical looms. They sewed the garments of family members and kept every piece clean by treading it in public pools or in streams that were often a mile or more away.

Furthermore, the various other chores performed by women in Israel and throughout the Middle East included the preparing of every meal, work considered a disgraceful act for a man. To accomplish this, women usually had to arise before dawn to build the fires necessary for cooking.

And all the while, they had the responsibility for keeping a tidy house and whatever other duties their circumstances required!

Poor women had even greater demands on their time. They often gathered grain by gleaning whatever was left by the reapers. This was something that had its well-entrenched roots in even earlier times.

For the famed Ruth and her mother-in-law Naomi, from the Old Testament period, gleaning was one of the few ways a living could be earned. Naomi gleaned for as long as she was able to do so, but there was a point at which, because of her health, her daughter-in-law had to work alone.

Every morning, Ruth would join the other widows, orphans, and poor women who waited to collect the grain left behind. These people epitomized the reason why Hebrew law required farmers to leave some of their harvest in the fields. According to Leviticus 19:10, this was to be done for the "poor and the stranger."

Ruth also threshed and winnowed the grain and carefully ground it into flour using a handmill or, if nothing else was available, a mortar and pestle.

Women had no conveniences of any kind to make their toil at all easier; even something as simple as a jug of water could mean walking a distance of a mile or more each way to fill it from the nearest well.

Hundreds of years after Ruth and Naomi, it became obvious that Rebekkah was seldom very good at this kind of labor, and she came to feel more and more useless, facing a suffocating feeling of inferiority.

Have I no value at all, no kind of worth, no function or purpose? she asked herself over and over. *Those around me work so hard, yet all I can do is cook a few meals, and I do not do even this well.*

While women were accepted as traditional participants in funeral services, where they provided the mandated Middle Eastern ritual mourning, they were not allowed to take part in public ceremonies of any other kind; they found themselves most often confined to their homes.

Restrictions against women began early in life since schools were exclusively for the education of boys. Even during temple worship, there was a marked separation, with women on one side and men on the other. Nor could men speak to women as they passed them on the street.

These often onerous manmade rules were the kinds of encumbrances maintained by the religious leaders as their method of maintaining control, and that control fell particularly hard on women. It all stemmed from what they viewed as the blame that rested on Eve for the plague of sin that infected the entire human race. For example: Many priests and rabbis believed menstruation was given to women as a sign of all the blood that the first woman, Eve, had caused to be shed.

Men were expected to pray daily, wearing *talits,* which were prayer shawls, as well as a fringed garment called *tzitzes* underneath their outer clothing. But women were exempt from such prayer obligations and from wearing any kind of ritual clothing except the black garments required for mourning. They were, however, to recite the grace after meals, but only by themselves, never in a quorum in which men participated.

Nor could a father ever teach his daughter the *torah,* because the religious leaders had concluded among themselves that the more a woman knew, the more unrestrained she would become, especially in her sexual conduct. After all, they felt, women were far more inclined to have loose morals than men!

The overall taboos and other restrictions applied to women in general were joined by those imposed between one group of women and another. An example was that if a wife's husband happened to be a *haber,* or pious scholar, she could not loan her cooking pots to another wife whose husband was perchance a tax-gatherer, since by doing so, she ran the risk of ritually polluting those pots.

Some men went beyond mere obedience to Jewish law when it came to women in their families or elsewhere. They would use their dominance in cruel and insulting ways, defying the other side of God's admonitions that women be treated not as cattle but as human beings, a man's control of his family never to be an excuse for overbearing and demeaning behavior on his part.

There was no divine sanction for a debasing and altogether worldly prayer that invariably made its way through various synagogues of that era, a prayer going back to even more ancient times: "Blessed You are, O Lord God, King of the universe, the One who hast seen fit not to make me a woman."

When Rebekkah could stand her circumstances no longer, she began accepting things from the men in her life in exchange for sexual favors. At first her parents were pleased with the gifts, but then they came to realize what was happening.

You would not understand, she said to herself. *You could not let yourself see what I was trying to do.*

A confrontation occurred, a confrontation that was to destroy any loving relationship that once held this family together, for when Rebekkah refused to stop what she was doing, her mother and her father left her alone.

I tried to stop you from abandoning me! her mind shouted. *But your shame forced you away, and you never came back to me or allowed me to return to you. It was to be long, long months before I saw you again.*

Lonely months, months of man after man in a blurring stream of them, sin after sin, with no real companionship.

Until she found her parents dead from exposure . . . on a side road leading out of Jerusalem. Their bodies had lain in that ditch for a number of days with no one caring enough to bury them, even in one of the mass paupers' graves that dotted the region.

After seeing Jesus . . .

Rebekkah was not keeping company with any men at that particular time, and she spent her time alone in the little room that served as her home.

Lonely . . . Darien thought. *This woman has had all the erotic adventures the world can offer her, yet always she returns to this wretched loneliness, no one to take her hand and chase the anguish away.*

That loneliness was hardly usual, for Rebekkah had concocted a pattern of rationalization in support of her behavior that seemed just what she needed to continue on as she had been living for a long time, without suffering the distasteful burden of living with an active and condemning conscience.

Rebekkah had convinced herself she was not an everyday street whore, but, in an era and a society that dictated the strictest moral conventions, such a distinction would have been moot because her way of life had become common knowledge throughout that area.

I take no money, she had declared again and again. *Though I sleep with men, it is never for money, only when I fall in love.*

Or so Rebekkah had deluded herself into thinking. Not coincidentally, it could be said that she managed to fall in love often.

Somehow she was adept at twisting the truth and ignoring the fact that, while money itself was not involved, gifts often were, and there was little difference, after having sex, whether a coin was placed in her hand or a beautiful scarf.

Some of those gifts were on the shelves or tables around her: precious gems set in rings and necklaces, several silk scarves, a bamboo chair from an island in the Indian Ocean, and rare alligator sandals from India, along with a colorful and intricate Oriental carpet that covered the entire floor and more.

"Never before have I thought anything of this." Rebekkah spoke out loud with strong emotion to the empty space around her. "The morals of others are not my concern, and I have refused to be bound by theirs."

. . . refused to be bound by theirs.

Or God's, for that matter.

"There is no hardened conscience for her, which is the same as no conscience at all," Darien had learned from God. *"In her case, her conscience has been buried with the hope that she could just simply forget it; but it is still there, it still lives, and she knows this now more than at any other time in her young and unsettled life."*

Then Rebekkah was hired as a midwife that one evening, and she saw Jesus, Mary, and Joseph, the warmth between them, the tenderness, and the overwhelming purity.

Afterward, she returned to her quarters but also to her freshly accusing memories, fostered by that collection of gifts that once had thrilled and flattered her, but now the sight of them dragged her back to images of what she had done with the men who bestowed them upon her.

King Herod himself . . .

An old man. A terribly sad man.

A tired, spent, and quite bitter husk of what he once had been, driven by musty and fading visions of his former conquests.

Awaiting that moment of death he dreaded.

Yet Herod would never admit this to himself, to his families, or assuredly, to any of the members of his court.

Many years before, he was great and noble, a man of aspirations profound and sweeping. But now he was merely old and sick and haplessly trying to convince himself that he had lost little or none of his virility, which was why Rebekkah was not the only woman to share his bed when his wife was not looking.

He had responded like a thirsty wanderer in a vast desert who was suddenly offered a cup of water. For Herod, Rebekkah was that, someone who could give him some sense of what once had been, and satisfy the thirst he had had for the past.

I lied to you every moment we were together, she thought. *Those fears of yours were justified, aged king.*

Then there had been the teenage boy, still a virgin.

I taught him so much during that one evening, Rebekkah recalled, *yet he ran from me afterward.*

Then she found out what happened to young Josiah.

You went and hung yourself, out of guilt. That was so foolish, boy! You did nothing to feel guilty about.

Her right leg was hurting her.

That, in itself, was an important key to what had become of this woman over the years. She had been born with weak tendons and walked with a limp. But she also had a devastating physical beauty that drew man after man to her.

Not a few came to her out of lust; others knocked at her door from a feeling of pity and an almost paternal need to reach out, put their arms around her, and give her the comfort for which she yearned.

None of her lovers had publicly revealed this secret life of hers, or else she would have been stoned to death in the village square a long time before by a conservative, outraged, and offended Bethlehem citizenry.

Conscience . . .

Conscience had been hardly a factor since Rebekkah did not feel she was doing anything wrong.

Until she had met Jesus . . .

Until she had midwifed that one baby in that one manger.

From that moment on, Rebekkah's most personal thoughts would never be the same, ripped out of their deluded complacency as they were and stirred by a no longer dormant conscience; she had seen pure, angelic innocence for the first time in her life. There had been other babies, countless numbers of them, but none could ever compare to the One who was named Jesus.

His little eyes, she recalled, wishing she had taken longer to examine them. *They were not the eyes of a normal child.*

She hugged herself.

This baby Jesus seemed to be looking into me instead of at me. How could a mere infant be like that? How could any human being possess such . . . ?

Power . . . that was what the woman saw in His eyes, a power unlike any other she had ever witnessed previously.

I felt so ashamed . . .

She had told this to the father, Joseph. And it was how she continued to feel.

Ashamed of everything I have been doing with men. Ashamed of those whose marriages have been affected, ashamed of—

She had totally forsaken the ancient moral and spiritual codes of her own people.

And now I have nowhere to turn.

She had been as intimate with scores of men as any woman could possibly be, but when she *needed* one of them, they were gone, busy with their families, their civic duties, and in some cases, their religious ones too.

Panic was beginning to thread its way through her body, the palms of her hands suddenly sweaty.

Though my lovers held to their promises by keeping our relationship secret, there have been so many of them, and they are now everywhere throughout the community. None would regard me seriously if I went to them and confessed any repentance on my part. They would think me a liar! Or possessed of a demon!

She gasped as she continued that line of reasoning.

And I cannot think of anyone who would want to help me even if they could. Some probably would prefer to see me die as soon as possible so they would have no chance of coming across me again, even by accident. What hypocrites! They use my body for their pleasure, then they cast me aside.

Her leg was throbbing. Rebekkah was used to that, had had to face it in some form or other all of her twenty-some years.

A moment later, it went numb.

This had not happened before! Panic grabbed Rebekkah. In the past, there had been pain, sharp needles of it in her leg, sometimes a shattering burst of pain as though someone had kicked her.

But not this!

Rebekkah tried to stand but had become too wobbly; instead, she fell back with a thud on the floor.

Paralyzed!

That spellbinding word was like a grotesque living thing buried inside her, threatening, sinister.

I must get help! Rebekkah's mind called out. *Surely there is someone who will hear me if I just raise my voice and let out my terror as loudly as I am able, someone who will come and be by my side, take my hand, and reassure me that I am going to be all right, that I am safe and whole.*

She screamed so forcefully she felt certain the sound of footsteps would come soon, that—

"Watch out, slut! We hear you. We are the ones who will be visiting you. You will never get rid of us once we arrive!"

Demons.

These creatures could not be seen, but Darien knew of a surety that they were coming, just as one of them had said.

He heard one of the demons, knew that familiar sound immediately, knew it from the earlier period in heaven when it once had been unfallen and very beautiful, but no longer. As with all the others of his kind, abominations from a place of fire and torment, it was being driven onward by a woman who was at a point where she could turn her back on them if they did not respond quickly and forcefully enough.

A demon named Legion.

Nearly as powerful as Satan, he had been given that name because Satan bestowed on him the command of a legion of evil creatures of darkness.

As soon as Darien saw the woman fall, as soon as he heard her cry out, he could hear the telltale rush of a demonic horde's passage.

Vultures . . .

Spiritual vultures getting ready to tear at another soul, to grab it and rush back to hell so they could trot out yet another damned victim before a gloating Satan.

"Father . . ." Darien spoke straight to the throne of God. *"Can I do this? Am I able? Dare I even attempt it?"*

God answered him across the void.

"You can, my beloved Darien. Surely you can, and when you are the victor, you will know the joy of My kingdom."

The angel entered the tiny room where Rebekkah had been living and sat beside the woman. While she could not see him, she sensed someone there, and she wondered if it was God Himself.

Then she heard the others.

"Is someone coming?" she cried desperately. "I cannot move. Something awful has happened to me!"

On the one side of her, she felt strangely at peace.

On the other, something was pulling at her. Rebekkah's soul was being pulled first toward Legion and his followers, and then toward Darien.

The demon leader spoke enticing words of sexual power.

"You will have more lovers than ever before," he cooed with images that struck into her inner being. *"And you will find yourself satisfied beyond any of your wildest dreams, my dear Rebekkah."*

The carnal nature of the woman found that appealing.

If sex had been repugnant to her, she would not have allowed herself to become trapped in the cycle that had surely been dragging her down for years. In moments of self-examination, which were rare, she had to admit that she found sexual gratification a compulsive source of the greatest pleasure of her life.

"But I cannot move!" she cried out again. "Who would want me now? I am a useless wretch."

Legion thought he had Rebekkah, thought he could use that flash of self-pity to further dominate her. But Darien would have none of it.

"What do you have now?" he confronted her. *"This is the extent of your life as you have lived it according to* their *enticements."*

Rebekkah heard Darien as well as Legion through her mind and her soul, not her ears.

She seemed confused, pulled to one side or the other, yet the room itself seemed as quiet as a . . . tomb.

"I am afraid," she admitted, her right cheek twitching. "I know God is going to punish me for my sins."

"Not if you accept the One you saw," Darien told her.

"But He was just a baby!" Rebekkah protested.

"Just *a baby? Can you be sure of that? Can you be sure the tiny form you helped bring into the world was only that?*

She had seen pure, angelic innocence for the first time in her life. There had been other babies, but they did not compare to the One named Jesus.

She hesitated, convicted of the truth of those words.

"What you have now is what you will be chained to for the rest of your life."

Rebekkah looked around at the familiar bareness, broken only by gifts that lust had brought her.

"This is all you will ever have," Darien told the woman, *"if you allow these gifts and how you got them to go on dominating you."*

"But who are those voices?" she asked from her ignorance and not a little from the feeling of oppression that was gathering around her.

"Unholy ones, things *feeding on your dreams and turning them into shrunken mockeries of what they once were. You no longer dream well, do you, Rebekkah?"*

She gasped at that.

"How do you know this?"

"How is not important. Am I right?"

She admitted he was.

"I dream only what is obscene; my previous acts come back to me at night and I can no longer fend them off. I could hear the groans of my ecstasy, and I want to shut it all out, but I cannot. My deeds accuse me, and I find myself guilty before them."

She would meet some of these men on the street, quite by accident, and she could only avoid their gaze as they avoided hers.

"Yes, I am guilty before men and before God Himself," she confessed. "I have done so much for which I know I can never be forgiven in order to avoid the flames of damnation."

"God denies only those who deny Him," Darien said with authority. *"You have to believe that."*

Legion was louder, more insistent.

"This other one is wrong!" he protested. *"Believe him not. He is the bearer of idle hope, and you have* no *hope, Rebekkah. Do not reach for what he offers. He has nothing for you. The time for your redemption is past."*

He paused, then spoke in a softer voice.

"Remember the pleasure," he said. *"Remember it well, dear Rebekkah."*

"I remember better the pain."

"But you buried that nonsense a long time ago. You turned from it as the useless emotion it was and is and always will be, embracing only the satisfaction that was yours each time a man had sex with you."

"All a lie!" Rebekkah blurted out, trying very hard to pull away from Legion, to kept his words from controlling her.

"No, it is not!" retorted Legion. *"You may* pretend *that it is a lie, but then your whole life has been a pretense, Rebekkah, my dear!"*

Her face went pale, and she could offer no rebuttal.

"You claim that you are not a whore, but there is no difference between you and one of those back-alley sluts," Legion thundered.

Rebekkah, who had managed to raise herself to her elbows, collapsed totally, falling over on her back and moaning.

"You have slept with an army of men in Bethlehem and Nazareth and Jerusalem," the demon kept on obscenely. *"You have no morals left, no dignity, no salvation. My kind and I await you as our plaything in damnation!"*

By contrast, Darien's insistent urging seemed almost weak, and yet—

"The other voice," she said. "The kinder one, the one that touched my heart, and from which I turned away, please, let me hear it again, Father."

"You have no *father like the one you say . . . ,"* Legion interrupted. *"Your earthly father is dead, and your heavenly Father ignores you because you have become so repulsive in His sight; He accepts only those who are without sin. You have a new father, Rebekkah, and he is calling you now into his awaiting arms."*

. . . into his awaiting arms.

Legion assumed those words would soften Rebekkah and surely make her easier prey, that she would accept a new father, no matter how loathsome, since this was better than having none at all.

But he was wrong, the wisdom of his master, the arch-deceiver, having suddenly deceived one of his own.

"I have known *that* father for too long," Rebekkah said weakly, but her voice gaining strength. "He has been responsible only for misery in my life."

Darien spoke now, knowing it was the right moment.

"Believe this, Rebekkah: God's hope is not idle or frivolous. It is the only hope that matters."

"The baby . . . ," she whispered. "Was that baby—"

Darien assured her He was what she had suspected.

"My hands touched God!" she said, able now to hold them out in front of her and remember that moment when she was easing Him out of His mother's womb and holding Him up so that she and the father could see what had been wrought.

. . . my hands touched God!

That thought took hold of her.

"He looked up at me as though He understood everything I ever was, everything I am. I saw in His eyes—"

She gasped as that fresh memory surfaced.

"Forgiveness, Rebekkah," Darien finished the sentence for her. *"He knew you would soon be one of His own redeemed ones, and what you saw was the forgiveness that was to be yours as a result."*

Her fear seemed to be dissipating by the second.

Legion was the one groaning now as he witnessed Rebekkah's manner changing so dramatically.

"Forgiveness." She repeated that word as though it was a drop of precious honey on her tongue. "I have never known that before. From the moment of my sin, the consuming pain of feeling rejected by everyone has been with me constantly, even as I tried to convince myself that I am going to be free of it, that someday I will get relief."

Rebekkah went back in memory to those times of wondering when someone would find out about her secret sin. How many knew but would never admit this to her? What opportunities for a normal life had she lost because her reputation preceded her?

"No more, dear woman," Darien assured her. *"Do you believe the baby you brought into this world is the holy and prophesied Son of the living God?"*

"I do!" Rebekkah exclaimed without hesitation because as soon as the angel had spoken, she accepted the truth of his words, "Oh, I do! I believe that. I want to go back to the blessed One and fall down before Him and give to Jesus the Christ all of my praise, my honor, and my adoration."

Feeling abruptly returned to every part of her body.

"I can move now!" she exclaimed.

"And there is nothing to fear," said Darien reassuringly. *"Be not ashamed nor afraid, but look into the face of the Lord and know He was sent so your sins might be washed away."*

"I feel so clean," Rebekkah said as she stood. "I feel *new!*"

"You are a new creature in Him. And you shall be for eternity."

"That other voice has stopped."

"He is now back with his own master. And you are with yours because He now dwells in your body, Rebekkah. He will never leave you nor forsake you."

CHAPTER 5

THE EVENING before the eighth day . . .

According to Hebrew law and custom, the new babe would have to be brought to the temple to undergo the ancient rite of circumcision, to which all Jewish male children were submitted.

Since there were usually other children waiting in line with their parents, the process was often one that took the better part of a day, so anything else they wanted to do had to be planned around this one event.

As Darien waited, along with Mary and Joseph, he felt a deep sense of rejoicing that he could be by the side of the incarnated Christ and share the growing joy of His earthly parents.

If you could only hear the hosts of heaven at this very moment, he mused. *If it could flood your very being as it does mine. If you only understood what wondrous new chapter is now being written in the history of the human race.*

At the moment the angel entered the rough-hewn stable, he saw something for which he had not been prepared.

Animals.

Several of them.

Gathered around the bed of straw where the days-old infant had been placed were a lamb, a goat, and a horse, and at the far end of the stable an aging donkey lay silently, its bloodshot eyes wide and staring over sagging lower lids.

Mary sat up beside her son, leaning over Him and starting to bathe His tiny, too-warm forehead with cool water that Joseph had carried by bucket from a well half a mile away.

"He seems warm," she said, a touch of alarm in her voice. "I fear our son might be ill, Joseph."

In addition, the baby was crying and seemed unduly restless.

"Mary, look!" her husband told her, pointing at the donkey.

Sighing with the effort, the animal managed to stand, though a bit uncertainly, and started to walk toward them.

Mary turned and saw the beast, slow in its gait, its aged condition sadly apparent, so tired, needing very much to continue its rest that evening but somehow drawn instead to the tiny form just ahead.

"Move aside for a moment, Mary," her husband asked.

She did so without question, as was expected of women in those days.

The donkey approached the baby and stood quite still before him for a brief period, cocking its oversized head slightly, as though puzzled. Then it lowered its head toward the squirming little body.

"Joseph, what is this—?" the mother said.

"Be still, my dearest," Joseph answered, gently grabbing his beloved's arm and restraining her from interfering.

The animal licked the forehead of Jesus, . . . once, twice, a third time.

Mary became annoyed.

"Jesus cannot have such close contact with that animal," she said. "It is not right, Joseph."

She pointed to the donkey.

"Joseph," she added, "it should be restrained."

But she fell silent when she saw what was happening. As a miniature hand reached up and gently touched the donkey's moist nose, the baby's discomfort seemed to pass.

"Jesus is smiling now!" Mary exclaimed in wonderment. "Look, my husband. Look at our son! That dear smile!"

"I see, Mary, I see," Joseph assured his youthful wife, accustomed by now to her excitable disposition.

For one brief moment, his serene gaze and the donkey's seemed interlocked. Then the donkey sighed in a manner that gripped its entire body and walked slowly back to where it had been resting.

"The animal knew our son was in distress," Joseph said. "He was trying to comfort Jesus the only way he knew how."

"But how could that be?" Mary questioned.

"I cannot say, beloved, but we can only accept the hand of God in this."

They both turned and looked at the donkey, which blinked once then fell back against its own bed of straw.

The rite of circumcision . . .

Darien had known about this ceremony from the moment of the first such act. He had been present often as parents submitted their sons to it.

He wondered if Jesus would be required to undergo circumcision, because as God-in-the-flesh, He was obviously not bound by the conventions of Jewish law or tradition, nor by those of any other society.

"Is it necessary, Father?" he asked God hesitantly.

"It is necessary that My beloved Son become a true man in every possible respect," was the reply. *"He is going to be tempted and tested as others are. Jesus will face what men face throughout their lives. He will eat and drink and be what they are in many ways, but without the sin that is theirs, imputed to them by Adam."*

God paused, then added, *"Are you clear on this, Darien?"*

The angel nodded, and in so doing, came face to face with one truth that had been part of his relationship with the Creator from the beginning.

Whatever He says is true. The Father cannot lie. He speaks, and the words of His mouth are as sure as the stars in the sky, as the tides that rise and fall . . . as heaven and hell.

If nothing else, this would always give Darien peace. For if God said the sky was purple or yellow, he and the rest of the unfallen angels could believe it as fact.

But that was not all.

Angels such as Darien had the guarantee that God would never tell them such a thing in the first place if it were not so, because, as some mortal men would say, the Father did not play games.

Circumcision was one of those rites or rules that God saw fit to maintain in the affairs of men; there were others following it that Jewish families also entered into within a short period after a baby's birth.

The purpose was to signify that the separation of the Jewish people from all Gentiles had been completed, and the designation of their unique relationship with Jehovah was declared for all the world to hear. Circumcision came as a commandment from God when He was in the earliest stages of forming Israel as His holy nation.

"Your human identity has become a prophesied part of God's holy covenant with Israel," Darien said in communication with the divine part of the baby's incarnated nature. *"But, I wonder, dear Lord, what joy can there be for your beloved earthly parents Mary and Joseph at this moment?"*

Darien hesitated, his emotions strong; then he continued.

"Their families have flatly rejected them, thinking that You were conceived in an illicit carnal act by Joseph and not by the Holy Spirit, and all continue to be deeply offended by this, continually accusing Mary and Joseph of grievous premarital sin. Because of that, this family of three surely will have to be alone at a time when they normally would be engaging in the most joyous of celebrations."

And a wonderful celebration it should have been!

Traditionally, new parents joined with family and friends for an event that, at its roots, was an age-old link between God and His chosen people from the nation of Israel. Invariably the celebration drew more than just those closest to the parents, with villagers who hardly knew them joining in for free food and drink.

Even so, God was honored and glorified in the psalms that were sung unto Him, voices lifted up in praise to almighty Jehovah. The prayers included petitions that He soon send the Messiah to liberate the Jews from bondage to yet another ruthless foreign power, this latest one the most powerful of all.

"Send Him to us so we might be free again," the whole group would shout, believing in their fervor that God was hardly capable of letting them down and would keep His long-offered promises at last.

This family of three surely will have to be alone at a time when they normally would be celebrating . . .

Darien had so convinced himself that Mary and Joseph would be denied the enjoyment of this long-practiced celebration that God's simple but powerful answer took him by complete surprise.

"It is not as you say," God replied without any immediate elaboration.

Darien had learned not to question in any strident manner, for that had precipitated his *Angelwalk* difficulties, and he pledged to avoid falling into that trap ever again. But he remained curious as to what the Creator meant.

God knew that this was so, that it grew out of concern for human happiness, and He decided to give the angel greater insight.

"Certain family members soon will be visited by Gabriel," said the Almighty, *"after which their hearts will be made tender and Mary and Joseph will have their loved ones back by their side at this happy time."*

It was what Darien had hoped would happen, and he thanked God for the grace that soon was to be poured out over a family he was coming to love very, very much, a love of which they perhaps would never be aware, with the exception of Jesus Himself, who had known from eons past about this blessed angel.

After the circumcision . . .

Circumcision was not the only ritual associated with a baby's birth. It was followed by a ceremony that involved what was called "the redemption of the firstborn," which occurred one month after birth as described in such Scriptures as Exodus 13:2 and 11:16, as well as Numbers 18:15–16. The purpose behind it was a public witness that the child was being bought back from God after originating with Him.

The third stage was named "purification of the mother," during which she could not enter any temple for a period of forty days because, according to Jewish religious law, she was considered ceremonially unclean.

At the conclusion of this period, the mother's cleansing was purchased by the sacrifice of a lamb in a burnt offering and a dove as a sin offering. If the parents could not afford a lamb, then a second dove was substituted. Since Mary and Joseph were far from being wealthy, this was what they chose . . . two doves.

"*My Son was not born above the law,*" the heavenly Father had told Darien. "*In His birth and His life, He will fulfill the law perfectly.*"

Darien, while not surprised, was glad to hear this, for God certainly had all the power necessary to abolish the law completely and start over through a new set of admonitions with Jesus at the center.

He wants to work within the structure of what He Himself created, Darien thought. *If Jesus, as a man, can be bound by the laws of men, then His sacrifice for them will have the meaning it should.*

Though the angel did not know the circumstances that had been planned for a long time, because God had not revealed them to him, Jesus would later testify in a similar fashion by saying to those who by then were eager to hear every word He uttered, "I have come not to abolish the law but to fulfill it."

Darien felt sadness coming from the Father whenever they spoke of what the future was to hold. But for the time being, he rejoiced in what amounted to a delusion on his part, that everything would go well, that his time with Jesus would be that of a virtually unending series of blessings.

The dedication . . .

Darien was at the temple when the new parents brought their baby to be dedicated to Jehovah. He saw an old man named Simeon approach Mary and Joseph directly after the ceremony was over.

"He is singing a song to them!" the angel exclaimed. *"He is!"*

It was to become known as the *Nunc Dimittus,* a song of praise and adoration as well as revelation.

"The Holy Spirit has revealed to me a wonderful truth about this baby," Simeon said to them. "He promised me that I will not die until I had seen God's anointed King. I was *driven* here this day by His words."

He reached out for the baby.

"Would you let me hold your son?" he asked.

Mary and Joseph exchanged glances, then allowed the old man to take the infant Jesus into his arms.

"Lord!" he said. "Now I can die content! For I have seen Him as You promised me I would. I have seen the Savior You have given to the world. He is the Light that will shine upon all of the nations, and He will be the glory of Your people Israel!"

Mary and Joseph could not speak, stunned by what they were being told about their beloved son.

As Simeon handed the tiny form back to His mother, the old man's expression, which had been joyous, changed drastically.

"What is wrong?" asked Joseph. "Are you ill?"

Simeon shook his head.

"A sword . . ." he started to say, then stopped, his ability to speak briefly overcome by the strongest emotions.

"What is this you say about a sword?" Joseph pressed.

Simeon was obviously struggling to control himself.

"A sword shall pierce your soul, woman," he finally managed to say, "for your Child shall be rejected by many in Israel, and this to their eternal undoing."

. . . rejected by many in Israel.

Mary was frowning as she said, "Who will do this—and why?"

"The whole nation," he told her, "from the religious leaders to the crowds. Few will be willing to stand with Him."

Simeon reached out and cupped his hand over the top of Jesus' head.

"But this One also will be the greatest joy to many others. And the deepest thoughts of many hearts shall be revealed."

The celebration and reconciliation . . .

Mary and Joseph expected that there would be little or none of this since their respective families had been acting so cynically throughout her pregnancy.

Having given up on an anticipated time of the most joyous celebration, which would have routinely followed under any other circumstances, Mary and Joseph were getting ready to retire for the night when they noticed someone standing in the entrance to the stable, his large form outlined by light from the moon that seemed to be directly overhead but his face obscured by shadows.

"Who is there?" Joseph called out, concerned about the intentions of any intruder who would come upon them so suddenly.

"I am the brother of your wife," announced the man.

"Nathaniel!" Mary exclaimed, surprised that he had come.

The tall, broad-shouldered farmer, just a few years older than she, stepped inside the stable.

"I could not stay away," he said.

"*Darien?*" The Son spoke.

"*Yes, Lord . . .*" the angel replied.

"*You did well, for you have brought something very special to this family that had been missing.*"

"*Thank you!*" exclaimed Darien, blessed by any compliment from the Deity.

"Are you listening?"

"Surely, Lord, I am listening."

"I had a visitor," Nathaniel continued.

"Who was it?" Joseph asked.

"I think he was from God, one of Jehovah's angels."

"Are you sure?"

"I am sure."

"What did the angel say?"

"That my sister has been truthful. Her son is not the product of sin but of pure righteousness."

As with Mary and Joseph, Nathaniel was seeing through a glass darkly. He had an impression of the truth but only vaguely so, and it remained largely unclear. The full significance of having a nephew such as Jesus would not become obvious to him until he became a Christian nearly thirty-five years later.

Mary stood and reached out for her brother. He walked up to her, and they put their arms around one another.

"If only our dear mother and our dear father could think as you do, Nathaniel," she whispered. "If only—"

"Mary, Mary, I—"

"I know you tried, my brother. But they can be stubborn. They—"

He gently grabbed her shoulders.

"Look at me," he said. "They believe you now."

"They do?" repeated Mary, longing to hear that but not quite believing that her prayers had been answered.

A familiar voice called to her from the entrance.

"Beloved Mary!"

"*Father!*" she returned his greeting.

Mary's father entered, along with her mother, but they were not the only ones. Joseph's own family was right behind them . . . his parents, brothers, and sisters all having gathered furtively outside the stable.

"We all were visited," said Joseph's brother Seth. "We know that the great Jehovah indeed has spoken. How could we remain apart from the three of you once we had shared such an experience?"

After that blessed evening of reconciliation . . .

As an archangel, Gabriel enjoyed the substantial privilege of being the first of the hosts of heaven, after Darien, to visit the sleeping incarnate One, and as soon as he arrived, he gasped at the sight.

"*Oh, what a wondrous baby the Lord is!*" the angel Gabriel exclaimed as he paid a visit to the manger while Jesus and Mary and Joseph were asleep. "*I can scarcely look without being overcome.*"

This unfallen one seemed so pleased that it was almost as though he himself was the father of this Child and not the Holy Spirit.

"*This is so blessed a moment, just as our Creator promised.*"

Gabriel sighed expansively.

"*All of us have been waiting a long time,*" he remarked happily. "*And now it has happened at last!*"

Darien realized that as much as did his comrade.

"*Wondrous, blessed, and holy,*" he agreed. "*If we only knew the end now that we have seen the beginning.*"

Gabriel chuckled over the anxiousness that he had learned to be so typical of his fellow angel.

"*Ever the impatient one,*" he said. "*But, then, I do understand. We are linked, you and I and the others, linked for eternity. We sense your feelings, Darien, though we are less anxious than you."*

Visiting after Gabriel were others . . . the angels Michael, Stedfast, Knower, Patience, Kindness, Charity, and Wisdom all came to see the Son.

And all went away with joy throughout their beings, though most became subdued, each of them deeply affected to the point of speechlessness which, for some of those angels, was a miracle in itself.

Night following night following night, one angel after the other, a parade from above, and yet unseen by either flesh-and-blood parent.

It was to happen like that every night before the little family was forced to flee from Bethlehem on a hazardous and lengthy journey to temporary safety in the land of Egypt—a place they dreaded out of fear of its heathenistic practices but went anyway because of a warning from a visitor from heaven. Before they left Bethlehem, angels by the tens of thousands left heaven for a brief while, one after the other, each standing in adoration before the incarnate God who had given them life from the birthplace of His mind.

"*What a sublime mystery!*" Darien exclaimed along with Gabriel.

"*How wondrous is this moment,*" the other angel said. "*I look upon the Creator born as a new baby!*"

"*He knows we are here while His earthly parents are oblivious to us.*"

"*If only they could see us and know why we are here, Darien,*" mused Gabriel. "*How very pleased both would be.*"

Oh, yes, dear comrade, that is so, Darien thought.

"*I wish the Father would summon us now so we could announce to the whole world what has happened.*"

"*Remember, Gabriel, that the shepherds know and have been here, falling on their knees before the Son.*"

"The Shepherd of our souls," the four men had proclaimed earlier in great wisdom. "We shall sacrifice a lamb in His honor."

Mary spoke cautiously seconds after they had finished, and she was surprised at her own words.

"Do as you have said just now, but that soon will no longer be necessary," she said, her voice trailing off.

Joseph leaned over, his lips at her ears.

"What have you told these men?" he whispered before any of the shepherds could respond, aware that such men could be babblers, gossiping among themselves about one matter or another, and he did not want his fragile young woman subjected to any more gossip than was already the case.

"I cannot say, my husband," she told him honestly. "The words came from my lips but I know not why I spoke them. They seemed to come from my very soul and not my mind. And over them I had no control whatever."

Joseph's eyes filled with tears, his momentary embarrassment gone.

"My dearest love . . . you, my wife, are of all women, I perceive, special. I am sadly ignorant of what lies ahead, but if it be by your side that I spend the rest of my life, then I am blessed beyond measure."

Mary and Joseph embraced and did not notice in the midst of their ardor that the baby Jesus, who had been observing them, sighed contentedly just once, then shut His clear little eyes and fell asleep.

Angels continued streaming in a long line from the streets of heaven to see the Son of the Most High wrapped in protective swaddling clothes, His skin slippery with the remains of that precious olive oil in which he had been bathed earlier, as was the Middle Eastern custom in that ancient time.

"*So quiet,*" Michael noted, his voice hushed. "*How I wish I were mortal, if only for a moment, so I could hold Him, and let Him know, by my tender touch, how very much I love Him.*"

"*There is no need for you to hold Him, for the babe can feel the love of all of us, my comrade,*" Darien ventured, "*yours, mine, ten thousand upon ten thousand others. We need not be human for Him to perceive this.*"

There were so many angels now around the still, sweet form of baby Jesus that if they were flesh and bone and blood and muscle, not all the Roman amphitheaters in the known world could contain them all.

"*Go now, Darien, for I have another mission on which to send you,*" God told him. "*After it is completed, you may return.*"

"*Where is it You want me to be?*" asked the angel.

"*There are wise men who will be sent by King Herod to find out where My Son is. Go with them and see that they are safe until they arrive here.*"

"*Then I shall be with Jesus through His mortal life . . . is that it, heavenly Father?*

"*You shall, Darien, . . . the most blessed of all my beloved angels.*"

Those words touched the very core of the angel's being.

"*Where are these wise men to be found?*" Darien asked, hardly able to speak in the aftermath.

"To the east, in Persia, near Eden."

"May I have Your leave to stop at the Garden, Father, to see True, the angel you placed at its entrance?"

"There is no time."

Darien was disappointed but could not dispute God's decision. Among all the unfallen angels, he best knew what the alternative was, for he alone had visited hell. And he knew that there were only two choices: to be with God or to be against Him.

He nodded without contest, thanked the almighty Creator, and then was on his way as he had been commanded to do . . . to a land of idolatry, astrology, magic, and other practices that had been condemned by the holy and sovereign Creator.

To a city where the group of priests called the Magi had come to be revered by the common people of that land, who knew no greater revelation than what they had been given in their spiritual darkness.

To three wise men who would be used mightily by the God of the Jews and turned from their previous ways once they met the One whom they had been seeking . . .

PART II

The angels may have wider spheres of action and nobler forms of duty than ourselves, but truth and right to them and to us are one and the same thing.

EDWIN HUBBELL CHAPIN

Mary and Joseph *had to contend with something wholly unexpected.*

Visitors . . .

Day after day, scores of them.

The baby Jesus was to draw to Him many human visitors in addition to those who were angelic—a variety of people compelled, it seemed, beyond their will to that stable at the fringes of that simple village.

Few could ever explain why they had come, except to babble something about a feeling that they should do so.

Men, women, even other children approached the little stable, having been drawn there, in some cases, as though Someone had wanted it to happen and they could not do otherwise.

None left disappointed.

All felt that they had had a special encounter, even if the specifics were beyond their ability to explain.

Months passed for Jesus, Mary, and Joseph. Until nearly two years went by after the Child had been born.

The most important of the human visitors proved to be three who met the Child long after the others had left—the three Magi . . . wise men from the East, their story one of the most amazing of all during that early period of the life of the King of Kings, and Lord of Lords . . .

CHAPTER 6

Many months later.

Ancient Persia.

A center of heathen worship, much of it based in the religion of Zoroastrianism.

It also had been the center of the Babylonian Empire at a time when the Jewish people were in subjugation to that once extraordinary world power.

The Magi were essentially a group of typically devout priests who had inherited their exalted positions in that form of worship that had once been popular but had been in decline for decades though it still wielded control over such men.

By their own choice, when they were old enough, each was given a chance to continue as followers of Zoroaster, as it was called in the Greek language, or Zarathustra, in Persian form, a giant figure in their history who had been a religious leader some twelve hundred years before. After starting out with a theology that at least was rooted in a single god, their theistic beliefs had deteriorated into a system of blatant occultism based upon an array of multiple gods, some of them good, the others quite evil. The good spirit was called *Spenta Mainyu*, and the evil one was *Angra Mainyu.*

Later, astrology became incorporated into their worship system. From there, their practices grew more and more occultic, though this did not deter a people who had been long steeped in heathenistic worship from their births to their deaths. They took it easily, their spiritual darkness deepening.

The Magi had come to be called wise men because they would spend most of their time studying the content of ancient scrolls and other parchments to which everyday, working-class Persians had little or no access, and also for examining the heavens for signs that could be called prophetic.

In addition, the Magi often interpreted the dreams of rulers, statesmen, and other high-bred individuals, thus solidifying their reputation for wisdom that seemed rare in that ancient society.

Named Gaspar, Balthasar, and Melchior, the three who would soon begin an uncertain journey suddenly found themselves given to some dreams of their own.

Afterward, in the early-morning hours, they ventured outside their respective residences, so quiet for a brief while, and looked up at the no longer dark sky, wondering what it had meant, that vivid scene in the middle of the night.

A traveling star or light, or that is what it seemed, but a star or light that moved from one side of their vision to the other, then seemed to stop!

None had ever dreamed that way before, and though apparently they were rightly deemed masters of the deepest significance of the dreams of others, these three proved not a little puzzled about their own.

"What could it mean?" Melchior, the oldest, speculated, when he had joined the others at breakfast and they were sharing their nighttime visions.

"Who can say?" asked Gaspar, the youngest but most cynical of the three. "This is much too strange. The visions of most of those whom we have advised seem rather easy to divine in comparison."

"And we were *together*, seeing what we did!" Balthasar exclaimed. "We have had our separate dreams until now, whatever these happened to be. But now it is something that we all *share*; think of that! Perhaps it is something we three are in the process of learning, the three of us, at the same time."

They ruminated about this peculiar matter from morning to midday, forgetting their scrolls and other meditations, until it came time for their rest before dinner and whatever else the evening held.

Abruptly Gaspar jumped to his feet and started walking in circles, his head bowed, muttering to himself.

"What disturbs you?" Balthasar inquired of his friend.

"I think I know what we have seen," Gaspar replied.

The other two waited anxiously, for he was not one given to wild fantasies.

"The Golden Light!" he exclaimed.

Dumbfounded, Melchior and Balthasar looked at him in astonishment, hardly believing they really had heard what he had just said, but at the same time realizing that he may have stumbled upon the truth.

The Golden Light . . .

Zarathustra, the prophet whose teachings had guided the lives of countless numbers of worshipers throughout that region, from about 1100 B.C. onward, Zarathustra . . . which meant . . . *He of the Golden Light.*

"*Could* he be the one who is being manifested in our dreams?" Balthasar mused, taken with the notion but not as yet convinced.

"We must find out," Gaspar stressed. "It is important that we be open to more such contact, whether this comes by dreams or whatever other channel Zarathustra may decide to use, if it is he."

As sleeptime came upon them, they slipped into that dream again.

On this new occasion, an angel spoke to them, though they knew not that it was such.

An angel whose name was Darien.

He told them what they were to do, that they were to gather together their camels and begin a journey that would take them west.

"But this is to be only at night," he said, "so that what you see in the sky can guide you to the destination that has been ordained. And you are to tell no one of your mission. You are to slip away without being seen so that none can follow you.

"For you three soon will be going to see the long-prophesied king of the Jews, the One who will change your lives as well as the lives of countless others after you for a very long time to come."

King of the *Jews!* They were not being confronted with ageless truths by or about Zarathustra but instead a king of the despised Jews.

"This is a sham," Gaspar argued sternly. "There is some trick to this, some attempt to deceive us. I would not be surprised if those loathsome Jews were behind the whole thing. If so, they are more clever than I imagined them to be."

Each of the three wise ones spit out that word *Jews* as though it were the bitterest of all poisons in his mouth.

"Why are you telling us this, master?" Melchior said in his dream, still clinging to the hope that it was Zarathustra who had made contact.

"I am not your master," Darien countered finally.

"But where is he? Where is Zarathustra?"

"He is not the One who has sent me."

"Then name Him of whom you speak," Melchior demanded.

"Almighty God . . . the very Jehovah written about in those Scriptures you recently have been studying."

"But we are *Persians,*" protested Balthasar in his own dream, or what he thought to be a dream and nothing more, however vivid and powerful it seemed. "The Jews are such a primitive, uncouth lot, unruly by nature."

This Magi straightened his shoulders in a gesture of superiority that was hardly typical of him.

"We are cultured and learned men," he added, "while most of the Jews seem little better than ignorant savages."

"Could mere ignorant savages have written the Scriptures you read with such zeal?" Darien asked tellingly.

Balthasar fell silent, unable to give any rebuke to that.

"But how will we know when we have reached our destination?" Gaspar spoke in the middle of the night. "For how long must we do this?"

"The light will stop over the place you are to visit," Darien concluded. *"Start by heading west of your native land, toward the Mediterranean. The rest of the journey will be safely guided as I now promise all of you."*

The next time the three Magi met, soon after morning light, there was little discussion or debate, an unusual situation in itself, and they felt compelled by the power of that shared dream to do as they had been directed without delay; thus, they prepared for their odyssey that night.

They did so, not expecting any revelation concerning the King of the Jews but convinced that He of the Golden Light was behind everything and was simply putting them to an elaborate and mysterious test.

Before they left, they ruminated on a coincidence, if it could be called such, that, as the voice stated, they had recently begun to share an interest in Hebrew history, documents, and prophecies, and only the week before had been speculating on certain passages of Daniel, Ezekiel, and other Jewish prophets.

"They all seem to have passages of great sorrow," Balthasar observed. "There is one in particular that I remember."

"Tell us . . . ," Melchior said.

"'He is despised and rejected by men, a man of sorrows and acquainted with grief. And we hid, as it were, our faces from Him.' This figure in Jewish prophecy was rejected even by those professing love for him."

"I agree," Gaspar said, very, very sad.

"There is more," Balthasar went on. "Listen to this: 'He was wounded for our transgressions, He was bruised for our iniquities; the chastisement for our peace was upon Him, and by His stripes we are healed.'"

"It seems," said ever-analytical Gaspar, "that the Messiah is going to have to sacrifice Himself for His people."

"That seems typical of the Jews," noted Melchior, "their own redeemer having to die like that. They are a violent nation, and their violence does not stop even at the feet of the One their prophets have been predicting!"

"Could it be that there is a connection?" Gaspar said, I mean, a connection between what the three of us have dreamed, and this? Could we be instruments of warning to this special Man and somehow be in a position to prevent His tragic death? Is that what Zarathustra would have us do?

The others had no answer, for any answer did not include Zarathustra, and it was this possibility that was beginning to give them considerable unease.

CHAPTER 7

AS THE three Magi traveled, they were observed in silence by a hovering angel named Darien who could not be seen but who would be guardian to their every step, and they looked for any occurrence of the predicted sign in the sky, which they were accustomed to doing because of their devotion to astrology.

"Zarathustra truly has deserted us!" Gaspar exclaimed in some fear because, at the start, the three saw nothing. "In the past, he has seemed so near to us, but now I feel nothing from our great prophet. It is almost as though the grave has finally stilled his magnificent voice and his boundless wisdom."

And this same willful, often morose Gaspar was not surprisingly the first to question what they were doing, and why.

"All these years that we have looked to the glorious heavens, all the charts we have drawn to plot the course of the lives of those who turn to us for help," he said, his tone bespeaking much, "and never have we encountered anything like we were told by that singular voice or the dream we have had on certain odd nights, depriving us of the needed rest that we were seeking after long, sometimes dull days of poring over one set of musty, ancient writings or another as we tried to make sense of what was written."

"What is your point?" Melchior asked a bit sharply and with more than usual impatience toward a friend not infrequently given to pronounced long-windedness. "If this is Zarathustra reaching out to us for some reason, how can we be other than on alert, waiting for him to speak the next time?"

"My point is simple, formed by but a single question: Are we perhaps pursuing something that is quite foolhardy this night? I remind you that we have been sent on our way with so little apparent justification yet a great deal of potential for calamity in this wild place, it would seem. And contrary as it is to our normal actions, we have done this without much protest or debate.

"Look at the dangers we all might face . . . wild beasts, roving bandits or serpents waiting to strike, rob us, or kill us. What is there that truly *can* protect us? My friends, I see *nothing!* Frankly, I dislike feeling so vulnerable. I suspect that I shall not be able to endure such a state very much longer."

It was Balthasar, the visionary, who intruded now, as the three of them rode their camels side by side.

"How long has it been since we have noticed that a certain disillusionment has taken up residence within each one of us?" he asked in response to Gaspar's typically melancholy pronouncement.

Balthasar was referring to the years of decline for the once-prestigious cult begun by Zarathustra, a decline that compelled those in charge to reach ever further into the dark practices of occultism in some desperate hope of halting it and rebuilding their numbers, all of which Melchior, Gaspar, and Balthasar opposed, calling such techniques forms of spiritual whoring.

"We cheapen ourselves," Gaspar had argued splendidly before the governing council. "And we also do something that is, if anything, much, much worse; for we surely open the door to the presence of a foul and powerful evil corrupting the purity of our faith.

"None of this would have pleased our beloved Zarathustra. You must stop your flirtation with the darkest of spirits. You must indeed stop now, or I warn you all, our entire religion is doomed!"

His two friends also joined in, sounding an alarm and telling of the consequences of departing from the original doctrines and adding to them what the prophet would have abhorred.

No one listened.

This led to a period of depression, not only for Gaspar but for his two friends as well. They all saw the foundation of their faith starting to crumble beneath their feet.

How long has it been now that a certain disillusionment, to give it a name, has taken up residence within each one of us?

Balthasar waited for comments in response to that despairing question, and when the others continued in their silence, he went on, "I would say some years, dear friends, as I recall, to speak a truth about which none of us here can be very happy. Be honest about this, I ask of you both.

"What we have believed for so long, the faith that has been within our respective families for more than a few generations, no longer provides what once seemed so sure, so clear, so blessed. If you can dispute this, do so, please; I beg you to do so, for it is my most earnest desire somehow to think otherwise, but on the other hand, it is not my desire to *delude* myself or either of you."

. . . no longer gives to us what it once did.

His words cut through to their very souls, for they realized their truth, truth so sharp that each felt a degree of real physical pain.

The camels were halted.

"I cannot deny what you have said," Melchior acknowledged candidly. "I look at the stars, as you do, and see none of them any longer as helpful signs put forth by the special beneficence of our gods."

Gaspar groaned when he heard that.

"Precisely how I feel every day of my life!" he said. "What is there left for us if everyone has arrived at the same dark conclusion?"

He glanced desperately at Balthasar and Melchior, a look of desperation on his bearded, pale face.

"From what source do we obtain our guidance now?" Gaspar asked, a plaintive quality in his voice. "How do we go about our lives with any semblance of our accustomed normalcy, advising others who seek the seeming wisdom we have been telling them we can surely provide?

"How do we conduct ourselves in any of this if it turns out that the very moorings of our youth are no more than . . . or perhaps never were . . . figments of someone's imagination and not appropriate to guide anyone through an earthly life that often seems so complex?"

Gaspar pointed upward at the many stars that once seemed to offer them everything, his manner both reverence and mounting trepidation.

"For how long have we bowed before deities who may or may not exist?" he spoke plaintively.

Usually boisterous, cheery Melchior was shivering.

"Or deities who are devils instead?" he ventured, the cheeks above his long, full beard drained of their normally ruddy color.

For the three wise men, that night suddenly seemed the very coldest of their lives.

CHAPTER 8

"*F*ATHER, *the star has not appeared to them yet,*" Darien observed nervously. "*They are anxious now, filling with doubts. They may decide to turn back any moment. Surely this should not be allowed to happen. What am I to do?*"

"*It is not a* star *that will guide them,*" said God.

Darien could scarcely believe those words.

"*But You said a light was to appear that would show the wise men the way to Bethlehem.*"

"*Yes, Darien, I said a light in the heavens would serve as their guide.*"

"*But there is none, Father. I can see nothing of the sort. Please help me; I do not understand.*"

"*There is to be no* star, *my nervous one.*"

"*But what then shall—?*"

"*Only you.*"

"*But what am I to do—?*"

"*Be that light, beloved Darien. Shine brightly. Lead them to the manger so that they may see my only begotten Son.*"

Abruptly, Darien understood, and joy beyond measure started to flood his very being. The more of it he experienced, the greater the light the three wise men saw, for some measure of the glory of the Father was contained in it. To them, this vision appeared to be a star beyond anything they had ever witnessed before.

"It glows!" Gaspar gasped, his rationalism reduced to nothing more solid than the sand at his feet.

"And it moves so deliberately," Melchior added with fascination. "Can it be a mindless *object,* then?"

"Jewish prophecy does speak of various signs and wonders," Balthasar recalled. "We are only now in Judea, and already look at what is happening before our eyes! If, as we have been told, there is to be a new king of this land, then the present one, this Herod, cannot be too pleased at such a prospect."

They rode a bit farther, and still the light was above and just ahead of them.

"When we stop, it seems to do so as well!" Gaspar said in awe. "When we go on, it does, too, as though it is linked to us in some unfathomable way."

The two others rather enjoyed the change in their friend, his pompous intellectualism giving way to the same sense of wonder that filled them.

"Shall we go on?" Melchior asked, chiding him a bit.

"Oh, we surely shall!" Gaspar said with an enthusiasm they had never seen from him over the many years of their friendship.

The journey, at night as it was, was no less dangerous for the three men and their camels than it had been for the shepherds and the herds for which they were responsible. Predators prowling the Middle Eastern sands were as eager to take down larger prey as sheep. And the Magi had left their homes with such eagerness that they neglected to take any kinds of weapons to protect themselves.

They approached Jerusalem, the largest city in Judea, and the capital of that nation. For a moment the star seemed to waver, but quickly continued on.

"Surely this is where we have been led," Melchior suggested. "There is only Bethlehem nearby, and that is a modest little village by any standard."

Breaking the stillness of the night were the roars of what seemed to be a full pride of lions, which must have been exceedingly hungry since they usually went after their prey only during the daylight hours.

"There is a saying among the Jews," Balthasar said as the three of them halted their camels at the sound.

"Yes, I know," Gaspar said. "It concerns Satan going about as a lion, seeking whom he may—"

"—devour!" Melchior completed the sentence for him.

They noticed vague shapes in the darkness.

"We should have gone during the day," Gaspar murmured.

"But there would be nothing above to guide us," Balthasar reminded him.

They were less than a mile from Jerusalem when the fully grown lions appeared out of the darkness, coming from their dens in the nearby hills.

They were crouched low to the ground, eying the camels and the figures on their backs.

"Up there!" Gaspar whispered.

He was pointing to other lions on the hard boulders to one side.

"We are trapped!" he gasped. "They will bring us down like flies swatted with the palms of our hands."

The camels had become nearly unmanageable, threatening to turn and run back toward Persia. Though quite fast for their size, they were no match for so many lions. One of them balked, trying to toss Gaspar off its back, but he held on, talking softly to it and getting it to calm down briefly.

"Pray to the gods!" Melchior said. "Close our eyes and send to them our desperate need for safety."

The three Magi prayed, but the lions on the ground were closer, surrounding the camels. All of them on the ground and on the boulders were getting ready to spring, their tails whipping from side to side.

"Not your gods, but One only, whose Son you shall soon see! From Him only comes your protection," called out a voice.

They realized it was the same voice as in their dreams.

"Be not afraid," Darien spoke soothingly. *"The lions about you are not your greatest danger. The earthly king you shall meet is far more of a beast than these simple creatures."*

"Who speaks?" Gaspar asked. "And from whence have you come?"

"A messenger from on high," Darien replied simply.

"We have been placed in great peril," Melchior said forlornly. "What can we do? What can we do?"

Darien did not reply.

"Look!" Gaspar pointed. "Look at the star!"

It seemed to be expanding, its brightness so piercing that wherever that light reached, the night fled. The lions also noticed and seemed to freeze where they were, looking upward, transfixed.

Something happened in the next few minutes that Balthasar, Melchior, and Gaspar could never forget.

The creatures on the boulders came down from their perches, joining the ones already on the ground, and walked ahead of the three Magi.

The ancient gates of Jerusalem loomed ahead as the cautious camels slowly followed behind the lions.

"The beasts guard us now!" Gaspar exclaimed. "They protect our every step. How can this be?"

Several more lions from another pride in that immediate area approached the three men and their camels with a manner that could only be called threatening, but they were turned away by a chorus of warning growls from those of their kind given a special mission of guardianship that night.

Finally the Magi were at the main gate leading into Jerusalem, that most important of all Jewish cities. They brought the camels to a momentary halt and looked a bit warily at the lions on either side of them.

"They seem to be waiting to make sure we are safe," Melchior observed. "What can this wondrous moment mean, my friends?"

The other two could provide him with no answer.

"We should go now," Balthasar said, "lest someone see us and assume we are about to be attacked, or worse yet, seek an explanation!"

As the three Magi entered Jerusalem, the lions meekly returned to their dens to sleep the rest of the night, their hunger now strangely absent.

"*I am very pleased, Darien,*" the Father told the angel.

"*I did not even have time to ask for Your guidance . . .*"

"*You acted in faith, believing. Could I have expected more?*"

"*More than faith?*"

"*That is what I ask, Darien.*"

"*No, Father, surely not more than faith.*"

"*Then feel blessed that you have done well this special night; truly rejoice in that, and go to the Holy Babe now, while these three wise men rest until morning, when they shall be granted a meeting with King Herod.*"

Darien obeyed, entering the stable, unseen as always, and crawling into the manger to be beside his Lord.

CHAPTER 9

UNKNOWN to the three wise men, King Herod, the most powerful authority in the land of Judea, could not sleep during that final night of their journey; he arose just minutes beyond midnight to stand before one of two large shuttered windows in his chambers, which he opened wide.

I am so tired, he thought. *I have remade the face of this land, and yet there is no one I can claim who loves me. I wonder even about the members of my own family. Will they be in sorrow after I die, or rejoicing?*

Coming from other men, those thoughts would have seemed deluded arrogance, the senile rambling of someone whose ego had been inflated out of all proportion to his impact upon the people and the nation he governed.

. . . *I have remade the face of this land.*

For decades, Herod had dominated the length and the breadth of Jewish history. But he was not a true Israeli. He became a Roman citizen while in his twenties and was appointed military governor of Galilee some time later. His initial mission, given to him by the emperor, was to clear that region of a plague of terrorists.

After being largely successful, including the devastating takeover of Jerusalem, Mark Antony finally gave Herod the kingship of Judea, a land that had been secured for the Romans in 37 B.C. Immediately, he ordered a national holiday under the guise of royal beneficence toward his subjects. As part of the celebration, he joined with Octavian, Antony, and others in offering a sacrifice to the Roman god Jupiter: a bull, a sheep, and a boar as part of a *lustrum*, or purification rite.

That was one reason why, from the very beginning of his reign as king of Judea, Herod would earn only the continual and increasing loathing of the Jews who deeply resented him for such an idolatrous system of worship; the fact that it was *Roman* as well was particularly galling.

But there were other causes at the root of hostility that would always linger, sometimes overtly, sometimes less directly, simmering like a volcano ready to spew forth its destruction. For one thing, the spectacular buildings decreed by Herod, designed to elevate the king's standing among the populace and which had kept more than a generation of workers employed, served as an inescapable reminder of the dominance of Rome.

But Herod was more concerned with maintaining the favor of Rome than gaining the affection of the Jews. He knew he would have to work hard to keep on pleasing the emperor, and one way he did this was outwardly, by erecting entire cities such as Samaria and Caesarea, the latter including a magnificent harbor utilizing the latest technology in hydraulic cement and underwater construction, and also building an extraordinary new temple, among other structures that were part of his rebuilding of Jerusalem.

One of the most impressive accomplishments was Herodium, named after himself and commemorating a battle he had fought and won against the Jews on that site.

To build this massive desert sanctuary meant hiring thousands of laborers: master stonecutters who worked on mammoth blocks of limestone, carvers and carpenters who hand-carved doors and window frames fashioned from huge logs, not to mention armies of glassmakers, plasterers, and fresco painters and men who worked their skills on stucco and in mosaics as well as ivory carvers, goldsmiths and silversmiths, and many more.

But his blood chilled in his veins when he heard that Octavian, later named Augustus, had defeated Antony and Cleopatra, and the king of Judea spent many weeks wondering if he would be allowed to hold on to his power.

Oh, how I waited for a messenger to come, he ruminated. *I could betray my nervousness, but it was continually grabbing my insides. I ate little. I slept little. I seemed disinterested even in sex, either with my wife or any other woman.*

A messenger on horseback finally arrived after a long journey directly from the emperor's chambers in Rome.

Emperor Augustus confirmed Herod as the appointed ruler of all of Judea!

But *within* the nation he ruled Herod never caught the love of the people, and he would always be thought of by most as a despised foreigner. He was forced to rule as an autocrat, with soldiers imposing his wishes, unlike David and Solomon and others whom the Jews obeyed out of respect and affection.

Ah, what could have been . . . beloved by my subjects, their undying devotion pledged to me through the years of my kingship, he thought, sighing with a wistfulness that nearly overpowered him. If only . . .

The air proved pleasantly chill against the aging ruler's face, which was showing the continual ravages of the life he had chosen to live, a face flaking and wrinkled for some time, seemingly every inch of it given to nearly intolerable itching that rarely gave him rest; a pallid gray look tinged the skin.

Perhaps I should return to Masada, he mused. *But that makes no sense. It would just mean more isolation. Though the terraced palace I built there is as grand as a man could want, it is still just stone and clay and a few tapestries and brightly colored mosaics. My family would not be joining me. They find it only a place for emergencies, not one where life can be lived with any kind of real joy.*

Herod scarcely knew the smallest measure of joy anymore, for he had found it necessary to spend so much of his fleeing time at the onerous task of constructing the most elaborate of plots against those lurking political enemies who were, in turn, spending so much of *their* time plotting against *him*.

As a routine matter, he was even forced into the desperate measure of having slaves sample each plateful of food, each goblet of wine; then he would wait impatiently to see if the contents had been poisoned. If so, the poor victim would drop dead at his feet, perhaps in great agony, and Herod would have to go through it all again with a fresh helping of food and drink, day after day, week after week, on and on for the rest of his life.

After many years of maintaining his royal rule through continual terror and brutality, he was now paying the price of the hatred he had engendered, years of planting spies throughout the populace, of sending Jews to Hyrcania, one of his fortresses, most of them never seen again.

Herod had become so egomaniacal with the exercise of his powers that he routinely violated traditional Jewish laws. One manifestation of this was the theater and amphitheater he had built at Jerusalem, where he staged gladitorial games and other forms of entertainment that were foreign to Judaism and repugnant to the majority of Jews.

His cities were generally pagan, as were his temples, and he invariably seemed to favor pagan and Samaritan factions over the Jews themselves.

Furthermore, he had a Roman symbol, a golden eagle, erected over Jerusalem's temple!

Along with all of the foregoing, there was Herod's oppressive taxation, which was periodically increased to pay for his latest building scheme.

But there was so much I did that was kind and good, he told himself. *I was very generous in the distribution of food when famines hit this land. All coins were struck without pagan symbols. Foreigners who wished to marry any woman from my household had to be circumcised. And what about the tax reductions I ordered again and again after most of the building projects were completed?*

Only the tyrannical elements of his rule were being remembered, though, the kind acts swept away by a tidal wave of selfishness and arrogance.

Ah, that breeze, he sighed with gratitude as a rift of cool air swirled by him, a rare moment of pleasure for which he did not have to pay a heavy price.

Herod felt momentarily refreshed after doing battle with dreams that were nothing more than nightmares spewed up from his past, replaying all the intrigues he had led, all the lives he had ruined, the blood of countless victims like a red tide sweeping back in on him from the darkness.

Herod raised his liver-splotched hand to rub a muscle that had started to twitch on his right cheek.

Shaking . . .

His vein-lined hand was shaking.

Herod quickly dropped it to his side, turning his attention toward the sky as he tried with some gathering desperation to find a fragile bit of solace in the ageless numbers of stars spreading their tiny but persistent lights with crystalline clarity in the midst of that typically beautiful, still Judean night.

Before I was born, he told himself, *they were there, and, I suppose, they will remain where they are long after this besotted and wretched body of mine has been turned into food for insatiable worms.*

In an instant, Herod's eyes opened wide, his attention riveted on an extraordinary sight above him.

A single star . . . larger than any of the others, brighter, and much nearer!

"What in the—?" he gasped.

A light more sparkling than any he had witnessed before seemed to be hovering above Jerusalem for a short while, then continued on in the direction of Bethlehem.

So beautiful, Herod said to himself, reaching his trembling hand toward it while the light still hung above the city. So—

And then it headed south.

Herod stood quietly, watching it go, restraining himself from calling out to it in a rather plaintive manner.

Please, whatever or whoever you might be, please do not leave so quickly. . . . Your beauty somehow has thrilled my tired soul this night. I think that I felt . . . cleansed . . . for one moment.

He waited at the window for several more minutes, hoping the light would return.

"Such nonsense!" he snorted. "I am old and sick, and my mind seeks to delude me in ways my enemies can never do!"

King Herod went back to bed, to sleep no better than before, pushing his vision of the light or star or whatever it was to some distant corner within himself.

Darien could feel the pathetic soul of this once-great man, yearning for peace, and he wanted to reach out, to minister to him, but that was not to be, for reasons only the heavenly Father knew.

"*Go to Bethlehem now . . . ,*" a gentle voice, full of love and patience, told him. "*And stay there with My Son while these three Magi linger.*"

As always, Darien obeyed; he went back to the baby Jesus, with no one but His earthly parents and a few livestock around.

"*I wish I could have reached out to King Herod as he did to me,*" Darien said. "*He seemed, then, so lonely, so burdened.*"

"*This one of whom you speak, however pitiful he may seem at times, this evil king, this Herod, is lost because of those crimes he has committed and those that are yet to come, without repentance for even one, offenses against Me and all the hosts of heaven,*" the incarnate One spoke only to the angel and nobody else, for even Mary and Joseph did not know that though His human body was young, it was but a fleshly shell over the rest of Him, which was older than time and eternity itself.

"*There are yet many more living for whom hope remains vibrant and real. Make these souls your companions, Darien, and none other. Turn away this very night from any of those who must be counted among the forever damned.*"

Darien winced at those words but understood the inescapable justice of them.

"*I shall, my Creator . . . I shall do as You say,*" the angel said in obedience and adoration.

The joy of fellowship with God-become-flesh overwhelmed the sorrow Darien felt for a soul that would remain lost for eternity . . .

CHAPTER 10

In the morning

The three Magi inquired throughout Jerusalem about the star, hoping others had witnessed it as they had.

They endured the noise of the ancient city, the dust and dirt, the often suffocating odors, the packed, narrow streets.

"How can they live like this?" Gaspar groaned.

"Pigs lie down in mud so long they eventually get used to it," Melchior said, snickering at the analogy.

"Your description is apt," Balthasar agreed, pretending to hold his breath and spare his lungs. "Just look at how uncouth most of these Jews really are. From the smell of them, I wonder if they know what a good bath is like!"

"I seriously doubt that they do," Gaspar interjected as a particularly stinking and very large middle-aged man in an old lamb's wool cloak bumped into him, muttered an apology, and continued on his way.

By Persian standards, Jerusalem and its often boisterous citizens seemed more than a little rough-hewn. But, then, the social and intellectual circles in which the Magi spent their time had been elitist from the start, a class totally separated from everyday association with the common people.

There were many legions of the poor back in Persia but none of the three Magi had ever come into contact with more than a few of them, let alone be surrounded by such people; they had been insulated by the cocoon that their long-held status as wise men had wrapped around them since they were quite young.

Gaspar sighed, thinking of the light, wondering if it could *ever* be worth what they were having to endure.

Dead ends everywhere they went!

Then they came upon a young woman wearing a skirt, a jacket, and an open coat, her head covered with a veil tied by a band. She sat on the ground in a little cul-de-sac at the end of a typically narrow alley. She was *chem'a*-making, using a process that involved pushing three poles into the ground to form a tripod on which a goat-skin bag containing *chalab* was hung. *Chalab* was a kind of milk that had been curdled and been left to turn sour by fermentation. The *chem'a,* or butter, was formed from this.

The Magi watched as the very disciplined woman sat down in front of the hanging bag and hit it with her fists many times, this "thumping" process not random at all because each punch was well aimed, continually shaking up the contents and commencing the transformation of milk into butter.

When she appeared to be taking a rest, Gaspar approached her and asked if she had seen the star. The woman looked up at him, smiled pleasantly, but said nothing, and then returned to her work.

He did not pursue the matter further.

"We can be sure that she saw *something,*" he told the others.

"But what makes you think that?" Melchior asked. "She spoke not at all."

"Her expression—there was something about it. I cannot describe at all well what I mean."

"That much is obvious," Balthasar said sarcastically. "Let us continue on our way."

Gaspar glanced back at the woman who seemed so at peace, oblivious to the raucous city all around her.

If only I could know what you do, he thought. *If only I could have the serenity that seems to be yours.*

A few minutes later they came upon someone else, an old innkeeper.

"I did see something," he told them, "but I thought only that I had imagined it, that it was just some kind of vision."

No one else had paid much more attention than that. Some admitted a quick glimpse, perhaps, and then back to sleep or lovemaking or gluttonous eating that would last well into the night.

Melchior, Gaspar, and Balthasar were becoming discouraged, thinking they had come to that city to find a newborn king.

"We have asked about the star," Balthasar chided them and himself at the same time, "but we have said nothing about what it means. Surely the Jews should be familiar with the contents of their own prophecies."

The other two were thankful that their friend had thought of this, for it stirred their own brains.

Gaspar snapped his fingers as he recalled a passage.

"There *is* a prophecy, I believe, regarding the king of the Jews, yes," he reminded them, "but it was only the voice we heard that announced any connection between what the old prophets had written and the star itself. This is something none of the old Jews seem to have known would happen."

"We should go out again and inquire of everyone," Melchior urged. "Surely we will find out something this time. In any event, we must not give up until we have been successful or until we know there is nothing but failure for us."

The very next day, they went to whomever would give them time and spoke of the Messiah, the king of the Jews.

"Where is He who has been born King of the Jews?" they asked again and again. "For we have seen His star in the East where we live and have followed it to this place. Please, tell us, if you will, for we have come to worship Him."

To say that they were seeking to "worship" him was a bit of a deception on their part since they had come more out of curiosity, intellectual or otherwise, but in no way would they have considered *worshiping* a Jewish king!

Their repeated inquiries soon reached the always attentive ears of King Herod, who became alarmed and, in his insecurity, turned to the Sanhedrin to seek information from its priests and scribes.

They told him that such prophecies did exist among the Old Testament books, to the extent that the Messiah was to be born in Bethlehem, that He would be a mighty king raised up to govern God's chosen people, that signs and wonders were supposed to accompany His birth and follow Him throughout His life.

"Signs and wonders?" Herod repeated, then demanded. "From whence shall these come? Tell me now!"

"Some will be in the sky, our king," one of the scribes told him, "like the star just one night ago."

"You saw it too?" Herod blurted out, thinking only he had been confronted with that singular vision.

"We did, sir. So did many of the common people, but they are largely unlearned, as you know, and could not understand any of its possible significance if any were attached to it."

"And you? What do you say? You sound skeptical, I must say."

"We think little of such occurrences. Certainly there is no reason to believe it came from God Himself."

Still, Herod was not at all reassured by that observation, the motives of the one who made it never less than suspect.

Oh, to shake the hand of another man and not wonder if he is planning some awful act against me! the king exclaimed to himself. *It used to be like that. How much I have lost during this long life of mine!*

In recent years, King Herod had come to think he could not trust any of the members of the influential Sanhedrin, for he suspected that more than a few of them were increasingly anxious to see someone else appointed by Rome to rule their nation, someone who could be more sympathetic to their needs than he had ever proved to be.

They seem to be serving me; they seem to be obeying all of my dictates, he moaned inaudibly, *but in truth the duplicitous lot of them merely wait for me to die so they can bring in a spineless puppet.*

Snorting with contempt, Herod looked away as aching regret chilled his age-weary mind.

To have contributed so much to this nation and yet to be surrounded by vultures ready to pick me clean!

Anger flashed across his deeply wrinkled face.

"Get out of my presence now!" Herod told them sharply. "I must consider these matters alone!"

As they were leaving, he looked at their backs and wondered, *How long will it be before you or one of your henchmen plunge a knife into mine?*

Finally Herod was alone with his fears.

When Herod summoned Gaspar, Balthasar, and Melchior, they knew they should not delay, for he had gained the reputation of possessing a ghastly temper. In those days, there was little or no safety guaranteed for foreign visitors; if a ruler such as Herod wanted to abuse them or even murder them . . . it simply happened, unprotested.

Herod was seated on his throne wearing a purple robe, the neck and sleeves of which were lined with material flecked with gold.

"You have found the king you seek," he said cleverly. "Now, I must ask, why is it that you have been inquiring so diligently about me?"

Only Gaspar felt sufficient courage to address him at that point.

"We seek the prophesied king of the Jews," he said, obviously nervous, "the One who had been called—"

"I *am* the king of the Jews," Herod interrupted. "Are you not hearing the words I speak from these very lips?"

"I have heard, sir," Gaspar said, his discomfort growing markedly. "The One sought by us is another. He is considered the Messiah whom Jewish Scriptures say is going to come to liberate His people one day."

Herod's anger was showing in his thin, white-bearded face.

"The Messiah!" he exclaimed, sputtering.

Herod paused, carefully examining the man before him and the other two a few feet in back.

They are Persians after all, he thought. *They worship other gods. They are here out of idle curiosity, probably because they are bored, and they need something other than lights in the heaven to occupy their minds.*

Herod shivered beneath the heavy robe and the layers of clothing under it; he felt a sudden chill strike deep to his very bones.

"But what makes you think the Messiah has been born as yet?" he said, carefully controlling the tone of his voice so none of the men would become suspicious of his intent.

Gaspar spoke forthrightly. "Because a strange light in the sky has been guiding us to this very spot, or so we thought."

"Or so you thought?" Herod replied mockingly. "You *may* be wrong then; is that not correct?"

"It *is* possible, yes." Gaspar spoke in as courteous a manner as he could muster. "If that be the case, then perhaps my comrades and I should return to our homeland as soon as the morning sun has arisen."

"Yes, perhaps you should," Herod added gruffly.

Just as quickly, the king made use of what little personal charm he had left.

"But then perhaps you should not," he added, his tone softening considerably. "Why do you not spend the night in my palace, with those accommodations that are truly worthy of men like yourselves?"

Some flashes of the old, ingratiating personality that had served him well showed through despite his age and infirmity and dissipation.

"Perhaps, in the morning, after you have rested sufficiently, we shall talk again," Herod added. "In the meantime, I will be able to ask my scribes and other learned advisers about this matter and pass on to you whatever wisdom they might have to impart . . . to help you in some way."

The three Magi reacted agreeably to this and thanked him.

"Our camels and some belongings are at the little inn where we have been staying," Gaspar told him.

"Give me the address, and I shall have my servants take care of everything," he said, smiling at the three of them.

When they were gone, Herod lost no time gathering the Sanhedrin together again in his throne room.

"Are you certain about the prophecies?" he asked them all.

"We are certain," one of the scribes spoke up. "As you know, sir, these foretellings have been passed down from generation to generation for hundreds of years or more. We have carefully preserved them through many meticulous copies as well as a great number of the original parchments.

"There can be no question, sir, at least in our minds about their contents. Having studied them diligently, we are quite convinced that these so-called wise men are here on a mere fool's quest."

"I am not as convinced as you are," Herod said.

"But you do not know the writings as we do."

"But I *do* know you, and you, and you," he retorted sarcastically, pointing to each one. "These writings, as you call them, may not be suspect at all, but it is the *interpretation* you give them that I must question. If musty old scribblings from long-gone centuries are as clear in what they convey as you have suggested, then your reluctance to accept them as divine raises some serious questions."

"We do accept the *writings,* sir," the scribe shot back, carefully modulating the anger in his voice so as not to insult a still-powerful king or blatantly contradict the man publicly. "It is merely any possibility of their *fulfillment* in this present day that we are disputing."

"And you *all* are in agreement, I suppose."

The scribe hesitated.

Herod grinned slightly as he noticed this.

"So . . . I believe I can safely assume that not everyone in your group shares this outlook of yours," Herod remarked with an acid tone, not letting this brief reaction pass without the sort of confrontation he had mastered over the years of his reign and which he could use to good advantage.

"One member . . . ," the scribe started to say.

"One member *what?*" Herod persisted sternly, now genuinely losing any patience he had tried to show.

"A man named Nicodaemus."

"I have heard of him. He is somebody who is considered very faithful. What does he tell you?"

"About the star, sir, the star."

Herod's expression froze as he waited for whatever else the scribe had to tell him about this Nicodaemus.

"He thinks the star may be a sign from Jehovah."

Herod's throat muscles constricted without warning, and it seemed he was close to choking.

What is it that has been placed so abruptly in the heavens above us? he asked himself a question that seemed tantalizingly without an answer. *Be this the light of some gods who have deigned to guide our steps through an uncertain future or, rather, an evil band of devils from the nether world beneath our very feet who have come to torment us at night? It was a light so bright and beautiful yet it brings only a clinging and chill darkness of the spirit, the soul . . . like a disguised shroud mocking us from the heavens.*

Herod knew that self-control before strangers and countrymen alike was important. He had to avoid any semblance of weakness that would encourage his enemies to attempt to overthrow him. Still, he nearly lost that control, nearly let it slip away from him as he pondered the meaning of what had happened.

"What of that strange light?" he managed to say out loud at last to challenge the scribe who seemed so self-satisfied from his years of study and learning. "Many of us have seen it. What *are* you blathering about?"

"Nicodaemus thinks it might be a sign."

"A sign of the Messiah's birth?"

"Yes . . ."

Herod fell back against the meticulously hand-tooled wood-and-leather throne that had been used by the various kings of Israel for many centuries. With a dazed grunt and a wave, he dismissed the scribes and others who had been summoned.

They left none too soon, allowing Herod to keep the secret that had plagued him for months.

May they never find out, he thought, shrinking from what would happen to him if his enemies became aware of his deteriorating condition.

His hand . . .

It was shaking again, this time much worse than before.

CHAPTER 11

THE MAGI met with King Herod the next morning after a breakfast consisting of eggs, dates, citrons, apples, and lemons, which were called *malum medicum* by the Romans.

All of this was sent by the king to the sumptuous private quarters he had turned over to the three of them the night before, giving each a large room, with hand-tooled leather furnishings, which greatly impressed and delighted even these men who had grown up in the midst of a luxuriant Persian culture.

"Bethlehem is where the prophecies indicated the Messiah is to be born," Herod told them. "It is close, just southwest of Jerusalem. Perhaps that is where this star you mentioned ceased its travels. Please consider this a possibility, my honored guests."

The king's manner seemed friendly, eager. He did not project an air of menace but, rather, one of true helpfulness, and they were won over by it as they glanced from one to the other. The king's words made some sense, especially considering what the astute scribes with whom he had been consulting surely must have told him.

"We shall do as you suggest," Gaspar spoke for all of them. "And I must say, King Herod, that we three are grateful for the kindnesses you have shown us. We shall be glad to cooperate any way we can."

"Good, good!" Herod exclaimed, feeling genuinely pleased and suddenly acting younger than his many years. "All I ask, now, is that you go and search diligently for the young Child, and when you have found the little One, bring me word again, that I may come and worship Him also."

Once again, his speech seemed innocuous enough that Melchior, Gaspar, and Balthasar had no reason to doubt the motives of this Jewish ruler, and they were to come to admire all that he had done for his nation, especially the beautiful buildings for which he had been responsible.

"Will you let me take you to Masada?" he asked quite eagerly, seeming more like a young man instead of an old, tired one.

"What is Masada?" Gaspar asked with great curiosity.

"The most marvelous place!" Herod exclaimed. "I built it to keep my family and myself safe during times of war but also as a retreat."

He told them of the grand three-terrace palace on a plateau more than a thousand feet high.

"The meticulous paintings, the marble columns," he went on. "And that view! It goes on for many miles in every direction, gentlemen. There are two smaller palaces near it and places where the water supply can be maintained for years. Rich soil for crops, a great deal of room to expand, and . . . and—"

Herod was nearly ecstatic as he talked, some of the encrustations of age falling from him, and a whisper of his long-dissipated youth returning.

"It is terribly isolated," he added, "and a day's journey from here, but I can promise a sight beyond any expectations you might have."

He leaned forward.

"Will you not let me take you there?"

Herod's passion for the impressive mountain fortress was so contagious that the Magi were tempted to forestall their original mission and let the king do for them what he had just suggested.

"We *would* like to see Masada," Balthasar admitted sincerely, "but I am wondering, your highness, if we could perhaps visit it upon our return from Bethlehem? We would have much freer minds and hearts then, and this would help us appreciate the full magnificence of your creation."

"Yes, of course," Herod agreed. "I shall have men ready to escort you to Masada when I see you again."

They had intended to start out for Bethlehem just a short while later, but Herod continued to engage the three of them in conversation, particularly about the beliefs that they had held all their adult life.

"I tire of this Jewish faith," he sighed wearily at one point. "It has lost any meaning it might have had once. Can you tell me more about what you believe?"

And they did so, expounding through the morning and during a multicourse lunch more like a banquet, that extended well into the afternoon, stopping just before dusk.

"I am very interested," Herod assured them with great smoothness, though only to guarantee that the three Magi would return to him with important news about the Child who now would be nearly two years old.

There was no way he could ever send his soldiers to search for the Child; that would seem far too threatening.

It would terrorize everyone, he thought correctly. *Those so inclined would be certain to hide the Child.*

The foreigners seemed better able to get the information he needed without generating suspicion, then he could carefully consider what to do with this potential new threat to his tyrannical rule.

Everything depends on these men, he told himself. *What a great coincidence that they have come here when I needed them most!*

A most hearty dinner feast marked the end of the Magi's stay at King Herod's palace . . .

Finally, amply filled with fine food and drink, Gaspar, Balthasar, and Melchior were about to travel the six miles from Jerusalem to tiny Bethlehem.

"We have to wait!" Balthasar urged abruptly. "Look! There is no star now. How do we know that we go to the right place?"

He pointed to the sky, which would soon have a full display of stars but not the brilliant one that had become so familiar to the three of them. Thus far, that particular star had not reappeared.

"Because of what the king's scribes said," Gaspar stated. "They did seem convinced, did they not?"

"But they are fallible men," Balthasar reminded him. "And we really do *have* to be sure. It is true that Bethlehem is but a short distance away, yet what if we find nothing, and someone else there has a different interpretation of certain Jewish prophecies? Would this not confuse us to the point of making us give up altogether?

"There is a danger that we become ensnared by the fallible opinions of men instead of looking up to the heavens, as we have been doing all of our adult years. It is from *there* that our help should come, my friends."

Melchior and Balthasar had to agree with him. So the three lingered a bit, sitting next to their camels, and carefully surveying the darkening sky.

"Now, Father?" Darien asked with mounting zeal. *"Should I not appear to the Magi as before?"*

"Yes, Darien," Almighty God told him. *"The time again has come for you to guide them where they need to go."*

"Oh, Father, thank You for giving me this task. It fills me with joy that is beyond measure."

"And so shall you shine forth."

The coming of night, a time that seemed somehow more serene than any they had known before now . . .

Gaspar, Melchior, and Balthasar had been sitting on the ground, barely able to keep awake as night advanced. Cooling breezes caressed their faces like the fingers of a beautiful woman. And there were the customary calls of animals and birds coming from the Middle Eastern darkness around them, acting like a kind of lullaby.

"It is really very nice right now," Gaspar sighed. "I have to say that there is something about this backward region that is beginning to seem so much more pleasant than our own land."

Minutes passed quietly, happily, none of them speaking, their senses taking in the feel of that place, the sounds of it.

They were about to fall asleep when—

That now-familiar and strangely comforting light . . . at last!

"Look!" Melchior said, pointing excitedly.

The bright star had returned.

The three men jumped to their feet, startling the skittish camels.

"It seems so much more vivid tonight!" Gaspar exclaimed with wonder. "I wonder why that is the case?"

"I feel as though it is saying something to me," Melchior remarked. "How can that be? How can—?"

Balthasar interrupted him.

"It does not speak," he countered. "You are filled with imagination. That is dangerous. We all *see* the star but you are the only one *hearing* anything. We must not be turned aside by any personal fantasies!"

Melchior nodded as he added, "It is just that I felt such peace then, as though a great, encompassing wave of it had washed over me."

As soon as he spoke, the light seemed to brighten.

"Look at that, my good friends!" he gasped. "It seems to be somehow communicating with us."

"Nonsense," barked Gaspar. "You are under some kind of delusion."

"If I am deluded, how can you explain *that?*" Melchior retorted, pointing toward the light. "Give me some rational answer to what is happening here, and I shall try very hard to believe what you have to say, old friend!"

Before their eyes, the star perceptibly dimmed.

Gaspar's mouth dropped open.

"Be happy!" Melchior said. "That is what we are being told. Can you not sense this?"

He hoped the other two could.

"Be happy with whatever lies ahead," he went on. "We have no reason, it seems, to be afraid, for we have come this far without harm, have we not? Remember the beasts and how even they somehow seemed guided to protect us."

Balthasar spoke up, an odd expression on his face, his eyes half-closed.

"I think Melchior is right," he said. "I begin to feel what he has mentioned . . . peace, Gaspar, peace beyond what I thought I *could* know."

"From something up there in the sky!" Gaspar exclaimed. "Have you lost your senses as well?"

"I have not lost anything," Balthasar replied. "I think—"

The star had begun to move.

"No ordinary *thing* does that," Melchior said. "We have been astrologers since the day we could speak our first few words, as were our parents before us. We have been taught that all wisdom comes from above."

"But only through Zarathustra!" Gaspar rebuked him, his nasal voice trembling with this unaccustomed display of emotion. "It is he to whom we should be turning, begging him for some kind of answer."

"Perhaps you are right, but then why is it that we have encountered nothing like that light or star or whatever it may be in all the years we have lived in this world, Gaspar? This one tonight is very different. I think it is far, far more meaningful than any of us dare to contemplate right now."

Gaspar could say nothing, could do nothing but stand there, frustrated, closing his hands into fists, opening them, closing, opening.

"We have to hurry," Balthasar begged. "We must not lose sight of the star. We must stay in its path."

Gaspar agreed resignedly, knowing that his instincts were suddenly failing him in the presence of this very special light that seemed to have a life of its own, however absurd that sounded to a well-educated mind.

CHAPTER 12

After midnight . . .

They arrived in Bethlehem and found a caravansary in which they could rest until morning—as if any of them could sleep after the expectations that had built up in their minds!

None of them could, as it turned out. All three would get up, at various times, and walk outside their little cubicle and look up at the sky, to find the light still there.

"I am right over the house where the Son and His earthly parents are staying, Father," Darien said. *"These three men are so close, and yet they do not know where He is."*

"Give them time," God said in a kindly voice. *"They are finite; you are infinite. It does take them longer to grasp the truth. Be patient, Darien. I know you are anxious to be by the side of the Child. It will not be much longer."*

"I shall try, Father, I shall try."

It was Gaspar who slept the least. It was also Gaspar who had been, over the years, by far the most faithful in his worship, following diligently all of the many precepts handed down by Zarathustra.

"And now I find myself confronting a force that may be more powerful than the great teacher ever was," he said out loud after walking down some steps to the courtyard below, and beyond it to an isolated stretch of sand.

Gaspar dropped to his knees, then fell forward onto his face, great sobs tearing through his thin body.

"Father?" Darien asked. *"Now?"*

"Yes . . . now," almighty God told the anxious one.

Suddenly, Gaspar *felt* the light, its warmth touching every inch of him, and he heard someone talking, not through his ears, but into his very soul.

"You shall find the One you seek after you arise in the morning." The voice spoke with great clarity.

"How will—how will we know?" he asked anxiously.

"You shall . . . in an instant."

"Please, I need to know more."

"How much can I say, Father?" Darien asked of his Creator.

"Speak what you feel burdened to say. Whatever it is will be acceptable to Me."

"Precious Father, I am so pleased."

"Do not delay, Darien. Seize the moment!"

Gaspar heard other voices, those of Balthasar and Melchior. They had awakened also and were coming down the steps. Immediately they were seized with the same spellbinding awe and fell on the sand beside him.

"Are you what we have been following?" Balthasar asked with awe.

"I am as you say," Darien replied.

"Are you the spirit of Zarathustra?" asked Melchior.

"Father?"

"Say what you want, Darien, and I shall stand with your every word."

Darien spoke clearly to the three of them.

"It is not this man who brings you what you see, what you feel, what you hear; for a greater One than he has been born in this place."

"We are Persians," Balthasar said. "If you speak of the king of the Jews, how can we accept Him as greater than our gods?"

"When you enter His presence a few hours hence, your questions will cease."

"No *man* can affect us as you say," Melchior added. "It is impossible."

"It is impossible if you close your mind, your heart, and your soul to Him. Many will do that and turn away, but not you."

Gaspar raised his head for a moment and was about to speak when his words were swept away in the beauty of what he saw.

The other two looked up as well and reacted as he had.

"So beautiful . . . ," Gaspar spoke for himself but for his friends as well. "You are more than a star. You are—"

More of Darien's kind joined him, and they began a joyful chorus unlike anything the three Magi had heard before, not in all the temples of their religion, not in all the crowds of worshipers, and not in private moments among the three of them, their faces pressed down into their prayer rugs, their chants rising in near-unison.

Gaspar reached out with his left hand.

"Let me touch you," he pleaded. "Let me *feel* you."

"*I shall touch* you," the angel said.

Darien brushed Gaspar's heavily wrinkled forehead with that touch for which the Magi had just petitioned.

The man started to fall back against the sand.

"I am faint," he said in a whisper. "Please, help me."

The angel took his hand and steadied him.

"You will be entering the holy presence of the incarnated Son of God," Darien told him.

"Not Zarathustra?"

"Not a mere man, NOT someone whose physical body has been in a grave for centuries and whose soul is elsewhere . . . but a living member of the triune Godhead, clothed for a time in mere flesh!"

"It is time to go, Darien . . . Return to the house where Jesus is staying; be by His side when they enter in the morning."

Darien hesitated then started to withdraw, as did the other angels, though the Magi pleaded with them to stay.

"*You three must go back to your beds,*" he told them, "*and let the next hours see you rest without worry so that you will be alert for the next day.*"

"And where are we to go?" Gaspar asked.

I am not surprised at your question, dear man, not surprised at all, he thought, for he knew that they were capable of accepting only tiny nuggets of divine truth at one time.

"*You will* truly *know.*"

And then, suddenly, ancient darkness reclaimed the night.

"Where is the king of the Jews?" Balthasar asked of a heavyset merchant who seemed to be alert to everything around him.

Obviously quite a jovial individual, this man, smiling broadly, started to roar with laughter.

"Sitting on a throne in yonder Jerusalem," he replied finally after getting control of himself. "You have the wrong place, stranger!"

He looked at Balthasar and seemed about to burst out in another uproarious display until Melchior interceded quickly.

"*Another* king," the Magi told him, summoning a degree of patience he did not normally possess, "the One revealed to us by your own prophecies."

"You mean the Messiah?" asked the other man, looking much more serious. "Is that He of whom you are speaking?"

Melchior nodded, thinking he and his friends could at last now get help in their search.

The man paused, his expression that of someone who had remembered a particularly fond dream but who had come to decide it would never be realized, a regret written across his heavily lined face.

"Here in Bethlehem?" the man spoke as he squatted on a sheepskin mat behind an assortment of clay pots and other items. Then he started laughing again, his laughter seeming forced this time yet nevertheless louder than before, so loud, in fact, that people in the narrow street stopped what they were doing and turned around to see if they could find out what was happening.

Gaspar, Balthasar, and Melchior saw that they would not get anywhere with him and soon went on their way. They spoke with others who either answered not at all or with scorn that had no humor whatever in it.

All three were becoming bitterly discouraged, Gaspar as usual the first to voice how he felt.

"What *are* we to do?" he complained forlornly. "We have come this great distance, met with a egomaniacal king, and wasted everyone else's time in addition to our own. There seems to be no supernatural message whatever in all of this, not from Zarathustra, nor Jehovah, nor any other god."

His exasperation was unmistakable.

"As it is turning out," he added, "we are simply three foolish and deluded men on a journey with no destination."

"Father, is there something You want me to do," Darien asked, *"perhaps to help these good men?*

"Fill that humble house of love with yourself," God told him.

"As brightly as before?"

"Yes, Darien, as brightly as before, but now it shall be here instead of in the heavens that you will do this."

Directly ahead, the three Magi saw a tiny structure seemingly aglow from within.

The three Magi saw that now familiar bright glow coming this time from the interior of the house.

And they walked toward it, their hearts beating faster.

We are doing something that our culture almost never allows, Melchior told himself, *walking boldly up to a stranger's house, uninvited.*

He repeated that last word.

Uninvited . . . perhaps not, the Magi thought, *perhaps not.*

Gaspar peered inside the doorless little structure, as did Melchior, who was followed by Balthasar.

Standing before them was a very young Child, not much more than a toddler, alert, wide-eyed, looking with great interest at them.

"See his eyes!" Balthasar exclaimed, surprised. "They show no fear at the approach of strangers."

Melchior noticed this as well.

"It is as though we are somehow, to him, not strangers at all," he said, gasping.

But it was, as to be expected, Gaspar who sounded an alarm.

"Where are the parents of this beautiful Child?" he whispered. "They risk too much by letting anyone they do not know so close."

"Over there!" Balthasar pointed. "In the corner."

Mary and Joseph were asleep in a modest bed to one side, unaware of what was transpiring in front of them.

The Child reached out to them, smiling, and they came to Him without question. Then the three Magi fell to their knees in front of Him, their heads bowed, not knowing what else to do in such a blessed presence as they felt themselves to be.

"*It has been good this day, Father,*" Darien said, great love and adoration for his Creator propelling his words.

"*Oh, I agree,*" God told him. "*I am proud of you. You have not failed me now, nor shall you ever do so, Darien.*"

"*Never?*" the angel repeated, more like a human Child reacting to a kind comment from his human father.

"*This is a happy time, and there are to be more of these times. But toward the end, you may be tempted to give in to a welling despair.*"

"*You will be with the Son and me, to guide and protect us?*"

"*As you shall be by His side, so shall I be with you, Darien.*"

"*Thank You for this mission, Father, and its blessings.*"

After seeing the joyful countenance of this special angel and bidding Darien to rejoin the holy Child in quiet little Bethlehem, God then sat back in His throne . . . and wept.

CHAPTER 13

THE THREE Magi fell to their knees in front of Him, their heads bowed, not knowing what else to do in such a blessed presence . . .

Gaspar, Balthasar, and Melchior lingered for some time after they first met Jesus but finally remembered the precious gifts they had brought from Persia, a land of exotic goods, to be sure, and went outside to get them from the backs of their camels.

Gold . . .

Balthasar gave Mary and Joseph an urn of solid gold (at a time when men and women of other cultures viewed gold with what could only be described as mystical appreciation, its value incalculable).

Frankincense . . .

Melchior presented a small bottle of frankincense, a fragrant gum resin gathered from the trunk and the branches of the *Boswellia* tree that gave off a sweet, spicy odor when burned.

Myrrh . . .

Gaspar's gift was a large earthenware container in which had been poured *murru*-based perfume, derived from a shrub or small tree in the *Comiphora* species. Of great monetary value, it was a component of holy anointing oil made by mixing the purest myrrh with sweet cinnamon, calamus, cassia, and olive oil. Solomon the king had been so enamored of this perfume that he wrote about its delicate scent.

Do any of these men realize, Darien wondered as he observed this tender little scene, *that these are symbols of virtue, prayer, and suffering? Or do they assume no special meaning other than the generous act the giving of each signified?*

The Magi spent more time with the parents and the Child than they had intended, for none of them wanted to leave, and they kept delaying their departure an hour, then another hour, and yet more hours after that.

All of the three Magi underwent drastic personality alterations while spending time with Jesus. None would ever be completely the same again, even after leaving the baby and His parents, and returning to their own homes some days later.

Of the three, the most profound change occurred with Gaspar, who seemed reluctant to leave this Child named Jesus.

"He is not quite two years old," he said in open admiration, "and yet He fascinates me beyond what I could ever have imagined."

"That is what we have found," Joseph agreed. "There is a sweetness about Him and yet an intelligence that seems beyond anything I have ever witnessed in such a young Child. He seems to *understand* everyone with whom He comes in contact. Though He cannot speak sentences as yet, He says so much with the expressions on His face."

"If only we could stay here and watch Him mature," Gaspar muttered to the parents. "I think it would be wondrous to witness how your son develops."

"You would be welcome," Joseph assured him, though the Magi's forlorn manner indicated what an impossibility it would be for them to linger even a short while.

"Should they stay, Lord?" inquired Darien, this time of the Son.

"No, guardian of My flesh. They should go back to their nation, where they will come to understand fully as the years pass all that has happened this day."

"And then they can spread by their mouths and their parchments the wondrous things for which you will responsible? Is that it, Lord?"

"My Father has taught you well, Darien."

The Child, who had been leaning against His mother, turned to His parents, telling them in a kindly manner, "*Rest . . .*"

With that, Jesus walked outside.

"Where is He going?" Joseph asked, concerned. "We should not let a two-year-old run off by Himself!"

"I think He shall not come to harm," Mary suggested.

Joseph threw up his hands in exasperation, obviously not as convinced as his wife that this was the case.

Gaspar, Balthasar, and Melchior nudged one another self-consciously and thanked the parents for their time. Mary and Joseph in turn expressed their gratitude for the generous gifts they had brought.

After excusing themselves and going outside, the three Magi noticed

Jesus sitting under the stars of that clear, beautiful night, looking up toward the heavens. He heard them nearby and turned in their direction, smiling.

"*Good-bye*," Jesus told them simply with a sweetness none had ever heard before.

And then Gaspar, Balthasar, and Melchior were on their way, with much to ponder during the coming weeks and months.

As the three Magi started the long journey back to their homeland, news they received of the slaughter of all Jewish boys two years of age and younger filled them with great guilt because they knew they had provoked King Herod by not returning to Jerusalem as he had asked of them.

It was to become a time of the greatest terror for every mother and every father of a young son.

Bloodshed and death reigned.

The streets of Bethlehem, Nazareth, Jericho, and many other places, even Jerusalem itself, were filled with cries of shock and pain and not a little anger.

Darien heard about what was happening from other angels assigned to the families who saw their sons torn away from them and cut to pieces by men who were merely following orders.

"*It was a scene out of hell*," Gabriel told him.

"*Were there demons?*" Darien asked.

"*Oh, yes, many, many demons. They could not take the souls of those so young but they chose instead to frighten them while they were still clothed by human flesh. Despair, Observer, and the others feasted upon the existing fear and magnified it.*"

"*Observer? He did not simply write down what was happening?*"

"*Despite his seeming reluctance to become involved in such ghastly business, all that fell by the wayside, Darien. He was no different from the others.*"

Just the stroke of an aged man's trembling hand . . . that was all it took.

With that single decree, Herod bred a wave of such intensified hatred of himself that threats against his own life became commonplace. Despite his dictatorial form of government, he found himself vulnerable during the latter years of his life and was forced to live at Masada more than anywhere else in Israel.

"*The blood on his hands!*" Darien exclaimed.

"*It will haunt him to the grave and beyond*," Gabriel added. "*There are no more restful nights of sleep for this king. He will be tormented without fail.*"

"And then the very demons who seized the opportunity he gave them will seize him after his heart beats for the final time."

"Once a man of greatness . . . ," Gabriel sighed, *"now to be thought of in ages to come as a barbarian, a murderer of the innocent."*

In the background rose the cries of dying children.

"It is our fault!" Gaspar exclaimed with anguish after they had returned to their safe homes. "We are responsible for the deaths of all those poor children; their blood is surely on our hands!"

Balthasar reminded him of why they had disobeyed Herod.

"We were warned," he said. "It was another of our dreams just before we left Bethlehem. Again a strange being came to each of us and—"

"I know," Gaspar said, still disturbed. "I know."

He had not so soon shorn himself of his many years of training imposed upon him by another culture, and groping with what had happened caused considerable conflict with his heritage since helpless children had been involved and Persian culture took great effort to safeguard its young.

Darien was the being they all had seen that final night in Bethlehem.

He had come to the three men, not in a dream, though these Magi assumed the visitation to be in that manner, but, rather, Darien was allowed by His heavenly Father to stand before them in space-time reality.

"You should not return to Herod," he warned the Magi. *"He is seeking only to kill the holy Child."*

"Kill?" Melchior repeated, hardly believing that he had heard correctly. "Why would even such a brute do so? Surely that little boy is a gift from some god. Herod should be asking Jesus to join him on the throne!"

"This is what he fears, that he will have to share his throne or give it up completely, another king taking his place."

"What will happen if we do not go back as he wanted?" Gaspar asked, alarmed.

As it turned out, Almighty God revealed the answer to Darien before the question could be asked.

"So many children will perish," he told the Magi. *"Much sorrow will grip families throughout this land. For their king, who should be protecting his people, soon will begin such a thorough and relentless slaughter of the innocent that it will send terror into the hearts of mothers and fathers in every town and village."*

"All of them dead because of one boy!" Gaspar muttered. "How *can* we anger Herod and allow that to happen?"

Again God had provided the angel with a reply.

"Many are going to die," Darien told him, *"so that One, later, can give Himself for all of mankind."*

The three men were strangely quiet though none of them had any idea why.

"We must warn Mary and Joseph," Gaspar said, his desperate tone showing how much he cared for the parents as well as the Child.

"They have been told," Darien said reassuringly. *"You need not worry. The three of them are now on their way to where they must go. They will be safe as they travel and safe where they stay."*

"Where is that?" Melchior asked.

"To Egypt."

"We have many friends there!" Balthasar exclaimed. "Tell us how we can help them, and we shall not hesitate to do anything that is asked of us."

"Send parchments to those you know. You will be instruments of almighty God in providing them shelter."

"How long will they remain in Egypt?" Gaspar inquired of the angel.

"Two years."

"Just two years?" Gaspar reasoned, ever the uncertain one of the three. "It seems hardly long enough."

The others glanced at one another, realizing that their friend's apprehension was hardly illogical this time.

"Surely the family *must* stay away for a far greater period of time than what you are suggesting," Gaspar added. "Herod's memory will not fade in just two years, nor will this horrible edict be done away with so soon."

"In two years, this king will be dead," Darien revealed. *"And his evil decree will die with him."*

PART III

Make yourself familiar with the angels, and behold them frequently in spirit; for without being seen, they nevertheless are present with you.

SAINT FRANCIS DE SALES

The three Magi were safely headed back to their own nation.

Life for these men would be much less troubled than for the little family they left behind, though they left only after trying unsuccessfully to convince the parents to come to Persia where they could be protected by the government where Gaspar, Balthasar, and Melchior continued to have the strongest possible influence.

Mary and Joseph considered this possibility with great seriousness, for there was much about it that was appealing, not the least of which was that they would have three now very good friends dedicated to their daily welfare without fail.

But then, the following night, the angel of the Lord appeared to the earthly father of Jesus in a dream, saying, "Arise, and take the young Child and His mother, flee to Egypt, and stay there until I bring you word; for Herod will seek the young Child to destroy Him."

Joseph wondered about the wisdom of fleeing to Egypt instead of Persia, especially in light of the fact that they would be strangers in a strange land, with no one to help them, whereas the three Magi were eager to be their protectors in Persia.

But finally, Joseph decided not to question the judgment of his strange nighttime visitor.

After recovering from the impact of that encounter, he realized he would have to act quickly, for Herod's decree would take effect immediately and there was no way of telling when Roman soldiers would tear through Bethlehem on their brutal mission.

Joseph hurriedly washed and dressed and, with his wife and son helping, gathered together whatever meager belongings they could bring with them. Then Joseph took Jesus and Mary by night and departed for Egypt.

To be able to reach that country, Jesus, Mary, and Joseph had to come to grips with the hardships represented by a very long journey that took them across the dangerous Sinai and Negev desert wastelands.

Finally, though, the three of them came to the eastern edge of the Mediterranean, where they found a coastal road that took them to the northeast border of Egypt.

For many centuries, the bountiful Nile Valley, a region of lush vegetation and fertile soil nurturing a variety of crops, had been a beacon to Jews. Such was true of Abraham during an extended period of famine, and also for Jacob and his sons, who fled to that land for the same reason. Their descendants settled along the Nile, not to mention Jeroboam, who had to escape into Egypt to avoid the wrath of King Solomon.

The land of the pharaohs, thought Darien. What an ironic turn of events from all that had happened so many centuries before, just before Moses became the leader of the Jews, back when they were slaves and treated as beasts of burden!

That once hostile country had continued as a secure place of refuge for Jews. More than a million of them lived in Egypt at that time, Jews who were finding it in some ways to be more hospitable than their own land, where the political intrigues fostered by Herod created an atmosphere of life-threatening danger for anyone who happened to disagree with the him.

Jesus, Mary, and Joseph stayed there until the death of Herod: that it might fulfill which was spoken of the Lord by the prophet, saying, "Out of Egypt I called My Son."

CHAPTER 14

THERE WAS to be a single confrontation between Darien and a gathering of various Satanic entities while Jesus and His parents remained for their two-year stay in the land of Egypt.

Since they had entered the very nation that once so brutally enslaved the Jews but was now itself enslaved to the worship of false gods, Satan assumed that, because the family was in a bizarre place of strangers, defeating Jesus there would not be difficult.

I have them where they will be surrounded by my handiwork, he thought as he prepared an onslaught much like a general getting together a plan for combat. *Everywhere they turn, they will find what Jehovah calls darkness but what I call evidence of my brilliance.*

Gods, so-called, for every purpose under the sun! Some of them, including Osiris and Horus, had been elevated to the status of national deities. Ptah, the god of craftsmanship, was another example, plus Amun and Re, who joined together and became Amun-Re, with the ability supposedly to materialize into the form of a ram or a goose. Thoth was another god, the one who bestowed learning and wisdom.

Animals were an important part of religious life for the Egyptians, many acting as live images for their gods. The apis-bull was thus connected with Ptah, the ibis-birds to Thoth, falcons to Horus, and cats to the goddess Baster. All of Egyptian life—political, social, economic—was interwoven with some form of homage to these so-called deities.

Demons strangle the entire nation, Darien observed as he wandered through the streets of the city where the little family of three had settled for at least part of their stay. *When the Israelites left the land and the Egyptian pharaoh tried to annihilate them, God showered His wrath upon their pursuers. With their leader snatched from them, with their military might crippled, with the economy of the nation ashambles because cheap Jewish labor was no longer available, the people turned more resolutely in the direction of the Deceiver for help.*

Abruptly, greater numbers of gods magically seemed to appear, though these gods were but predatory demonic entities from the corridors of hell, sent in disguise to present themselves as benevolent spirits and help the Egyptians out of their time of tribulation but, in truth, only chaining the people to a far worse destiny.

Darien saw fathers willing to sacrifice their children if demons were to require this of them. He saw mothers killing their unborn babies with abortions and the bloody fetuses being used in the most loathsome of rites.

It matters not to any of Satan's emissaries whether the worst sort of infamy is being performed, for these creatures gain a great deal of pleasure from the pain of those so helpless.

Darien smiled then as he thought, *Even so, the Father snatches their souls from the grasp of Satan. For no aborted baby is sent to hell. All are taken into His kingdom where no further pain can affict them, and where angels are their companions.*

Perhaps the most blatant manifestation of Egyptian occultism was seen in the belief that each pharaoh was himself a god. Below him in the religion's hierarchy were the chief priests. Next came a host of astrologers, readers of texts long considered sacred, and singers and musicians, the latter providing the only means of service considered suitable for women. At the bottom tier were the common clergy, whose tasks ranged from burning incense to interpreting dreams. Egyptian prayers were not always directed to gods in temples but to the statues of favorite deities kept in Egyptian homes in little shrines, the design of which became a family project in each case. Two of the most popular deities in this respect were Bes, the god of the family and newborn children, and Taweret, goddess of pregnant women. Neither was what could be called attractive figures: Bes was a ghastly looking creature, part dwarf, part lion. Taweret was little better, looking like a bloated hippopotamus.

The practice of magic in one form or another had become interwoven into every facet of Egyptian life, as was the wearing of amulets that were supposed to protect the individual from the dangers of life, including disease, accident, and whatever else. These charms were made of many different materials and represented a range of deities or sacred symbols.

Supposedly, some of the stones of which the amulets had been made, such as lapis lazuli, themselves had protective qualities.

The son of Ramses II was supposedly gifted with special magical powers. Other noted magicians abounded, including Imhotep and Djedi, respected members of the elite social circles, and treated in almost god-like fashion by the lower classes.

Only once before had Darien been plunged into such a hellish center of demonic activity. That had occurred during his *Angelwalk* odyssey, when he was taken to visit hell itself and had to be rescued by an angel named Stedfast . . .

"*You turn the warm and protective womb into a graveyard that spits out its tortured and dismembered dead,*" Darien had said to the master of evil standing before him, "*and call this a battle won in your war against the Almighty. Your weapons are the bodies of babies with bloated stomachs—your elixir the blood of victims of senseless slaughter throughout time itself, mixed with the fluids of perverse acts in dark places of passion.*

"*You shout brazenly of a hard-won victory, and yet all you have left before you is the ceaseless damnation of hell! Your trophies are nothing more than the twisted bones of a demented grotesquerie—your former majesty become an eternal mirror held up to the rotting filth that you now call your very being.*"

Darien's anger was spent. He had only the shreds of some pity left. And he told his former friend that that was so.

"*You are without hope,*" he had shouted, watching Satan cringe at the sound of his words, "*and this is by your own choice. But as for myself and my destiny, I choose, now, my Creator and yours. Take me back, Lord!*"

Suddenly Darien had been lifted upward. Through the volcanic-like geysers below, there is for an instant, barely visible, the bent-over shape of a wretched creature falling to his knees and weeping . . .

Yet Satan would continue to fight fiercely and in desperation. It was not that he had chosen to ignore the truth but had convinced himself that he could defeat it, turning the truth of God into a lie. And there was nowhere that he proved more active with his acts of deception than throughout the Egypt of that early period dated 2 A.D.

Though the reality of their Son Jesus being incarnate deity was not comprehended by Mary and Joseph, it was notably obvious to the unclean spirits in Egypt that they could not let God Incarnate stay in that country without one devastating onslaught that they hoped would destroy His physical presence. If God's Plan were thwarted, Satan and his demons would have an advantage that would surely be monumental, giving them confidence to be more bold in the future.

And this was why Darien's presence became critical, for in that Jesus had to appear as human as possible, and in His fleshly body itself He was human, any strictly *supernatural* defense needed to be carried out by the angel assigned to Him as His guardian, a duty that necessarily included protection for Mary and Joseph.

They possessed few belongings, but much of what they did have was stolen either by snatchers as they walked to the market from the one little room they occupied, a room paid for by the meager revenue from carpentry jobs Joseph was able to find periodically from Egyptians who valued the quality of his work above their prejudices against anyone who was a Jew.

Mary and Joseph would wake up in the middle of the night and hear the strangest of noises nearby, often, it seemed, right in the room with them . . . whining sounds, scraping sounds, a bizarre howling, all of which seemed far more ominous than anything that would have come from mere animals.

They often found themselves sweating, their hearts beating wildly, as they anxiously surveyed the darkness, only to be met with nothing more, it seemed, than the mere foolishness of their own fears.

But not their son.

Not this Jesus, this God incarnate . . . He always slept soundly, no disturbance bothering Him, either at night or during the day when He would nap.

Serene. Oh, yes. There was a serenity about Jesus that seemed of itself to ward off intrusion by anyone of flesh and blood.

But the demons tried. Oh, how desperately they tried! And that was when the battle was joined, when Darien stood up to their onslaught but also needed Gabriel, Michael, Stedfast, and others to stand by his side when the fury of Satan's soldiers became too intense.

He remembered what Stedfast had told him about True, an angel given the duty of standing firm before the entrance to Eden . . .

I was at the entrance to the Garden of Eden, guarded as always by my dear comrade. True had remained there for thousands upon thousands of years, alone much of the time except when other angels had been able to pay our friend a visit, and to talk with him, to tell him what had been going on in the world.

"There have been so many tragedies," I said, my mind swirling with the history that had elapsed since the last time.

"I can understand that," True replied. "I remember the awful darkness that fell upon this place just after Adam and Eve left in shame."

His radiance dimmed momentarily, a sign of intense sadness.

"Oh, what they gave up, Stedfast, what they gave up," he said, the sorrow he felt almost palpable.

"And what they brought upon the world!" I reminded him.

"How can the Father forgive them?" True asked. "How can even mercy itself be so merciful with such as those two?"

We talked a bit longer and then I said, "You were the only angel who could endure staying here until the end of time."

True looked at me, believing my words because no unfallen angel is capable of lying but, still, he was astonished by what I had just told him.

"Out of so many of us, I was the only one?" he asked.

"That is my understanding."

The weariness that had attended him a moment earlier seemed to have dissipated.

I sensed that True was looking at himself through a kind of mental mirror and recalling the vast multitude of loyal angels, obedient from the beginning, to whom he had belonged before being called to duty at the entrance to Eden.

This splendid True, this comrade, must continually try to cope with the severe isolation imposed upon him by that mission to which he, above all the others in heaven, had been assigned . . .

"Be faithful," Darien whispered, remembering what Stedfast had told him. "Be true, my friend, be as you always have been, dear True."

And now Darien had a similar mission of his own . . .

As a guardian, like True.

True's mandate had been to stand against demonic intruders at the uninhabited Garden of Eden.

But for Darien, it was a far more profound circumstance . . . to defeat those who would claim the earthly life of the Son of God.

CHAPTER 15

NIGHTTIME . . . the air was humid, an odor of age and death constant.

First among the demons to reach out and attempt to take the life of the young Jesus in that darkness-shrouded country was one named Despair.

Darien saw him coming, rising up from the rancid depths of hell, a blood-red entity not unlike Satan himself, the souls of many who had succumbed to him clinging to his countenance until he shook them off like a grotesque dog shaking off water.

A demon named Despair.

"I come to claim the sleeping forms of father, mother, and Child," this one spoke. *"Stand aside."*

His manner was domineering, but Darien knew better, knew that this particular fallen angel was not one of Satan's most spellbound followers.

"I shall not!" Darien declared forcefully to the intruder. *"Nor will you be permitted to enter."*

"I am more powerful than you," Despair said, his tone a theatrically smirking one. *"I am certainly more fierce."*

He moved a step forward.

"You cannot resist. I shall roll over you and squash you as a man with a large foot squashes a hapless bug."

Suddenly Darien was joined by Gabriel and Michael. Despair stepped back.

"Nor am I *alone,"* Darien said defiantly, grateful that he was being given some help but not completely certain that he needed it.

A horde of demons suddenly joined Despair. Darien recognized among them the familiar countenances of Mifult, DuRong, Torment, Adultery, and scores of others long beautiful in their unfallen state but now hideously misshapen. And there was also Observer, the personal journalist of Satan, standing to one side, recording the events as always.

"Can you resist us?" asked Despair, centuries of evil and corruption carried forth in his shrill voice.

"As it is the Father's will that we do so for the sake of the Son," Darien declared to him, *"surely it shall be so."*

The demons began babbling and shrieking, sending forth a fierce cacophony of hideous sounds and fostering the most loathsome and often fetid images in the minds of Darien, Gabriel, and Michael.

But it was not any of this sort that could ever have succeeded in weakening the defenses of the three angels at the threshold of that home where Jesus was sleeping, for they had encountered the reality of these many times during their own travels over the centuries of history that had passed, and though still affected, still repulsed, still sickened, they were not overwhelmed, as doubtless Despair and the others were hoping.

Instead, more powerful, to be sure, were the gentler scenes, various recollections of moments from heaven itself, before the casting out.

These had the greatest pull, the most tempting potential, to undermine the determination of any unfallen angel.

"We once were comrades," Despair pointed out. *"You and I, Darien, could scarcely have been closer."*

He snorted, the foulness of his form sending chills through Darien and the angels on either side of him.

"Why did that have to end?" Despair continued. *"You could have come with us, all three of you. Surely you cannot dispute* that!"

"And you could have stayed," Darien retorted. *"If you had, it would have remained between us as you have just said."*

"We chose to follow a new master. What is so wrong with that?"

"What is so right *about following the* wrong *master?"*

Darien briefly had paid heed to the beguiling images from heaven, but he, of all angels, was not to be seduced by them. Before his travels along *Angelwalk,* that might have been the case. For he had begun that journey in an attempt to uncover the truth about Satan, and he had found it in every stinking, sinful, perverse act that ever occurred, from the first moment of disobedience in the Garden of Eden to the present, when that very sin that had been encouraged by Satan had made it necessary for the Son to become flesh.

Darien stepped forward.

"Look at yourself then," he said. *"Look at the glorious body you once had. That body was given to you by the Master you forsook eons ago."*

Despair hesitated, as did the others, no sounds whatsoever coming from them now, no movement. They just stood where they were, on that dirt street at the edge of that sprawling city in Egypt. Beyond the three unfallen ones remained the prize they desperately wanted but were not being allowed to have.

. . . . that body was given to you by the Master you forsook eons ago.

Despair's memories, intended as a weapon to wear down the resistance of Darien, Michael, and Gabriel, became the opposite in a moment of divine irony, for those three unfallen ones still could claim heaven as their own, while Despair and the other hordes had only hell and a master who cared nothing for them.

"*You* must *let us through!*" Despair screamed. "*Darien, you cannot imagine what he inflicts on us when we fail.*"

"*So we should disobey the Creator* you *deserted so you can avoid punishment from the devil you inherited?*" Darien asked. "*What would such an act make us, Despair? No better than you! For we would be throwing away the redemption that will keep countless souls from being lost and headed for damnation and turn them instead toward salvation and the streets of heaven forever!*"

"*The torment!*" Despair cried out. "*Every moment of our lives is filled with anguish anyway but when we go back empty-handed from even a minor assignment, Satan subjects us to what you could never conceive, Darien.*"

His form shook with the anticipation of what would be awaiting them if they did not achieve the goal of destroying the incarnate One.

"*We have to do this!*" he pleaded. "*If that means destroying* you, *then, yes, it must be done.*"

Darien did what Despair could never have expected.

He stood still, saying nothing nor calling into that arena any more of the Father's unfallen angels.

"*We can destroy you,*" Despair chortled. "*Surely you* must *realize that. Surely you must fear—*"

"*Your master is the prince of lies,*" Darien finally spoke. "*And you are now believing one of them. We can* never *be destroyed.*"

Darien leaned forward.

"*Nor can* you *be destroyed, Despair. But do not ever forget that heaven is* eternally *our home, while* hell *is yours until you are cast into the lake of fire* forever!"

"You lie!" Despair shrieked. *"Satan told us we can surround you and others and by sheer numbers eradicate you."*

"Go ahead. Try what you must. See for yourself."

Despair turned around to the other demons and told them to attack. As they were gathering on their cloven hooves and getting ready to charge, they heard a sound coming from inside the little house, a movement, a murmuring.

Then a two-and-a-half-year-old Boy appeared in the doorway.

Despair gasped at the sight of Him.

Jesus looked up into his face.

"How sad you seem, Despair," He said.

"Oh, Holy One, we have known nothing but sorrow since we left."

"You can change. You can turn your back on Satan. You can come to My side right now, and stand with Darien, Michael, and Gabriel."

"That I could do so, I would give up everything . . ."

"Give up just one. The devil whom you serve. Turn your back, and walk forward, Despair, become Joy again."

Despair moaned at the mention of his former name as an unfallen angel. Joy had truly described every moment of his existence then, and he had given others the overflowing joy he felt as they gave back to him that much and more besides.

"I remember the stars coming into being," he said wistfully. *"I could reach out and actually touch them. I could go from galaxy to galaxy as easily as I—"*

"As easily as you can walk forward and bring along with you any of those who no longer want to return to the ever-consuming flames of your present habitation."

Despair looked into the wise, pure young face of that Child and could feel nothing but love coming from it.

"I cannot give up what is now my very being," he said, groaning with a great and unholy mournfulness deepening his voice.

Abruptly, he reached out for the Child, and Darien was about to stop Despair when Jesus motioned him away.

"But I also am unable to bring myself to harm any part of you," Despair acknowledged finally.

"You will go back to the greatest pain you have ever known," Jesus reminded this former occupant of His holy kingdom. *"Yet that need not be. You alone make the choice, Despair. Choose righteousness! Reject evil!"*

Despair shook through his entire self.

"Yes, I know, but it shall not be any different for You, for me, this or any other day. You will return to Your usual sound sleep unharmed and, as must be my own terrible fate, at the same time I shall submit to the punishment that is ahead, meted out by the most despicable of creatures."

"Good-bye, Despair," Jesus said, bidding him farewell.

"Good-bye, my Lor—" The demon tried to speak but was unable to finish, drawn to the flame-punctured darkness that beckoned.

The Child did not smile in triumph, for there was nothing over which to gloat, one tragedy avoided while another, the continued damnation of a once beautiful creature, went on as before, as always.

And then the Child went back inside to sleep again, while Darien, Michael, and Gabriel stood vigil the rest of that night and well into the hot afternoon that followed, no more demons intruding until the final days just before Jesus, Mary, and Joseph were to depart Egypt and return to the Holy Lands.

CHAPTER 16

King Herod has died . . .

That announcement was spread rapidly throughout the known world, carried by boat and on the backs of asses and even by carrier pigeons as well as by ordinary foot traveler. There was jubilation among the inhabitants of the Holy Lands but also some degree of reluctant sorrow, since this man had been responsible for many of the most glorious buildings known in the history of Israel, buildings the construction of which had given countless numbers of men much needed work.

"He was arrogant," some observers opined, "but along with that came a grand vision that will be hard to replace. There is no one on the scene now who seems quite able to carry on as he had been doing in his better moments."

Since 37 B.C., King Herod had cast an inescapable cloak of influence over the Holy Lands. Not for many hundred years had any king of Israel become as pervasive in his impact upon everyday life. He had succeeded in imposing a period as politically stable as anything could be in those days. Suddenly, after decades of this one king being in control, of Jews seeing the outward manifestations of his rule everywhere while hating his ties to imperial Rome, Herod the Great was gone, and the glue that held together different political and cultural factions abruptly was gone forever.

Sadly, after King Herod's death, the kingdom disintegrated and ended up being parceled out by the Romans among Herod's sons. Judah itself was placed under the control of Roman procurators seated at Caesarea, the Roman administrative headquarters, ironically a port city built by Herod.

But, for the parents of Jesus, the news was a blessing beyond description.

After being told, the two of them literally danced in the streets of the Egyptian city where they had been staying.

"Crazy Jews!" some of the townspeople were saying as they witnessed this joyful behavior. "They surely have taken leave of their senses."

"No, no, it is more than that," others suggested. "See how very happy they are. How much happiness have we known?"

Early morning . . .

The three members of that special family had neatly packed their few belongings and piled them on the back of the same old loyal donkey that had licked the brow of the baby Jesus four years earlier.

"*You are so tired,*" Darien said to the animal, his tone soothing, taking its mind away from a myriad of aches and pains assaulting its tired body, muscles once strong now waiting patiently to rest for eternity.

Mary and Joseph knew well enough that this would be the last journey it would ever take with them, for its age had made the beast increasingly slow. Simple walking became an obviously great effort producing an uncertain gait at times. Neither parent comprehended how aware of the donkey's state their son was also.

"We cannot inflict this journey upon our friend," Joseph said shortly before the return journey was to begin. "He was given to me by *my* parents, and now this family has had him since the beginning."

Joseph's manner was sad.

"Our friend has given so much of himself to us," he added with no joy about the prospect of what might have to happen. "I . . . I fear that he will not make it back and we will have to leave him for the vultures and the hyenas or else find some place where he might be buried safely and not be dug up later by the same predators."

Joseph's eyes were filling with tears, ashamed that he was displaying such emotion over what many other men would consider just an animal; but for his family the donkey had proven to be so much more over the years.

"I could not bear that, dearest Mary," he went on. "I surely could not, you know. I think we should keep him with us for as long as possible and pray that he will be shielded safe along the way."

"I think you may be right," agreed Mary, not unsympathetically, but speaking realistically. "Yet what are we to do for another to replace him, Joseph? We have no money to spare. And beasts of burden are expensive in this country."

Jesus had been looking into the weary old face of that faithful donkey.

"Are you able to do this, dear friend?"

The animal gazed at him through eyes whose sight had dimmed more than Mary and Joseph could have realized.

"We must take the bundles off his back," Joseph observed. "He might be in pain, from the look of him."

"I know what you feel. Will you be able to serve Me this one last time?"

The donkey groaned, trying with some desperation to find a source of renewed energy within itself.

Once a strong, tough male, this one's condition had begun deteriorating gradually for a number of years, but there was yet no thought or instinct within him to simply give up by resolutely sitting down on the ground and not moving, as others of his kind might have done, resisting the best efforts of their masters to make them stand and continue working and then breathing a final time before they died.

"One day, one of your offspring will carry Me through the streets of Jerusalem as crowds sing 'Hosanna!' all around."

Suddenly, the donkey was holding its ears up straight instead of letting them droop as before. It shook its head in a quite human-like gesture, as though trying to clear some mental cobwebs from the corridors of its brain.

"I can ask My Father to relieve you of your burden now, and we will find another if you cannot do this. You will not be disappointing Me."

The Child leaned over and kissed the animal between the ears.

Mary's eyelids shot open wide.

"Joseph, look!" she said excitedly, pointing at the two of them.

In an instant the donkey, having seemed so wobbly a moment before, now appeared to have somehow gained new strength, unsteadily at first, and then—

Pawing the ground! And snorting impatiently!

"Our friend is ready, Mother, Father," announced young Jesus. "We can begin the journey now."

His parents glanced at one another but did not question what they had just witnessed, for both had long ago decided there was no way they could have afforded all the parchments necessary to have written down everything that had come about thus far in the young life of their son Jesus.

"Someday, my wife . . . ," Joseph once remarked wistfully. "Someday we will make a record of everything."

Mary humored her husband, for this was something she, too, wished they could do, but she also sensed that it would not fall to them to do this but rather, it would be left as a task for others.

PART IV

The devil is no idle spirit, but a vagrant, runagate walker, who never rests in one place. The motive, cause and main intention of his walking is to ruin man.

THOMAS ADAMS

There was to be a single confrontation between Darien and a gathering of various Satanic entities while Jesus and His parents remained for their two-year stay in the land of Egypt . . .

That battle passed quickly enough, but Satan had not given up this very early stage of his fight against the incarnate Deity. Centuries of time would never temper his mad rush toward his own punishment, undeterred by acts of remorse or moments of even the most tentative kindness. No other name but evil could be his, and he came to wear it with great arrogance as he trotted out for the unwary his great panoply of infamy, before which they, if unsaved, could not hope to stand.

Satan understood that he must stop Jesus before the three of them left Egypt.

"I cannot let Him return to the Jews," he ranted in hell, "or face a much harder contest with the forces of God in Israel."

Despite the hard-line domination of the pharisaical religious rulers in that country, he knew that the Jews had been anticipating their Messiah for centuries and would be ripe for an extraordinary individual to come upon the scene and stir up a following, whereas the deluded and long-corrupted Egyptians had no such expectation. The vast majority of them already viewed the pharaoh in that role, bowing before him as though he were Jehovah incarnate.

Satan now planned to move against Darien in an attempt to disable him so that an assault on Jesus, Mary, and Joseph would be less likely thwarted.

"I shall do it alone!" he declared to the multitude of demons spread out before him in the main meeting chamber of hell.

His ego left him no choice but to claim all the ability necessary without the help of any others.

"I would be happy to join you," Despair called out, hoping to make the master once again proud of him and thereby erase the stigma of his earlier defeat earlier at Jesus' doorstep.

But Satan would have none of it.

"I shall not even begin to listen to any one of you who has failed me so miserably!" He spat out the words with special contempt that made the vast lot of them tremble. "You had a chance and failed. Only I can do this!

Seeing an opportunity to deter further onerous displays of Satanic wrath, the various assembled demons burst out with boisterous acclamations of shrieking approval, hoping to hide their insincerity as they tried to win favor with him instead of the punishment that had been meted out to Despair, DuRong, and those others who had return from the failed mission.

Despair looked about at his haggard comrades and saw Observer to one side, compiling everything in his book; he shuffled over to him.

"He does not realize the futility of it," Despair whispered.

"He never will," Observer lamented.

"Then why do we continue to follow him?"

Observer looked up, a strange expression distorting his already hideous features, and replied, "Because we are him."

Despair was about to ask Observer to elaborate when it suddenly became apparent that Satan was ready to leave hell for his self-appointed mission.

"I shall be back with the head of a child," boasted the Prince of Darkness vaingloriously, "and the heart of God."

CHAPTER 17

As Jesus, Mary, and Joseph were at last walking away from that temporary dwelling of theirs, ready to embark on the dusty, primitive road across Egypt and into Israel, the land of their birth, they were stopped by a small but enthusiastic group of local Egyptians standing directly in front of them.

"I have baked some special cakes for your journey," one of the women said, handing to Mary a small, brown leather pouch into which she had carefully placed her little gift, just made that morning and still warm from the oven.

Another woman approached them with a second pouch, this one a bit larger and packed full with strips of dried meat that would not spoil throughout the hot days of travel that were ahead.

One of the men had nothing that they could eat but instead gave Jesus, Mary, and Joseph something quite different.

A small cloak of leopard skin.

"Very warm," he told them. "It will be good for the nights."

He turned toward Jesus.

"This is my gift to Jesus," he continued, "my gift to this most remarkable Child whom we have been privileged to know."

Jesus walked up to the man and gratefully took the cloak from him.

"May My Father bless you," He said, "and keep you throughout the rest of the days of your life."

The man's gaze immediately turned toward Joseph.

"How can *he* do as you say, Jesus?" he asked. "In a moment or two, the three of you will be gone from our presence."

He cleared his throat and added, "I am grateful for your thought, Child, but how is this ever to be?"

Jesus' expression was a serene one.

"It is through the Spirit of My Father that this shall be revealed to you, friend," He said with great warmth.

"I give you a mere cloak, and you seem to promise so much more."

"You give of your love to the Son, and the Father shall remember what you have done for all eternity. Do not be anxious. Let peace be yours day after day. For it *is* to be that you *will* come to know in due time who I am, and you will then accept My Father's salvation out of a trusting heart and humble spirit."

The man scratched the top of his head, pleased by such words but also deeply puzzled.

"I *will* miss You, Jesus," he admitted. "I will miss the strange thoughts Your mouth speaks in riddles."

"They are riddles only for a time."

"But how can I accept them if I know not their meaning?"

"When your children were conceived and then born, was this not a mystery of life itself? Yet you accepted it without question."

"But it was something that happens every day in this place and elsewhere and continues on to this very moment. But that is not so with much of what You have said during the past two years and just now, Jesus. What You say is not ordinary. Nor can it be accepted as easily as a child coming into this world."

Jesus nodded in appreciation of the man's befuddlement.

"Yet there will be a time when believing the truth is for you and the others gathered here at your side the same as accepting the reality of the birth of a child," He said, "the rising and the setting of the sun, the warmth of your wife in your arms. It will be as natural and as wonderful as any of these."

The man's eyes narrowed.

"You are greater than the pharaoh whom we worship . . . ," he said in a whisper, as though he had been given sudden knowledge that no one else possessed and was seeking confirmation. Though You are but a mere boy, is this not so, good Jesus? I would be very happy if You would tell me now whether I am correct about this or not. I would not be pleased to be carrying within me a delusion that is idle fantasy."

Without hesitation, the Child leaned over, spoke into his ear, and then stepped back.

The man's face broadened into a smile unlike any that had graced it before then, and he swerved around to look at his wives, his children, and the other villagers who had accompanied them.

"We must let this dear family go!" he proclaimed. "They have a tiring trek ahead of them."

Long after Jesus, Mary, and Joseph had left, this man was being pestered with questions about what the Child had whispered, and he would tell them nothing other than simply, "When it happens, we all will know, with joy leaping in our hearts. Until then, be of good cheer, my family, my friends."

He reached out his arms toward them in an encompassing gesture.

"Above all, beloved," he added, "do not be afraid."

CHAPTER 18

AN EARTHQUAKE so devastating that it was to reach halfway across Egypt . . .

Satan did not cause it. He had no such power. But he chose to take advantage of the catastrophe, as he often did in the midst of the various hardships that befell mankind, along with the chaos and suffering they generated.

Darien remembered his encounter with Satan in hell during his *Angelwalk* journey, and clearly words from those lips came back to him as though just spoken . . .

"You talk of conscience. Goodness. Mercy. Such silly stuff, Darien . . . for the weak. My strength is pain, my energy from the bloodshed of wars, my ecstasy from the dying of hope and the birth of despair.

"Your men of God rant and rave about my punishment sometimes someday somewhere. For me, and my exercise of power, there is no wait. I mete out punishment now. I grow stronger from the cries of countless starving millions. Plagues are my rejuvenation. I dine on what your redeemed ones call anarchy, barbarism, hedonism. I relish the perverse acts of the homosexual and call them my baptism."

Only a handful of earthquakes ranging from moderate tremors to those that leveled entire villages across the country had been known to occur in that North African region over thousands of years.

In such a primitive time, quakes of any severity at all were capable of producing disastrous results since building codes as such were unknown and homes were packed together without regard for any kind of safety.

And yet few of those in the past or later would prove to be anywhere near as strong as the one hitting Egypt that morning. In an instant, villages and isolated homes as well as ancient monuments, temples, and other buildings trembled, swayed, then crashed into rubble.

Joseph pointed with awe and terror at the sight now spreading before his family and himself.

Dunes moving like animated figures!

Several of the sandy forms were several stories high, and suddenly they started shifting like sugar in a bowl held in a trembling hand.

Mary gasped. Jesus put His arm around her and spoke some comforting words. She reached over and touched His cheek lovingly.

"What a different child You are," she said in admiration. "I should be talking to You as You have just done with me."

"My Father has made me a comforter," Jesus told her.

"But more," His mother said knowingly and with a touch of pride. "My dearest Jesus, You *are* much more than that."

Her words seemed to show that she understood much about Jesus, but in fact Mary did not, at least not with the knowledge that she later would possess. For she, as so many others, was looking through a glass darkly, seeing flashes of the truth, tantalized by these glimpses but nothing more.

"We are on a sea of sand . . . ," Joseph was muttering. "The dunes are waves tossed about before our very eyes."

It was a sight none of the three would ever forget; it may have given rise to Jesus' later parable comparing faith to a house built on solid rock while another nearby, that of someone with no sound faith at all, rested on shifting sand.

Fortunately, Jesus, Mary, and Joseph had not as yet left what was solid ground; they were only on the very edge of the desert but not into it, a circumstance for which they were grateful since otherwise, all three of them would have been sucked under by what had become a huge amount of quicksand. But they *were* safe, even as they were given no choice but to witness the terrifying event before them.

The rocky surface beneath them seemed more like a welcome hand holding them safely in its palm, and Joseph kissed it with considerable gusto.

A minute passed, then two, three, then four.

After five minutes, they had started to get to their feet when, less than fifty yards ahead, the earth was opened up by an aftershock that exceeded the severity of the original quake and was accompanied by what seemed to be a loud booming sound.

They were thrown to the ground again by the force of it, which subjected them to a violent rolling motion.

Even their normally surefooted donkey tumbled, falling over on its side, and staying in that position; whether unable to move or scared to do so, the result was the same, leaving it to look dazedly from side to side, wondering what had happened and seeing no place to hide, no shelter to seek.

But none of them, human or animal, was hurt, since they were by then considerably away from any buildings in the village, though the damage there and elsewhere throughout that region was appalling.

"*Lord, Lord!*" the angel cried to the Son.

"*Yes, Darien,*" Jesus replied.

"*Do You want me to stay here or go to those behind us who are so unfortunate?*"

"*Go to them. I will be safe here for the moment. I would have asked you to do this if you had said nothing.*"

"*Thank You, dear Lord . . . I . . . I do not know, but I think there is some need for me to be there.*"

"*There is, Darien. There is a need as you say. Hurry to your task.*"

People sobbing, bleeding, with broken arms or legs, many, many dead in the debris-choked streets of the village.

Screaming . . . the very young and the very old, their sounds equally pitiable . . . and others, terrified, in pain, suffocating.

A deafening din arose from the men, women, and children wrenched out of the comforting familiarity of their everyday lives, lives lived according to a routine that had been going on for many years and now suddenly plunged into an existence more intensely frightening and disturbingly uncertain than anything that they ever before experienced.

Darien could feel the pain, could feel the cold and terrible panic, could feel the despair, with thousands of people wondering if their lives *could* get back to normal, given the catastrophe around them.

And no organized help.

No resources or planning for this disaster existed on any significant scale.

While the leaders invariably made sure that they were as well protected as possible, the lot of the common people was anything but secure. Basically they were being left to their own devices.

Countless numbers of families were made, in a matter of seconds, homeless and possessionless and forced over the ensuing days and weeks to be beggars in an era where social responsibility to the poor was nearly nonexistent except for occasional, very public displays of supposed generosity, in reality no more than ploys to maintain public admiration of the rulers and the upper class from which they invariably came.

Loss of property was only one immediate and traumatic consequence of the quake.

Injuries.

These were another part of the nightmare. Many of the victims would never walk again, many would never be "in their right minds" again, and many would lose one or more limbs in a time when amputation was hardly humane.

And the dead . . . scores of villagers were dead, either killed instantly or dying under debris before they could be rescued.

The immediate effects of the earthquake were severe enough. But there was also a residual impact that would become apparent as days and weeks passed.

Casualties among livestock. Hundreds of cattle died along with thousands of chickens, dogs, and cats.

Food stores became contaminated, which meant that some sort of famine was virtually certain as time passed.

The elderly and the very young would succumb to both hunger and the outbreaks of disease that would follow.

Oh, Father, Father, Darien thought. *So many, so very many!*

Darien saw people dying everywhere, their souls leaving their bodies as repulsive demons grabbed them and took them, screaming . . .

To hell.

All had linked their souls with the occultic forces that were dominating Egypt before the new Christians, forty or more years later, would bring some relief from demonic activity.

Darien could not do anything at first but stand, stunned by the extent of the destruction and the ferocity of it.

Those close to death would see Darien clearly, would reach out in desperation for him because of his sheer beauty, the majesty of his appearance, but as they did so, demons would spring forth seemingly from nowhere, and the doomed unsaved would be surrounded by Satan's cruelest henchmen.

"Please, help!" each one would plead. "Do not let these creatures take us to the flames. We can feel the heat even now."

"I can do nothing," Darien had to tell them without exception. *"You worshiped them as statues of strange gods. You must go with them."*

"But can that be so?" most retorted, not unreasonably. "How can I be damned for what I did not know?"

"You never read the Scriptures?"

"Yes but—"

"You never felt a tugging at your heart, a still, small voice nudging you?"

"Yes but—"

"So you read, you felt, you sensed?"

"Yes but I—"

"And you rejected the truth, then? Is that not right?"

Demons hissed and chortled, and each soul entered the blazing corridors of that awful place that Darien knew so well. But there was one who did not, one near death but not quite to the point that the scurrying *things* were ready to claim him as well.

Hakki was a scribe, one who had served the pharaoh with great loyalty. But as a scribe, he had access to a vast library of parchments, scrolls, tablets, and other sources of knowledge. Like the Magi, his mind was a questioning one, open to truth wherever that truth could be found, even in Jewish writings.

And he was now dying. Some blocks of stone had fallen on his chest. Bones were broken. One of his ribs had punctured a lung. He had little time left as he lay on that little street in that village not far from the most populated center of Egypt.

"I think it is too late, angel," Hakki said as he saw Darien approach.

"You know me to be what I am?" Darien asked, surprised.

"I do; that I do, angel. I have read about you in some writings I discovered by a few old Jews."

"You take those Jews seriously?" the angel probed, hoping the man was as genuine as he was beginning to seem and not just engaging in some rambling ruminations as the dying often were prone to do.

"I *must* take them seriously," Hakki replied without any hesitation. "There may be much great wisdom in what so many of them have to say. Not that there are not boring genealogies but once I get past those, I find a true enlightenment offered by none of those who are counted among our so-called wise men.

"Yet I also understand that the wisdom of a group of ragged Jews is hardly something to give me any confidence that I have truly stumbled upon divine truth rather than man-made or evil fantasy."

"*How* could *a few backward Jews have anything worthy to say?*" Darien said, deliberately snorting for emphasis. "*Perhaps you are possessed of some sort of sorcery if you believe as you have told me?*"

"If they are as ignorant as you imply," Hakki proposed, "how is it that they were so strikingly correct about you, angel?"

Darien came closer.

"*I believe you,*" he said. "*What is your name?*"

"Hakki. And yours?"

"*Darien.*"

"That is a good name. Has the Lord God Jehovah sent you?"

Despite himself, Darien gasped, not prepared for such directness.

"Your manner seems to suggest that I am correct," Hakki observed in the face of the angel's silence. "I can see that you have made the same mistake about an Egyptian that I used to make regarding Jews . . . that we are a heathen lot at best, bereft of any intellectual or spiritual validity."

He smiled, though weakly.

"I have studied much, indeed, about angels," he said. "I was skeptical at first but then realized that we had them in our religion also, only they were not beings of sparkling countenance but loathsome creatures instead. When I read about fallen and unfallen angels, I began to realize that there was a connection. The unfallen ones supposedly served the Jews, but we were left with the . . . the—"

"*Demons?*" Darien offered.

"Yes, the demons . . . the demons. Even our high priests acknowledge the presence of demons from the underworld. They rejected, however, that, for the Jews, there were only angels like you."

His forehead wrinkled, and he seemed disgusted as he recalled the time he had spent with those religious leaders.

"The questions I posed went very much unanswered: 'If there are *only* the demons as far as we are concerned, what happened to the countless other angels?' My voice getting louder, my tone more incredulous, I added, 'Are you saying to me that these beings do not exist, perhaps never did? If so, who, then, decided that *we* get the evil angels while the Jews are left only with their fantasies? However, if unfallen angels do exist, the same question must be asked.' I waited for a response, and got a dismissal."

Abruptly, the man coughed up some blood.

"I have little time left," he said, his voice progressively weaker. "Leave me alone. I do not have to be told by you that I am going to hell."

"I would not have said that," Darien replied quickly while expecting the onslaught of demons any moment.

"But I have done nothing to accept your God and turn away from the many gods of this accursed land."

"Are you so sure, Hakki, that you remain so far from salvation?"

"Of course I am. I—"

He looked at Darien with some intensity.

"Why are you here?" he asked. "I would have thought that your God had better things for you to do."

Darien knew he had to be patient with this man and also alert to any "signals" that Hakki was sending his way.

"Nothing could be better than to talk with a man who has an opportunity to find himself in God's presence any moment," the angel assured him. *"That is why I am here. Little else matters right now."*

. . . an opportunity to find himself in God's presence any moment.

Hakki repeated those words out loud.

"You talk as though there is hope for a lifelong heathen," he observed, trying to seem cynical but not entirely succeeding. "If you are an angel sent by God, then one of you is not very astute."

"Until the last moment of life, yes, there is hope."

Darien was at the man's side now.

"You asked why I am here," he said. *"Do you still want to know the answer?"*

The Egyptian nodded as he replied. "I did ask that. And you may be assured that I am still curious."

"I stand here now because of the prophesied Messiah . . . ," Darien announced abruptly, waiting for Hakki's reaction.

The Egyptian blinked several times then closed his eyes, rubbed his forehead briefly but in a frenzied motion, and proceeded to recite rapidly a passage of Scripture that he happened to have read a long time before, "'He is despised and rejected by men, a Man of sorrows and acquainted with grief. And we hid, as it were, our faces from Him; He was despised, and we did not esteem Him.'"

Hakki seemed to enjoy seeing the angel's nonplused reaction.

"Is *that* the Messiah you mean?" he asked pointedly. "Have I perhaps quoted the appropriate verses?"

"*Yes . . . ,*" Darien answered, barely able to speak, for never before had he encountered such insight from someone who remained unregenerate in the midst of it.

The Egyptian smiled as he spoke again, this second time reciting another verse of Scripture, "'Thus says the LORD your Redeemer, and He who formed You from the womb: "I am the LORD who makes all things, who stretches out the heavens all alone, who spreads abroad the earth by Myself.' "

"*You have read from Isaiah, I see,*" Darien remarked, trying to regain some control of himself.

"And more, much more, angel Darien. I appreciate several of the other passages from yet another pile of parchments very much. The ones I saw . . . they . . . they . . . seem . . . to have . . . so . . . much hope."

He started crying then.

"*That I could reach out now and hold you as though I were flesh like you,*" whispered Darien, greatly moved by Hakki's tears.

"That I could feel you do so; then I would not be so afraid to die."

Darien knew that Hakki had given him a striking look inside his very soul.

"*You do not have to know that fear. You can be at peace.*"

"Peace? There is no such thing for this lifelong servant of demons."

Just then there was the sound of rushing wind and the sensation of heat, not from any fires caused by the earthquake.

"I smell—" Hakki started to say, while experiencing some difficulty in swallowing. "I see such horrors."

They were in a mad rush for him, a shrieking crowd of them, foul, twisted creatures, creatures reeking the rancid odor of death, centuries of decay wrapped around them like a worm-infested shroud.

"I thought how wonderful it would be to see your God," Hakki said, terror written on his features.

"*You can! It is not too late.*"

"I believe the Jews *will* have their Messiah. I believe He will be more than just for them but for the whole of this world."

"*You accept this, Hakki? You accept this with all your being?*"

The Egyptian's expression brightened.

"I think I do, angel Darien. Yes! I think I do."

The first demon reached him and extended a jagged talon to rip his infinite soul from his finite body.

Not fast enough.

Ten thousand unfallen ones like Darien burst forth from heaven to earth.

At the front of them stood the resplendent archangel Michael, with the sword of righteousness given to him by almighty God.

Evil could not stand before him.

Evil immediately retreated, evil slithered back to hell, and evil lost another soul that could not be added to the eternal flames.

Hakki was no longer sobbing, for he had witnessed the veil between the finite and the infinite being parted.

"I see heaven, Darien," he whispered in awe. "I see the almighty Father and the Holy Spirit but not the blessed, only begotten Son, not the—"

The Egyptian turned from gazing upward to looking at Darien.

"He is here!" Hakki, the pharaoh's scribe exclaimed. "That is it, is it not? He has come to be among us, and—and—"

"Come," Michael said, gently taking his soul, helping it step out from the worn-out, battered, old flesh that had encased it. *"You are with us now. The demons can never threaten you again."*

Hakki went with that throng of angels to stand before the throne of God as he started earnestly singing, "Let all those rejoice who put their trust in You; let them always shout for joy, because You defend them; let those also who love Your holy name be joyful in You."

CHAPTER 19

MAJOR CRACKS appeared across scores of locations where there was dirt rather than sand, but the biggest "wound" in the earth was the one ahead of where Jesus, Mary, and Joseph had stopped.

A jagged, wide crevasse!

Running for miles in a north-south direction.

A crevasse so wide it seemed to mandate a substantial detour for them since they could not possibly get across it.

"We will have to continue our journey another way," Joseph told his family. "This obstacle may go on for miles. We cannot tell exactly how long it is. And we have no way of crossing it where we stand."

He looked back from where they had come.

Smoke. Clouds of it billowing toward the sky.

"When I think of what must have happened back in the village," he said, moaning. "I wonder if we should not delay returning to Israel and go back instead to those good people to see what we can do to help them."

Joseph had expected Jesus to agree with this and be eager to do His part. But that was not what he heard from his son.

"They are being helped as much as possible, Father," spoke up Jesus. "Angels of mercy are attending their steps."

. . . angels of mercy are attending their steps.

No four-year-old ever before spoke in that manner. Joseph could no longer count the number of times this Child had astonished him.

"Always so confident," Joseph remarked, smiling. "How is it that You can know so much for one so young?"

He walked over to the edge of the crevasse . . . pitch black within its depths.

Joseph thought he could see shapes below, moving shapes, but he assumed they were only shadows of rocks, that his vision was otherwise playing tricks on him.

"Please step back, Father," Jesus told him while standing perhaps twenty feet or so behind the man.

"I am not so careless as you may fear, my son," Joseph retorted gently. "You need not be concerned that I shall stumble forward and fall in."

He was starting to chuckle at the Child's apprehension; then, before Joseph knew it, Jesus had rushed to his side, looking up into his eyes with an intensity that neither he or Mary had seen before.

"Is there something below of which I should be afraid?" he asked, deeply moved by the fervent expression on the boy's face.

"Only the one who would take your soul to hell if he could!" replied Jesus, a frown on His soft young forehead. "He is not down there, but what has happened is a symbol, Father. Demons can come from anywhere."

Joseph turned to this Child whom he loved with mind, body, and soul.

"Are you speaking of Satan?" he asked rather dumbly.

"Yes, Father, I am," Jesus replied with a patience that was typical of Him, arising out of His love for Mary and Joseph.

"Why would the devil want to have anything to do with the three of us? Is he not after more important men and women, those who hold the destinies of many more than you or I or your mother will ever influence in all of our lifetimes? We would be a waste of time to Satan."

"Father . . . ," Jesus said lovingly. "It is not you he is after, but if he can take you along also, he would be very happy."

"If not me, then who? Certainly not my dear Mary. Who then? Can You tell Your father what is—?"

Suddenly, Joseph's spine felt as though it was being encased in solid ice.

"Is Satan after You, Jesus? Is that what you are saying? He wants to destroy a four-year-old boy?

Neither Joseph nor Mary were as yet fully aware of all that had come to be embodied in Jesus. But they knew He was not as other children, and they could hardly miss the flashes of brilliance that were so extraordinary.

Both had had more than a few hints along such lines since before the birth of Jesus and on to the present, of course, and there were suspicions as a result, especially when they were able to locate parchment copies of some of the old prophecies and the clues they provided, but any full awareness would not come to Mary or Joseph until nearly thirty more years had passed.

Looking through a glass darkly.

At present that was what they were doing, having been provided only as much knowledge as almighty God felt they could handle.

"Lord, I am here," Darien said to the Son.

"I know . . . ," Jesus replied, though not with spoken words. His earthly father and mother would be kept unaware of what was taking place, for they could not comprehend it and would be deeply troubled were they to catch the slightest glimpse.

"Tell me what I can do!" Darien implored the Son of God.

"Just be by My side, as My friend and My guardian."

"I guard only Your physical body, which is subject to every frailty and infirmity of the flesh. No demon can touch Your Spirit."

"It is that body of which you speak that shall be in danger soon, Darien. Satan must try to stop Me in a very short while although he knows he is doomed to failure. But he can never admit failure in anything. His ego will always force him on and on, like a poor, doomed lemming, until he reaches the brink of his own damnation."

"Yes, I know. Then, Lord, tell me what I am to do in order that the Father's mission might be fulfilled."

"You will see, My loyal companion; you will see soon enough . . ."

Joseph was becoming anxious, for Jesus had not answered him, and this was unusual.

"Is Satan after You, Jesus?" he repeated. "Tell me if this is it, please."

Joseph was perspiring, large drops of sweat stinging his eyes and trickling down his sun-toughened cheeks.

"Is that what You are saying?" he repeated again. "Satan wants to destroy You, a four-year-old boy?"

Jesus knew that Joseph was a devout man, that he would never intentionally scoff at the predictions of Daniel, Isaiah, and the other major and minor prophets.

But, still, full understanding was being divinely kept from the two of them, for if they knew in full the reality of His incarnation, they would no longer treat Him as flesh and blood but God-in-human-form instead. Since that could never be allowed, Jesus would have to live as a boy child, then as a man, and be tempted of the flesh as were all others.

"More than a boy, Father," Jesus replied. "He is after greater bounty than this flesh with which I am surrounded."

CHAPTER 20

JOSEPH had become accustomed to a son who was like others physically but not like typical children from Nazareth in other ways.

"His mind is so active, with questions and ideas and so much more than a boy His age would normally think of," Joseph said, nearly gasping as he discussed Jesus during a quiet time with Mary. "It is never at rest. I find myself surprised when I see our son *sleeping* at night. I half-expect Jesus to be sitting up in bed, His eyes flashing as He thinks about something beyond even our comprehension.

"None of this is what children are supposed to be like, Mary, we both know that. What is it that compels Jesus to act as He does? I am not sure whether we should be pleased or frightened at what we see happening."

"I have noticed, Joseph," she agreed, her usual serene manner very much in evidence. "His speech is much like an adult's. His thoughts seem to be far beyond those of even the wisest men."

Joseph nodded at the truth of what she said and added his own recollection, "Our son walked at just over a year. He called us by name a short time later."

Joseph had become the parent who wondered about his son Jesus, indulging in a certain curiosity that ebbed and flowed but never left him. For Mary, there was a simple acceptance, which was as it should have been.

Only I experienced what I did that one night, she realized. *Only I will ever know what it was like.*

She would continually find herself returning to those memories of that night when she had had a visitor unlike any other, and a moment that no one else could comprehend without having been at her side when it happened.

"Rejoice, highly favored one, the Lord is with you; blessed are you among women!" the being had said.

Oh, how troubled she had been when she heard that voice after seeing the most beautiful creature she had ever met.

Those wings, so pure white! she exclaimed to herself as she recalled them. *That face, as bright as the afternoon sun.*

Mary had barely been able to look at this radiant being for fear of doing damage to her eyesight. Instead she had gazed beyond the angel and perceived that he seemed to be standing in some kind of doorway.

And beyond it she saw—

I saw, oh, I saw . . . Mary again recalled, and not for the last time, the memory still causing her to gasp as she had done when she first faced the form that night, the light filling her room from wall to wall and floor to ceiling.

Heaven.

She knew it could be nothing else, this place that spread out in every direction behind the figure in front of her.

"Are you from God?" she had asked. "Are you one of His angels?"

"It is as you say," the angel told her.

"Oh, Father, I truly did rejoice when my friend Gabriel was given that assignment," Darien told God.

"You did not wish it for yourself?"

"You have given me so much already, Father. How could I wish to have Gabriel deprived of such joy?"

God could not have been more pleased . . .

Mary had fallen on her knees before the visitor, in wonder but also in fear and trembling, for she had begun to worry that her senses were deceiving her.

"*Do not be afraid, Mary,*" Gabriel had spoken with extraordinary jubilation. *"For you have found favor with God. And behold, you will conceive in your womb and bring forth a Son, and shall call His name JESUS."*

Gabriel had paused then, his brightness becoming ever greater, and then added: *"The child within you will be in truth the only begotten Son of the Most High, and in due course, the Lord God shall give unto Him the throne of His father David, and He shall reign over the house of Jacob forever; and of His kingdom there shall be no end."*

It was then that Mary had been quite overwhelmed. She had not yet been married, though she and Joseph had set a wedding date.

And she was a virgin. In a society that treated such matters with gravity, and where unwed mothers were considered a source of shame to any family, pregnancy before marriage was not a prospect that Mary or any other woman would greet with any enthusiasm.

Yet, if what the visitor said proved to be true, Mary would in fact become pregnant, perhaps before that very night ended.

But how could she explain this to Joseph, without having him seek to put her away because of what he and others would think had happened? Was not a dreaded stigma the only possible outcome?

She had voiced her doubts by saying, "How shall this be, for surely you know that I have not been with a man?"

The answer was immediate and utterly unexpected.

"*The Holy Spirit will come upon you, and the power of the Highest shall overshadow you; therefore, also, that Holy One who is to be born will be called the Son of God.*"

Gabriel had seen her doubts melting, but they were not quite gone.

"But nothing like this has ever happened before," she had protested. "It is far too unusual for anyone to believe us when Joseph and I explain—"

"*With God, dear Mary,*" the angel had interrupted, "*nothing should be considered impossible, for by Him was everything made that ever was and ever shall be.*"

"But my poor Joseph! He will think me a loose woman, someone who has betrayed her premarital vows."

Gabriel knew that Mary was in awful turmoil, and he sought to calm the teenage girl's troubled heart.

"*Another such as I will go to Joseph,*" he said, his tone filled with the sort of peace that he hoped would become hers. "*Rest well, for your beloved will not abandon you when he finds that you are carrying a Child within you, Mary. He will come to understand that this is a special One, and he will know that you are not a common prostitute of the streets but someone chosen by God for an honor above all other women until now and for the rest of time.*"

For the time being, she had been quiet.

And then the Holy Spirit, third member of the triune Godhead, had entered the room as the angel stepped aside.

Just as God had breathed life into the dust of Eden and made from it a living soul named Adam, so the Spirit came upon a virgin that night and gave her the life that was to begin growing steadily within her womb. Where once no tiny form had been, now there was One, the touch of Deity upon her body.

Afterward, when Mary was again alone, she thought of her dear Joseph . . . with a peace unlike any before in her young life.

CHAPTER 21

"POOR JOSEPH!" Darien explained. "*He cannot cope with what Mary has tried to explain to him.*"

"*What happened to her is beyond anything he has experienced before now,*" God spoke sympathetically from His great white throne in heaven. "*It would be the same with any other man, Darien.*"

"*Am I to have a part in this, Father?*" Darien asked, anticipating the holy Father's next directive.

"*You shall. Indeed you shall.*"

Darien knew the habits of his Creator, and he awaited the next command.

Joseph loved Mary, but when she told him what had happened, he thought she had become quite mad.

"You say that you are with child, and you expect me to believe that no man has touched you?" he said incredulously.

Mary could have taken offense at the two levels of doubt manifested by that single statement: One, that she was pregnant in the first place, and two, that she had become so without a sexual relationship with another man.

Instead, she had smiled as she replied. "We are most blessed among parents, Joseph. There can be no greater joy for us."

"How can you seem as happy as you do? What about the scandal, Mary? Our families will think that you and I—"

In those more circumspect times, to speak plainly about such matters of intimacy was considered sinful in itself and very vulgar. Discretion of speech was taught to every child from the earliest age.

So Joseph just threw up his hands in a gesture of extreme frustration without finishing what he had been about to say. Civility between the sexes was a way of life for the Jews since the men all wanted children as a mark of their masculinity, and it was a rare occasion when potential mothers were mistreated.

"Do not worry," Mary reassured him. "There shall be no scandal from what has happened. God's messenger has promised this to me."

But Joseph had been uncertain of that. He seemed to have only two unappealing choices available to him: He could drag young Mary into the village square and make a public example of her, as was the law. Or he could decide to put her away, which meant that she would become little better than a prisoner for the rest of her life in exile. Either way what he would be doing was nothing more than sending her permanently out of his life.

"*He is so sad, Father,*" Darien had said.

"*He knows nothing other than what experience and custom have taught him,*" God observed. "*The way he feels is understandable.*"

Before leaving Mary, Joseph hugged her, surprised that she seemed so radiant under the circumstances.

How is it that you are so peaceful? he thought. *Surely you cannot be unaware of what is likely to occur.*

Then, as he walked the short distance between their two residences, Joseph had found his mind filled with sad and turbulent scenes of what it would be like if they were never to be together again, if he had to go on without this special woman because, according to laws and traditions, she would have to be cast out and either stoned or left to wander from place to place, perhaps eventually starving to death.

How could I go on without her? he thought. *How could I enjoy anything if she is no longer to be with me?*

By the time Joseph had returned to his humble residence, he was feeling exhausted of body as well as of spirit, and it was not long before he thankfully fell asleep once he was back inside.

A dream.

For a man such as Joseph who had dreamed little over the years, this was an uncommon event in itself. At first strange, it soon became quite wonderful.

"*I can go to him now, Father?*" Darien had asked hopefully. "*I can be to this good man a comfort such as he needs?*"

God looked at the angel.

He saw the change in Darien, from seemingly ceaseless questions about the justice of Satan's punishment to complete trust, adoration, and acceptance, plus a growing eagerness to serve God as well as man.

"You can do that, Darien," He had said. *"And you can go now. Tell him that there is nothing to be ashamed of. Tell him to rejoice instead, for a miracle has happened to his beloved which will change the course of human history."*

Darien became exuberant.

"I will be with him instantly, Father. Thank You for giving me this new duty. Praise be to Your name, O Lord."

God smiled.

As He could weep, so could He smile.

And heaven shone with the glory of it.

Joseph felt fearful only for a short while, until the sudden visitor in his dream (or in his reality, whichever was the case) bespoke nothing of dark terror and lurking demons but only such kindness as Joseph could not contain within himself. As he listened, he was driven to a kind of weeping that came from within his very soul.

You gave me life, showed me great kindness, and in Your providence watched over my spirit.

Remembering those words from the scrolls of Job that he had read years earlier brought a certain peace that soothed him.

"*Joseph, Joseph . . .*" were the words he heard first.

The top of his head was lightly touched, and he looked up into a countenance that went far beyond the most beautiful sunset he had ever seen.

"*Fear not . . . ,*" Darien said.

"Are you Jehovah?" Joseph asked innocently.

"I am not God but one sent by Him to be at your side in this moment when comfort is needed."

Joseph trembled at that.

"I am unworthy," he replied. "You should be spending your time with someone else."

"It is not for you to decide this matter of your worth," Darien had admonished. *"It is your Creator's, and only He should do so."*

"Surely you are mistaken," Joseph had persisted. "I am of so little consequence. The woman I was going to marry, and who was to bear my children, is now pregnant with the child of another man."

"Yes, Mary is *expecting a baby,"* confirmed the angel, expecting Joseph to

react as he did, falling forward on his bed and groaning with the anguish that was flooding his being as Mary's words were confirmed.

"I must bring her to the square!" Joseph shrieked in desperation. "I must present my dearest to be judged by the assembled religious leaders, and . . . and undoubtedly to be stoned as her punishment or made to drink poison in the sight of everyone I have known since earliest childhood."

"Is what you say out of love for this young woman," Darien said, his words needle-like, *"or instead from concern about your position in the community? You must choose that which you care about the most."*

The angel's words had their intended impact, for Joseph was suddenly silent and unmoving upon his bed.

"Sit up, Joseph," Darien said. *"Look at me, and have confidence in what I shall say. Truly believe that you should not be ashamed of your Mary. Believe instead that, as young as she is, she will bring into the world Someone long prophesied and much needed because of the sins of mankind."*

Joseph jerked up to a sitting position, some remnant of defiance continuing to cling to him.

"This special young mother is most blessed among all women," the angel said as soothingly as he could.

Joseph's eyes opened wide in anger.

"Stranger, are you perhaps a devil after all?" he had asked harshly, as yet unconvinced. "A devil posing as an angel of light?"

"I am not what you now fear," Darien assured him.

"You may not be, but still nothing is changed. I have never known Mary, yet she carries a baby."

"No man is the father, Joseph. For that which is conceived in Mary is of the Holy Spirit, sent by God Himself."

Joseph audibly sucked in his breath. He was a devout man and had become more than fleetingly familiar with the parchments on which the ancient foretellings had been written.

"How am I to be sure of this?" he asked, his doubt dying but still capable of one last question. "How can I know that these words of yours are true?"

"This woman whom you love shall bring forth a righteous son, and you shall call His name JESUS. For He is being sent by the Father so that His people may be saved from their multitude of sins."

"Can you tell me if my . . . my dear Mary was still a virgin before all this ever happened?" Joseph added hopefully.

"Yes, she was," Darien assured him. *"Mary has not been unfaithful to you. This same Mary truly is keeping herself only for the joys of your marriage bed and for the many blessed years ahead when other children will join your household and thereby grace your lives."*

Suddenly liberated from the prospect of losing this young woman who had come to mean a great deal to him, Joseph held his hands above his head, palms upward, and began to shout exuberant praises to almighty God.

"All this was done that it might be fulfilled which was spoken by the Lord through the prophet," Darien announced, "'*Behold, the virgin shall be with child . . .*'"

Joseph repeated those words, then called out, "Oh, Father God, what blessings You confer on those so unworthy."

He looked up at the angel.

"What am I to do now?" he asked, a bright eagerness replacing his skepticism. "Tell me, and it shall be."

"Go to Mary, put your arms around her, and speak to her of your love. Forbid her not to become your bride, nor forestall being her bridegroom."

Joseph's expression showed how very pleased he was.

"Then, as the Lord has decreed, you must wait until the Child is born before you and Mary consummate your marriage," Darien said, realizing that, for one of flesh and blood, however devout in the faith, this would prove the most difficult task of all. *"Make known to me now whether you are able to do as your Creator wishes."*

Joseph replied instantly and with considerable zeal.

"Oh, yes!" he agreed. "My soon-bride and I truly shall obey the Lord God Jehovah all the days of our lives, honoring Him with our thoughts, our words, and our deeds. And if there is more that we can do, we need only be told."

"Be it as you say," Darien declared with great happiness before vanishing from his presence that night.

Then Joseph, being awakened from sleep as he was and not able to return to rest again that night, had finally left his bed in the early morning and did every thing the radiant visitor sent of the Lord had bidden, making arrangements to take unto him the young woman Mary as his beloved wife.

Much attention was paid in those days to the way a bride was to be dressed. For there was an air of joy and celebration abounding in and from the marriage ceremony since marriage was thought of as lifelong, the most important commitment anyone could make apart from faith in almighty God.

"I will greatly rejoice in the LORD God, my soul shall be joyful in my God; For He has clothed me with the garments of salvation, He has covered me with the robe of righteousness, as a bridegroom decks himself with ornaments, and as a bride adorns herself with her jewels."

So wrote the prophet Isaiah, and so was the sense of anticipation when Mary and Joseph were married.

They had to forego the usual display of jewels and other ornaments, and there were in attendance only the very few friends who did not think that the couple had violated God's directives by having had intimate sexual relations before their marriage. No family members joined them; that reconciliation was not to happen until after the birth of their son.

After pledging their vows to God and to one another, Joseph, a bit nervously, lifted the veil over Mary's face.

Thank You, Holy Father, for bringing us together this day, he thought. *May neither of us ever act in a way that brings shame to You, O Lord.*

At that precise moment, he said, "In the name of God, merciful and gracious . . . this day is blessed, this moment is sacred."

Though now married, Joseph resolutely abstained from knowing Mary carnally until she had brought forth their firstborn son.

Meanwhile, after that remarkable event, the only such birth in the history of the world, Mary, being only a teenager at the time, chose to further heed the clear and wonderful admonition issued by that certain angel named Darien by bestowing upon this most blessed Child the cherished name of JESUS . . . who they did not know as yet to be the prophesied King of Kings and Lord of Lords.

PART V

Many have puzzled themselves about the origin of evil. I am content to observe that there is evil, and that there is a way to escape from it, and with this I begin and end.

JOHN MILTON

So it was that, eventually, Jesus, Mary, and Joseph stood so dejectedly in front of that immense crevasse, death and destruction outlined against the sky behind them, the land of their ancestors ahead but now seeming so far out of reach.

And Satan, unknown to the parents but not to Jesus, was rapidly approaching the scene, utterly obsessed with his intention of destroying the thin, young, physical body of a Boy named Jesus. The former Lucifer could scarcely wait, the prospect of thwarting this plan of almighty God driving him onward, up from the bowels of hell itself.

"It shall be so!" he declared venomously to the empty air around him. "By this plan, then surely another, and yet more after it, my thirst of victory growing ever stronger and my ability to achieve it enhanced."

He saw them just ahead.

"Jesus is limited by the mortal frame in which He has encased Himself," Satan gloated. "Yet I do not have such a constraint!"

Waiting for him among the flames of hell were those demons enslaved to his will, eager to hear the report of his victory.

Suddenly Satan stopped.

"Whence came all those people?" he asked slowly, a chill passing through his malevolent and misshapen presence.

He thought of his followers, their expectations fanned, ready to welcome him back as their victorious Lord.

Ahead and below, Satan heard the verses of psalms being sung, proclamations of praise and thanksgiving, saw the smiles of the young and the elderly as their happiness shone forth.

There! In the midst of the gathered throng. A four-year-old Boy with the golden light of heaven touching His bright young face.

Already the familiar taste of defeat was beginning to spread its sour poison through every part of Satan's spirit, propelled as he was by desires unspeakable from eternal light to darkness abiding, as its perverse and unholy prince . . .

CHAPTER 22

WHAT HAPPENED exceeded all hope that Mary and Joseph could have had, and yet if they had reconciled their son's miraculous incarnation with all the special abilities and the vaulting intelligence that Jesus had been showing ever increasingly, they would have been far less surprised and stunned.

Still, unlike following generations, which benefited from greater revelation and understanding, these parents could not grasp who this boy of theirs truly was while at the same time knowing that He was a gift from God.

Standing at the edge of the crevasse, they had been about to give up and try instead to figure out another route back to Israel, one that would have involved, a road here, a mountain range there, a stretch of desert, and on and on, not knowing if a man, a woman, and a child could survive the rigors of such a long, uncertain odyssey.

Their first route had the advantage of being the shortest, with no mountains in their way and more than one oasis at which they could rest, replenish their water supply, and then head out again.

"Father, *look!*" shouted Jesus after the daylight hours had passed and dusk was coming, the darkening sky lit by still-active flames near the horizon, reminding them that though they were gone, many others were trapped by the catastrophe.

Mary and Joseph saw a caravan, a large one.

It was snaking toward them from the direction of the village they had left so recently, a caravan comprised of camels, donkeys, and horses, all burdened by boxes, leather satchels, and considerably more.

The caravan's original schedule had not included spending time with anyone from that devastated village. But when the wealthy family members who owned the caravan and the goods it was transporting from one residence to another, the ownership of two homes a rare luxury in those days enjoyed only by the upper levels of Egyptian society, saw what devastation had been visited upon that humble place, they felt true compassion for the many homeless and injured people in the aftermath of the quake, and they did not hesitate to extend their help in any way possible. They shared whatever food had been brought along for the trip, warm clothing, and certain other supplies as well.

And now the caravan had left the village and was heading toward the spot where Jesus, Mary, and Joseph had found their plans thwarted.

A short while later, the lead camel stopped as it approached the family.

Someone slid down its side, a tall man, thin-faced, with a hawk-like nose and a prominent forehead.

He was speaking as he approached.

"What can we do to help out here?" he asked, making that offer seemingly without limitation.

"Your offer of kindness is appreciated, stranger," Joseph told him, touched by what the other man had said, "but I have very grave doubts that there is anything for us to do now except return to our own land along another, much more difficult route, with greater dangers attending our every step."

He sighed, his shoulders slumping, a slight shiver racing through his body as he considered the coming days and weeks.

"In the meantime, stranger," Joseph added, "there is nothing left to us except to pray that, somehow, my family and I will make it back to our homeland without grievous harm befalling any of us."

The Egyptian frowned at this, fully understanding Joseph's distress.

"My name is Baktar." He introduced himself in a rather courtly manner. "And you are Joseph, I presume. Perhaps we can do something to overcome your dilemma."

"How did you know my name?" the earthly father of Jesus inquired, momentarily taken aback by the recognition by a complete stranger.

"My family, my slaves, and I have come from the poor village just behind us. Many of the citizens there told us of your family, especially your son, and the two years you spent among them."

Baktar turned toward Jesus.

"A handsome lad," he observed. "Big for his age, and, I understand, with the mind of an adult, or a god."

Joseph blushed at that.

"Jesus is an ordinary boy," he protested, uncomfortable with having his son described as the stranger had done.

"No, Joseph, he is not," the Egyptian countered, correcting Joseph as an elderly scribe might correct a younger student. "There is more to your son Jesus, I suspect, than you might guess, my good man."

Baktar walked the few steps to where the Child had been standing and knelt down in front of Him.

"All my life, I have worshiped at the feet of a multitude of severe graven images crafted as embodiments of our many gods," he acknowledged, frowning as he did so. "But in recent days, I have felt that all of this is little better than ritual, the meaningless bowing and muttering of a few gestures and payment of some coins for the dubious privilege, and then it is over."

"Empty . . . ," Jesus said.

Baktar looked up into His face.

"Yes!" he exclaimed. "That is precisely what I am describing. It is all form and proscribed motion and, yes, cold, cold emptiness. I leave a large, beautiful temple or one of the altars in my home, and I am no longer affected as I once was. It is the same with my wives, my sons, my daughters."

"You see nothing but darkness," offered Jesus, "where once joy and peace seemed present instead."

Baktar fell back.

"Such words from the mouth of a child!" he gasped. "But even more than that, what You say is truth itself."

"*Lord?*" the angel asked.

"*Yes, Darien?*"

"*How can this Egyptian be so perceptive?*" the angel mused. "*He seems more open than a great many Jews are.*"

They were communicating in a direct, nonverbal link between Darien's spirit and the spirit of the incarnate Son.

"*Who are more open to revelation, those who have convinced themselves that they have everything they need and have stopped looking for anything else, or those others who hunger and thirst after righteousness?*"

"*Those who hunger, Lord.*"

"*Then you have the answer you sought.*"

CHAPTER 23

BAKTAR soon happily introduced Jesus, Mary, and Joseph to all the members of his own family, especially his seven beautiful wives over whom he beamed proudly, as well as his numerous sons and daughters and, in a few cases, *their* sons and daughters, which explained why the caravan was such a large one.

And well into the evening, they gathered together and shared whatever allotments of food were at hand, including what little was left after parceling out most of the caravan's allotment to the villagers. Those present had to eat sparingly, but the mood of companionship made it all take on the joviality of a feast.

Everyone was drawn to Jesus as He sat quietly before one of the campfires, acting more self-assured than any other four-year-old the Egyptians had ever seen, His calmness a beacon.

As far as the adults were concerned, His personal manner was intriguing, yet not off-putting. The same seemed true of the other children, who were comfortable in His presence, even those who were older than He was by several years.

After a bit, Jesus eagerly launched into a series of stories He told in animated fashion to the younger ones, simple but captivating parables about wheat farmers, rich men, servants, kings, and others. This went on for nearly an hour, with the children watching Jesus and listening to Him as though *nothing* could distract their attention.

After He had finished, each of them, smiling, thanked Him and went off to play alone. Jesus remained where He was, seemingly content in His sudden solitude.

"Lord, that was wonderful!" the angel commented. *"You planted seeds within them that could change their lives."*

"Not could, *Darien . . . their lives* will *be changed. The images created will*

remain deep inside them until a time in their lives when they will need the Father's intervention."

"They will not be among the lost then?"

"They will be among the redeemed for all eternity."

Shortly thereafter, Baktar sat down beside Jesus.

"I have had at my homes the best of all intellects from Egyptian society," he commented, thinking of those stimulating occasions that would stay with him until the day he died, refreshing times that eschewed cheap or even casual talk and concentrated instead on vital topics that were of the profoundest substance. "But not a single one of those scholars seemed to me to be what You are. I could fancy a situation where you were to stand in front of scores of these elite thinkers and best the whole lot."

"Their wisdom is not from above," Jesus told him.

"But if not from above, as you say, whence doth it come?"

Jesus paused . . .

"What will You tell him, Lord?" inquired Darien.

"He must face the truth," Jesus replied.

"But if You tell it to him without warning, he might pull back. He might reject what you say altogether?"

"Or it could set him free."

Jesus spoke again, His voice starkly serious.

"You can decide to have one of two masters," He said, obliquely answering Baktar. "You must hold to one and reject the other."

"But I asked You about the wisdom of the finest minds of Egypt. What kind of answer is this, Jesus?"

Baktar was beginning to feel that, despite the genius of this Child, he had finally bumped up against the inevitable limitations imposed by Jesus' youth.

"One master is almighty God," the four-year-old went on. "The other is the Prince of Darkness."

"Those wise men I have known for so long now, those to whom I have been turning for years—!"

Baktar's expression changed then dramatically as he comprehended finally what Jesus was saying.

. . . the Prince of Darkness.

He bowed his head.

"Yes, something like what you say has been worrying me, Jesus, though not in quite the way you have offered it. Yes, I must admit that that has been worrying me very much. Often they seem not wise at all but ordinary men, making me doubt that their *guesses* come from a greater source than what I myself might reason."

"*He knows!*" Darien exclaimed. "*He knows about Satan.*"

"The Egyptian aristocracy is well read. Some are as familiar with the Jewish prophecies and other scrolls as the three Magi became. Sadly, they may know more about these than countless thousands who were born and raised in Israel itself.

"*And yet theirs is only a head knowledge. They themselves have been in the grip of Satan for a long time but are too blind to realize this. Baktar's soul is opening up to enlightenment that he will spread to others.*

"*I should never have wondered about Your holy words to this special man. Lord, I do fear greatly for how long Your patience with me will endure. Do You want me right now to return to the Father?*"

Darien had become genuinely distraught over a simple matter but one that had implications he loathed, reminding him of when he traveled the path known as *Angelwalk* during a period of similar, even more profound questions.

The Son did not let him remain this way for long.

"*No, stay here. I understand you. It is your nature to question, Darien. We have long known that. Remember this, and be of good cheer: It is far better to question and arrive at the right answer than never to ask at all, and receive nothing in return.*"

Jesus' divine Spirit within that flesh-and-blood boy's body spoke then with the sweetest joy as He said to the angel, "*I love you not one bit less for what you are.*"

The next day, shortly after sunrise, Baktar approached Joseph and suggested how the family's impasse might be broken.

"I know you are anxious to return," he said, "and that the alternative way you mentioned is very hazardous. I think I can suggest something."

"It would be wonderful if you could since I just do not perceive anything else," Joseph replied dejectedly. "Perhaps if, somehow, we had passage by sea, then we could make it in from the coast."

That remark grew out of little more than a touch of daydreaming, not anything like a real suggestion that should be taken seriously.

He saw Baktar's eyes widening, a little smile crossing his face. Joseph's mouth dropped open.

"Surely you were not thinking of sending us by sea vessel, were you?" he asked, not willing to believe that this was possible.

"Not only that," the Egyptian told him somewhat mischievously.

"We could not possibly accept—"

"Be quiet, Joseph," he said with mock sternness, then added, "for two years now, you have been helping so many other people. Let it be that someone at last brings you relief in return, please."

Baktar pointed to Jesus.

"That Child must be protected at all costs," he said. "I doubt that anyone realizes this more than you or Mary."

"Lord, this Egyptian has so much wisdom!" Darien exclaimed.

"He will come out from under a lifetime of spiritual darkness and do great acts in My name," Jesus said. *"You will see him walking the streets of My Father's heavenly kingdom before his eighty-third year."*

"A short while ago, I saw Satan coming here with great ferocity, but now I cannot find him anywhere."

To be sure, Darien looked as far as the horizon.

"There he is!" the angel exclaimed as he noticed his former comrade now a very long distance away. *"He seems to have retreated."*

"Satan has felt the pure and beautiful reality of ennobling love here, a willingness to sacrifice, to do unto others with the greatest human kindness. These deeds, so fine, so pure, are like a deadly potent to him.

"Mere acts, of whatever soaring magnitude, are no keys to salvation. Yet in the case of Baktar the Egyptian, what has been revealed is a hungry soul ready, even eager, to receive redemption.

"Satan is being pushed back, though he desperately waits until the last minute for an opening of which he can take advantage. That wait will prove to be futile, for he will fail and not be able to find one."

"Then I do not have to be on guard, Lord?"

"This time you need not be."

"So Satan will soon return to hell?"

The Son nodded as He replied. *"For a period of time, until My fleshly body reaches its thirtieth birthday."*

"There will be no attacks by demons until then?" Darien asked, astonished by such a possibility.

"None."

"Satan never gives up, though."

"Yes, but he must regroup because he now loses the respect of the other demons as a result of his failure this day, though they continue to be enslaved to him like the brute beasts they have become after being held so long in his sway. He will spend the next three decades planning another series of attacks against Me."

"So Your earthly childhood will be one of peace?"

"And love . . . between Mary, Joseph, and Myself."

"That is wonderful to hear, Lord."

"To be truly loved by the Father as well as by His earthly parents? Yes, it is . . . truly a blessing, Darien."

"And for me? If there is no danger to your physical self for a time, how am I to serve as your guardian, Lord?"

"Enjoy the gift of peace while you have it. Get to know the parents as you already know the Child. There will be times when they sense your presence. They will stop and listen but think there is nothing but their imaginations, and they will go on their way."

"For that brief moment, though, some portion of the barrier that exists between mortality and the infinite will lift, and it shall be glorious for you, dear Darien, something you will never be able to forget."

The angel sighed in anticipation.

"Do not worry about tomorrow," Jesus the Christ told him, *"for tomorrow will worry about itself, Darien. This is the day your Lord has made for you, My faithful servant. Let it be a source of great blessing . . . as long as it lasts."*

CHAPTER 24

So Jesus, Mary, and Joseph were befriended by a stranger named Baktar, who escorted the three of them to the port city where he had a luxurious home and allowed them to stay for some days of welcome rest.

Then they were helped on-board a ship that originally had been scheduled to travel straight to the southern tip of Italy, but, as the owner, Baktar ordered the captain to take a detour to the coast to Judea.

"I will accompany you to make certain everything is done properly!" Baktar spoke rather grandiloquently, enjoying any reasonable opportunity to display his generosity; but since what he was doing came from a sincere heart, his verbal flourishes did not come across as objectionable.

He stepped onto the flat, wide vessel, and stayed with them until the brief trip was over and the three Jews were safely on home soil.

They turned and waved to him, then were on their way.

Baktar hesitated, a bond having developed between him and the three family members stronger than he had anticipated.

"Wait!" he ordered the captain.

"But it is time to pull up the anchor and—"

"No!" Baktar said sternly. "Wait for me."

A small boat was put over the side, and he was taken to shore.

Jesus, Mary, and Joseph had already started inland when they heard Baktar shouting after them.

They stopped and waited for this special new friend to catch up to them.

"I could not let you go just yet," Baktar told them, his chest heaving from unaccustomed exertion as he stopped running.

"What can we do for you?" Joseph asked.

"May I spend just a few more minutes with your son?"

"Of course . . . however much time you need."

Baktar shook Joseph's hand with great enthusiasm, then he led Jesus away from Mary and Joseph a short distance and sat down with Him on the bare sand.

Often they seem not wise at all but ordinary men, making me doubt that their *guesses* come from a greater source than what I myself might reason.

"I am dismissing all of my advisers," he remarked. "After what You told me, I cannot feel comfortable with any of them."

Jesus said nothing.

"But I do not know who or what to put in their place," Baktar confessed. "I now feel both more at peace and yet more uncertain at the same time. How can that be? Please help me understand this, Jesus."

"You are being torn between two masters . . . ," the Child told him simply but with a power that could not be ignored.

The Egyptian lapsed into silence.

Then Jesus proceeded to speak intently to the Egyptian about the need to serve God and not man.

"All those years I spent worshiping so faithfully in the past are as naught?" Baktar asked plaintively, his forehead lined with deep frown marks.

The Child nodded sadly.

"What can You give me in return?" the Egyptian asked.

Jesus leaned forward and touched the man's hands, so big in comparison with His own, still the hands of a young boy.

"Close your eyes," He said. "Pray with me."

Baktar did that eagerly.

Moments later, Jesus opened His eyes and spoke expectantly. "Do you accept? Do you believe?"

"I do!" the man exclaimed. "I accept more completely than anything else in this entire life of mine."

"Then go and be at peace."

The Egyptian's eyes filled with tears.

"You are not the child here," he said, his voice husky. "Nor am I the master now as I once was over so many others."

Sighing, Baktar reached out and placed his hands on that special Child's thin, narrow shoulders.

"There will be many more who believe You," he said. "And there will be many who believe me when I tell them of You."

Then he left Jesus and the parents to continue their journey to Nazareth, where the father would teach the son the trade of carpentry, and the son would give both his parents continuing hints of the eternally proscribed mission that was to be His many years hence.

"I shall be back with the head of a child," the Prince of Darkness had vaingloriously boasted, *"and the heart of God."*

And that was what the other demons were expecting of this fallen creature, once so astonishing in his magnificence, the one for whom they had been willing to give up all that was formerly holy and just and good and honorable in their lives.

They merely assumed that what he promised was what they would see upon his triumphant return.

A promise he was never allowed to keep.

Yes, Satan had told his fellow demonic entities what he intended to do, the victory over which they would gloat.

But now, their master was forced to go back to hell with only another defeat to present to its vast hordes.

Despair was the first to approach him.

"Master, you surely have nothing for us!" the demon exclaimed. *"You sounded so certain when you left. And yet—"*

Satan knew Despair's reaction would mirror how the others were likely to feel, but there was nothing whatsoever that he could do about this except agonize over what had happened.

"It seemed so right at the time . . . ," he mumbled to himself in a far corner of hell away from any of the other fallen creatures.

Satan had been ready to intervene, not in any fleshly manner, for he had no physical form and had wisely determined that materializing in plain view would only scare everyone away from his repugnant self and push them closer than ever to the comforting presence of the incarnate Deity.

Waiting . . .

That was what he decided to do . . . wait for an opening to move into a darkened soul and then possess it. Through this victim, he would move against the Son of God.

"Oh, what a hold I once had over that man!" he exclaimed with frustration, thinking of Baktar. *"I have been so confident of his eternal destiny that I maintained a place for his soul not far from where I am right now."*

Satan stood then, walked down several red-hot corridors, the walls of which were crammed full with writhing souls, the pain of one shared as the pain of all.

"*Ah!*" he exclaimed, looking at the familiar surrounding and gorging himself on the pain of the damned, a kind of ecstasy radiating through him.

He passed by Cain, Goliath, Darius the Great, all of the pharaohs of Egypt who had ever lived, plus innumerable others.

Sodom and Gomorrah . . .

Thousands of the damned souls from Sodom and Gomorrah and other cultures that had come and gone glared out at him: the Sumerians, the Hittites, the Moabites, the Ammonites, the Assyrians, all defeated and cast aside because they had stood against God's people.

"*Right there is where you were to have been, Baktar,*" the devil said as he stopped before another wall in another section of hell. "*I could look forward to plucking you out at any time of your spot and giving you new pain such as I had devised.*"

Absent-mindedly, Satan grabbed a hapless, screaming soul, stuck it slowly into his mouth, chewed on it for some time, then spit the thing out, watching with no joy whatever this time.

The twisted and pathetic remnant of a once mighty king of a once dominant empire plopped in front of him, looking up with an agonized pleading as a cry escaped the tortured lips. "Mercy, Satan, mercy! I gave you everything when I was of flesh and blood. Now return to me just a little mercy, just a little—"

"*What you gave was not enough!*" the devil growled fiercely. "*I have even your wretched soul, as you know all too well, and still it is not enough to satisfy my desires! No one can ever give me enough, not now, not ever!*"

The former Lucifer, the most beautiful of archangels amidst the endless and sublime majesty of heaven, now swung around and around, gesturing wildly with those twisted talons of his, not an unusual act for this creature as those in subordination to him had known all too well across the millenniums that had passed.

"*Baktar, your darkness was fleeing!*" the devil screamed, his frustration oozing out of him. "*But, alas, I did not move nearly fast enough to catch you before you got beyond my grasp. You saw too much light there in the presence of Jesus the Christ, and you heard too much truth from that . . . that damnable Child.*

"*You . . . you were exposed to the holy presence that I despise so much, Baktar. I myself soon had to shrink from the One called Blessed, but before I was gone, I saw you reaching out, becoming as a child yourself, you and everyone with you, your entire family—and I hate you for this, Baktar. How I hate you!*"

CHAPTER 25

For just under *thirty years, Satan would be restrained by divine edict while Jesus was given time to mature without interference, in His human form, from being a boy to a man. Peace would last for a while longer for Him and for those He loved.*

Darien looked forward to that respite promised by God, a sweetly nurturing childhood for Jesus that would be founded on growth and nurturing for the Son as His flesh-and-blood self matured.

And that was what followed the family's unheralded return to Israel from Egypt after leaving Baktar's sea-going vessel.

How sad the Egyptian seemed when he waved good-bye to Mary and Joseph, Darien thought. *He had known that family so briefly and yet the impact would stay with the man for the rest of his life.*

The angel recalled petitioning the heavenly Father for an angel to stay by Baktar's side during the years ahead.

"*It is already done,*" was the Father's response.

"*Thank You, oh, praise Your holy name!*" Darien exclaimed joyfully. "*I should not have thought otherwise.*"

"*Stedfast will be with him until the moment he enters My kingdom,*" God added, knowing how much this would please Darien.

Stedfast! Wonderful, comforting Stedfast! The angel who had pulled him out of hell at the end of that monstrous encounter with Satan.

"*And after Baktar, there will be many men, women, and children whose lives this man will have influenced, and they in turn will touch others on through the centuries of history until the end of time,*" God continued. "*Stedfast will be to each a guardian and a comforter.*"

He looked directly into Darien's very being.

"*But it is for you only to be steadfast by My Son,*" He said with the greatest tenderness. "*There are coming those monstrous times of the deepest tribulation, times that will bring even you to the edge of despair, Darien; but do not give up, for I shall not leave you powerless."*

The angel caught something in God's words then that seemed new and most intriguing to him.

"*Am I to be comforted when I need it, Father?*" he asked in awe.

"*So the need shall be, and the comfort with it.*"

The angel could not speak but reached out for the Father and touched Him.

To touch God!

What Darien felt could not be described. A thousand libraries comprised of ten thousand volumes each would not do the experience the justice it required to be understood.

When mortal children were blessed with moments of sitting on their father's lap, they underwent one of the most satisfying pleasures of flesh-and-blood life, a closeness beyond the mere physical act itself. They felt close to the man whose love had helped make them what they were, the one whose responsibility of caring and protecting and teaching was shared with their mother.

Yet with angels and their Creator, it was so much more!

Those who were unfallen not only communed with Father, Son, and Holy Spirit, as did Darien, but they entered the Trinity, spirit merging with spirit, in much the same way as the Godhead itself existed, separate but one.

Though just temporary, this was, above all else, the most sublime of experiences in an angel's life, so much so that even Satan, in the sulfuric murkiness of hell, remembered from time to time what it was like not merely to be close to God but to be in God, to be one with Him. If there were ever regret deep within the devil, it would come in the midst of such flashes of recollection, from which he would turn abruptly and look at the multiplied fruits of damnation strewn with immeasurable cruelty around his very being. Perhaps then he would weep, or something like it, if weeping had not eternally run its course with the cruel and dispassionate father of all sin.

"*But it is for you only to be steadfast by My beloved Son . . .*"

"*Yea, Father, I shall be what You say,*" Darien told God at the gates. "*Not even an onslaught from hell itself will deter me, Blessed One.*"

Then Darien withdrew from God's presence and returned to Nazareth where Jesus, Mary, and Joseph had settled, doing as the Creator had instructed and commencing those thirty years of fellowship in the presence of the King of Kings . . .

The family of three settled in the village of Nazareth for that long period. It seemed to offer more opportunities for Joseph as a carpenter, and they found a very small but pleasant residence that suited their needs.

A time of physical as well as spiritual growth for the humanness of Jesus.

And a time of being nurtured openly by His earthly parents and secretly by His heavenly Father.

Some of the Child's traits surfaced early on, such as His relationship with that loyal donkey that had been with Joseph's family for so long. During their second year in Nazareth, it had finally reached the end of its long life and could no longer stand.

Mary and Joseph were saddened, thinking they soon would have to hasten along its death because periodically their friend would moan, its large head shaking pitiably from side to side.

Once Mary had happened upon the donkey as its legs were jerking in spasms, first forward, then backward, forward, then backward; dark-colored spittle drained from the corners of the donkey's mouth.

"I cannot bear what I see any longer," she told Joseph. "That animal never let us down when it was needed. Now, my husband, you and I have to do something to help in return. We have to—to—?"

She buried her face in her hands, tears flowing freely.

"Mary, look!" exclaimed Joseph.

Jesus was walking past the two of them, through the doorway leading outside, to where the donkey was plopped, a sudden harsh howling sound coming from deep within its age-ravaged form. He bent down beside the creature and started talking with a tenderness that brought a different kind of tears to the eyes of His parents.

"Be at rest, beloved friend." Jesus spoke soothingly to the donkey. "There is now to be no more pain for you. Look up . . . look up, see My Father. Hear the words He speaks to you . . . understand them."

"It is time to go now, faithful servant. It is time to say good-bye to those you have loved for so long. Come, I will help you."

Mary and Joseph saw the donkey turn in their direction for a moment, just a moment, then it sighed a single time as it laid its head back against the soft sand.

"Do not be afraid, loyal friend. You need not be afraid ever again."

Jesus sat down and held the animal's head on His lap, swaying gently back and forth.

"Joseph!" called Mary.

"See the love our son has for this creature."

Jesus had reached out and slowly closed the donkey's eyes.

"Wait here," Joseph told her, his voice cracking.

He walked outside, and stood next to the Child. Jesus looked up at him.

"He must be buried now, Father," he said.

"We will do it together, son," Joseph assured Him.

Together, father and son walked to the makeshift cemetery that had been set aside by a few Nazarenes for the disposal of their animals.

Joseph could not bear to read the poignant words written on some of the wooden markers; he proceeded to dig a grave, then together they placed the donkey's body in it.

"I loved him, Father," Jesus admitted, tears trickling down His soft young cheeks. "He served us without question . . . out of a simple and ever-present love. How many of those who are professing my blessed heavenly Father's name will continue to do so during the dark days that are to come?"

Jesus reached out a small, thin hand, and Joseph took it in his own.

"Son, son, I *am* your father," Joseph said. "What is this You say about people professing my name? I cannot understand."

The Child looked up at him, then, and smiled with such bountiful joy that any more questions were silenced.

A gentleness and a kindness also showed up in all of Jesus' relationships with other children from the village of Nazarene and various communities nearby, for it was invariably He who was the one to step in and squelch fights, even those between children who happened to be much older. As soon as He was present, with His calmness and His intelligence, and with the peaceful way He spoke, any desire for fighting seemed to end, drained from the would-be participants in a miraculous way.

There was something about their youthfulness, before the many corruptions of adulthood had spoiled them, that responded guilelessly to Jesus.

While none of the children could understand what it was about this Child that drew them to Him, any explanation about such matters became irrelevant at best, for the young ones knew only that when Jesus broke them apart and told everyone, "Let there be only peace between you," they could no longer fight. They would go their various ways, puzzling among themselves about why they would ever listen to a simple carpenter's son yet feeling no more hostility toward one another just the same.

In many respects, though, Jesus was just another boy among many. He played rough-and-tumble games with other children as well as quieter ones that involved gaming boards.

Boys, Jesus among them, often used slings and stones for target practice. A sling, made from a woolen pouch held between two strings, would hold a stone that was whirled round and round. When the slinger, as he was called, let go one of the strings, the stone was propelled toward its target.

Competing with slinging was shooting bows and arrows.

Jesus became adept with both, much admired for his ability in target and distance shooting. And he was a fine wrestler, another sport also popular throughout the Middle East. The form of wrestling most widespread was hip-and-thigh, which involved holding on to the other boy's belt, precisely as Jacob did in his struggle with a heavenly manifestation.

Still, despite all this, Jesus' differentness would come out again and again.

Neither Mary nor Joseph were blind to the displays of Jesus' ever more intriguing ways. They had often discussed this remarkable son of theirs, frequently with joy, but sometimes with a certain amount of fear as they considered the future.

His mind is so active, with questions and ideas and so much more than a boy His age would normally think of. It is never at rest. I find myself surprised when I see our son sleeping at night. I half-expect Jesus to be sitting up in bed, His eyes flashing as He thinks about something beyond even our comprehension.

Joseph's earlier words were recalled, a mixture of admiration and uneasiness, as though he were saying, "What has been put here in our midst? This son of mine is much more than either Mary or I comprehend."

But for the first years of His life, Jesus never acted less than totally obedient to them or sensitive to their needs.

That ended shortly after His twelfth birthday.

The three of them had gone to Jerusalem for the feast of the Passover.

This was a supremely important aspect of Jewish life. On the one hand, Passover represented and celebrated the freeing of the Israelites from Egyptian bondage thirteen centuries earlier.

But there was another important dimension to the festivities that had to do with the spring migration of the flocks, a busy time for farmers after which they looked forward to journeying to Jerusalem and engaging in a kind of citywide party—a real beacon for all hardworking Jews throughout the whole country, making it an important and coveted part of the year.

The Passover celebration was kicked off with a special *seder,* or ritual feast, and a retelling of the familiar but always inspiring Passover story.

Mary and Joseph were in the habit of going to Jerusalem every year for this purpose, making the occasion something of a vacation, though this was the first time Jesus had been allowed to accompany them. His parents wanted the trip to coincide with His twelfth birthday in commemoration of His initial step toward being a man.

Joseph shut down his successful carpentry business, partly because so many other businessmen in Nazareth traditionally did the same, everyone deciding to become part of the general exodus from that village and others largely deserted during Passover week.

Food was served from morning until evening, with lamb the predominant meat. Jesus also liked the dried fruits that were always available in overflowing abundance, including grapes and figs, which were His favorites. He especially enjoyed the delicacy made of ground-up figs rolled in dough, then pressed into square cakes and baked in outdoor ovens. Similar to Turkish *baklavas,* these were much sought after by every child in the area, and Jesus was no exception.

Throughout Judea, spring was a time of year blessed with better conditions for increased travel since the long period of winter rains was over by then and the roads were no longer reduced to intimidating rivers of mud.

Jesus joined in with Mary and Joseph, showing unbridled enthusiasm while enjoying the sights, sounds, and general activity of the ancient city.

After spending the rest of the year in the comparative isolation and quiet of Nazareth, entering the much larger and bustling Jerusalem would have been an adventure of no small proportions to any twelve year old. Despite His divinity, Jesus was fully a boy, with all the gusto of any child His age.

Before long, He was separated from His parents, but they paid no particular attention to this, nor was there any alarm . . . at first.

The way of life in Israel at that time was far less troubled than it had been during other historical periods, unless one happened to be in the budding insurrectionist groups, and then everyday existence was altogether different. Imperial Rome was determined to stamp out all such activity.

Whether or not the people admitted it, this was in part due to the Roman occupation of their country. Whatever the weaknesses of imperial rule in other respects, especially on a moral plane, the emperor and those serving him did not tolerate lawlessness. They felt that everyone in Italy itself or anywhere else throughout the empire had a right to expect protection from unlawful elements.

Furthermore, children of that era tended to be very self-reliant, for they were having to live in an often inhospitable land, their survival attacked by wind, snow, rain and unrelenting winter cold as well as marauding beasts or poisonous snakes and spiders.

Darien could see what was capturing Jesus' attention from the outset . . . beggar children. He was immediately drawn to these pathetic wanderers, who were a large part of the street population of Jerusalem. They lived or starved based strictly upon the generosity (or lack of it) of residents as well as strangers.

"Nearly all these poor children have no families," Jesus told Darien. *"Some of the ones who do are forced to take back anything that they have collected at the end of each day and turn it over to parents who do little or nothing but build up private hoards that benefit them—and seldom their children!"*

The angel was as saddened by this as Jesus was.

"You have had a special bond with young children since before Your incarnation, Lord," he remarked. *"They are as yet not lost spiritually, though most are not very far from the abyss."*

It was clear that the Son of God was in distress, though Jesus the Child was showing none of this.

"I see these precious children reaching the age of accountability and then being swallowed up by the adult world of knowing sin, choosing sin, participating deliberately in sin, and so many will go beyond the reach of redemption."

Despite Himself, Jesus groaned at the disturbing whirlwind of images thrusting forward in His mind.

"I want to reach out to them and take them into my arms and succor them as their Savior and their Lord, Darien. But I cannot do that now because it is not in My Father's Plan that I be other than what I appear until the time He has appointed in His Plan for the Ages. Only later will I be able to shed this cloak of flesh."

Darien asked, "*Where are You to go now, Lord?*"

"*To the temple,*" Jesus replied. "*That is where I must be very shortly, for it is time to start challenging those religious leaders who have held sway over the lives of My people far too long and have abused their power to such an extent that the stench of their transgressions reaches up to My Father in heaven.*"

But Jesus was stopped by one of the street children who had touched His heart.

This one, just nine years old, jumped in front of Him. Though not rich, His parents had dressed Him as nicely as they could afford to do in a handcrafted white tunic.

"I need to eat," the boy said. "Can you spare a coin?"

Jesus looked at him and smiled.

"If you only knew who I am," He said.

The boy frowned and started to turn away. Unlike most other children, he did not feel comfortable around someone who spoke as an adult but looked every bit as young as he was.

"You seem hungry," Jesus added without pretense. "Would you like some bread?"

"Bread?" the boy repeated, blinking repeatedly at that cherished word. "Yes! I can take bread."

"The baker down the way . . . go to him."

"I have been there. He is a skinflint. He would give me nothing. I told him my mother is ill and needs food. But he would not listen."

Jesus smiled in a kindly manner.

"Let Me pray now to the Father for His help," He said.

"I do not know my father."

Jesus knelt without speaking for a moment.

"Father, help this boy," He prayed aloud. "Change the heart of that baker. Melt his coldness. Please, Father, help his mother so both will be witnesses for Thee until the last days of their lives."

The boy stepped back, suspicious that this young stranger knew anything about his mother, for they had been keeping to themselves, and he could not be sure that anyone knew her name or his, for that matter.

Jesus stood then, and turned to the boy.

"The baker will have sufficient bread for you both . . . ," Jesus continued, "and your mother is well now."

Instinctively, in a familiar gesture of disbelief, the beggar boy spat on the ground at Jesus' feet.

"You are only a little older than I am," he said with the contempt of someone much more mature, "and yet You talk like—"

Jesus did not react at all to this but seemed only to be waiting with an extraordinary degree of patience.

"Lord, he is insulting You," Darien said. *"You are not obligated to take this kind of abuse, especially from one so young."*

Jesus smiled not at the boy but at the angel, though the grimy little street child in front of Him could not have known that.

"Darien, do you think Me to be so ill-prepared that I am unable to handle this one encounter, yet at the same time you claim to have confidence in Me to provide for the salvation of the world?"

Darien apologized to Jesus for misspeaking and continued to observe, but in silence this time.

Suddenly the boy's manner softened as he looked at Jesus intently, the words spoken by this stranger having carried such conviction that all his defenses were suddenly disabled.

"There . . . is bread . . . waiting?" he asked uncertainly, wanting very much to believe what he had just heard but having been disappointed a great deal in so few years of hard, hungry, cold life. "And my . . . my mother is well?"

"The sickness *has* left her," confirmed Jesus. "She awaits you. Go, child, and be by your mother's side."

"Please, sir, do not say this if it is untrue."

Jesus' expression was one of great tenderness.

"She is as I said. And she soon will be offered work, with a place to stay."

The boy rushed to Jesus and fell at His feet.

"It is the will of the Father who sent me," Jesus told him. "Be with your mother now, and remember this good day."

The street child started to scamper off, then stopped, turned, and asked, "Will I ever see you again?"

"In a place with streets of gold," Jesus assured him, His voice clear and strong, "and angels on every side."

The boy nodded, tears glistening on his cheeks, and then was gone.

CHAPTER 26

After the celebration ended, Mary and Joseph started back toward Nazareth, but Jesus stayed behind. His parents did not miss Him at first, for they assumed He was with friends further back in the caravan. But when He failed to show up that evening, they started to look for Him among their relatives and friends, and when they could not find Him, they went back to Jerusalem to search there. Three days later, they finally discovered Jesus confronting the learned scribes and Pharisees at the temple . . .

At first they could do nothing but watch their son, seated confidently on a tool and virtually surrounded by white-haired, bearded men ten times or more His age.

"He is talking with them as though He understands the ancient writings better than they do!" Joseph whispered, both astonished and embarrassed.

Mary was less startled, her reaction bordering on awe.

"Remember this, my husband . . . ," she said. "Remember that our son has come to this knowledge without the training other children might have. You are a carpenter. You hope that He will follow you in a business that has lasted for generations. That is why you have been teaching Jesus to use His hands. But this is something more, something for which neither of us has been responsible."

Joseph's thoughts were similar to Mary's.

"And now He is holding His own with a gathering of men destined since birth to be what they are, and He has done so without ever reading the parchments and other materials they have had for a long time," Joseph added, "realizing how correct his wife was. I have shown this boy of ours how to build homes and stables and carts. He does well, He learns quickly. And I have been very proud of Him."

"Are you not still proud?" she asked. "*Listen* to what He is saying, see how these men respond."

Joseph did as she had requested.

"Everyone is expecting the Messiah to come soon," a middle-aged Pharisee said. "What do You think about this, boy?"

"Lord, this . . . this man is so forward!" Darien exclaimed. *"Surely You will ignore His impudence?"*

"He is acting this way because it is difficult for him to see anyone other than what My physical form suggests—a young child. I shall not lay the blame for this on his shoulders as a condemnation of his words or his manner."

Jesus looked at the man and smiled.

"Before your seventieth birthday, you will know that which you seek," He replied solemnly. "You are to be to the Messiah a friend like few others, coming to His side when others have fled."

The Pharisee stepped back, and the others in that temple, built by Herod the Great, gasped, murmuring about this child. Some were drawn to what they considered His audacity; others were displeased by what they saw as presumptuousness.

"How can You know this?" Nicodaemus persisted. "And my name! You *know* it as well. But I am not someone famous. How can this be? What resource do You have that none of us here are aware of?"

"There is knowledge that is not of this world," Jesus said simply.

"But You and I have never met. Please, I must know."

"In time, Nicodaemus."

"Can You not tell me more now, boy?"

Judging by the expression on Jesus' face, He seemed to take pity on the puzzled man; He went on to say, "One day years hence, you—and you alone—will come to the Messiah at night, when everyone else is asleep, and you shall learn from Him the sacred way to eternal life."

Few subjects had been debated more among those often cloistered members of the Sanhedrin, including the specific nature of heaven and hell, the existence of demons, and other weighty matters.

Immediately other men approached Jesus.

The sight of this immediately overwhelmed His parents because their boy Jesus seemed trapped, surrounded by men with a vast number of years of study to guide them.

"What do they want?" Joseph asked. "We have to stop this now. That son of ours is but twelve."

Mary agreed finally, and they pushed through the group that had been surrounding their son.

"Why have You done this to us?" she called to him. "Your father and I have been frantic, searching for you everywhere."

Other children would have felt ashamed, especially in front of men who were now so anxious to get as close to Him as could be managed.

But not Jesus. He remained calm, even serene.

"Why did you feel you had to search so diligently for me?" he asked them both. "Do you not know by now that I have to be about My Father's business?"

As usual, Mary and Joseph did not understand what He meant.

"Come, son," Joseph said. "We need to be heading home."

Nicodaemus approached them.

"We have been captivated by your boy's wisdom," he told them. "Speaking for myself, let me say that I would like to get to know Him better. He is quite remarkable. He could become a brilliant teacher. Even today we have learned something from Him."

"From our Son?" Joseph questioned. "He is but a boy. And you are a grown man of some years. So are the others here in the temple."

"Can you be so sure this Child is *just* a boy?" Nicodaemus probed earnestly. "He could not be as ordinary as you claim. If he were, then we would have turned from Him hours ago as an arrogant nuisance."

He extended his arm and indicated the other men who were listening.

"Look at their expressions. See how intent they are. And tell me that a *boy* would be able to evoke this kind of reaction!"

In back of him, the rest of the Pharisees and scribes clamored for the parents to let Jesus spend more time with them.

"We see something in Him," one of them said anxiously.

"All our lives we have dedicated ourselves to *learning*," another emphasized. "At His age we knew only a small portion of what He does. Let us spend more time with Him. The past few hours have gone by all too quickly."

And so they pleaded, one after the other.

But Mary and Joseph were not prepared for anything like that, and they took Him back to Nazareth with them.

PART VI

Around our pillows golden ladders rise,
And up and down the skies,
With winged sandals shod,
The angels come, and go, the Messengers of God!

RICHARD HENRY STODDARD

For the next thirty years minus twelve, Jesus of Nazareth remained in loving and strict obedience to His earthly parents.

A blessed time of communion between them.

A time during which the family circle was enlarged when his brothers were born, all of whom He loved and who loved Jesus in return.

Except Jude.

That one brother would remain doubtful about Jesus' identity, even antagonistic toward Him for many years.

Jesus learned well the trade of a carpenter at the hands of His beloved earthly father. In due course, the Child became an adult and increased in wisdom and stature, and in favor with God and man.

Joseph developed varying periods of illness, his physical condition weakening a bit more each time. So, Jesus had to take over more and more of the family business and managed, over the next dozen years, to save enough from its revenues to support His parents when he ultimately left to begin His ministry . . .

CHAPTER 27

DUSK had come, the sounds of early nighttime beginning sporadically at first, only to intensify as stars became visible in that clear Middle Eastern sky.

"Oh, Lord, these years have been good ones!" exclaimed Darien in that treasured moment of peace at the side of Jesus, who was sitting under an ancient sycamore tree near Joseph's prospering carpentry shop in the center of Nazareth.

"They have," Jesus agreed.

"Especially with Your earthly father," the angel added.

Jesus nodded, fully in agreement with that.

How He loved the man!

Joseph had had to grapple with the knowledge that the Child his wife bore was not his own. While he tried very hard to accept Mary's explanation of what had happened, as well as view the visitation he had witnessed by an angel as something other than a delusion, he could scarcely deny, if he wanted to be honest with himself, that his doubts had never ceased completely, that they continued to surface every so often, unbidden and dreaded. He would have to beat them back the only way he knew how . . . by engaging in long periods of emotional prayer, sometimes well into the night.

But always Joseph would come out of such troubled times resolved in his mind, heart, and soul to go on, to accept by faith what had been revealed to him by the very young woman he loved so deeply and by that messenger who had confronted him one night, apparently sent from the God to whom he had been devoted long before Mary entered his life, the God who had guided them to Egypt before it was too late to escape the madness that grew out of Herod's murderous decree.

None of these insecure, uncertain moments were allowed to harm the developing relationship involving Jesus and Joseph, and because of this, years of incomparable human closeness between father and son followed that astonishing birth in Bethlehem and the fascination it garnered among shepherds and wise men alike.

Mary and Joseph resisted the temptation to keep their son cloistered.

They did not completely understand who He was, but they could hardly be unaware of how unlike other children He constantly proved Himself to be in a bewildering variety of ways during their everyday lives.

But one thing both understood, and clearly so.

"If He is kept isolated," Mary had said, "it will not be good for Him."

Joseph agreed.

"I knew someone before I met you, my wife," he told her. "He had a young son who was very, very smart, the brightest lad you could imagine. His parents kept him away from other young people, forcing him always to study, study, study and never go out to play, for they considered childhood game-playing to be useless and wasteful of his time."

"What happened to him, Joseph?"

"He ran away . . . my friend has not seen him since. But he has heard that his son, now a man, leads a dissolute life, whoring, and much else."

"That will never happen to our Jesus!" she declared.

As a result, those were also years during which God-in-the-flesh experienced what many of His other creations were like, boys and girls the same age as He, and also the adults with whom Joseph came in contact in the conduct of his carpentry business.

"*That is true,*" Jesus said, agreeing with Darien. "*There has been joy and love. You are an important part of all this.*"

The angel sighed, refreshed by his Lord's words.

"*Do You yearn for heaven?*" he asked.

"*I do yearn for heaven.*"

"*When will You return?*"

"*When My work here is done.*"

"*The Jewish people expect their prophesied Messiah to free them from bondage. How will they react when they learn that the bondage You will free them from is not that of Rome but of their own sins?*"

Darien had no doubt that this would come as a wrenching shock to many Jews who had clung to the prophecies of the Messiah as sources of hope during the many calamities that befell their nation.

Jesus' next remark underlined this.

"They will not understand, Darien. It will take a very long time before some of them begin to perceive the truth, and then I will be gone."

Darien did not expect to hear that.

"You will leave before this occurs?" the angel asked, trying not to appear as concerned as he was.

"It is because of that very departure of which I speak that it will happen," Jesus replied calmly.

From the beginning, Darien knew that full awareness was to be kept from him for a time, that God had a purpose for doing so.

Often, Darien would sit by himself and watch Jesus with those people who somehow found out His location and wonder where this time on earth truly was heading.

The angel could discern no reason to believe that life for the two of them would remain as it was forever, literally and figuratively. Not knowing anything more than that prompted him that evening to ask the Son of God a question he could no longer keep himself from raising out loud.

"You know the end from the beginning . . . ," he began. *"But I do not. Can I perhaps be told more, Lord? What we are enjoying tonight is not all that will ever be, I know, but what else is to come, Lord?"*

Jesus leaned back against the tree.

"Are you sure your dedication would not change if you knew the full extent of what you are hungering and thirsting for?" He asked. *"Can you be sure you would be able to persist in this mission regardless of the good or the bad of whatever I might tell you?"*

"*I am with You through whatever happens,*" Darien asserted. *"Nothing will ever deter me in the course that has been set before me by the Father."*

"So Peter will say . . . ," whispered Jesus.

"What do You mean, Lord? Who is this Peter? Have You glimpsed the future and seen something just now?"

Jesus nodded.

"Before the joy at the end, there must be pain," He muttered sadly.

"And Peter is involved somehow?"

But Jesus spoke no more about this subject, and Darien did not persist, though the images of that little interlude would remain with him, persistently recalled at idle moments until his time on earth was no more . . .

CHAPTER 28

It was time.

Darien did not have to hear an announcement that this was so. No chorus of angels would sing out from heaven in proclamation.

It was time for Jesus' ministry to begin, a moment Darien had known was due to come though he could never be certain when it would be upon them.

He had been awaiting it for a long while now, with anticipation but also with considerable uncertainty, for he knew that the beginning of Jesus' ministry was an epochal event unmatched in the entire history of the human race, and it was to mean a massive change in the relationship between them.

Until then, while the fleshly Jesus was asleep each night, the Son was fully awake, with no need for rest, and He and Darien spent hours together in blissful communion. This had seldom been possible to the same extent in heaven, where the Trinity's attention was demanded by redeemed souls and angels alike.

To be so close to the Creator of everything that ever existed and ever will, Darien would think happily.

But it had to end; he understood this and remained grateful for the period when there were no attacks by Satan, when Jesus could be a boy, then a young man, with little to occupy His time except working with Joseph and speaking with people who came to Him with questions.

Ah, those gatherings . . . Darien recalled, *strangers would gather around Jesus, sometimes asking Him questions, sometimes just listening to the questions of others.*

The rich came despite themselves—after all, Jesus was the son of a humble carpenter and not as educated as many of them could well afford to be. The scholars as well as the poor sought Him out, ostensibly for the most ordinary of reasons, yet Darien knew they gathered around

Jesus because there was no doubt He had qualities to which they had not been accustomed no matter how much learning they had assimilated over the years, a joy, a peace, a confidence they wished to find in their own lives.

When they were alone, the angel told Him how wonderful it was to see Him sharing Himself with everyone and how eagerly people responded to Him, though He was, as far as they were concerned, a very young man, younger than many of them, and yet He drew them to Him in a way that was beyond their comprehension.

"It is only the start," Jesus remarked, *"before the religious leaders and the politicians become involved. The people are open, but those who rule them will not be. It is from* them *that trouble will come."*

"But for now it is so pleasant," added Darien. *"There is trust and rapport . . . so beautiful, Lord. That it could be like that always!"*

"You call Me Lord, and well you should," said Jesus. *"But when the time comes, those who have no demands on themselves* now, *none at all but to sit when it is convenient and listen or ask uncomplicated questions about crops or building homes or tending to their animals or other such matters, how many of* them *will find Me so easy to be with when the accusations start? When one after the other turns against Me and speaks no longer respectfully but mocks Me to My face, sometimes behind My back, which of them will stand by My side then, Darien, or flee from Me?"*

But aside from such moments of melancholy, there were far more times when Darien watched Jesus touch the lives of people in Nazareth.

Apart from the obvious questions about carpentry and other such matters, He was approached by people who wanted His advice about moral issues, about having a temper, about disciplining their children.

"But I am not married," Jesus would respond to them. *"What help can I be?"*

"There is something about You," one mother told Him, fumbling for the right words, "something wise in the way You speak, in the way You seem to think. I have been watching You for a while, Jesus, and I cannot ignore what my eyes and ears perceive."

"You are closer to the truth than you know, dear woman," He told her.

She smiled and proceeded to ask what was on her heart.

"My son has been rebellious," she said. "His father wants to discipline him, but we worry that this will make matters worse. Should we just ignore the bad things he continues to do?"

"He who ignores discipline comes to poverty and shame," Jesus said slowly, "but whoever heeds correction is honored."

He took her hand between His own and added, "A fool spurns his father's discipline, but whoever heeds correction shows great prudence. Your son will be grateful to you once you and his father show that your actions are in love, not anger. That love will surely bring him back to you both."

"You are barely more than a boy Yourself," the mother observed. "From whence come your wise words?"

"From Proverbs," He replied. "The wisdom of God can prove sufficient for all that life brings to every man, woman, and child."

She kissed him on the lips, not out of passion, but in a common gesture of that time, a gesture of appreciation.

Other mothers came on subsequent days with additional problems, and He spoke to them all.

His own earthly parents never interfered, never questioned what He was doing, though between themselves, they would stop and wonder. And amidst their pride, they asked themselves what was going to happen to their beloved son, and always Mary would be the one to hug herself and shudder.

Heaven on earth . . .

In a sense, that was what Jesus represented, an important part of heaven transplanted to earth and encased in human flesh.

How He had to control Himself as a boy and as a man whenever He saw sin, and despite the constraints that bound Satan, sin itself went on unabated because it was embedded in human nature, Darien told himself. *There was no need for the devil to waste his time with those who were so far from God already.*

But there were common, garden-variety sins that seemed not particularly noteworthy because they were part and parcel of every human being born since Eden . . . the little lies, the minor conceits and deceits, the piddling dishonesties that arose in everyday relationships but were sins just the same, barriers between God and man.

Jesus saw them all.

"Oh, Darien, Darien," He would speak in anguish, *"few realize how sinful they truly are. They will say, 'Oh, it is only a tiny lie,' or 'I have to do this, you know; my business depends on it.' They are choosing the chaff when the wheat is also available to them."*

Darien knew his Lord better than ever after those thirty years of being continually at His side, and he had no doubt that seeing the corruption of His Father's creations was, in a sense, a bit like hell for Him.

"I would gather them together as a mother gathers her chicks," Jesus said more than once. *"But even if heaven itself should open up before them, so many would look, yes, even gaze intently for a short while, and then go about their lives as before. It would have little or no impact on them, Darien."*

Jesus found that almost inconceivable.

"If someone came up to any of these people and held out a gold coin in one hand and a scorpion in the other, all would most certainly turn from the poisonous creature in a hurry and grab the gold. Yet in a far more important sense, a spiritual one that determines where they will spend eternity, they will make the opposite decision again and again without ever being fully aware of the deadly consequences!"

There were times when He would witness an act of sin and want to reach out and shake the individual committing it and say, *"Do you not realize who I am? You are* Our *creation.* We *made you from the dust of Eden. And now you have turned Eden into dust by your rebellion against the Triune Godhead!"*

Righteous anger, anger that came from a holy God confronting the stinking filth of unholiness, any act of sin a filthy rag waved before a perfect Jehovah . . .

But sinners were basically dumb, brute beasts, wallowing compulsively in their own unworthiness. Many centuries later, certain groups of arrogant men would gather together to try to deny this, saying that such a view fostered a destructive self-image and should not be allowed, but they were wrong, very wrong.

Throughout the course of human history, Darien would discover, vast numbers would learn well the choice before them—essentially that of heaven or hell as their destination—and embrace the flames of damnation with a zeal that betrayed their allegiance not to almighty God but to Satan, the deceiver.

"If only I could take them in My arms, Darien, and protect them," Jesus told the angel time after time as anguish danced across His strong and handsome human face, which mirrored the incarnate divine sorrow over what had been happening to humanity since the Fall.

And yet Jesus could *not* reach out as He wanted, could *not* take all the sinners He would ever meet in His arms and hug them to Himself. He could do none of this, for that was not the Plan for the Ages, it was never the Plan, which was something else altogether, more profound and far reaching and blessed in the long run, but still a wrenching struggle for the fleshly part of Jesus, a struggle to remain patient, to restrain impulses that were an outgrowth of His goodness and mercy but would tamper with what His Father had been so carefully fashioning for so long.

Later, when the fate of Jesus was revealed to Darien, he thought back on those words of concern for the souls of his Lord's creation, souls that would decree the madness to follow, and this angel would know, then and ever, what forgiveness was all about.

CHAPTER 29

IT WAS TIME . . .

And John the Baptist was to herald that this was so.

"He has been chosen," God revealed to Darien. *"Already he proclaims that the coming of the Messiah is at hand."*

"Have any listened, Father?"

"Some have. They are being prepared to follow My Son. Several are fishermen. One is a tax-gatherer. They pretend to ignore the words of the Baptist but those words are seeds planted in their very souls."

God paused, then spoke again. *"Go to this man with great speed, Darien. Spend whatever time is needed with him. He will think back upon the time between the two of you, and it will give him strength."*

"Strength for what, Father?"

"My dear servant is going to die soon."

Darien felt the deepest sorrow come from God then.

"Father, You are weeping."

"I weep not for John the Baptist who shall soon be welcomed into My presence but for the souls of those who will conspire to end his precious life. That sin will follow them into the very pit of hell."

"Who are those You mention?"

"The son of Herod the Great, his wife, their daughter Salome, and others."

"I will go on, Father."

"Be to this man whatever your spirit leads you to be. No greater has ever walked the face of the earth."

"When shall I return to the side of Jesus?"

"Do not be concerned about that. My Son shall follow you and the Baptist. And then you will witness the beginning of wonders."

. . . the beginning of wonders.

Darien puzzled over exactly what the Father could have meant. There had been wonders already. Was something greater in store?

But this time he did not question. He simply thanked God and briefly left the side of Jesus to go to John the Baptist.

Darien came upon the tough-looking, bearded prophet skinning a rabbit he had caught. Shortly after that, he stuck the body on a spit made out of a tree branch and roasted it over an open fire.

Some people were more sensitive to the presence of angels than others. Some felt their nearness while others had no idea that angels actually existed.

John the Baptist was different from all of them. He did not suspect or hope or guess that angels were nearby at any given moment.

He knew!

This took one of those angels, Darien, by surprise.

"Welcome, stranger," John said cheerfully, as though he had just seen a man step into the clearing. "What is your name?"

Darien told him.

"I had no doubt that some messenger from a Holy God had come," he went on, cocking his head. Then he played with the lower part of his gray-flecked beard and mused, "I wonder if this means I am soon to die."

. . . I am soon to die.

The angel gasped, once again taken by surprise.

"I thought that would get a reaction from you," John said, chuckling heartily. "Will I be able to *see* you?"

"Only when—," Darien started to reply.

"My soul is leaving my body and I am ready to be taken up. Is that it?"

"Yes . . ."

"I know angels cannot eat, so please excuse me if I indulge in one pleasure that only flesh-and-blood creatures know."

After the rabbit was well cooked, John started to eat it as though he had not had a meal for many days.

"Big man, big appetite," he said a bit apologetically.

"I can see that," Darien finally ventured.

"You and your kind are one reason why I am thought by many to be on the crazy side," John remarked.

Darien did not understand what the prophet meant by this, and he said so.

"I have talked with angels before." The Baptist's reply was completely unexpected.

Darien had no words, so stunned was he.

"I can tell by your silence," John observed, "that, as of this moment, you can be numbered in with that group whose members steal glances at me out of curiosity over what a wild man such as myself, given to such childish fantasies, really does look like."

Darien was puzzled. This man did not seem at all what he had expected, obviously crude in his conduct and eccentric as well.

I cannot blame those who treat him with derision, Darien told himself. *He is obviously a strange character. If I were someone of the flesh and I saw him and heard him, I would reach the same conclusion.*

"*What angels have you talked with before now?*" he asked.

"One named Stedfast," John replied.

Darien realized there was no way the Baptist could have known about that angel unless there had been communication between them.

"*How recently was Stedfast with you?*"

"Just yesterday."

John's manner was pleasant, even boisterous. He had finished the rabbit, and was now downing some water from a tiny stream nearby.

"So good to the taste," he sighed. "But it is still not the water of life."

The angel had begun to relax.

John was friendly and obviously dedicated. Nor would God have sent Darien to the man's side with such words if they were not true. The only barrier that had stood in the way was the trap of judging the Baptist by his outward appearance, one into which Darien regrettably had fallen.

"A few may pass by and hear me, you know," John said almost wistfully. "They will look for somebody else here with me, and seeing no one, they will only conclude that I talk to the air around us."

He roared with laughter.

"And it will hardly surprise them considering what they think of me already!" John exclaimed.

He washed his hands in the stream, and then, as he was standing, asked, "Why did God send you?"

For a moment, Darien did not know what to say.

"There was Stedfast, and before him—"

"*Others, John? You had other angels visiting?*"

"Virtue was one, as I remember. Faithful was another."

Darien knew them both, as every angel knew every other angel.

"*Only recently?*" he inquired.

"Only recently."

Darien wept in the same sense that almighty God wept, his emotions so strong they could hardly be contained, but not wholly the tears of sorrow, for there was great joy as well.

"You are sad," John observed.

"How could you know?"

"How could any of God's prophets know certain things we have known over the centuries? Is that what you ask? Well, the answer is simple: Jehovah gave us gifts other people do not have."

John stood, the full size of the man, from his six-foot-four height to the width of his shoulders making him a formidable physical presence, his bulk accentuated by the double-layer of animal skins he wore.

"Why were you weeping?" the Baptist asked, a tender tone belying his rugged, muscular appearance.

Before Darien could say anything, John spoke again but with no trace of concern. "But then, I know why—at least I think I do."

. . . *I wonder if this means that I am soon to die.*

He repeated that and went on to add, "I have heard that angels come as you and the others came to me only when death is near. I spoke partly in jest a moment ago, but in that was some truth, was there not?"

Darien admitted what the Father had told him.

John groaned, straightened himself up to his full height, pushing back his shoulders, then folded one hand around an old sheep's rod with a gnarled handle.

"Send me where You want me to go, Holy Father!" he declared as he left that secluded place and headed for the River Jordan.

CHAPTER 30

WORD had spread about John's baptisms.

Crowds of varying size would form along the banks of the Jordan, waiting out of curiosity in most instances since the Baptist had been gaining more than a little notoriety for some while. But for a few, it was also an eagerness to take a public stand for Jehovah, which was exactly the opportunity he offered.

While John was not able to baptize anyone in the name of the Father, the Son, and the Holy Spirit, he spoke of almighty God alone; he said the water was a symbol of cleansing without realizing how this act would be repeated for countless millions of men, women, and children throughout the two thousand years that were to follow.

One by one, they approached him, and he immersed each beneath the waters of the Jordan and brought them up again. Only half a dozen came that day for this ceremony, but John was not disappointed. He had often said that heaven would rejoice if he ministered to only one soul throughout the whole of his life.

"I am God's instrument," he once said to some men who had become his friends. "Is the harp to say to the master harpist stroking it that it is not satisfied, that only one melody has ever been played on its strings? That instrument *or any other* is in existence only to respond to the touch of whoever owns it. My holy Father in heaven owns me. Whatever He wishes, I am ready to do."

Once John had sensed Someone saying to him, *"Would you even die for Me, John?"*

This encounter had come at a time when John was sitting on the side of the Jordan, having just learned that Herod was interested in seeing him but that the king's wife was agitating against the visit because of all the Baptist's diatribes against the immorality that was rampant in the royal household.

"Yea, Father, I would die for You," John replied, as he always did whenever he suspected God's hand in evidence.

"Would you ever stop spreading My Word, even if this meant earning the fatal condemnation of your earthly principalities and powers?"

"I would *never* do that. I would go on telling others of You until the very last breath from my body.

"Am I everything to you, John?"

"Everything, Father, for now, for eternity."

It was over quickly enough, that contact between finite and infinite. But the memory of it would never leave John. In fact it returned vividly to his mind one extraordinary afternoon when he decided to respond to a summons delivered to him by one of Herod's messengers. He went to the king's palace.

"I fear you," the king admitted to the Baptist that day.

"You need not fear me," John contradicted him, "but you should fear the holy God who has sent me, and His Son soon to follow."

Herod's temper was beginning to flare up, but he managed to keep from unleashing it because his respect for John was far greater than his heated emotions.

"I think you are a righteous and a holy man," the king acknowledged. "Your words are strong but there is some truth in them, and I would like to listen to you now, if you will speak some more."

John went on to repeat what he had said before but with special impact now.

"You have taken as your wife Herodias, who was married to your brother Philip. This is unlawful."

"I will change the law," Herod retorted.

"The law is not only man's; it came from God Himself."

The king fell back against his throne, surprisingly ill equipped to dispute what he was being told.

"Also, you would like to escape from the shadow of your father," the Baptist said, speaking less harshly this time.

Herod's shoulders slumped as he tacitly admitted what the other man had said.

"You are so wise," he remarked, admiration in his voice.

"It is not my wisdom, for it comes to me from above."

Herod looked at him earnestly.

"My father was a great man . . . ," he pointed out.

"But a man dragged down by his passions," John reminded him. "It is that debauched side of Herod the Great that you fear, thinking you have inherited it and there is nothing you can do to stop it from taking over your life."

Herod groaned in light of such honesty.

"I would *never* have ordered the slaughter of all those poor children two years old or younger. What a ghastly act that was on my father's part! But then he also was responsible for most of the beautiful temples and other buildings that abound throughout the land."

Herod could not look directly at John for the next few moments, his body becoming drenched with perspiration.

"It is as though he wanted the people to look at the outer facade," he muttered, "and ignore what was inside."

Finally he glanced at John.

"I do not want to end this now, Baptist. Will you continue further with me later on this day?"

John indicated that he would, grateful for the unexpected opportunity to witness to such a man who was desperately in need of the truth of God's Word.

So the king and the Baptist spent the rest of that afternoon and well into the night discussing the weightiest of matters . . .

. . . while eavesdropping servants dutifully reported everything to Herodias, who was not pleased.

CHAPTER 31

"I DO NOT want to end this now, Baptist. Will you perhaps continue further with me later on this day?"

John indicated that he would, grateful for the unexpected opportunity to witness to such a man who was desperately in need of the truth of God's Word.

Sighing from that fragment of recollection, the Baptist was ready to go back to shore when suddenly he froze where he stood, the water up to his knees, his gaze on several of the men whose attention was fixed unwaveringly on his every move.

Pharisees and Sadducees.

There were an unusual number of their kind present that day, and John was greatly angered because he knew they had come to entrap him if they could since he upset them as well.

"Brood of vipers," he called out, pointing to each one. "Who warned you to flee from the wrath to come? Therefore bear fruits worthy of repentance, and do not think to say to yourselves, 'We have Abraham as our father.' For I say to you, that God is able to raise up children to Abraham from these stones.

"And even now the ax is laid to the root of the trees. Therefore every tree which does not bear good fruit is cut down and thrown into the fire. I indeed baptize you with water unto repentance, but He who is coming after me is mightier than I, whose sandals I am not worthy to carry. He will baptize you with the Holy Spirit and with fire. His winnowing fan is in His hand, and He will thoroughly clean out His threshing floor, and gather His wheat into the barn; but He will burn up the chaff with unquenchable fire."

The people, including those of the Sanhedrin, were stunned by the power and eloquence of the Baptist's proclamation, coming as it did from a man most of them considered uncouth to the point of bordering on the barbaric.

"John!" Darien cried. *"He is here. The One you have been seeking all your life is the last to be baptized this day."*

"Where?" the Baptist asked, momentarily confused.

"On the west bank. He is even now entering the water," the angel told him, anxious that the man be properly alerted.

The Baptist saw Jesus as the tall, broad-shouldered figure stepped into the chill, clear water.

"I am ready," Jesus told him.

John's face flushed red, not with that rage that he so commonly directed against the hypocrites among the Sanhedrin and elsewhere throughout the land, but with embarrassment.

"I need to be baptized by You, my dear Lord," he said humbly, "and are You coming to me?"

John bowed his head reverently, but Jesus made him raise it up again.

"Permit it to be so now, John, for thus it is fitting for us to fulfill all righteousness."

. . . *for thus it is fitting for us to fulfill all righteousness.*

John started weeping, an unusual sight for those on both banks of the Jordan who were familiar with him since he was far better known to them as a vehement man, regularly spitting out words of condemnation.

"Do not weep for Me," Jesus pleaded, "nor for yourself, but for those lost ones who hear the message I shall be giving—and you have proclaimed before I came—and choose to turn away from it with ears deafened by disbelief."

The Baptist nodded, wiping the tears away as he said, "I will do this very moment as You ask of me, my Lord."

"*Lord,*" Darien said, "*now?*"

"*Yes, now.*"

As Jesus was turning back to shore, heaven opened up before them.

In an instant, a pure white dove appeared and settled on Jesus' right shoulder while a voice of great majesty and power came out of heaven, saying, "This is My beloved Son, in whom I am well pleased."

Some saw what had happened and heard those words, but others did not, their souls not receiving such things due to their hardened disbelief.

John fell to his waist in the Jordan's waters.

"I see . . . ," he muttered, stymied for words, this man accustomed to using them in the most arresting manner.

"What you *see* is where you will go soon," Jesus told him.

"Soon, Lord?"

"Angels will welcome you past the gates as others sing a chorus of exaltation while you stand before the throne of the Most High."

Every nerve in the Baptist's body seemed to stir.

"But I am so unworthy," he sobbed. "I am dung on the spotless golden streets of Jehovah's kingdom. I—"

"Arise now, dear John. Men will soon come for you and cast you into prison."

"Will it be Herod's doing?"

Jesus' tone was sad as He told John this was the case.

"He reached out to me in need, and I witnessed to Him as fervently as I could," the Baptist recalled.

"Some can never be brought to the truth and have it in their hearts. Their minds are reprobate, sold out to the master of evil."

John gasped, repeating, "I see . . . almighty God."

"My Father Himself will embrace you."

"And I see others waiting with Him."

"Those who *have* accepted the message you announced to the world and have gone on to Jehovah before you. It will not be long, John, until you join them."

"They seem so loving . . ."

"Because you were the instrument. Eternity is theirs for that reason. Their gratitude will never end."

"Will there be much pain for me?"

"It will be done with in an instant. You shall be absent from your body and present with My Father in the blink of an eye."

"Good-bye, my precious Lord," John said in farewell.

Jesus touched the Baptist on the forehead with the palm of His right hand.

"Only for a season," He said. "Just as surely as spring follows winter, we shall not be parted for long."

John watched as Jesus waded to the Jordan's bank, then turned for a moment, whispering words that the Baptist nevertheless heard, even from that distance, "Be still, and of good courage, beloved John."

By the time, John reached the bank, Jesus was gone, but not those words, those precious words that would sustain him among the darkness and the rats.

CHAPTER 32

THEN was Jesus led . . . into the wilderness to be tempted of the devil . . .

During His childhood, only a small number of people became suspicions about Jesus' true identity. But from now on, it would be different. Any demonstrations of deity were going to be more overt, leaving observers to accept or reject Him. But first the fleshly dimension of Jesus had to be tested for forty days and forty nights in the worst region of the Judean wilderness.

It was an area not only of wild beasts but also of criminals who fled capture, along with another group no one wanted, the lepers of Judea, rejected by "normal" Jews who could not run the risk of infection.

In the distance, the granite slopes of Mount Sinai could be seen, changing color by the hour as the intensity and direction of the sun's rays altered. Closer were numerous, smaller rock formations, some sculpted by the winds and the rare rains into various shapes that were often human in shape. At night, when illuminated by moonlight, these formations seemed eerie, intimidating.

"*Why must You go through this?*" Darien asked ignorantly after he had been told what was to happen.

"*So that, as the prophets have said, I shall be tempted and tested in all points like every man,*" replied Jesus.

The Judean wilderness was perhaps the harshest anywhere in the known world. During the day, almost unimaginable heat pounded the surface. At night, the chilliest of winds whipped across the barrenness.

Scorpions and poisonous snakes were a persistent hazard for foolhardy travelers, along with constant thirst, murderous thirst, because in all those miles of land, there was little or no water.

Even the plentiful sand could play fatal tricks on the unwary, seeming safe in one spot and, then, a foot or two further on, giving way completely as quicksand and pulling the victim down.

And in the caves of the mountains that ran through the area hid ruthless robbers and other vicious criminals as well as the poor lepers, moaning away their lives.

But there was something else . . . madness. Again and again, people wandered back from the wilderness or were found at its fringes acting as though they had become possessed, ranting about foul spirits in the night, phantom demons beckoning to the edge of hell itself. They could be heard at night, like rabid creatures, their cries tearing through the darkness, chilling the blood of people in nearby villages who found their sleep shattered.

A hint of hell . . .

This was where Jesus would spend more than a month. The God that He was could not die, could not thirst, could not feel hunger, but the Man that He was could die if bitten by a scorpion or a snake, could waste away from dehydration without adequate water to drink, could starve without food, could be attacked by fierce and desperate men, could be contaminated by the dreaded affliction of leprosy.

The Man faced grave danger; God did not. But it was the *Man* who Satan would connive to destroy, for it was only with the *Man* that he had any hope of success. As before, in Egypt, he knew if he could take the body of Jesus and rend it asunder, then God's Plan of redemption at least would be significantly delayed because it would have to be started all over again with another incarnation many years hence, and all the while, the devil's intention would continue as it had been: to stop that body as well, and the one after it, on and on, every day, week, month, and year of delay meaning multitudes of other souls dragged to hell.

"*I* live *to see them die!*" Satan had declared to the demonic hordes a long time before. "*The flames of damnation represent my desire for all men, all women, all—*"

He stopped short of saying children because they were protected by God's providence until they were a certain age. After that, Satan could go after them with some expectation of success since then their souls *would* be at issue.

And so he was to begin his wilderness assault, more ferocious than ever before, tempting the humanness of Jesus, trying to disengage it from the Deity He also embodied. If he could get Jesus to sin, sin bringing about separation from God, then God would have to abandon that fleshly body, letting it fall to the ground and die to be consumed by the beasts of the wilderness, especially the vultures always on alert.

But if Satan failed, if Jesus remained free of harm, if He successfully resisted Satan in His flesh-and-blood personification, nothing else could be done *at the source of redemption.* That would mean the devil would have to continue doing as he had always done, trying to corrupt those who were candidates for salvation.

For a full thirty-plus days, Satan did nothing at all but stand aside and look and wait, like a hovering bird of prey, ready to swoop down. There was to be no temptation just yet. He reasoned that if Jesus the Man were weakened sufficiently by hunger and thirst over that long period, His resistance would be diminished as a result, and then gaining control of Jesus would be easier when the time came for Satan to rush into the arena and confront Him.

Darien was not aware of any of this. As far as he was concerned, he was not to prepare for any onslaught. He assumed that Jesus' confinement to the wilderness was something that had to be done as a kind of ceremonial act.

But it did prove to be far more, for it was intended as a war cry flung in the very face of Satan.

"Here I am!" Jesus seemed to be saying. *"Take your best shot at me, Satan. But you must realize that you shall fail; I can tell you that. When will you learn, son of the morning? The master deceiver has once again only succeeded in deceiving himself!"*

Otherwise there was no reason for Jesus to face the dangers of that wilderness and torment Himself so long. It was a spiritual metaphor for the sins of man. If it had not been, then after the baptism by John, He would have returned to His home in Nazareth and avoided the anguish that became self-imposed.

The wilderness was essentially a symbolic forerunner of one of those places of amusement to be created in Rome decades later. Before Christians were forced out into the open arenas and thrown to lions and other beasts, they would spend many days jammed together in dungeons, fed only enough scraps to keep them from collapsing and given barely sufficient water—and often polluted water at that.

What those Christians would later face was precisely the sort of confrontation Jesus endured now: physical abuse in an arena in which Satan ruled as he prowled about like a roaring lion seeking the moment when he could easily "devour" God-in-the-flesh. Just as they would come to be tempted to renounce God, so would He, in His humanity, come to an identical point.

Only Jesus Himself standing against the instigator of all evil committed since the beginning of time . . .

A member of the Triune Godhead did not have even the community of suffering embodied in a dungeon filled with scores of Christians, some modicum of comfort derived from their *shared* ordeal.

Later, many would die on their knees before ravenous beasts, their hands cupped together, expressions of the profoundest peace shining from their faces, provoking the most hardened of witnesses to exclaim, "How can it be? They are smiling. Look at their joy! Look at their joy!"

Jesus was physically alone, but not spiritually.

As time passed, other angels, including Gabriel and Michael, joined Darien to stand by *his* side as well as to be with their Lord.

Thus it was for their Lord during that wilderness period. As the days passed and His body craved food, gradually that body grew weaker.

Animals came and briefly stood at Jesus' side. A pack of wolves, passing through the wilderness on their way to more fertile locales, stopped before Him, as did one or more lions, surveying the situation and then leaving without troubling the still form.

Darien saw Jesus' face become pale, His steps slow, pain evident in the little whimpering sounds that escaped from His mouth. Again and again toward the conclusion of that seemingly endless period Jesus did not have the strength to stand for more than a minute or two at a time, invariably toppling over onto the sand.

Once, after more than thirty days, He came upon a solitary water hole and walked to it as fast as He could, but the liquid was so bitter it could not be consumed, and Jesus had to spit it out, gagging from the taste.

"*You are dying!*" cried the angel.

As far as the human part of Him, yes, that was true. Darien had long before confused the physical appearance Jesus wore with His real identity, the spiritual, divine part of Him, forgetting that any mortal, corruptible body was merely a cloak of flesh hung over a human soul.

"*I cannot let this happen!*" Darien said.

"*There is no choice,*" replied Jesus. "*I live or I die according only to the will of My heavenly Father.*"

The Son did not speak harshly, touched by Darien's concern and not wanting to add to his misery.

Other angels came immediately, heeding the sudden anguished cry of one of their own, as the Word of God would later relate in the Gospel of Mark, saying that during Jesus' travail, "angels ministered to Him."

"He is dying!" Darien repeated. *"There has been no food, no water. He is too weak to live. He cannot last—"*

Jesus had fallen yet another time and was unable to get back on His feet.

He lay on the sand, tremors of pain shooting through His chest and stomach as well as His head.

"I shall go right now to the Father," Gabriel indicated. *"I shall appeal to Him for help without delay."*

"We both will go," Michael added. *"We—"*

He stopped speaking.

"What is it?" Darien asked.

And then it hit them, the truth that their emotions had caused everyone to overlook.

"The heavenly Father is in charge," Michael added. *"We cannot allow ourselves to be so much like His flesh-and-blood creations that we become plagued with those doubts of a similar kind."*

A murmur of agreement rippled through the multitude.

Jesus' eyes had closed in the meantime, His breathing more labored now than at any time before.

Angels moaned, distressed by what seemed an important battle about to be lost, the Messiah dying before them as they all stood by, unable to do anything but futilely witness the ignominy.

"The shell only lies there . . . ," Darien said. *"We should all repeat just that in our minds. The shell only lies there. The Son Himself is untouched, the Son is—"*

And then His voice swept over them, as rich, as reassuring as ever, the same voice that had spoken to every one of the unfallen angels during the Casting Out when each gathered together at the side of the Trinity and watched the legion upon legion of fallen former comrades leave heaven, never to return.

"You have spoken as My Father hoped you would," He told them in the midst of that wilderness. *"Your strength becomes the strength of that fallen mortal form in which I must remain until My hour comes."*

The angels looked at one another and then back at the body of Jesus.

He stirred, the eyes reopening, the lips moving, and He was able to lift Himself weakly to His elbows.

"Satan is coming," Jesus the Christ spoke ominously, His voice far stronger than any of them could have expected. *"Thirty-five days have passed now. I am weak and near death. The temptations begin."*

CHAPTER 33

SATAN came, not his demons.

It was a mission he had set for himself, and only himself.

This time, as so often previously, this mission was one that his ego, which had been the root cause of the Casting Out in the first place, could not allow him to delegate to any of the other demonic entities constantly hovering in his presence, waiting for the slightest command so that they could prove their loyalty to him, though others, like Observer, could no longer stand the wretched being their master had become. Still, they had been chained to him for so long that the link between them was unbreakable, and they knew that whatever fate was in store for Satan would prove to be their own as well.

Alone . . .

The devil was alone, though a vast cackling horde of demons stood behind him at the entrance to hell, waiting, ready to surge forward, bickering among themselves as to who would lead the shrieking charge.

I am so tired of them, he thought, *so tired of their Medusian appearance, as I am of my own, which is not so different.*

Satan remembered what he once looked like as he walked the beautiful avenues of heaven, seeing only others who were sublimely beautiful in their own right.

I was the most beautiful of all. None could equal me. Not Darien. Not Michael or Gabriel. Not Stedfast. They paled in comparison to me!

And then there were those times when he was forced to realize in sudden, shocking bursts of truth, that the demons all around him in hell were but mirror images of himself, replicas of what he had become.

I would will myself to ignore this, will myself into a kind of self-imposed amnesia, and it would work for a while, work very well, or so it seemed. Then I could lose myself in the pretense that my slaves had been pathetically corrupted but I was still able to retain a measure of the beauty I once had, and I dreamed that in my day of victory over Yahweh I would reclaim what was once mine and rule heaven as its all-powerful king.

The battle ahead . . .

It was to be a key battle in the war that Satan had been fighting so long.

Destroying the incarnated Christ!

I will succeed, Satan had convinced himself. *Only Darien stands by His side. That angel is no match for me. I would have kept him in hell if it had not been for Stedfast, who rescued him an instant before it would have been too late.*

As he had done in Egypt, Satan began his approach directly from the environs of that fiery place like a bird of prey swooping down, but this time no one stopped him, knowingly or otherwise, though the unfallen angels at Jesus' side begged their Lord to let them hold the devil off and prevent him from assaulting that body in which Divinity dwelt, a body made weak by the deprivations of the past several weeks.

Of all the angels, Darien spoke up most vehemently.

"*You cannot withstand any sort of attack,*" he protested, aware of his mission, a greater challenge than any of the others had been given to date. "*The Father has asked me to protect You, Lord. What else am I to do?*"

It was clear that this angel was in spiritual anguish, torn between Jesus' plight and almighty God's clear admonition.

"*The Father and I are One,*" Jesus reminded him. "*You were to be at My side. And that is where you are.*"

Darien continued his protest.

"*To protect You from harm!*" the angel replied, "*to see that demons not take Your flesh and rend it asunder.*"

Jesus was trying to be patient.

"*I am safe. You need not be concerned. I must face this, not as the Son of God, but as a man.*"

"*Lord, You are dying . . . I mean, that earthly physical body is dying. How can You say You will be . . . safe?*"

As soon as he had spoken, Darien wished he had not done so, for this outburst demonstrated that he was suddenly slipping back into the regrettable habit that had made the journey along *Angelwalk* necessary.

But in this case, he rationalized, *my attitude is not connected in any way to my own self or any lingering doubts or anything of the sort but is directed at the welfare, the very survival, of the incarnated Son of the living God. Surely I must—!*

Shame . . . it hit him hard. He was doing what million of human beings had always done, trying to suppose that they knew more about a given situation than almighty God did.

Darien hesitated, the other angels intently looking at him, quite ready to listen, since he seemed to have become, in that remarkable moment, their *de facto* leader, more so than even Gabriel and Michael. Whatever it was that he spoke, they certainly would accept and obey. All he had to do was tell them.

Satan's crime in the first place, the truth hit him with great, almost blinding clarity. *And yet here I am, spouting much the same rebellious talk: Oh, yes, yes, I know as much as God does. Surely I can conduct matters as well or better than He does, and thus, I have every reason for questioning His divine judgment—which, after all, I must do since I cannot quite bring myself to trust it completely.*

Darien stood accused by his own spirit, and he lapsed into silence, the lessons he learned from *Angelwalk* not altogether forgotten.

I must step aside, he acknowledged to himself. *I must step aside without further dispute and let the blessed Son do as He has declared.*

The angel shivered at the prospect.

The Son of God, wrapped in fallible human flesh, was to face the maestro of damnation alone!

"*We will remain here, dear Lord,*" Darien said in final, though still reluctant, acquiescence, "*if You should need us.*"

Then he and the multitude of other unfallen angels stepped aside, forced into the role of frustrated bystanders, powerful beings allowed to do nothing but watch the events about to transpire, orchestrated as these were by a vile mad spirit fanatically bent on destroying all that was holy.

. . . they hovered behind him at the entrance to hell, waiting, ready to surge forward at his command.

Each group of angelic creatures, fallen and unfallen alike, was promptly relegated to the sidelines as their masters met in the Judean wilderness arena for the spiritual battle that was to come.

A moment later, Satan arrived.

CHAPTER 34

THE CREATURE seemed huge, repulsive, and ever so powerful, yet in his voice there was a hint of his former heaven-based magnificence, and it was easy to see that he was accustomed to issuing commands and expecting them to be obeyed by his own kind.

He stood before the unmoving body of Jesus, sneering as his gaze roamed the pitiable form.

"*Within that lump of flesh and bones dwells a member of the Triune Godhead!*" he said, a sarcastic and sadistic edge to his voice. "*Behold, the Savior of the world.*"

He strode around Jesus, chuckling at what he saw.

"*The pale, pale face,*" he went on, "*the bloodshot eyes, the dry, cracking lips specked by patches of blood, strength turned to spineless mush, every muscle weakened and spongy instead of hard and firm—a sight surely destined to inspire whole masses to trod the path that leads to heavenly redemption!*"

He bent down, closer to Jesus' face.

"*Give up!*" Satan shouted. "*You are losing the battle, and soon the war itself will be lost.* I have won! *You will be buried right here, in the stomachs of the grateful beasts that sniff out your cold, lifeless corpse!*"

Jesus said nothing.

Satan looked at the angels who were standing to one side.

"*Ah, do I see the formerly rebellious Darien there with the other simpering servants of a God who deserves none of the adulation that has been His for far too long!*" he roared theatrically. "*You thought you had the last laugh, did you not, when good old reliable Stedfast reached down and pulled you out of my domain?*

"*Wrong! The real truth is in front of you at this very moment. There, in the ancient sand, lies the hope of the world! There, useless and wretched, is the so-called blessed Redeemer. But now, it seems, He cannot even redeem*

Himself from such a pathetic and miserable wasteland as this one. This Jesus I see is hungry, He is thirsty, He is in terrible pain, and He will be dead quite soon if—"

Satan's wings stretched out straight in a grotesque motion that sought to imitate their former glory, but his features betrayed his pain when he grimaced as the effort proved too much for him, and he had to tuck them in again.

Jesus continued to be still, hardly breathing, it seemed.

"Obviously your Father has abandoned You," Satan went on. *"But* I *will not. God has been lying to You from the beginning. If You will serve me, instead of Him, I shall bring You out of this ghastly place and give You whatever You desire."*

Jesus moved slightly, groaning.

"You must be so hungry that even a stale slice of bread would seem a feast to You," Satan growled.

Jesus slowly turned His head and looked upward, squinting against the overhead sun as a thin line of spittle dripped out of His lips, which had become nearly as pale as the rest of His face.

"You do not look so gloriously triumphant now," Satan mocked. *"You would hardly be a worthy opponent for a lame old beggar—or a blind one, for that matter!"*

He stepped back, pretending as the deceiver he was to be suddenly filled with pity over Jesus' plight.

"But then it would be cruel *of me not to give You a chance,"* Satan cooed. *"And it will be a much better chance than You could ever have expected of me."*

He pointed to a large stone near Jesus' feet.

"See that!" he went on. *"I have an idea. If you are indeed the Son of God, all powerful, then it should be quite a simple matter for You to command that stone to become bread."*

Satan waited for an answer.

At first it did not seem that Jesus was about to say or do anything. Then, seconds later, He raised Himself up from the sand by pressing both palms against its surface and stood with great effort, though He staggered briefly before becoming steady.

In the next instant, He faced Satan, and said, *"It is written, 'Man shall not live by bread alone, but by every word that proceeds from the mouth of God.'"*

Now it was Satan's turn to be quiet.

"He did not expect that," Darien whispered to Gabriel, pleased about what they had witnessed.

"Did you . . . did any of us?" the other angel replied. *"If* we *who have spent eternity with Him were startled, think of how the devil must feel just now!"*

Darien turned his attention to the bodily form of Jesus.

"Lord, Lord, not Your spirit, never Your spirit, which is incapable of weariness, but Your human self, the very incarnation . . . You are still so very tired and hungry. None of that has changed. How much longer will You be able to hold on?"

"Follow me to the top there," Satan continued, pointing to a small pile of rocks that had been formed into a miniature peak. It was not very high, but it might as well have been Sinai or Ararat to someone in the condition to which Jesus had deteriorated.

Satan reached the top in an instant, but Jesus was sorely limited by His battered physical form. He could only *attempt* the climb one rock at a time.

Darien stepped forward again, no longer able to control Himself.

"Lord!" he screamed. *"You are the Son of God; yes, I know that. But You live now as a human being, as a man!"*

Before Darien could say anything else, Jesus spoke to him in a voice that was loud, strong, and clear. *"Only those who obey Me can truly cry out, 'Lord, Lord.'"*

There was nothing else, just those eleven words, but they might as well have been a dagger aimed at a human heart. Immediately Darien's iridescence dimmed almost to the point of causing him to disappear altogether from that privileged company of fellow angelic creations.

"Be still," Gabriel whispered to him sympathetically. *"Show your own kind of courage. Be a comfort to Jesus that way, my brother."*

Darien nodded and thanked his brother angel, then stood quietly and watched what happened next.

The devil led Jesus up to a high place and showed Him in an instant all the kingdoms of the world.

"Look at them!" Satan exclaimed. *"They are laid out before You, all the treasures of the wealthiest empires since governments on earth began. There are riches beyond compare and the greatest power in history.*

"I am the god of this fallen world. I will give all this to You; I will raise You up in an instant from Your weakness, hunger, and pain, if You will but worship me.

That is all it takes, Jesus. You are on Your knees even now. Simply remain there. Bow Your head, and claim me as Your master."

Somehow Jesus had been able to make it to the top of that peak which, though small, represented a daunting challenge for one who had been battered by nearly forty days of isolation in the wilderness.

"*Get behind me, Satan, and stop such blasphemy,*" said Jesus, "*for it is written, 'You shall worship the* LORD *your God, and Him only you shall serve.*'"

The devil shuddered with simmering rage and an all-too-familiar sense of futility. But he was not yet willing to turn away, acknowledging his own defeat, and leaving the incarnated One alone.

The chill desert night had come, and a full moon was visible in the sky.

"*A time of madness,*" Satan said, pointing to it. "*This is my time, you know. All the acts of depravity that I have ever fostered are symbolized in each night of the full moon when the sins of mankind shall burst forth unrestrained throughout this the night of endless legends and myths that are closer to reality than any man knows.*"

He turned in the direction of Jerusalem, the faint outline of which could be seen in the early glow of beginning moonlight.

"*There!*" Satan proclaimed. "*My final temptation, the one even You will not be able to resist!*"

He expected Jesus to follow him back through that wild, ugly place to the edge of the ancient city.

"*Lord, the distance is too far, it—!*" Darien started to say before catching himself and then uttering nothing further.

"*Good, my brother . . . ,*" Gabriel whispered. "*It is hard for all of us. You are surely not alone.*"

Satan had turned and was going back down that peak as he motioned for Jesus to follow after him.

I want You to go with me so that You will die on the way, Satan thought. *Yes, drop by the side of the road and never rise again, for that means I shall be able to stand over You and celebrate with my legions of demons.*

Without looking back, Satan started to walk away toward one of the dirt roads at the edge of the wilderness, one of which connected with the main thoroughfare leading into Jerusalem. He stopped every so often, waiting to detect any footsteps directly behind him.

"*Good!*" the devil muttered out loud the first time he heard the step, his self-satisfaction uncontrolled.

Fainter . . .

He was counting on this, the footsteps growing fainter, the sound fading until it had ceased altogether. Satan planned to go back along that road and find the body, then call forth a Bacchanalian party of the damned.

I almost feel sorry for Him, he told himself. *Oh, glorious He was, there at the right hand of the Father.*

Satan stopped again, for the seventh time, not to hear once more the faltering footsteps of a suffering Jesus but suddenly recalling heaven, moments of peace he had had there with the eternal Trinity, of which the Son was a part, and the love constantly emanating from God, love that in his rebellion, Lucifer-become-Satan cast aside as though it was an old rag suitable only for some garbage heap. As he did so, as he remembered, he understood more than ever that he was not doing *anything* to the Son of God but to the finite shell wrapped around an infinite member of the Godhead.

I can kill this One and surely the One who comes next and the One after that, the Prince of Darkness speculated out of his ignorance as to what Jehovah had planned, *but it will not change anything for me, for the others of my breed. A Redeemer will have to keep coming, incarnation after incarnation, until I fail for the last, awful time, and that final One is the One who seals my doom.*

Footsteps crunching in the sand behind him intruded upon his reverie. These were not the faltering footsteps of a Man about to die but those of Someone strong again, those of Someone whose inner being had been miraculously replenished and revitalized, Someone who had emerged from the wilderness, no longer subject to its siren song of death.

Satan did not turn, could not bear the sight he knew would greet him: a strong Jesus, a Jesus standing tall and straight, a Jesus walking with firm step, a Jesus against whom he would fling one further temptation.

I will bring You to the temple, make You climb to its pinnacle, he thought, *and I shall say to You, "If You are the Son of God, throw Yourself down. For it is written: 'He shall give His angels charge over you,' and, 'In their hands they shall bear you up, lest you dash your foot against a stone.'"*

As they entered through the main gate and, a short time later, approached the temple, Satan looked at Jesus finally, looked into the clear bright eyes of the only begotten Son, seeing Him in precisely the physical condition he feared he would and, thus, his careful plan was reduced to tatters at his feet.

. . . in their hands they shall bear you up, lest you dash your foot against a stone..

After the two of them had climbed to the pinnacle of that holy temple, the sinister master of all evil repeated those sly and insinuating words out loud, laced as they were with the very taint of hell. When the last venomous word spewed forth from his cankered mouth, he knew in the pit of his being what the answer would be before the Redeemer spoke it, for time and eternity.

PART VII

In this dim world of clouding cares,
We rarely know, till 'wildered eyes
See white wings lessening up the skies,
The angels with us unawares.

GERALD MASSEY
Ballad of Babe Christabel

SATAN LEFT the presence of Jesus for a while, stung badly by yet another failure to harm or destroy the Son of God in His incarnated body. For a time, the devil seemed to have given up altogether; unable to mount any more attacks, his determination seemed fatally depleted.

It was as though God has restrained him yet again . . .

Shortly after those forty days in the wilderness, but some weeks before the tragic circumstances that were to claim His life, Jesus the Christ started His ministry.

His teaching did not begin on the dusty roads of that often barren land, though later this was exactly where He would head.

The synagogues.

Jesus started spreading the good news in synagogues throughout Judea as well as in a number of other different places such as meeting halls owned by curious men interested in what He had to say, and when nothing else was available, He stood on street corners and in the midst of rolling grain fields.

At the start, everyone praised Him, beguiled for a while by the striking brilliance of His ideas and His wise-sounding speech. Then Jesus went back to the village of Nazareth, where He had been brought up by His earthly parents . . .

CHAPTER 35

And when the devil had ended all the temptation, he departed from Jesus for a season. Then Jesus returned in the power of the Spirit into Galilee: and there went out a fame of Him through all the region round about . . . And then He came to Nazareth where He had been brought up, and then went into the synagogue on the Sabbath . . .

As Jesus was sitting down to listen and to learn, someone in the congregation recognized Him and handed Him a scroll of the prophet Isaiah. At each end of the scroll was a wooden roller called the "tree of life." The parchment itself was wound around these in such a way that whatever had already been read that year was wound together at one end and held tightly by a special pin attached to the wood. The other end held the unread portions of parchment.

After pausing as required by the applicable ceremonial law, Jesus unrolled it and found the place where it was written, "The Spirit of the Lord is upon Me because He has anointed Me to preach the gospel to the poor."

He paused, glancing around at those who seemed almost to stop breathing so intent they were on what He was reading out loud. Some pressed their lips so tightly together that they appeared not to have lips at all.

A few were frowning. Others played absent-mindedly with their earlobes.

"He has sent Me to heal the brokenhearted, to proclaim liberty to the captives and recovery of sight to the blind," Jesus continued, "To set at liberty those who are oppressed; to proclaim the acceptable year of the Lord."

Then Jesus rolled up the scroll, holding it in His hands as though reluctant to let go of it, His half-closed eyelids gave the appearance of His being in a swoon; then solemnly he gave it back to the same attendant and sat down again.

The attention of everyone in the synagogue was fastened on Him, and he added with confidence but not arrogance, "This day, truly this scripture is fulfilled in the hearing of all who are listening to My voice."

They reacted instantly to what Jesus had said. Anger . . . Darien could see it on the faces of the learned men who were present in the temple, their expressions betraying the emotional response that every one of them was feeling.

"Are you not the son of Joseph, a simple carpenter from Nazareth?" one older individual said bitingly, looking at Jesus with sudden contempt.

Jesus said to that one and to those others who were similarly dubious, "You will surely say this proverb to Me, 'Physician, heal yourself! Whatever we have heard done in Capernaum, do also here in Your country.'"

He looked at them with an expression that seemed at once angry and regretful.

"For it is with much feeling that I say to you, no prophet is accepted in his own country. But I tell you truly, many widows were in Israel in the days of Elijah, when the heaven was shut up three years and six months, and there was a great famine throughout all the land; but Elijah did not minister to them because of great unbelief that had taken hold of everyone."

His gaze roamed over the gathered philosophers, scribes and others.

"Or think of the prophet Elisha, who healed Naaman, a Syrian, rather than the many Jewish lepers needing help. If this is as I have said, what does that say about each one of you, who have learned so little since then?"

"If you are as my colleague earlier indicated," added another, "how can it be that You speak with such presumption, telling us that a prophecy such as the one from our revered Isaiah is fulfilled in You?"

Jesus' reply was caustic.

"If I could prove to you that I am whom I say I am, you still would not listen in the way that you must for My words to have any value."

They were grumbling more loudly by now.

"Your unbelief is not directly against just Me this day only," continued Jesus without hesitation, "but others over the past many hundreds of years have felt it also, including Elisha and Elijah, who were prophets without honor in their own land until a long time had passed and you belatedly gave them the recognition they deserved. If they had not been lifted up to the Father and taken out of the presence of unbelief, they would have known more of your scorn.

"And only recently there has been someone like John the Baptist, who lives with the threat of death every day because he chose to try and accomplish the mission given to him by My heavenly Father. It was this man with so much truth to offer the world who proclaimed that a greater One than he would follow in his footsteps, and that One is—"

Possessed of a great frenzy as a unified group, they snorted with disgust, and all clamped their hands tightly over their ears, for they assumed that they knew what Jesus was going to say next, and it was not anything they were prepared to hear, bound as they were to the worship of tradition more than the heavenly Father Himself.

Their collective wrath rose up, and the men of that gathering dragged Jesus to the edge of the hill upon which Nazareth had been built.

"No man uttering such words should be allowed any longer the breath of life," someone shouted as the rest roared their own disapproval.

Jesus was about to be toppled over.

"Lord, shall I act now?" Darien asked, compelled to speak up.

"You shall," replied the King of Kings. *"You shall."*

Suddenly Jesus extricated Himself without harm and passed through the surrounding crowd which was now abruptly silent, none of them attempting in any way to stop the Son of God. He left Nazareth shortly thereafter but not before seeing His earthly parents, Mary and Joseph, to tell them He had to be on His way, that it was no longer safe to live in the quiet village of His birth.

"Thank you, Darien," Jesus said as He left that place behind Him and began the first of the travels that would take Him throughout the land of Israel over the next three years.

"It is the desire of my existence to keep You safe, O Lord," the angel replied. *"God the Father would not have it otherwise."*

As an angel, Darien had done in that moment what he could, for he knew not what else was left to do unless the blessed heavenly Father Himself would miraculously intervene. So it was that he had decided to suddenly shine forth with such transcendent brightness that those present thought it had to be something to do with the afternoon sun and not the actual cause, which was being kept from them.

The result was that the men at the base of the mountain could not look straight up for a moment or two, and, also, those surrounding Jesus had to step back, focusing their attention on the uneven rocky surface beneath their feet until the encompassing glow had passed, which they hoped would happen soon since their eyes were beginning to hurt.

"The light they saw was so vivid that they seemed blinded for a while," Jesus said admiringly, *"until after I was safely away from them."*

"I did not want their sight to be taken from them for the rest of their lives," Darien confessed, wondering if Jesus was gently criticizing his action.

The Son detected this and added, *"Do not be concerned. Most of them will go to their graves having no idea of what happened here. Their ignorance is not only of that moment in itself but of the precious truths that it embodied, for none of them could have killed Me. My death is in My Father's hands, and His only, and no man can alter what He has had planned since the foundation of this world."*

"You said 'most of them'? Do You mean that some will change what they think about You and will accept all this before it is too late to change their eternal destiny?"

"That is right, Darien . . . some are going to change. They will be in heaven before that grand moment when you and I have returned to My Father's kingdom."

Darien felt relieved.

"I did well then?" he asked, less like an angel then and more like a child eager for an adult's blessing.

"You did well. Praise be to the blessed Father in heaven for sending you to stand here by My side!"

CHAPTER 36

JESUS had finally completed the task of gathering together all twelve of His apostles by the time He found out that John the Baptist had been imprisoned by King Herod, son of Herod the Great.

"*His last night of life, Lord?*" Darien asked, steeling himself for the answer that would amount to a dreadful prophecy.

The silence greeting him told this angel as much as any sudden outpouring of words could have.

Several days had passed.

John was being given only some stale bread and a little water, and he had nothing to sleep on except a few patches of hay. He developed a chill early on, but it passed after a kindly guard slipped some herbs to him.

"*Not unlike the surroundings for Your birth,*" Darien remarked as he reported back to Jesus about the condition of the Baptist.

"*He never knew the comfort of lavish palaces, fine clothing, and banquets, nor the ease of servants waiting to meet his every need,*" replied Jesus with a mixture of sorrow and respect. "*Those who are wealthy cling to their riches, loving their well-guarded treasury of money, and the vast accumulated holdings that that money has secured while willfully ignoring how this perverse love is at the root of all the evil that has infested their lives.*"

"*Would it be all right, Lord, if I stayed with him?*"

"*Why do you want to be there?*"

"*To comfort him, to welcome his soul from his body and send it on to the Father.*"

"*I was hoping you would say that. Go ahead. And bless you for wanting to be by the side of this great and wonderful servant.*"

John looked about the dungeon to which he had been confined.

"*Lord, is this to be my end?*" *he pleaded.* "*Sick and cold, waiting for the judgment of a mortal man?*"

"*It is not the Lord, John,*" Darien told him.

"The angel then?"

"*Yes . . .*"

"You are here because you know, as I do, that I am going to die soon. Is that not it, angel?"

His height was such that when he stood, the Baptist came very close to the rough-hewn rock ceiling of that place. He reached up and touched its hard surface with the fingers of his left hand, smiling as he did because he knew how deluded Herod showed himself to be when he had ordered John's imprisonment.

"They think by putting me here, that separates me from Almighty God," he said out loud. "But I know that God is with me on the highest mountain peak or down in the deepest valley. Nothing can come between us, not even the hatred of a Jewish king's sin-ridden and vengeful wife!"

"*Is there anything you want to tell Jesus*?" Darien asked.

"Just say that I shall go to my grave loving Him."

Several minutes later, the door to that dungeon swung open and a familiar, obese figure stood in the doorway.

John had been praying, pouring out his soul to God.

"King Herod!" the Baptist blurted out, surprised that the man would be willing to face him under the circumstances.

"John . . . ," Herod said sadly as he entered. "Have they fed you yet?"

"They have given me nothing."

Herod swung around, angrily ordering the guard to make sure the prisoner's dinner was served by the time Herod left, and he indicated what each of the courses was to be.

"My finest dinnerware also!" he demanded.

The guard assured him this would be done.

Herod approached the Baptist.

"No locusts for you tonight," he said. "I wanted you to have a good meal, and I did not think you should be alone."

The awkward silence that followed was broken for them by the sound of wings. Both turned, startled, as they saw a dove land in the window, a tiny opening set high up in the wall facing west, allowing a modicum of light into the dungeon.

"I am never alone," John remarked. "Even when the moment of my death comes, even then I shall have the angels of my Lord taking me to His kingdom."

"How can you tell me that you honestly believe this will happen?" Herod asked, mystified. "I find you to be exceptionally intelligent, courageous to an extraordinary degree. Why waste your time with fantasies?"

"God's wisdom is as foolishness to man," the Baptist retorted.

"And that is it? That is all you have to say? I hold your life in my hand, John. You should not trifle with me."

"You can do nothing except by leave of the heavenly Father, who created us all and whose salvation or condemnation shall envelop every human being who has ever lived."

"I am king because God permitted it," Herod mused. "But then what have I made of this position of power? My father became a monster, but he left behind majestic buildings. I, too, am a monster, yet I leave nothing but your death, Baptist."

As Herod turned to go, the dove immediately flew off its perch and landed on the king's right shoulder.

"A sign!" John exclaimed.

"To save your hide," the king barked.

"My hide, as you call it, is doomed; this I know. I spoke of a sign by Jehovah to save you and the nation you rule."

Herod stood still, his head tilted, his eyes closed as he remembered some starkly vivid images.

"I have been having the most terrible of dreams, John, dreams about this city of Jerusalem, so ancient, so holy, suddenly being surrounded by conquering Roman soldiers and ultimately, Jews by the hundreds, or perhaps the thousands, being starved into submission. But before the few who are left surrender to the will of Rome, they are compelled to resort to certain acts, unspeakable acts."

"Cannibalism," John anticipated, "mothers taking their own sons and daughters, and fathers—"

"Yes! I know!" Herod interrupted the Baptist with more loathing of the truth than anger at John for speaking it. "Is this a warning? So that I will change my horrid ways and become an inspiration to the Jews I rule? And try to get them to turn away from the shameful acts for which I have served as a royal example?"

"It is what you have just said. If you go on ignoring this, it will be at the certain peril of your own destiny."

"My destiny? What in this tired and corrupt world of ours are you talking about, Baptist? I know what every moment of every day for the foreseeable future is going to be like as far as I could ever be concerned. I have known all this from the moment I assumed the throne of Israel.

"It is necessary that I control everything in my life, which is as it should be for a monarch with enemies such as mine who lurk in the shadows, ready to assassinate me should I be so foolish as to give them the slightest opportunity."

"In this life, that may be true. You can be guarded, and you can surely escape whatever your enemies would wish upon you. Though God is not your enemy, Herod, His punishment will prove to be many times more severe than anything they could brandish about, if you continue to turn your back on Him."

Herod's face became a cold mask, more like the face of a stone statue, no emotion whatever showing on it.

"I have lived in sin too long, too long," he said, nodding his head resignedly, "for me to have any hope of wrenching myself out of the pattern and the substance of this wretched life of mine."

With that, the king of Israel grabbed the unsuspecting dove in his huge right hand, bloated like the rest of his immense frame, and squeezed it to death in an instant then tossed what was left of the pathetic little body on the cold stone floor.

"The bird did not even struggle or utter a sound," observed Herod wonderingly, the faintest hint of regret in his voice." It never—"

He shook his head, clearing it of any emotion, and then said coldly, just before leaving the dungeon, "I wonder if perhaps Satan already has a place set aside in hell for me, with my name engraved in blood."

Abruptly this powerful man shrugged his shoulders and went outside. As he started up the steps leading back into the extraordinary palace his father had built, he stopped for a moment and looked back over his shoulder.

"If I could . . . ," Herod whispered, "if I could . . ."

Then he hurriedly continued on his way, for Herodias and Salome were in the main banquet hall, ready to start a festive dinner, and he dare not keep them waiting.

"If only that man could have been reached," John said as soon as he was alone with Darien.

"*The very corridors of hell are filled with the souls of men who were almost saved*," the angel reminded him.

"Yes, I know that. But the tragedy remains, the thoughts of what could have been if Cain had never killed Abel, if the pharaoh at the time of Moses truly had repented, if Herod's father had been benevolent instead of the beast he became."

John the Baptist wiped away some tears.

"I asked you to tell Jesus that I loved Him?" he asked.

"*Yes, and I will do that.*"

"Something else?"

"*Just ask, John; just ask.*"

"Stay with me until they kill me."

That is why I am here, Darien acknowledged.

John sighed with relief.

"Will my soul be able to see you, angel?"

"*And ten thousand upon ten thousand more like me.*"

He got down on his knees and bowed his head as he started to pray, "Precious heavenly God, how much I yearn to be at rest in You."

Darien was there by his side and would remain so throughout the night until morning light broke through that single window and stern-faced men came and took him and could not imagine why he died with such words as they heard coming from his lips.

"I forgive you all," the Baptist told them, smiling, cocking his head as he listened to the first sweet sounds of heaven's angels singing a welcome hymn. "You send me to my beloved Creator."

And then he was gone from their midst in a joyous way that all the kings of earthly time and the men who carried out their every whim could not possibly understand.

CHAPTER 37

WHEN JESUS was told what had happened, He went into seclusion for a time.

It was there, in an isolated place near Jerusalem, that Darien was to see a bit more clearly the shape of things to come.

"*Lord, what can I do to help You?*" the angel asked.

"*Be here, just as you are now,*" replied Jesus warmly. "*You are My link with the heavenly Father. While I remain in this body, I cannot be with Him. You are able to go back and forth to heaven, but I am not. If I were to leave this mortal frame in which I find Myself, it would surely die.*"

Though the Son of God was incarnated and separated from His former home, He could pray to God as any man did. But He also carried within Him those sweet images of fellowship with the rest of the Trinity, images that were so precious they would help to sustain Him over the times of testing that were yet to come.

"*John . . . ,*" He spoke softly.

The humanity of Jesus was speaking what the divinity was feeling.

"*He is with the Father now,*" He said.

"*In a whole, perfect body,*" Darien offered.

"*Yes, whole and perfect. Oh, but he deserved better in this life. The religious leaders accused him of having a demon. I shall soon have to confront them face to face, and they will feel more hatred toward Me than they ever did toward John.*"

"*But it is they who were seduced by demons.*"

"*You are correct, Darien. But none of these men could ever admit that, could ever admit even the* possibility. *It would destroy everything that has become important in their lives, the position they enjoy in the community, and more. John threatened the foundation of everything that they were, and they could not allow that to happen.*"

"So they pressured Herod, Lord?"

"They pressured Herodias, the king's wife, appealing to her own deep hatred for the Baptist. It did not take much effort to persuade her to confront Herod and demand that he do something.

"But she knew that it had to be done in some clever way. So that was when she had their daughter Salome dance for the king and so entrance him that he would give her whatever she wanted."

"You miss him so very much, Lord. I can see that."

"My human nature misses him. He was a courageous man and a humble one, though his enemies thought him arrogant and wildly emotional."

"Those who condemned him stand condemned by their actions. Upon their deaths, they will surely know the eternal torment that was never to be the Baptist's."

Jesus became angry then.

"You sound pleased, Darien!" He exclaimed.

"I suppose I am. Those who did nothing to stop John's death, who secretly wished for it to happen, are now—"

"No!" Jesus cut him off, His voice quite loud. *"You must never look at the loss of a single soul in that manner. If all the angels in heaven* rejoice *over the salvation of just one soul, should* you *rejoice over the loss of one?"*

Darien knew now how deeply he had misspoken.

"I was thinking of the justice of—" he started to say.

"But you still gloat, Darien. You still feel some small shred of joy that they are being punished."

Darien had to admit that he did.

"I confess it to You, Lord," he said contritely.

"Look at it this way: What if their lives were to be changed, and they were to forsake the ways that were like millstones around their necks, and, instead, they reached out and became instruments of righteousness instead of what they are now?"

"That would be wonderful, Lord. A victory!"

"But if they die before they are reborn and do not use their influence truly *for the salvation of souls, this means that many of those who look to them for spiritual truth will* not *be redeemed, as the Father requires, and will go to the same hell as the Pharisees and Sadducees who kept them in darkness."*

Jesus' manner became even more intent.

"Therein can be found the heart of it all, Darien," He went on. *"Therein*

rests the tragedy of tragedies. That is why you should never be pleased when you come to know where their kind go after they die. These men, these rigid taskmasters encrusted with manmade doctrines, spinning their unholy entrapments like spiders, snaring many in their tradition-laden webs, these men take with them so many others who are duped into trusting them, swelling the confines of hell and causing celebration among the foul and malevolent creatures of damnation."

Jesus had been sitting on a large flat rock.

As He stood wearily, He said, "*The worst battles are ahead. Until now, our confrontations with the religious rulers of this nation have been mild, you know. But these were only hints, the vaguest suggestions, of what still lies ahead of us.*"

"*But they would have killed You, Lord! Is that so mild?*"

"*If you only knew what will happen . . .*"

Jesus the Man's expression reflected what Jesus the Son knew as an omniscient member of the triune Godhead.

This time Darien did not ask the Son what He meant. But he did perceive that Satan would no longer be restrained, that the wilderness temptations and the death of John the Baptist were but the beginning of a part of God's Plan that would determine, more than ever, the course of human history.

"*Where do they go now?*" he asked.

"*Where Daniel went.*"

"*Into the lion's den?*"

"*There are different kinds of lions, Darien.*"

They left that secluded spot. The apostles were waiting, seeing only Jesus and not the angel at His side.

"Are you well?" Peter, the fisherman, asked.

"I am well," Jesus replied. "Do not be alarmed when I go off by Myself."

Peter was relieved, as were the others since all of them had been similarly concerned about Jesus.

"Where do we go now?" Matthew, the tax-gatherer, spoke next.

"To the sick and the lost who need us."

"Where are they, Jesus?"

"Turn around and you will see."

They had been gathered atop a low hill just outside the main gate leading into Jerusalem.

Ahead was a typical line of blind beggars dressed as usual in ragged clothes and pleading with passersby for a coin or two so they could buy some bread.

"Bring them to Me," said Jesus.

"We have nothing to give to them," young Andrew protested. "We are hardly more than beggars ourselves."

"Bring them to Me," Jesus repeated.

Andrew nodded and went with the others. Each brought back a blind man and stood before Jesus, who touched them all, one at a time, placing His thumbs on their eyes. There was grumbling among the others in line until He had finished.

"You have now received your sight," He said simply.

Within a very short while, all twelve were no longer blind. They looked with awe at Jesus and the apostles.

"Who has done this for us?" one of them asked enthusiastically. "Who has performed this miracle?"

Peter pointed energetically to Jesus.

The twelve beggars fell at His feet, thanking Him for giving them what they had not had for many years. Each kissed Him on the cheek, as was the custom in those days.

And then they were gone.

PART VIII

That there is a devil is doubted by none but such are under the influences of the devil himself. For any to deny the being of this devil must be from an ignorance or profaneness worse than diabolical.

COTTON MATHER
A Discourse on the Wonders of the Invisible World

THE MIRACLE of the healing of the blind beggars represented the earliest of many for Jesus the Christ.

But it was followed by countless others, a remarkable variety of human needs being taken care of by this extraordinary Man with a gift unlike any the people of that land had ever before witnessed.

As the fame of Jesus spread throughout the land of Israel, more blind men and women came to Him as well as those unfortunate individuals who were lame or deaf or dumbstruck or afflicted with a variety of other ailments. And there was the raising of Lazarus from the dead, perhaps the most astonishing of all the miracles.

The latter was not an isolated instance. There was also Jairus's daughter, who was given back her earthly life.

How derisive they were, Darien recalled of the minstrels and others engaging in the customary mourning rituals.

Jesus said to them, "Give Me room to pass. For this beautiful girl is not dead."

They looked at Him in disbelief.

"She only sleeps," He said.

They laughed scornfully at the Son of God but stepped aside. In less than a minute, Jesus was back outside, holding the little one's hand as she smiled serenely at the doubters.

Later, there was also the widow's son and others along the way, causing the fame of Jesus to spread ever faster.

But healing and resurrection were not the only miracles Jesus was able to perform, often in front of huge crowds . . .

The casting out of demons from those who were possessed!

The first instance to occur would always be thought of by the apostles as the worst. For in one of the men so afflicted there was not a single demon but many.

Previously, throughout the length and breadth of Darien's sojourn on earth, he had not been witness to anything of the sort . . .

CHAPTER 38

A DEMON-POSSESSED MAN . . .
It all started toward dusk, this unforgettable and initially chilling encounter, and ended just after sunrise in a triumphant outcome that no one except the Son of God and Darien, His guardian angel, could have guessed.

A victory for God and a mighty defeat for the forces of darkness . . .

Jesus and the apostles were encamped on the northern shore of the Sea of Galilee, northeast of Jerusalem. Darien, as usual, was with the group, but only the Master was fully aware of this.

There was one exception among the twelve followers.

John . . .

From time to time, John, the youngest apostle, caught hints, often vague, but also occasionally more compelling, hints of what was going on beyond the realm of the normal senses, particularly sight and sound. This was one of the reasons God had chosen him to record the graphic series of revelations of future events to be given to him several decades later on the Isle of Patmos.

John cleared his throat before he spoke.

"We are here together as always," he said that night, "but I also sense that we have visitors from time to time."

"Lord!" exclaimed Darien. *"He knows somehow."*

"John has been selected by My Father for special duties. And along with these, special gifts have been bestowed upon him."

Everyone was startled by John's statement and proceeded to press him for what he meant, but he did not go into it further.

Darien was intrigued by the fact that John was young and healthy and energetic, hardly an example of someone whose life is ebbing away, which was when angels usually became apparent to flesh-and-blood men, women, and children, the separation between finite and infinite gone at last.

Later that same night, Virtue came to be with Jesus and Darien.

"Lord Jesus," Virtue spoke with reverent concern. *"Satan is going to be fully active from now on, is that not true?"*

The Son of God nodded but did not reply otherwise.

"Without demonic activity, man is bad enough," Virtue went on musingly. *"If Satan were to be confined to the environs of hell, and hell only, that still would not stop the depravity of human beings."*

Jesus agreed again with a nod of His head.

"Unfortunately that is true, Virtue," He finally said. *"Once someone contracts a disease, and sin is like a disease Satan has been spreading for thousands of years, he does not need to linger, for those who have become contaminated go on infecting others. The master of evil simply sits back and enjoys the horrible fruit of his labors."*

"Without a physician, they have no hope of a cure," Virtue added.

The angel had noticed an upsurge in demonic activity since the wilderness temptations had ended.

"It is as though he is punishing your creations because he can no longer punish You directly, Lord," Virtue remarked.

"Sadly, you are right," Jesus assured this angel. *"Satan has been held back for so long now that he is anxious to make up for that period of restraint. And he will try to harm anyone and anything he can."*

"Will it get worse?" Virtue asked.

"Worse indeed. Only that antediluvian time before Noah was able to complete the ark and the time after that when Sodom and Gomorrah were destroyed can compare, though in many ways that which lies ahead will be far, far worse."

Virtue left then, but it was the same with other angels who visited, spending moments with the Son of God and with Darien, undetected by any of the apostles, with the singular exception of young John.

"This one is special, is he not, dear Lord?" Darien probed delicately that night, already convinced of what the answer would be, especially in view of what he had learned just a short while before.

"John is very special indeed," Jesus confirmed warmly. *"Through the many visions My Father will give him at the end of his long life, which will turn out to be terribly lonely toward the close, so completely isolated as he will be from anyone he knows, John is going to have the task of preparing those holy words that will help bring about the salvation of countless numbers of souls for the rest of time."*

Hardly more than a teenager now, John's influence over the coming centuries would be transcendent, with millions upon millions of people conducting their lives in conformity with various interpretations of the prophecies he would expound under the guidance of the Holy Spirit, writing on parchments while sitting on a bare, flat rock on a small mountain in the middle of a Mediterranean island.

Darien studied the apostle, who was sitting beside the Sea of Galilee, his feet in the water, his head thrown back as he looked up at the sky, which was not as yet filled with stars.

"John's mind is on heaven," Jesus commented knowingly. *"Wherever we are, whatever we might be doing, those thoughts of his are seldom very far away from heaven. Already, these years before his exile on Patmos, there are being given to this young man flashes of what is to come, hints that My Father in His providence is allowing John to glimpse, preparing him for those final days of revelation."*

"His exile, Lord?" asked the angel, startled by what was a revelation in itself. *"Why would this good man be forced into exile? What crime could he ever have committed to warrant such punishment?"*

"Believing, Darien. He dares simply to believe."

Darien already had a sense of that consequence from what had happened to John the Baptist. Basically, that had been his only crime, proclaiming the message of almighty God that men were to repent and believe, for the kingdom of God was at hand.

"And for that he is to be isolated on a barren isle?" Darien asked, hoping he somehow had not heard correctly.

"He will be the last survivor of this group," He said.

Inexpressible sadness had been wrapped around Jesus' every word. Darien felt it radiate throughout himself as well.

And, as it happened, John seemed to be affected also.

"Lord, look at him!" Darien exclaimed.

"I know," Jesus said. *"I know."*

The apostle had gotten to his feet and was going off by himself, even further away from the others than he had been at seaside.

"Should I go with him, Lord?" Darien asked.

"No need," Jesus replied. *"John has to be left alone, to deal with what has been put on his shoulders."*

CHAPTER 39

IT WAS NEARLY midnight now, a cool Judean breeze drifting over the water, and carrying with it a familiar mixture of pungent scents, reaching Jesus and the apostles as they were falling asleep.

"I like those odors," Peter confessed contentedly, his stomach full of fish he had caught for himself and the others. "No perfume I have ever smelled can compare to what we are enjoying this very moment."

Jesus smiled as He listened to the fisherman, glad that everyone could rest from what had been long days of hard travel.

His human side relished such moments with the apostles, for He loved them all, and He knew what remained ahead for each one of them as a result of their devotion to Him.

But there was something about Peter that seemed particularly appealing.

This boisterous man was earthy without being vulgar. And he did not seem inclined toward any of the pretensions Thomas was prone to from time to time since Thomas considered himself the reigning intellectual of the group, set apart from the others yet a true member of their group, and he frequently lost patience with Peter's more flagrantly emotional approach to life.

Neither Darien nor the indwelling holy Son of God slept, though the physical form through which He was incarnated did. It was an outgrowth of that very incarnation that, while Jesus had not given up His divinity to become flesh, God's only begotten nevertheless did take unto Himself many of the limitations of that finite body. Jesus the Christ was meant to *experience* the distress of hunger and thirst, or else the wilderness travail would have been a meaningless charade, play-acting of the most manipulative sort.

As with all men, He could feel heat and cold, the summer and the winters of that ancient land at times nearly intolerable for Him as well as for the band of twelve who followed Him throughout Israel. There were also moments of extreme tiredness bordering on exhaustion due to the many hours of walking they all found necessary. When He cut Himself accidentally, He bled. When He stepped on a small stone that bit into His flesh, He knew pain. And that physical body He inhabited could become ill from the same germs to which ordinary mortal men were susceptible. But the eternal spirit at the center of His humanity was untouched.

"*For many mortal men, after you and I leave this world, Darien,*" He had said some time before, "*what I represent will seem to them to be an unfathomable mystery, a perplexing one for that reason.*"

It was understandably difficult for the finite mortal minds of men to wholly understand that which was infinite. This spiritual reality stirred up another question as far as Darien was concerned.

"*Then why not make it all clearer to them so they do not have to struggle so much to understand?*" the angel asked respectfully.

Jesus had stopped walking and was pointing up at the sun.

"*Is there any doubt that it will remain there forever?*" He asked.

"*I cannot suppose there is any doubt, Lord.*"

"*So you need not have faith, then, that this will be so.*"

Jesus waited for the angel to respond.

"*I need not have faith that it will be so because I can take it for granted,*" Darien suggested. "*Faith is not involved in certain matters. When a shepherd orders his loyal sheepdog to do something, it is not faith but training that takes over at that point, or perhaps love—yes, love has a part in it but that is all.*"

Darien thought of other examples that illustrated a most compelling and yet very basic truth: Where routine and habit took over, faith was pushed to the background and people were inclined to say, "I do this or that, not because of soul-deep faith, but because it was the way I was raised or how I trained myself or something of that sort. I do what I do because I do not know how else to do it."

Yet there was no way around the truth that redemption was not given on the basis of childhood conditioning. Nor was it a course that could be completed, with redemption the award to be bestowed at the end.

"*By keeping some facets of His Plan from His human creation, My Father sees to it that faith is given a chance to flourish, knowing that men are intrigued by the unknown,*" Jesus responded appreciatively. "*They either have faith and accept even that which confounds them, or they do not.*"

Jesus paused, reflecting for a moment, then added, *"Faith could be called the substance of things hoped for, the evidence of things that are not seen."*

Darien began to ponder these words, simple and yet profound, anticipating that, later, there would be perhaps another opportunity to discuss it all again.

John has to be left alone to deal with what has been put on his shoulders.

The apostle did not go very far from the rest of them, just far enough to come upon a graveyard on a large plateau atop a promontory that jutted out nearly to the edge of the Sea of Galilee.

A desolate spot of caves that had been turned into tombs.

The poor of that region buried their dead relatives and friends there, using rocks as headstones.

John stood at its very edge, the cold, dead feel of it striking through to his soul, not helping the melancholy that had afflicted him then.

"How many there in that bleak place are now in hell because they rejected You?" he spoke out loud.

This was a statement that would characterize John's compassionate outlook until the end of his days. Daily, it seemed, he would stop and look at a crowd of people and be concerned with little but their spiritual health. If they were starving, yes, that would bother him, and he would try to feed whatever number he could. If some were old and not far from death, he would spend time by the side of each one, uttering words as comforting as he could manage from the center of his soul.

But, above all else, it was their eternal destiny that took hold of this apostle, for it was not enough, he knew so well, if someone happened to have ample food and water and be well clothed and yet went on to face the devastating ravages of hell; it was not enough if they avoided suffering the plight of the lame or the blind and could perform in their daily lives like the finest Greco-Roman athletes, only to end up in a place of torment far worse than whatever they were saved from while alive in the flesh.

. . . how many are in that bleak place?

That night, it was a cemetery. Another night it might be the back alleys of Jerusalem or a ditch beside a road through the countryside.

"Wherever souls are in anguish . . . ," he whispered, turning away from that musty place of the dead.

Until a howl stopped him short.

At first he thought it might have been an animal of the night, howling at the full moon.

But not this time.

Once . . . again . . . and again.

Then—

Gone.

John sighed with relief, and was about to continue back to the campsite when he heard the sound of footsteps.

He swung around to face the cemetery again.

"Is there some need that you have? Can I help you?" he asked characteristically, not letting his fear dominate him.

Silence.

"I shall stand here as long as necessary," the apostle spoke calmly. "You need not be afraid of me."

Laughter, coarse and chilling.

"And why is it that we should *be afraid of* you?" the voice seemed to leap out of the darkness. "*We can do you more harm than you could ever hope to inflict upon us. We are beyond harm, stranger. We can never face any more of it than we have already in this miserable world of yours and elsewhere!*"

John looked around for others but could detect no one else.

"You are *wrong!*" he said, raising his own voice. "Anything you have experienced is little but a hint of what—"

"*—will happen in hell,*" the other interrupted. "*You were going to say that, were you not? Do not lie to us now!*"

The hint of a shape, jumping over one of the rocks . . . and red eyes, eyes that pierced the darkness.

"How is it that you have heard of hell?" John asked.

"*We have not* heard *of that place,*" the voice retorted savagely, changing in a way that made the apostle tremble. "*We have come from the very depths of hell itself, and there are many of us within reach of you right now!*"

John was tempted to run.

"*We are more than you can count,*" the words chased him. "*You can never hope to escape us.*"

Ashamed, knowing how cowardly this was of him, he nevertheless could not stop himself and started to back away, then turn, and—

Behind him the shrieks of many demons filled his ears, along with the pitiable cries of the man they had possessed.

Ashamed of his skittish behavior, John decided not to tell the eleven other apostles what he had encountered.

Instead he slipped quietly back into the camp they had set up not quite a mile away and found his spot close to where Jesus was resting on His back, His sturdy but trim body stretched out straight, not curled up fetal-like as were some of the others, nor turned over on His stomach as the rest were positioned.

Sleep did not come for this apostle until nearly two hours later, terrible hours for him. Yet, thinking of the others, he was careful not to make any noise, despite his restlessness, resorting to looking up at the stars in order to calm himself after hearing those frightful voices and sounds.

By morning John had gotten far less rest than usual, and he was one of those apostles who needed as much sleep as he could grab. But he proved effective at hiding from the others how nervous he felt.

After they all had eaten some pleasant-tasting little sweet cakes and three loaves of unleavened bread an elderly woman from a nearby village had cooked for them, Jesus walked a few steps to the shore of the Sea of Galilee and waited, His hands clasped in back of Him, His eyes surveying the terrain on either side of Him as well as whatever he could see across that body of water.

The day before, His apostles had spread word where He could be found that morning, and it was not long before a great multitude could be seen approaching from the north and south.

"They come as sheep for a shepherd," He said. "But how many of them know that it *is* a shepherd they need?"

In only a few minutes they gathered around Jesus, waiting for Him either to speak or to touch those obviously in need of healing. But this time the number of people proved so great that Jesus had to climb on-board a nearby fishing vessel and begin the day's teachings from there.

"Behold, a sower went out to sow. And as he sowed, some seed fell by the wayside; and the birds came and devoured them. Some fell on stony places, where they did not have much earth; and they immediately sprang up because they had no depth of earth. But when the sun was up they scorched, and because they had no root they withered away.

"And some fell among thorns, and the thorns sprang up and choked them. But others fell on good ground and yielded a crop: some a hundredfold, some sixty, some thirty—"

Jesus cut Himself off and looked at the multitude briefly without saying anything further for more than a minute. Then He added, "He who has ears to hear, let him hear!"

It was immediately after this that Jesus launched into other parables for the remainder of the day, captivating everyone so that not a single man or woman left before He finished.

"What value is it, dear Lord, if Your message proves incomprehensible to so many?" Darien asked.

"What value is it if My message is so simple, so superficial that it does not lodge within any of them for very long?" answered Jesus. *"The good news should never be made so palatable that it leaves a man as easily and as quickly as it entered him.*

"It is far, far better for wisdom to be like the tiniest of seed—like a mustard seed perhaps—that grows mightily and becomes a large tree for the shelter of many and lasts for the remainder of the hearer's life—even if this means that, at first, the human mind has some trouble digesting it. Would you not agree with this, Darien?"

"Yes, Lord, I would agree."

Some in the throng seemed to grasp perhaps some small portion of what He was telling them, but most did not, often scratching their heads in puzzlement. Yet, despite this, nearly everyone agreed that they would come again to hear this remarkable teacher because, while His words were difficult, He spoke as no other man did, and they wanted to perceive His true meaning rather than just give up and stay away the next time.

Later, after all those people had started to go their way finally, Jesus climbed down out of the boat and momentarily sat on the ground, explaining the meaning of the parables to the apostles, starting with the first one. Among men much older than he, only young John had already grasped the truth that He had been teaching.

"The seed is the Word of God," he heard Jesus tell the others. "When anyone hears the Word of the kingdom, and does not understand it, then the wicked one comes and snatches away what was sown in his heart. This is he who received seed by the wayside.

"But he who received the seed on stony places, this is he who hears the Word and immediately receives it with joy; yet he has no root in himself, but endures only for a while. For when tribulation or persecution arises because of the Word, immediately he stumbles.

"Now he who received seed among the thorns is he who hears the Word, and the cares of this world and the deceitfulness of riches choke the Word, and he becomes unfruitful.

"But he who received seed on the good ground is he who hears the Word and understands it, who indeed bears fruit and produces: some a hundred-fold, some sixty, some thirty."

The tenderness Jesus felt for those twelve men who had given up everything to follow Him was apparent as he added, "Take heed what you hear: with what measure you mete, it shall be measured to you: and unto you that hear shall more be given."

There were other matters Jesus taught these men within the next several minutes, but none of the lessons was any more profound than what He offered in that first and simplest of parables, one of many He would use as effective tools of learning throughout the three years they spent together.

The same day, when the evening was come, Jesus said unto them, "Let us pass over to the other side of the sea."

The twelve men did as He had asked without knowing very much about His intentions.

Fortunately, the boat from which Jesus had just spoken to the large multitude had not yet been hired by anyone else, so Matthew bargained for its use and they all climbed inside and set sail across the Sea of Galilee rather than walking all the way around it.

Wind.

It kicked up suddenly, sweeping over the normally quiet surface and transforming it into a maze of dangerous turbulence.

"*The waves!*" Thaddaeus screamed. "We are doomed!"

They were in the middle of that body of water when large waves struck the ship broadside, rocking it mightily and threatening to roll it on its side, plunging everyone overboard, likely to their death.

"*How afraid they are, Lord!*" the angel remarked.

"*They are only human, Darien,*" Jesus told him. "*Fear is part of the curse of Adam and Eve that burdens them. No man, no woman, no child will be free of it entirely during mortal life on this planet.*"

"*Not even these good, devoted men?*" the angel asked.

"*Not even them, Darien,*" replied Jesus, "*though long after you and I leave these apostles and return to My Father's kingdom, their courage will more than outweigh their fear.*"

The angel was relieved, yet he wondered in what sort of situations "courage" would be required as much as Jesus had just implied.

The ship was now nearly full of water and about to sink.

"Where is Jesus?" Peter shouted. "We have to find Him. What if He has been washed over the edge?"

John located Him, asleep, His head on a soft pillow at the opposite end of the boat from where they had been standing.

"Teacher, Teacher!" they all spoke at once, panic sending them into a frenzy, "do You not care that we are perishing?"

Jesus was awakened by their tumult and jumped to His feet, His expression stern, accusing them.

In an instant the Son of God had rebuked that destructive storm and commanded the sea, "Peace . . . be still."

The wind immediately ceased, and once again the Sea of Galilee became as before—a placid lake.

Jesus was disappointed in their conduct.

"Why are you so fearful?" He asked, making them feel ashamed of the way they had acted in His presence. "How is it that you have no faith? Do you think that I would have allowed any of you to perish? If you are not safe while I was with you, how then could you be safe anywhere?"

Once they had reached the other side, several of them, though not John, spoke among themselves, saying, "Who can this be, that even the wind and the sea obey Him?"

That was when they heard the sounds in the darkness of night, howling sounds, but not of wolves or other creatures they could recognize.

"What could that be?" Thomas asked, more frightened than he was willing to admit. "Nothing from hell could seem worse!"

He was shivering. So were Andrew, Matthew, and the others.

Finally John spoke up, telling his comrades what he had encountered on the other side of the lake.

"His eyes seemed like red lights," he said. "I cannot describe how it felt to see them moving through the darkness as though they had a life of their own. And that sound! I detected such agony in it!"

Jesus had been quiet, but now He spoke. "This man has thousands of demons in his body."

"Thousands?" Thomas repeated. "One would be enough. Why would Satan waste so many on a single man?"

"Because Satan is eager to destroy the ministry that has been started," Jesus replied. "He wants to spread terror through everyone here so you will think he and the other fallen angels are capable of thwarting—"

More sounds.

Louder this time.

Closer.

"He has been following us," John said ominously. "He must be coming very fast for us to be able to hear him. Surely he will soon be here."

The other apostles were ready to leave, not wanting a confrontation with this man. It was John who admonished them otherwise.

"Do we run when the forces of darkness seem near?" he asked, aware that he was bordering on hypocrisy by doing this. "I myself ran, and throughout the night, I could not rest well because I was convicted within myself about the cowardice of doing so."

John's candor disarmed the others, and none of them flung cruel accusations back in their friend's face.

"Go on, my brother," the often brusque Peter told him, showing a sensitivity that was to increase over the coming years of his life.

"Every moment any or all of us spend in retreat is surely a victory for the enemy," continued John. "If we allow our fear to rule us at even the *suggestion* of danger, we are no better than those savages in Africa or elsewhere who, chained to spiritual darkness, cower ignorantly in their huts and their caves when lightning snaps all around them, thinking it to be the sudden wrath of some malevolent god."

The others murmured reluctant agreement.

"Now," spoke Jesus. "He is here now."

They could not hear anything or see an intruder, but Jesus did, and that was all they needed to know.

Moving.

A shape at last.

To the left. Then the right.

And now, snarling, the man burst into the midst of them.

Clothed in dirty rags, holding a tiny leather satchel in his left hand, he was covered with scratches and open sores. His torn clothes were stained with blood.

At first the apostles thought the intruder was a pitiable leper, like so many of those in that region, perhaps one who had been roaming the countryside in an ever more desperate search for whatever scraps of food could be found. Because of this, they backed away from him, fearful of contagion.

"Look!" Matthew shouted. "In his right hand!"

A stone.

It was flat, nearly round, with sharp edges covered with blood.

"He is no leper," Andrew observed. "Look at him!"

"He has been cutting himself," John said, his own fear gradually being replaced by pity. "Those demons have driven him to—"

At the mention of "demons," the man's face contorted wildly, lips twisted, a grotesque frown on his forehead, pale, splotched skin made even more ghostly in the light of the night's moon.

"We are greater than you could imagine!" The crude, guttural sounds burst from the man's throat as he surveyed each of the apostles, one after the other, a dark red tongue darting out from between thin, peeling lips. "We have seen what evil is. We *are* evil. And no mortal man can stand against us!"

Then the man's gaze fastened upon Jesus, who was standing a bit to the right of the apostles.

Peter, the biggest of the twelve, stepped forward.

"You shall not harm this Man!" he declared, ready to defend Jesus.

The intruder dropped to his knees.

"What have I to do with You, Jesus, for You are the Son of the Most High God?" he blurted. "I adjure You by all that is holy that You torment me not!"

Jesus walked to him and bent down beside him, placing His large, rough, carpenter's hands on either side of the man's face.

"Look at Me!" He demanded. "You know who I am. You know that the battle within you can be won. Do I have your faith? Do I have *all* of your faith?"

"Yes!" the possessed one cried. "I have been given over to *them* most of the days of my life. I can stand it no longer."

"And you shall *not* have to for another minute!" Jesus assured him.

He grabbed the man's neck.

"Come out of the man," the Son of God demanded of the fallen angels. "Come out, unclean spirits."

"*We have no place to go,*" a mixture of voices shouted stridently. "*How can we leave?*"

"What are you called?" Jesus asked, though He knew already.

"Legion, because we are many."

Darien knew that that was a false identification because he had previously encountered a single demon with that same name but, then, he was not surprised that such entities would try to lie even to the Son of God.

"If you send us out now from this one man, we will have to go directly back to hell," the voices continued pleadingly. "We must attach ourselves to one body or many right away or our master assumes we are foolishly idle, and for that reason he will punish the lot of us in unholy ways."

Jesus glanced up and saw that dawn was beginning to send its gentle light over that region.

Ahead was a small hill, and on it a large herd of swine grazed on patches of grass.

The possessed man turned in that direction as well.

"*Yes!*" the demons spoke. "Send us there! Please do that, Jesus. That will forestall our punishment, if only for a short while"

Jesus ordered them to depart from the man, and they rushed instantly into the nearby swine, two thousand fallen angels taking over two thousand animals, which was virtually the entire herd. The animals panicked and ran over the edge of the hill, plunging into the Sea of Galilee.

The demons were cast free.

An entrance to hell opened up before them, and they were sucked into its recesses, screaming.

Only John saw them in their natural form.

Jesus rushed over to him as the young apostle became dizzy and started to fall.

"They were monstrous!" John began, teeth chattering, but not from any morning chill. "They had splotched faces like those of dead corpses that had been allowed to rot in the sun before being buried."

His left cheek was twitching.

"And yet I felt sorry for them," John went on. "I saw on their countenances what seemed to be regret."

"Regret?" Thomas repeated. "What do you mean by that?"

"That they had given up the joy and the peace and the glory of heaven to follow a master who had no compassion or forgiveness, only the hatred that consumed him, hatred he passed on to them."

"Did you see where they all went," Andrew asked, "after the swine had plunged into the sea?"

"Yes . . . ," replied John. "I saw."

Blood had drained from his face.

"Hell," he said. "I saw them pulled through the entrance to hell."

He fell back against Jesus, who was standing next to him.

"I saw the damned, lost souls from many centuries being tormented by those very loathsome creatures."

"*Will John recover from this, Lord?*" Darien asked, deeply concerned.

"*He will, yes,*" replied Jesus, "*but this encounter will have changed him for the rest of his life. Despite his age, he will no longer be a young man. Within the next three years, every hair on his head will become gray, his face will lose its youthful color, and his mind will never be able to relieve itself completely of those dreadful images.*"

"*But why was it that the Father allowed this to happen, Lord?*"

"*To prepare him for what he will face on Patmos, for those images will be far more extreme than any he has seen today.*"

"*Lord?*"

"*Will any of the angels be at his side?*" Darien asked.

"*Yes, together with the Holy Spirit.*"

"*Is it me?*"

"*It is you, dear Darien. It is you.*"

John's fellow apostles had become so engrossed in what he was telling them that they all forgot about the demon-possessed man.

"I am whole now!" they heard the man exclaim in a normal voice.

The twelve swung around and looked at him.

"His rags," Peter said, pointing. "They are on the ground, and he has put on a fresh garment that had been kept in that leather satchel."

The man ran up to Jesus and fell at His feet.

"Please, please, let me go along with You," he spoke fervently. "I shall do nothing but serve You all the days of my life."

Jesus smiled in a kindly manner.

"It is better that you go and tell others what has happened," He admonished, "Tell them what a wonderful miracle God has given you this day. Make sure they learn of His great mercy."

The man was crying, wanting to please Jesus in any way he could.

"There is nothing more, Lord?" he asked.

"It is as I have said. Go, and make no secret of what has happened this morning. I ask no more than that."

"*Lord?*" said the angel.

"*Yes, Darien?*" replied the Son of God.

"*I see Stedfast. Is he going to accompany this man as his guardian?*"

Jesus nodded.

"*Yes . . . until we are at the gates of heaven to give him entrance.*"

"*What a wonderful morning, Lord!*"

For a moment there by the Sea of Galilee, Darien perceived that the hosts of heaven were singing a glorious and jubilant, "*Hallelujah, and amen!*"

PART IX

And Jesus went about all Galilee, teaching in their synagogues, preaching the gospel of the kingdom, and healing all kinds of sickness and all kinds of disease among the people. Then His fame went throughout all Syria: and they brought to Him all sick people who were afflicted with various diseases and torments, and those who were demon-possessed, epileptics, and paralytics; and He healed them.

Matthew 4:23–24

THE FIRST few miracles and the striking initial growth of Jesus' ministry formed the basis for a feeling of invincibility that would soon creep into the apostles. They were beginning to assume that no one could stop what was happening, not the religious leaders whose opposition was still anemic, and not all the demons at Satan's command.

Peter was often the most vocal.

"My friends, we will eventually go on right to the very steps of the emperor's palace in Rome," the big fisherman would say in his typically expansive manner, meaning well with his words but also very much swayed by what seemed to be the brightest future any of them had ever hoped to visualize for themselves.

Peter, though more outspoken than the rest, was not alone in his confidence.

Andrew felt similarly. So did James and most of the rest. Only Thomas and young John seemed almost immune.

Like a Shepherd, Jesus would bring them back to reality each time this great surge of blind expectancy burst forth among them, but He knew that He had to guide the men without breaking their spirit, and this was difficult because their sinful natures interfered with them as it did with all men.

CHAPTER 40

DURING the next two and a half years, Jesus the Christ's ministry extended to every boundary of the land of Israel, virtually no region in the country left untouched, from Bethzacharias and Hebron in the south to Caesaria and Samaria in the north, as well as to Jericho and Lydda in the central part of the nation.

The twelve apostles, ever alert, received innumerable reports of sympathetic travelers who returned to their own countries after hearing one of Jesus' messages; these men subsequently sent back word of dynamic interest in their homelands, but with such messages there was also intimations of frustration that seemed to say, "We know enough to find what You offer appealing, and so it is with our families and our friends when we tell them of what we heard, but we do not have sufficient understanding to go any further, to expand our knowledge, to be completely at peace with what the Nazarene told us. Our ignorance could be our undoing if we are not helped along."

This meant that many new disciples had to be recruited as soon as possible, and trained and sent off to spread the good news beyond Israel itself, another milestone for this group of dedicated men.

But along with such mushrooming growth came increased opposition, which surprised the apostles at first but not Jesus Himself. At the beginning, they were considered by the members of the Sanhedrin as merely an annoyance, hardly more worthy of a response than John the Baptist had been.

The Baptist's death had come about, not from the discomfort of the Pharisees and Sadducees nor any of the scribes, but from a vengeful Herodias. If she had not instigated a plot against John, he presumably would have lived many more years. So the ruling religious council of the Jews happened to be blameless in this regard; in fact, some of them had cautioned the king not to make John a martyr.

But Jesus was different. He had called the religious leaders nothing more than sepulchers full of dead men's bones. He seemed to be trying to destroy the very basis for the way they lived!

"Lord," said Darien as they sat atop the Mount of Olives during a mild, serene spring evening while the apostles were asleep below, *"it has been a remarkable period of time, has it not?"*

"It surely has," Jesus replied, thinking back over all that had happened. *"We have been blessed."*

And blessed was the only adequate word to describe what had transpired. A variety of miracles had become almost commonplace: the healing of lepers, the giving of sight to the blind and the ability to walk back to those who had been lame, demons purged from the possessed, and life restored to those who had died.

Always Darien was deeply affected, for he was seeing the powers of divinity applied to flesh-and-blood sufferers.

Though this angel had known heaven throughout his existence and was aware of all of that which the Trinity was capable, to actually *see* people freed from agony, from disability, to witness the joy that engulfed them when this happened, was a far greater experience than he had anticipated.

"I think most it has to do with the expressions on their faces," Darien recalled early on, talking out his impression in the presence of the Son of God. *"To see such terrible pain replaced by health and strength that must seem to them to be incomprehensible; and the surprise, Lord, the surprise they show when sight returns; when they find their bodies made whole, with no sores remaining, with limbs lost to leprosy generated; when their hearts beat without pain; when their minds are clear and are no longer subject to the grossness of demonic manipulation—oh, Lord, I can scarce describe my own feelings!"*

"What they are given is a suggestion of heaven," Jesus said. *"I can never touch* all *of those who need healing. Others will die in their infirmities, but if they have accepted Me as their Savior, their Lord, they will be admitted into My Father's heaven with new, unblemished bodies and will never again know illness or infirmity for any reason."*

. . . I can never touch all of those who need healing.

For the first time, Jesus revealed an emotion bordering on impatience or frustration or perhaps both. His human nature wanted to reach out and immediately heal *all* in need. But there was a specific timetable that the almighty triune Godhead had established, a timetable of which Jesus was fully aware and by which both the finite and the infinite were bound.

Yet the *need* for healing continued.

Once the people saw that it was possible, that they were not necessarily chained to their infirmities, they sought out Jesus wherever He went, hoping that by merely touching His garment they might receive what they desperately craved.

Since Jesus was bound by His fleshly limitations, He could not be everywhere people were suffering. This provided an opening for the false prophets, the insensitive hucksters who, having seen the example provided by Jesus, decided to do counterfeit healing on their own, sometimes claiming to do it in His name, sometimes not bothering even with that tenuous connection with divinity.

"*They lead so many astray,*" Darien remarked. "*When people find out they are not healed, both the messenger and the message are rejected in disillusionment.*"

"*Not all who claim My name are of Me,*" Jesus confirmed, anger flashing on His human face. "*Deceivers are rampant now, and there will be times when they hold even greater sway over the unsuspecting, manipulating them at will.*"

Widows wanting to see their husbands raised from the grave, as Jesus had brought Lazarus back to life; children crying for a mother and a father . . .

"*Multitudes will be chained to their every word, believing whatever they have to say while they secretly line their pockets with money and puff up their vanity with the adulation that is heaped upon them as they spread nice-sounding doctrine that has a form of godliness but denies its power.*"

That was a new and very disturbing thought for the angel, and he asked if Jesus would elaborate.

"*The chief priests and others are slaves to the religious system they have concocted over the centuries, adding a maze of rules to simple commandments. They bind people to such a cold, hard system of belief* and practice *that the people become ripe for the fakers who offer up a more palatable approach to faith.*"

"*The leaders are more puppets of Satan than genuine teachers of God's infallible word,*" Darien suggested, and Jesus smiled in approval.

"*The Pharisees and Sadducees are trapped like rats in a corner,*" Jesus continued. "*They are unable or, by this time, unwilling to figure a way out of their self-imposed dilemma. They have had power, influence, and wealth for a long time. None are not eager to change any of that. And due to the way they have turned worship into a crass commercial enterprise, through the money-changers in the temple and other means of fattening their own treasuries, their gross sins will rise up at judgment time and become the acts that will surely condemn them throughout eternity."*

Jesus paused, sighing in a way that told Darien how much He hungered for the redemption of every member of the Sanhedrin but how little was the likelihood that any would be saved from damnation.

"And the frauds will be dealt with just as harshly. They twist the Word of God and the miracles they have seen Me perform. These miserable men have no real allegiance to anything that is good and holy. They talk about salvation but their words are hollow facades because the men uttering them have only reprobate minds and they use what is sacred for their own ends."

"How they will suffer when judgment is meted out!" Darien exclaimed. *"Satan must be anticipating them with special glee."*

"Oh, he is, he is. Satan will have the pleasure of tormenting such false teachers in hell as well as many of those they have led astray by their perverse doctrines. For corrupters of the spiritually innocent, we should not waste our pity, for they know fully what they do, and there are few among them who ever seem willing to repent, for they have been permanently seduced by their own deceptions.

"But the members of the Sanhedrin are another story, sadly enough. They once were quite different from what we see today, Darien, since, back then, they only wanted to serve God and be His interpreters before those who looked to them for wisdom and guidance. They knew they had a holy responsibility, and they did not take it lightly.

"But, so many years later, these leaders have become not more than pallid shells of what their kind were generations ago. Their so-called holiness mocks those days of the past. They are intelligent men who are physically close to the greatest truth *in the history of the world because they have vast numbers of parchments that are available to no others, treasured copies of ancient Israel's most important writings, writings given to them by My Father, but they nevertheless are influenced by their own self-interests, letting the spiritual health of their nation become a casualty. They sell what are free gifts from God and heap unto themselves damnation as a result."*

Jesus' expression showed His frustration, which Darien shared.

"They have had the matchless opportunity of studying these precious documents every hour of every day if they wish," Darien said, musing for a moment. *"But most fail to do this or, in the case of some, having done so, they allow their musty* traditions *to cloud their thinking, and they go so far as to discard anything that does not agree with those traditions rather than judging* every *tradition by the inspired and written Word of God."*

"Excellent, Darien," Jesus congratulated him. *"I will build a very fine parable around what you have said."*

The angel glowed more brightly at the thought that he had been somehow helpful to his Lord.

"Can nothing be done to set their thinking straight?" Darien asked. *"What instruments of righteousness these religious leaders could become with this resource of knowledge at their disposal and the intelligence they could bring to any mission to reach others with the good news! To use all this only for self-glorification!* Could *it be otherwise?"*

Jesus left no doubt, though not cruelly, that what the angel hoped for was just that, mere hope, pleasant enough to contemplate but with no expectation that any of it would ever come about.

"Not as long as they, men of flesh and blood as they are, remain captive to their sinful natures and continue to puff themselves up with swelling vanity, doing good deeds to be seen of men with little thought for their heavenly Father."

The Son of God spoke even more sadly than before when He added, *"They are leading participants in My Father's Plan, but it is to be to their shame."*

CHAPTER 41

THOUSANDS of people were gathered, men, women, and children alike, some sitting, others standing, all waiting.

Some were quiet. Others were engaged in conversation.

One rather obese man, an Egyptian, sat on a three-legged stool under the shade of a large tree. A soap dish had been placed on the ground in front of him while his barber cut his hair, using a primitive "barber's razor," essentially a flat stone with edges that had been honed to sufficient sharpness.

Another man, a Jew from Lachish, wore a long tunic but no sandals on his feet. He was by himself, playing a lyre. Some distance away, a woman had a harp, an instrument of eleven strings strung obliquely across an ornate soundboard decorated with a mosaic swirling to a ram's head at one end. Two tall, muscular men, obviously slaves, stood nearby, waiting to take the harp out of her way when she was finished playing it.

It was the largest crowd to which Jesus would ever speak. And the human part of Him knew that the message could not be less than the best of which He in the flesh was capable.

Still, Jesus did not rehearse His words in any way.

As incarnate Deity, all He had to do was open His mouth and speak. He did not even need to think about what to say, for He was the embodiment of all wisdom and whatever He said would be the perfect essence of that wisdom.

But none of this meant He could take lightly His momentous opportunity before such a massive crowd. For Jesus was going to speak to those thousands of people about eternal matters that came from the infinite mind of God the Father, and was nothing less than a holy responsibility.

If it had been His Father's wish that He speak to them as pure spirit, without the facade of mortality, that would have been different, for words would have meant little and He could have communicated directly to their own souls in each case.

Yet Jesus as a Man required the medium of words. While existing within a body of flesh, if He had contracted a sore throat or a cold, his clarity of speech would be impaired as a result, and He would have had to cancel everything and look to another day instead. There were no provisions by almighty God to provide for invincibility of His incarnate state of being.

Illness and disability could come His way, as hunger and thirst did during the wilderness temptations.

Yet He was sinless.

Incarnate Deity, the embodiment of all that was good and holy and perfect in every way, could not sin.

"*There are some who say that illness is a result of sin,*" the sinless Lamb of God had once told Darien.

The angel could scarcely believe what he was hearing.

"*If a baby becomes ill, it is because that baby has sinned?*" he exclaimed, astonished at the stupidity of that notion. "*If a man is sick in his stomach, they will claim that sin is the cause? That every bug, every—?*"

Darien was sputtering, unable to finish his sentence, a certain righteous rage suddenly filling him.

"*According to what the Pharisees are saying, yes,*" Jesus answered.

"*But then, since You have been sick periodically in Your physical body,*" Darien reasoned, "*they will be suggesting that You have been sinning.*"

The very notion sent angry tremors through the angel.

"*That is a damnable error from the hand of Satan!*" he exclaimed.

That it was. But nothing of the sort would deter such men. They would come to spout many such dishonoring pronouncements with no regard for the truth.

"*Oh, it will prove far worse than even that,*" said Jesus. "*One heresy after another even now tumbles from their misbegotten lips, and it will not end with the next generation or the one after that.*"

Darien recoiled from what his Lord told him about those men who would claim that the Father was powerless unless they aggressively prayed Him into action, that He was scarcely more than an impotent figurehead until they spoke, claiming it was their words that gave Him power.

"*Oh, Father, Father . . .*" The angel fell to the ground, deeply upset by this glimpse into what was yet ahead.

Jesus sighed, feeling entirely as Darien did.

"*Untold numbers are being led astray by such teachings,*" He added wearily, "*as they choose to listen to cunningly devised fables.*"

Darien looked up at Him.

. . . cunningly devised fables.

Jesus then told him of one such individual, a supposedly spiritual Galilean, who claimed to have great insight into the supernatural. He went so far as to announce that he had been with a sick man besieged by a grotesque, monkey-like demon, and he had ordered this monstrosity to depart its victim.

"*As soon as it did, howling and screaming, according to this man,*" Jesus said, "*the sufferer's illness promptly disappeared.*"

The Son of God's fleshly expression was a mixture of embarrassment and pain, and Darien knew why: That sort of carnival-like approach to something as holy as healing bordered on the blasphemous and was repugnant to a holy God.

Initially, Darien thought he might have burst out in laughter, partly to get some relief from the miserable way he had felt seconds before, that horrendous image so intrinsically ludicrous and far too bizarre, it would seem, for anybody to take seriously; but after a moment, he knew that Jesus regarded it with obvious gravity, and Darien did not let any levity minimize the impact of what He just said.

"*The only ones howling and screaming will be the deceivers themselves when they face the pit of hell rather than the gates of heaven,*" he reasoned. "*It is a tragedy when* anyone *must face damnation, but for such deceivers there is great justice in the punishment they will be receiving.*"

"*Yet they are putting forth claims against anyone who dares to disagree with them,*" Jesus told him, "*people they call 'heresy hunters,' are condemned by My Father and will end up being handed over to Satan. Men like this are here today and will be here in every age to come.*"

CHAPTER 42

And there followed Him great multitudes of people from Galilee, and from Decapolis, and from Jerusalem, and from beyond Jordan.

And seeing the multitudes, He went up into a mountain, and when He was set, He started to teach . . .

"He is here now!" someone exclaimed in a whisper, pointing to the tall, broad-shouldered Man who was being followed by His twelve apostles.

"Yes, yes," another added. "I have heard so much about Him. I hope what He has to say is worth the trouble of getting here."

Having just arrived from a camp less than a mile away, Jesus started to walk through the throng to reach the top of the mount.

A woman stood up before Him.

"My child is dying!" she pleaded. "Can you heal him?"

Jesus spoke, "Go home, woman. Your son is now well."

She ran from the spot, shouting joyfully.

He had almost reached the gradual slope that led to the top when a man approached Him.

"I have just said good-bye to my blessed daughter," he cried. "She died in my house an hour ago. I have heard of you and your healings. Can you bring her back? I love this dear, dear child very much. She was only five years old. My wife is grieving so badly that I wonder if she, too, will die soon."

"Do you believe I can do this?" asked Jesus.

The man studied Jesus' face for a moment, then replied, "I believe, yes, I believe that You are that special One sent by God, His only begotten Son, whom the prophets told us would be coming."

"Then go home. Your daughter is alive."

Word about the two encounters spread quickly, and even before Jesus had begun to address the crowd, people were whispering excitedly.

"This is the Messiah, come to free us from our bondage!" one heavyset man exclaimed to his wife.

"How can you know that?" she asked him.

"It is prophesied in the old writings. He is practicing miracles of which no mere man would be capable."

A young man standing next to them added, "I overheard you talking just now, and I agree. What He will give us today is a speech exhorting us to overthrow the Roman conquerors. All he has to do is ask that of everyone here, and most of us will follow Him to the battlefields!"

This sort of talk spread throughout the multitude, and so much emotion surfaced that Jesus had to stand quietly, with great patience, for quite a long time before the noise finally died away and became five thousand whispering voices that sounded more like a hive of bees.

Jesus' voice carried to each individual there.

"He will tell us to rally against the soldiers," a strong-looking man, nearly as big as Peter, said as he waited for those first words. "This Jesus will raise His fists into the air and demand that we revolt."

But he fell silent as Jesus gently began His sermon on that mount: "Blessed are the poor in spirit, for theirs is the kingdom of heaven."

What is He doing? That is not what He should be telling everyone! the man thought, a sick feeling already beginning to grip his stomach. *The poor are not the problem. We have always had them with us, with or without the Romans.*

All whispering and other sounds ceased as the people listened, some beguiled by what He was saying, others disappointed, their silence not arising from their approval but, rather, from their despair.

"Bless are those who mourn, for they shall be comforted," continued Jesus. "Blessed are the meek, for they shall inherit the earth."

Darien decided to leave the mount for a while and walk through the crowd, trying to found out more about how they were reacting. He had not been asked to do this but decided, on his own, that it was appropriate.

"Blessed are those who hunger and thirst for righteousness, for they shall be filled," Jesus was telling the thousands before Him. "Blessed are the merciful, for they shall obtain mercy. Blessed are the pure in heart, for they shall see God. Blessed are the peacemakers, for they shall be called sons of God."

Darien soon encountered a group of half a dozen men who were part of the overall throng but stood back near the edge of it. Though they could hear Jesus clearly, and they rather grudgingly marveled at this fact, none of them were pleased by the content of what He was saying thus far.

"He utters the words of a weakling," the tallest and toughest-looking of them observed. "I *thought* there was reason to suspect that He is the Messiah."

The others had gotten him to come based upon that very expectation.

"Barabbas will be disappointed," he said. "He was hoping to link up his men with the forces of the Nazarene and at last wrestle this land of ours from the iron-fisted rule of the Romans."

"But, Elias, He seemed so promising not long ago," another protested. "We have heard him mention wickedness in high places and talk about resisting Satan. He said if we do, the devil will flee from us. Everyone here assumed he was talking about Rome's government and about the emperor and his soldiers!"

"You were wrong, were you not?" The first man spat the words out. "Just listen to Jesus now!"

"Blessed are those who are persecuted for righteousness' sake," the powerful voice continued, "for theirs is the kingdom of heaven. Blessed are you when they revile and persecute you, and say all kinds of evil against you falsely for My sake. Rejoice and be exceeding glad, for great is your reward in heaven, for so persecuted they the prophets who were before you."

Elias became more distressed.

"Jesus talks of heaven! But little about this life, this domination we endure by a brutal foreign power. He says simply that we should be patient, that we will get our freedom *after* we die!"

He paused, closing his eyes; then the lids shot open.

"I think it is possible that that Jesus up there may prove to be nothing more than a Roman stooge!" he blurted out. "I think He has been set up to take our minds off the present situation of unrest and focus our attention toward the future. That way, a clever one I admit, Rome is able to retain control *now*, subversion is handily quelled, and we go on as we have been doing for these many years."

As much as they all hated to admit it, that made some sense to the five other men. Angry and feeling betrayed, they decided to push through the crowd and confront the Nazarene directly.

"You are the light of the world," Jesus was continuing. "A city that is set on a hill cannot be hidden. Nor do they light a lamp and put it under a basket but on a lampstand, and it gives light to all who are in the house. Let your light so shine before men, that they may see your good works and glorify your Father in heaven."

"*Lord, the men are going to challenge You!*" Darien quickly warned, not certain whether He was aware.

"*I know . . . ,*" Jesus told him.

"*What am I to do?*"

"*Nothing.*"

As they walked past hundreds, then thousands of people, the angry men noticed the expressions on many of the faces.

"*They cannot take their eyes off Him,*" the tall man remarked. "*And they seem to be listening to every word.*"

Truly that was so; especially to His latest words.

"You have heard that it was said to those of old, 'You shall not murder, and whoever murders will be in danger of the judgment.' But I say to you that whoever is angry with his brother without a cause shall be in danger of the judgment. And whoever says to his brother, 'Raca' shall be in danger of the council. But whoever says 'You fool!' shall be in danger of hell fire."

Elias stopped walking.

"What is it, friend?" one of the others asked.

The tall man waved him into silence.

"Therefore if you bring your gift to the altar," Jesus went on, "and there remember that your brother has something against you, leave your gift there before the altar, and go your way. First be reconciled to your brother, and then come and offer your gift."

At that moment, Jesus seemed to turn and glance at Elias to the exclusion of all others.

"*Lord, has there been a barrier between them . . . between this man Elias and his brother?*" Darien inquired.

"*His brother is dying, and the man called Elias refuses to go to his side,*" the Son of God explained.

"*I hope that will change, Lord, because of what You are saying.*"

"*It will, Darien.*"

Jesus walked a few feet down the slope.

"You have heard that it was said to those of old, 'You shall not commit adultery.' But I say to you that whoever looks at a woman to lust for her has already committed adultery with her already in his heart."

The other men had stopped beside Elias. Two more seemed as transfixed by the words of Jesus as he suddenly had become.

"It has been said, 'Whoever divorces his wife, let him give her a certificate of divorce.' But I say to you that whoever divorces his wife for any reason except sexual immorality causes her to commit adultery; and whoever marries a woman who is divorced commits adultery."

By now, all six men were listening, no longer interested in exposing Jesus as a traitor but entranced by the wisdom He was giving the multitude, wisdom that seemed to hit each of them in a very personal manner.

Elias groaned at the next words Jesus spoke.

"Again, you have heard that it was said to those of old, 'Do not swear falsely, but shall perform your oaths to the Lord.' But I say unto you, do not swear at all: neither by heaven; for it is God's throne; nor by the earth, for it is His footstool; nor by Jerusalem, for it is the city of the great King.

"Nor shall you swear by your head, because you cannot make one hair white or black. But let your 'Yes' be 'Yes,' and your 'No,' 'No.' For whatever is more than these is from the evil one."

So it was that these six men became truly aghast and troubled in their very souls. So it was that they neither stood at the base of the mount and accused Jesus as they had planned nor stayed to hear more.

His words had pierced, arrow-like, into their hearts, for He had spoken of "secret sins" of which they all had been guilty, though they had assumed no one knew and no one could ever find out.

"*They act so strangely, Lord,*" Darien observed.

"*Because they have been found out,*" Jesus told him, "*and the truth has been the harsh accuser of each of them.*"

"*They were determined to falsely judge You and subject You to the derision of this throng after they had turned it against You.*"

"*They did not succeed because darkness shall always flee before the cleansing light of the Word,*" Jesus answered.

"*I will stay and listen now, Lord.*"

"*Good, Darien. There is much more to be said.*"

Jesus smiled slightly as the six men started walking from that spot, their step quickening into a run.

Only Elias looked back over his shoulder before running faster, anxious to leave the presence of a Man who seemed able to peer into their souls.

"Do not worry about your life," the Son of God continued telling those thousands who had gathered to hear Him, "what you shall eat or what you will drink; nor about your body, what you will put on. Is not life more than food and the body more than clothing?"

He had seen scattered among the multitude several wealthy women who had donned the finest imported apparel, with bright, intricately dyed colors. Their manner was haughty. As they periodically glanced at the crowd, their expressions betrayed a contempt that Jesus found repugnant.

"Look at the birds of the air, for they neither sow nor reap nor gather into barns; yet your heavenly Father feeds them. Are you not of more value than they? Which of you by worrying can add one cubit unto his stature?"

The well-dressed women appeared oblivious to what He was trying to tell them, except one, the oldest, a woman more than sixty years old, who wore the most extravagant garb of all. She could not meet His gaze and turned away hastily.

"And why do you worry about clothing? Consider the lilies of the field, how they grow; they neither toil nor spin; and yet I say to you that even Solomon in all his glory was not arrayed like one of these.

"Now, if God so clothes the grass of the field, which today is, and tomorrow is thrown into the oven, will He not much more clothe you, O you of little faith? Therefore do not worry, saying, 'What shall we eat?' Or 'What shall we drink?' Or 'What shall we wear?' . . . For your heavenly Father knows that you need all these things.

"But seek first the kingdom of God and His righteousness, and all these things shall be added to you. Therefore do not worry about tomorrow, for tomorrow will worry about its own things. Sufficient for the day is its own trouble."

Suddenly the older woman broke away and nervously approached the base of thc mount.

"I perceive that what you say is true," she cried to Him. "But I know not what I am to do. I have had much wealth since I was a child."

"Give what you have to the poor," Jesus told her.

"But then I would have nothing!"

"It is better to enter the kingdom of heaven having left behind few of this world's goods than to be sucked into hell, trying to take great treasure with you. Those who are rich in this life may be poor and in anguish in the next."

"Can no one with much money and many belongings enter heaven?" the woman asked, tears trickling down her cheeks.

Jesus' voice became more tender as He told her, "It is harder for such a one than for a camel to go through the eye of a needle."

One of her companions approached her.

"We must be gone," she urged, "you are being overwhelmed by this Man's spell."

Esther spun around and confronted the other woman.

"No!" she declared. "You are the one who is overwhelmed, not by the simplicity and the beauty of the message we have heard but by your baubles, your fine silks, your hand-carved ivory statues."

"But you have more of those than I do!"

"No longer," Esther declared. "I give what I have to the Nazarene's blessed work."

Jesus came down from the top of the mount and touched the woman gently on the shoulder.

"Please do not give any of this to me or those with me," He said. "We have no need of such things. I ask not for a single gem but have said that you should sell what you have and give the proceeds to the poor.

"There is no hunger among My apostles and Myself; we have sufficient clothing to protect us; we are content to sleep in stables or to wherever else we may be guided. My heavenly Father takes care of whatever our needs might be because we have pledged ourselves entirely to His honor and glory."

"But what can I do for *You*, Jesus?" Esther asked, desperately anxious not to simply go off and do nothing.

"You can take care of those who are truly needy. To do it for the least of them, the hungriest of them, the most destitute, is to do it for Me, Esther."

She fell back, not prepared for that.

"How did you know my name?"

Even those of colder hearts who had tried to get her to go with them a moment before were surprised by this.

"It has been given to Me to know even the innermost thoughts of your being," He told her.

She fell at His feet.

But she was not alone. Two other women did likewise.

"*I shall sell what I have and benefit the poor,*" Esther said.

"And I will add my own belongings to yours," one of the others promised.

The third woman hesitated.

"I feel so weak, so uncertain," she admitted. "I do not know if I can do what it is that You ask."

"Whatever you will, do it out of a willing heart, not grudgingly," Jesus said. "My Father loves a cheerful giver."

She glanced at her two companions.

"I am not ready," she said as she got to her feet. "I am not ready to give away everything I have accumulated."

She turned from them and walked back through the multitude, then disappeared over the side of another hill.

But not Esther. Or her other friend.

"My friend is so weak," Esther said. "She has chosen the material things in her life and now—"

"Yes, she has," Jesus interrupted, "but there may be a time when this woman will change the way she acts. Do not condemn her so harshly just yet, for your angry words can only harden her heart further."

Then he went back up to the top of the mount and continued speaking to the throng. "I say to you this day: Judge not, that you be not judged. For with what judgment you judge, you will be judged; and with the measure you use, it will be measured back to you.

"And why do you look at the speck in your brother's eye, but do not consider the plank in your own eye? Or how can you say to your brother, 'Let me remove the speck from your eye'; and look, a plank is in your own eye? Hypocrite! First remove the plank from your own eye, and then you will see clearly to remove the speck from your brother's eye."

Esther and her friend nodded to one another as He concluded that passage, and both were taking the jeweled adornments out of their hair and off their ears with the intention of selling them and then using the money to buy meat, bread, cakes, and wine to distribute to the poor.

Addressing the matter He and Darien had discussed earlier, Jesus told the attentive multitude, "Beware of false prophets, who come to you in sheep's clothing, but inwardly they are ravenous wolves. You will know them by their fruits. Do men gather grapes from thornbushes or figs from thistles?

"Even so, every good tree bears good fruit, but a bad tree bears bad fruit. A good tree cannot bear bad fruit, nor can a bad tree bear good fruit. Every tree that does not bear good fruit is cut down and thrown into the fire. Therefore by their fruits you shall know them."

Jesus clearly had continuing concern over the dangers of the deceivers who would claim His name as they convinced many of their genuineness.

"Not every one who says to Me, 'Lord, Lord,' shall enter the kingdom of heaven, but he who does the will of My Father in heaven. Many will say to Me in that day, 'Lord, Lord, have we not prophesied in Your name, cast out demons in Your name, and done many wonders in Your name?' "

Jesus paused, then added, "And then I will declare to them, 'I never knew you; depart from Me, you who practice lawlessness!' "

The Son of God was nearing the end of what He intended to say on the mount that day as the multitude listened.

"Therefore, whoever hears these sayings of Mine, and does them, I will liken him to a wise man who built his house on the rock; and the rain descended, the floods came, and the winds blew and beat on that house, and it did not fall, for it was founded on the rock.

"But everyone who hears these sayings of Mine, and does not do them, will be like a foolish man who built his house on the sand; and the rain descended, the floods came, and the winds blew and beat on that house; and it fell. And great was its fall."

Finally, the Son of God ceased speaking and came down from the mount, His apostles walking along with him.

So intrigued were those in the multitude that many did not disperse as they would have normally done and go back to their homes or places of business. Instead they stayed with Jesus, eager to hear anything else He might say before dusk or see any acts of healing He might perform.

They were not disappointed, for a leper soon had approached Jesus, and begged to be healed.

"Make me clean, Lord," the middle-aged man pleaded, falling in front of him.

Upon seeing the man, his features just begun to be distorted, the crowd stepped back hastily and so did the twelve apostles, leaving Jesus alone with the leper.

The Son of God reached out His hand and touched the man.

Some in the crowd gasped.

"Why would the Nazarene do this?" one asked, aghast. "He could become diseased like that poor man is."

Suddenly his words ceased, his eyes widening, as He saw what was happening.

"I will . . . ," Jesus replied to the leper's entreaty. "Be clean."

None in the throng had *seen* any of the other miracles. They came that day only because they had *heard* about them.

The leper was cleansed.

Before the eyes of all present, his skin was healed, his limbs made whole, his body straightened.

There was no longer any stench about him.

The man danced around in a circle, jumping, laughing, holding his arms before his eyes and looking at them in joyous amazement.

Then he ran forward, stopping here and there in front of the crowd, showing them his wholeness.

At first they all moved away from him again but then, seeing that their eyes had not betrayed them and the leprosy had indeed been cast off this man, they gathered around, his own amazement becoming theirs.

CHAPTER 43

JESUS sent away the multitude, and took a ship, and came upon the coast of the region named Magdala. As this was happening, Darien was still thinking of some of the wisdom that Jesus had imparted while the apostles were miraculously feeding the four thousand listeners from a boy's lunch that had consisted of just seven loaves of unleavened bread and a few small fish caught less than an hour earlier in the Sea of Galilee.

And enough left over to feed the residents of a small village!

Seven basketfuls remained after a number of hours and the people had finished eating all that they could!

"*How many truly understood the extent of that miracle, Lord?*" questioned the angel. "*They were filling their bellies at the same time they were paying attention to what You were teaching, without fully knowing what was taking place all around them, the astonishing multiplication of a meager amount of food that otherwise would have been adequate for barely a handful of people, perhaps 1 percent of all those who had journeyed to that place.*"

It was then that the Pharisees and the Sadducees came and sought to tempt Him, desiring of Him that He would show them a sign from heaven.

Jesus looked at them with great pity and said, "When it is evening, you say, 'It will be fair weather, for the sky is red.' And yet, in the morning, you change all of this by telling everyone that foul weather is coming, for the sky is red and hints of a storm."

He pointed His finger at each one.

"Hypocrites! You pretend to discern the face of the sky and know all there is to know, discouraging others from questioning your judgment and telling them not to seek anything further. Yet you yourselves pursue this sign or that sign, looking at every shadow, every cloud in the sky, listening for every wind that blows, hoping to know what is being revealed in all of this.

"But I tell you truly that only a wicked and adulterous generation does what you do. You might as well give up. Any new signs are figments of your wishful thinking. Whatever is necessary has already been shown to you, not in the sky above or the earth below but in the books of the ancient prophets, for it is the truths they have offered up that should be your concern."

And Jesus, weary of their kind, departed from them, along with His twelve apostles.

When they all had reached the other side of a large lake, those apostles in charge of keeping together food for the group discovered that they had forgotten to take the leftover bread with them.

Jesus then spoke of bread but of another kind, admonishing them not to be concerned with food for their bodies but, instead, that which would replenish their souls.

"Avoid the false spiritual food of the Pharisees and the Sadducees," He urged them. "This should be your greater concern."

His humanity was tired.

The loving Son of God had taken care of so many others; now was the time for Him to replenish Himself in the flesh, to spend time alone with His disciples.

"Who do men say that I, the Son of Man, am?" Jesus asked of them.

At first the apostles, caught by surprise, said nothing, glancing sheepishly from one to the other and then back to Jesus. Then Peter, James, and John all responded in much the same manner, telling Him that He was the Messiah prophesied by Isaiah and others centuries before.

"But who do *you* say that I am?" Jesus repeated, either not satisfied or not hearing properly what they had said.

Thomas replied, "Some say You are John the Baptist; others say you are Elijah; and others Jeremiah or one of the other great prophets."

"But who do you say that I am? He repeated.

"You are the Christ, the Son of the living God," Peter interjected, then added. "I already told You that, Lord." Peter replied with a touch of irritation. "You are the Messiah."

Jesus looked at him and replied, "Blessed you are, Simon Bar-Jonah, for flesh and blood has not revealed this to you, but My Father who is in heaven. And I also say to you that you are Peter, and on this rock I will build My church, and the gates of Hades shall not prevail against it.

"And I shall give to you the keys of the kingdom of heaven, and whatever you bind on earth will be bound in heaven, and whatever you loose on earth will be loosed in heaven."

Then Jesus began to tell them what was ahead, that He must go into Jerusalem and suffer many things at the hands of the elders and chief priests and scribes; He told them He would be killed and then be raised again the third day.

Peter, disturbed, took Him aside and began to rebuke Him, saying, "Far be it from You, Lord; this shall not happen to You!"

"Get behind me, Satan!" Jesus responded. "You are an offense to Me, for you are not mindful of the things of God, but the things of men."

He turned from Peter and faced the others.

"If anyone desires to come after Me, let him deny himself, and take up his cross, and follow Me. For whoever desires to save his life will lose it, and whoever loses his life for My sake will find it. For what profit is it to a man if he gains the whole world, and loses his own soul? Or what will a man give in exchange for his soul?

"For the Son of Man shall come in the glory of His Father with His angels, and then He will reward each according to his works. Assuredly, I say to you, there are some standing here who shall not taste death till they see the Son of Man coming in His kingdom."

Six more days passed. Jesus took Peter, James, and John to the top of a mountain that rose right in the midst of the plain upon which all thirteen had been encamped.

Jesus got down on His knees and began to pray with great earnestness.

Assuming that He wanted them to do similarly, Peter, James, and John slipped to a like position on the hard rock surface of that mountaintop. But they were so tired by then from the rigorous climbing that they dozed off, only to be awakened a short while later, confronted by a sight so vivid it would seem fresh in their memories until the end of their days.

John gasped loudly, and the others followed his gaze.

The face of Jesus!

"See what is happening!" James spoke with such awe that he could hardly be heard. "He is—"

Changing . . .

The figure of the Man they had come to know and love was altering before their eyes, His face shining with a coruscating brilliance that stopped just short of blinding the three of them as they watched, transfixed.

The garment Jesus was wearing . . .

No longer the homespun cloth of typical toga-like apparel, it was now a transformed white, embodying the most effulgent purity they had ever seen.

Surrounded by shimmering light that moved and danced flame-like, Jesus stood in the very center of this resplendent display.

"He is a god!" James whispered.

"Not *a* god," John told him without elaboration.

Peter could not speak at all, could do nothing except point at what the others themselves already noticed.

Jesus was no longer alone!

Two other figures appeared next to Him.

The apostles heard their Lord greet the others.

Moses and Elijah . . .

There was a striking similitude of appearance among the three figures. Both great men spoke with Jesus about a matter that Peter, James, and John could scarcely endure hearing about so abruptly.

The death of their beloved Friend.

Moses and Elijah talked of His coming execution at the hands of wicked men, which must occur in accordance with the divine Plan of His heavenly Father.

And then the two figures were gone, leaving Jesus standing alone before the apostles, His appearance as it more customarily was, devoid of the brilliant light.

Peter, hoping not to seem stupid, felt it necessary to say something and said "Lord, it is good for us to be here; if You wish, let us make here three shelters: one for You, one for Moses, and one for Elijah so that none will be unprotected if a storm arises. James and John and I can erect something for the three of us."

For such a big man, such a strongly masculine one, the fisherman was acting more like an awed child who was finding it a Herculean effort not to become unhinged by what he and the others had encountered.

Just as Peter was ending his offer, a bright cloud shot down from the sky, not unlike a powerful bolt of lightning, and surrounded the three apostles as well as the Son of God.

The three men looked at one another and at their Master.

They seemed wholly shut off from the world around them. There were no sounds from beyond that remarkable cloud, no sensations of being anything but suspended between heaven and earth.

Only a voice could be heard, a magnificent voice, a voice that was clear and seemed so close the speaker might have been in their midst.

"*This is My beloved Son, in whom I am well pleased. Hear Him!*"

And then it was gone, that voice, and along with it, the cloud.

As abruptly as silence had descended, so it was that the three apostles once again felt the mountaintop beneath their feet, heard birds singing nearby, and felt the rays of the overhead sun on their backs.

Their finite understanding tried hard to grapple mightily with the taste of the infinite they had been given that afternoon. On their way back down the mountain, John tried to get Jesus to talk in detail about their shared experience, but the Master would not refer to it any further, and ignored the young apostle's inquiry.

During the days and weeks to follow, Peter, James, and John would think often of what had happened, and look at their Master as never before.

PART X

Blow, blow, thou winter wind,
Thou art not so unkind
As man's ingratitude.

William Shakespeare
As You Like It

In time, many people became impatient with the sermons of Jesus, though these were the most inspired words of implicit holiness they would ever hear, divine words of redemption and spiritual cleansing that could change their lives if they only chose to listen with their understanding, and not their easily manipulated emotions, emotions stirred understandably by the promise of freedom from pain.

"More miracles!" they would collectively shout.

The volume of their voices seemed ever greater as the days passed, and they were inclined to demand more and more of Him.

"We shall worry about matters of the soul later," people would say, in so many words. "But, in the meantime, it is our bodies that need to be taken care of. Nothing else matters for the moment."

Jesus was sought after for the touch of His hands while the wisdom from His mouth was increasingly ignored.

The Son of God knew this, of course; He was not loathe to criticize the people for seeking with such passion after signs and wonders and turning their backs on the substance of the very gospel that He was on earth to teach . . .

CHAPTER 44

AT THE START, great hordes of people viewed Jesus the Christ as a new and impressive teacher. They were eager to hear those words He spoke so beautifully with an authority that none of them had ever heard from anyone else.

But then the very *nature* of the multitudes changed.

More and more, the sick, the disabled, and the demon-possessed could be seen along with grieving husbands, wives, sons, daughters, but fewer and fewer men and women who were present simply to gain the benefit of His spiritual wisdom.

The Son of God was greatly saddened.

"*People want the healing but little or nothing else,*" He said one night while the twelve apostles were asleep. "*They say to themselves, 'Sometime later we will return and listen, but not now.'*"

Darien, too, had noticed this tendency among those who were gathering around Jesus day after day.

"*I have seen what You are indicating, Lord,*" Darien replied, knowing the Father had wanted him to be a *guardian,* yes, but also a *comfort* to the physical part of what the Son had become.

To comfort God-in-the-flesh, Darien thought. *Can there be a greater privilege?*

"*How sad,*" Jesus continued rather morosely. "*Not that they were healed, for this is a blessing I shall continue to be happy to place upon them, but it is sad that many will go on with their lives, seeing with their restored eyes, hearing with their restored ears, walking with their restored legs, and at the same time, forgetting how it was they were made whole in the first place and by whom this came about.*"

Darien had followed more than one of the men who were healed. Only a few were to have changed lives in addition to changed bodies. He remembered one in particular, a man blind since birth but born into a family of great wealth so he did not have to hit the streets to beg for money or food.

His mother and his father had resisted his desire to seek out the Nazarene and that touch of His that was supposed to restore a body to wholeness, whatever the affliction that had settled upon it.

"Foolishness," the father had declared. "You go after fables instead of resigning yourself to reality."

But their son Benaiah, eighteen years old, was determined, their entreaties not stopping him.

"I *shall* go!" he declared firmly but in a kind manner.

"You go alone . . . ," his father told him sharply. "There will be no one by your side to help you this time."

Benaiah's mother drew the line at this, not wanting any harm to come to their son, and she tried to persuade her husband to send a servant along with the young man.

"If anything happens to him because you did not decree this," she said, "you would never be able to forgive yourself."

"I will not!" he declared stubbornly. "I have said what I have meant, and that is it, woman."

So Benaiah went outside, nervous at the prospect of whatever might await him, nervous that he had no one at all to lean on, even though he knew the immediate neighborhood well enough.

Once he got to the marketplaces at the center of Jerusalem, he could make out nicely since he had been *taken* there many times and everyone knew him, one of them typically calling out, "Hello, Benaiah! How are you today, young man?" To this one he would reply appreciatively, "Fine, Abiathar, I am quite well this afternoon. How are you?"

And there were the others, names he connected with voices but that was all. Only two or three ever invited him into their homes, the rest assuming he could not be bothered since his home was obviously so much grander, with servant after servant committed to taking care of his every need.

"But I cannot *see* anything," Benaiah would say to one of the merchants who did show him some hospitality. "It could be a shack or a palace, and it would not matter. I respond to what I *sense* from the people inside. Are they kind, loving? Are they happy?

"I can tell all of this well. I can tell *very* well because I cannot, I do not look on the outward appearance. What I 'see' comes instead from *within* each man, each woman. It matters little whether I am sitting on a dirt floor or, instead, on some precious handwoven Persian rug or a fine lot of Italian marble."

Benaiah was more mature than most of the other eighteen-year-olds, and that, too, set him apart.

"I have no one who truly understands me," he would say to another of those rare hosts from the marketplaces at the center of Jerusalem. "My father does not. Nor is there much understanding in my mother. They see me only as someone blind, someone who would be helpless without them."

"But *I* try, do I not?" Abiathar spoke up. "Surely I have never been less than willing to listen?"

"Oh, you have, you have," Benaiah agreed. "But none who have their sight can ever know what blindness is like."

"I concede that. But is it not better to have parents who overprotect you than being out on the cruel streets?"

The eighteen-year-old nodded.

"I feel ashamed about my complaints," he acknowledged.

"You are searching," Abiathar said. "All young men do the same. With you, due to your blindness, it is even more difficult."

Periodically, Benaiah would be invited in to have dinner with Abiathar's wife and children. Normal custom mandated that the servant who had accompanied him be fed separately. But neither Benaiah or Abiathar would allow anything of the sort to happen. The servant, a different one each time, would sit at the table with the rest.

The last time this had happened had been three weeks earlier. Abiathar was in an especially good mood.

"I feel the closeness of God!" he exclaimed after they had finished dinner. "I can almost sense one of His angels in this house."

"He is a wise and good man," Darien told the Lord.

"He has witnessed to many about Me," Jesus replied. *"And He has brought along his entire family to hear Me speak."*

"What will happen, Lord?"

"Something beautiful."

Benaiah continued sharing his thoughts.

"I wonder sometimes," he said, "if the fact that I have been blind all my life has meant that other senses have become sharper. I do not mean just my hearing and my ability to smell but *other* ones."

"Including those of the spirit?" Abiathar asked, genuinely intrigued.

"Especially those."

"Give me some examples."

"When I was very young, I would tell my father that during the night I thought there was someone in the room with me."

"And he thought it was just your childish imagination, I suppose."

Benaiah blinked several times in surprise and blushed, startled that his friend had guessed the answer with such accuracy.

"That is exactly what he said."

"It is a convenient way adults have to brush aside any truths that cannot be dealt with comfortably," Abiathar observed. "I have done it with my own children. Your father is a normal man. His response was neither evil nor stupid."

"*Could* I have felt the presence of an angel?" Benaiah asked.

"I think you did. Your world is one of darkness, young man. It may have been that our precious Creator wanted to assure you that you would never be completely alone, whatever the circumstances."

. . . a world of darkness.

Again, Abiathar spoke correctly.

Ever since then, Benaiah had spent moments, quiet moments reflecting back on his life, those occasions when a possible accident had *almost* happened but he had been saved from it, many, many instances of death or injury avoided.

. . . a world of darkness.

And in the midst of it, he now wondered if perhaps someone had been sent by God to share it with him.

CHAPTER 45

BENAIAH'S FRIEND *Abiathar had seemed so healthy then with a strong voice, the same as always . . .*

Somehow, though Benaiah left home with no one to help him, he was able to reach the marketplaces. He fell more than once, cutting his knees on rough-edged stones, and he was sure there were bruises on other places on his body.

But there he was, large numbers of people around him, some glancing, puzzled, at a blind man, a very young one, adorned by such fine clothing as his parents' wealth had been able to provide, yet alone.

"Abiathar!" he called out.

No answer.

He shouted louder this time.

Still no response.

Then a voice. An unfamiliar one.

"Can I help you, sir?" it asked.

"Yes, I . . . I cannot find Abiathar," replied Benaiah. "Would you be kind enough to take me to him, please?"

A pause.

Benaiah was about to speak again when the man's voice said gently, "Abiathar is dead. Your friend died of a pain in his chest this morning."

Dead! his mind screamed that brutal word, though, momentarily, nothing came to his lips. *Oh, my friend, my poor, poor friend!*

"Let me go to him!" Benaiah begged finally. "Let me spend a last few minutes at the side of my friend."

"I think that would be fine," the voice agreed. "I will help you inside."

"I know the way. Thank you for your kindness. But I think that I can still make it on my own."

"He is on his bed."

Benaiah stumbled and groped his way to Abiathar's home, then walked carefully inside, his fingers touching the doorway and guiding him past the furniture that was still in all the familiar locations.

He approached the bed, got down on his knees beside it, reached out, and placed a hand on Abiathar's shoulder.

So cold, so hard already, Benaiah told himself, pulling back instantly from the unwelcome touch.

He reached again for the body, found his friend's right hand and held it in his own, sobbing.

"Lord?" Darien started to ask.

Jesus knew what he was going to ask before anything was uttered.

"Yes, dear angel, do what you can."

Suddenly Benaiah thought he heard someone speaking to him even though he knew he was alone in the room with Abiathar.

Go . . .

A single word.

He cocked his head to one side, listening.

Nothing.

No one else had entered behind Benaiah, he knew that. And no one else was there. He would have detected movement.

"Is anyone here?" he asked, just to be certain.

No reply.

Go to Jesus . . .

Again!

It was during such times that he cursed his sightlessness all the more. It would have been so simple if he could just *look* and see!

"I am here with my poor friend." He spoke with special pleading. "Please, show some kindness and do not disturb us. He is dead, and I did not get here until it was too late. He comforted me time and again, but I could not be with him when comfort was what he needed. Depart, stranger, and let us be!"

Go to Jesus, and fall before Him.

"That was where I was heading," Benaiah said, "before I learned of what had happened to Abiathar here."

Go now. Do not delay.

He clamped his hands to his ears.

"Be quiet!" he screamed. "Leave us alone!"

The words continued without letup.

Finally Benaiah could stand it no longer. He jumped to his feet, stirred into action by the persistence of whoever had been speaking.

"I will do what you ask of me," he said. "And then, be sure of this, whoever you are: I will return to my friend here and mourn by his bed. From this moment on, I do not want to hear from you again. I must attend to my sorrow without being disrupted."

As soon as Benaiah made it outside, he stopped.

"This was not meant to be," he said out loud. "My father tried to warn me, and I did not listen. If I go on now, there might be worse tragedy ahead."

Go . . .

Benaiah wanted to object, wanted to tell whoever it was that, just because he was young and blind and struck by sorrow, he should not be considered someone who could be played with or manipulated without conscience.

Go to Jesus.

He felt an impulse to be obstinate, but that passed quickly enough.

Then, abruptly, Benaiah remembered that his original intention had been to contact this Jesus anyway.

"How did you know?" he asked. "No one but my mother and my father had any idea about what I was going to do."

He will touch you and make you whole . . .

Benaiah started stumbling forward, crying as he did.

"Yes, *yes!* That was what I hoped this Jesus would do . . . touch me and give me my sight," he said. "But I understand that there is no reason why I *can* expect Him to do that. I am but a stranger, like other blind men. There is nothing that makes me special, that would draw His attention in any way to my plight."

He does not need anything but your faith.

"But I have so little of that."

His voice broke for a moment, then he said, "I have seldom prayed. Such things have never been important in my house. My parents have always seemed to show more faith in their wealth than I could have in anything miraculous."

Afterward, use your sight as an occasion to witness to others.

Benaiah raised a fist in front of him.

"But that will *never* happen!" Benaiah shouted so loudly that people in the narrow street behind and in front of him looked at him as though he were rather odd and carefully avoided any contact with him.

Go . . . He awaits.

Benaiah decided he had nothing to lose, that he would simply continue ahead for the same reason that brought him into Jerusalem in the first place.

He managed to reach the main gate, then stopped to ask someone if they knew where the Nazarene was holding His latest meeting.

"Directly ahead, at the base of Golgotha," the man told him. "I am heading there now. Do you need help, young man?"

"I do," Benaiah replied gratefully. "I am not familiar with these paths. I doubt that I could make it by myself."

"Take my arm then. One of my wife's relatives is blind. I am used to this sort of thing."

The two of them walked slowly forward. The distance was not great, but the way to get to the Mount of the Skull was rock-strewn and there was a narrow creek to one side with treacherous footing.

Benaiah heard the voice of Jesus only seconds later.

"Rise, and walk . . . ," He was saying.

"Can you see anything?" Benaiah asked.

The other man did not answer him at first.

"Can you—?" he started to repeat.

"On a stretcher," his benefactor mumbled.

"On a stretcher?"

"Yes . . . his legs were twisted badly . . . so thin and fragile-looking. He just stood up, and . . . and walked."

Benaiah could sense that the man was struggling with his emotions.

"Those legs are no longer as they were," he managed to continue. "His steps are strong, a light seems to shine on his face."

"Will you take me up to Jesus?" Benaiah asked, his excitement growing. "Can you get me through the crowd?"

"I will try. I—"

The man fell silent.

"What is wrong, stranger?" Benaiah asked.

The multitude, which had been quite noisy, grew quiet.

"Tell me, please!" Benaiah begged. "What's happening?"

And then he heard the most wonderful voice that had ever reached his ears, a voice that was calling out *his* name.

"Come to Me, Benaiah," it said.

"I . . I need help. I am blind. I cannot make it by myself."

"Come to Me now . . ." the voice urged again without the slightest hint of impatience. "Do not delay. The Lord desires to make you whole."

Suddenly Benaiah found himself walking straight ahead without stumbling. He could hear people stepping aside to let him pass.

After the first few steps, he found himself walking more steadily, all fear gone, replaced by an eagerness to stand in front of the Nazarene.

A hand touched Benaiah's shoulder. He knew it was not someone from the throng.

"Look up . . . ," that same gentle voice said.

"But I cannot see. I—" he protested.

Fingers touched his eyes.

And then a strange thought rammed its way through Benaiah's mind.

My dear friend Abiathar died so suddenly. He left a family behind. How are they going to be able to survive without him?

He pulled away abruptly.

"Would you—?" Benaiah started to ask, then acknowledged the likelihood that he was guilty of the most insipid stupidity by throwing away an opportunity for sight.

But I loved Abiathar far more . . .

For that reason, Benaiah felt compelled to continue.

"I am willing to keep my blindness if you would give a friend back his life," he said, wondering if anyone from the multitude, hearing this, would shout the likely accusation of "Fool! Fool!" at him.

Perhaps I am just that . . . a fool, he wondered about himself. *Abiathar is beyond help, but here I am, desperate for one of the greatest of all gifts. How sight would change the rest of my life!*

"Your friend has been given what you ask," the Nazarene announced so abruptly that Benaiah did not grasp what He had said at first; he just stood without moving, as though nothing had been said.

"Go, young man," that magnificent voice told him. "Share in the joy of your friend's precious new life."

Benaiah had heard about the raising of Lazarus after three days in a tomb. And there had been other accounts of similar miracles. But he had found these much harder to believe than any of the others.

He turned away from Jesus, then realized he had offered no words of gratitude. He turned back to face Him again.

"Thank You, Jesus!" he said, any other words failing him.

"You and Abiathar will remain friends until one of you dies a final time, and beyond that, after the other is called out from this mortal life, you both will be reunited in My Father's kingdom," the Nazarene said. "This will happen because you were willing, in faith, to give up what you have coveted for so many years."

Jesus smiled, the most reassuring, comforting smile that anyone in the crowd had ever seen.

"Go to Abiathar," the Son of God added. "Let him and his fine family take you into their arms."

The man who had helped Benaiah moments ago came up to him.

"I will go with you," he volunteered.

"No, you came here for a reason. Stay. I shall make it back alone."

"I have heard and seen more than I ever thought would be possible. That is enough for now. Let me do this for you, young man."

Benaiah nodded, and the two walked back to the main gate in the huge wall Herod had built around Jerusalem.

"If He is right, your friend will have been brought back from death," the man reminded him. "Are you prepared for that? To have given up sight for the welfare of another?"

"I am prepared."

"He will have regained what he lost, but you will still be blind. Is that truly pleasing to you?"

Benaiah thought of the eighteen years he had spent at home: eating foods that had been prepared by skilled chefs, wearing finely crafted clothes made of expensive imported fabrics, taking baths in water scented with the finest oils, listening to poets and musicians and others who were paid generously to provide entertainment at well-attended banquets given by his parents, having no concern for the provision of any of his other needs, whatever these might have been.

Except sight.

A wealthy blind man could appreciate the music of a harp and the sound of tambourines, the sensuous feel of fine clothes. He could enjoy the delicious taste of all that exquisite food his parents provided, with its bewitching blend of sauces and spices—but he was denied what even the poorest of sighted beggars could enjoy every morning and every evening: beautiful Middle Eastern sunrises and sunsets.

Nor could he exchange glances with a woman as a prelude to falling in love with her. There was no possibility of taking a piece of wood, working with it, turning it into a finely carved work of art and immediately *seeing* the results of his talent, a privilege the lowest of woodcutters enjoyed.

I have never seen a reflection of myself in a stream, he thought. *I do not know what my father and my mother look like.*

But for Abiathar, life was much more important. Benaiah felt the edges of regret nipping at him, but he ignored them and filled his mind instead with what he knew would be the joy of hearing Abiathar call his name. He envisioned his friend's amazement as he described the miracle that had happened.

Nearly ten minutes later, they were approaching Abiathar's house.

A small group of people had gathered in front of it.

"Go inside!" one of them said. "We have already seen Abiathar. He is alive. He is well. And he is as crabby as ever, thank God!"

The man with Benaiah helped him up to the entrance. Benaiah stood quietly there for a moment, praying.

"I hope the one inside knows what you have sacrificed for him this day. I hope he appreciates—," the man started to say.

"Lord?" the angel asked, having suspected moments before that the Son of God planned something quite wonderful.

"Yes, Darien?" Jesus responded.

"Is it now that light comes into his darkness?"

"Light, yes, as though from heaven itself."

"I had no choice," Benaiah interrupted the one who had been so kind to him. "My friend's life for—"

He stopped talking, strange images flashing through his mind . . . light and shadow and faces and—

Suddenly Benaiah felt something happening inside his head that he had never felt before. He started to flail his arms out in front of him, as though trying to resist an unseen attacker.

"What's wrong with him?" a woman shouted excitedly.

The throng gasped collectively at the abrupt change, several of the men whispering to one another, wondering if some demon had entered Benaiah's body.

His behavior had become so bizarre that everyone started to back away from him, not sure of what was happening.

Just as quickly, he calmed down and hesitantly touched his eyes, which had been filled with sharp pain.

Then Benaiah reached out and touched the front door.

"What color is this?" he asked.

"Very dark brown," the other man told him.

Benaiah touched the frame around it.

"And this?"

"White," his benefactor replied.

"And those large shutters on either side of the window on the second floor?" Benaiah asked. "What color are those?"

"The same as the door, they—" the man replied, then nearly choked. "How did you know that they were there?"

Benaiah spun around on one heel.

"Your beard must be pure white, too, sir," he exclaimed with jubilation, "for it is the same color as this building."

Benaiah then pointed to another man, a taller, thinner one who was closest of all to him.

"You have a scar on your right cheek," he said. "It has been there for many years, for it has almost disappeared."

And to another.

"And you, sir . . . your eyes are bloodshot, probably from too little sleep over the past few days."

He pointed to the sky.

"I think those are clouds! Tell me, someone. *Are* they clouds?"

"They are, young man. They are," a woman called back to him.

Benaiah went on and on like that, pointing out a dog that was running past, a bird that flew by, a—

A voice called out to him, so familiar.

"Benaiah, you see!"

The eighteen-year-old turned around at the sound of it.

"Abiathar, you live!"

They hurried into one another's arms, kissing one another's cheeks and pounding each other's back.

"What a miracle!" Abiathar sobbed, having lost any control of his emotions despite the presence of dozens of people who were observing everything that happened.

"But yours is the greater one," contended Benaiah.

"But what *you* did was the greater act," his friend argued.

Benaiah had hoped his friend would never find out.

"What do you mean?" he ventured, hoping he sounded dumb enough to be convincing.

"Do not pretend, my dear Benaiah. Just before I opened my eyes, I saw a wondrous angel. He came to me and told me what you had done."

"That was good, yes, so very good," remarked Jesus.

"I did not know if You would approve," Darien answered.

"I could not do less, My guardian, My dear friend. You have made Me very proud of you this day."

Benaiah bowed his head.

"I wanted only your life," he said, his voice breaking.

"And I know that I gladly would have remained dead," Abiathar spoke honestly, the passion behind his words evident, "if it was to be that you, Benaiah, could be given such a wonderful gift."

Just then, Abiathar's wife and four children came outside, and the seven of them joined hands and offered up their praises to a holy and merciful Creator. As they did so, several from the watching multitude, now considerably larger than before, fell to their knees and prayed on their own, attesting to what had happened that day in their presence. Soon the whole of Jerusalem and for many miles beyond would hear of the wonder of it, the glory, and the joy.

CHAPTER 46

SURPRISINGLY, only a few were to have changed lives in addition to changed bodies . . .

Despite that encounter involving Abiathar and Benaiah, news of which spread rapidly, many who were healed took the reality of this miracle and did nothing to change the direction of their lives.

Darien knew how dangerous it was for people to act this way.

While confronting Satan in hell, he had seen the destiny of people who played with spiritual matters, with matters divine and holy. The opportunities they had for getting their lives on track were gone, only damnation replacing them.

His mind pummeled with despairing images, Darien trembled greatly as he asked, "*Will many lose their healing, Lord? Something wonderful happened with those two. But what about the others?*"

Jesus paused, thinking over the angel's question, and then said, "*Sin is separation from God. If they sin so grievously that My Father must chastise them, then any such miracle in their lives might be withdrawn.*"

Darien was distressed.

"*So foolish . . . ,*" he muttered.

"*Some are believers because they find themselves in danger of one sort or another, and they will seek the Father's protection accordingly. Some are believers in the hope that their pain, their sorrow, their poverty will be banished. Some get what they hope, then give back nothing in return.*"

"*They are using God, then?*"

"*They are, Darien; they are.*"

"*But how valid is their faith then?*"

"*It may be that their belief is sincere but their motives are faulty. My message is not that salvation comes if they believe only for the right reasons. A man who is dying of a disease cries out to God for mercy, in faith believing, and he is healed and will still enter the kingdom of heaven upon his death later. Nothing has changed there. Even a broken vessel can be used of My Father, whatever the motive might be."*

"But what of this *life, Lord?"*

"In that will be seen the difference," Jesus emphasized. *"In that will be seen also the condemnation of those who bring such souls to what seemed like salvation but who do it for the wrong reasons."*

Darien was puzzled.

"I know not what You mean," he admitted.

"For some, a cry of 'Lord, Lord' will be sincere, coming from the center of their souls. But with others, it will be only as deep, as substantial, as the miracle they have received in return. Once they have had their freedom from pain for a while, the memory of who bestowed it upon them will fade from their recollection. And their 'faith' will be seen for what it is, a means to an end, not the God who heard their prayer and answered it so graciously."

Jesus' body was trembling with righteous anger.

. . . the condemnation of those who bring such souls to what seemed like salvation but who do it for the wrong reasons.

He thought of the many hapless souls they were leading to a false belief that heaven was their future home.

"In the marketplace," He went on, *"a customer will buy what a merchant has to offer. He does not have to* know *that merchant. He simply offers his money and takes away what he has purchased."*

"I need more help, Lord," asked Darien, more obtuse than usual.

"Those who tell others to 'buy' healing by offering 'faith' as payment put the miraculous on the earthly level of any mundane business deal, nothing more. Once healing has been obtained, the 'faith' that bought it becomes a devalued currency. It has been spent. It is forgotten. It no longer matters."

The angel suddenly grasped the truth Jesus was expounding.

"Those others who are *redeemed will* be *redeemed because they have stopped to ask the merchant his name,"* Darien suggested, continuing the allegory, *"and have invited him into their home for dinner. Soon both are united by the common bond of being loyal and deep friends, one with the other."*

"The purchase has then led to a relationship that will last the rest of their lives," Jesus confirmed. *"But with the others, it ends the moment they have what they wanted, then they go on their way, never to return."*

"*How much longer will it go on, Lord?*" Darien asked, dreading what the Son's answer might be.

"*Many will turn their backs. Many will suddenly—*"

His physical form shook as a chill abruptly gripped him.

It was not that the Son of God was afraid, for there could never be fear in Him. But just as He was subject to temptations, so it was that Satan could fling against Him a sense of foreboding that would assault His finite nature without touching His incarnated divinity.

"*Is it to be soon, Lord?*" asked Darien.

Jesus had bowed His head.

"*So soon . . .*," He said, His voice trailing off.

In heaven, then, God wept, wept for the awful things that were to happen within the next week . . .

PART XI

God clothed Himself in man's vile flesh so that He might be weak enough to suffer woe.

JOHN DONNE
Holy Sonnets, XI

"LORD?"

"Yes, Darien?"

"It is so cold now."

Silence.

"I am not speaking of earthly temperatures. This is different."

"I know what you mean. Your spirit . . . you are referring to a chill across your very spirit."

"I have known that only once before."

"Amidst the flames of hell, Darien?"

"Yes . . . though there were flames, I felt even more this awful chill as well."

"The absence of hope . . . it comes with death when only damnation is ahead."

"But how is it that I feel this, Lord?"

"Because what you sense emanates from Me, Darien."

The angel's form shook.

"But, Lord, Lord, you are not damned!"

"Upon Me will be heaped the sins of the whole world. That is what you feel. The voices of millions upon millions of sinners crying out."

"I do not understand, Lord."

"Oh, you will . . . you will, my dear Darien . . ."

CHAPTER 47

THE VOICES *of millions upon millions of sinners crying out.*

Darien could not shake the impact of those words.

Jesus had delivered scores of sermons as short as a few minutes or going on for several hours over the past three years, all containing great theological truths; and He had, in the process, nearly always held spellbound anyone who would listen to Him with something other than a totally closed mind.

Unlike all human listeners of whatever age or sex or circumstance, Darien knew it was God's Son-in-the-Flesh who was talking, not just a young preacher walking dusty roads in one small Middle Eastern country; this made *everything* from His mouth carry a breath of eternity itself.

Remarkably, Jesus has brought together heaven and earth in a single flesh-and-blood body. The angel considered this overwhelming fact. *It is not something whose significance has faded with the passage of time, but, in fact, it grows ever more profound with each new hour, truly ever more blessed.*

The activity of the next day was to involve a triumphant emergence by Jesus from the countryside into the center of Jerusalem, while thousands of jubilant people gathered around Him, singing their adoring hosannas.

The attention of the entire nation will be upon Him, Darien told himself. *And many will be expecting the Nazarene, as some call Him, to announce His intention to free Israel from the yoke of Roman occupation.*

But that was not what the Son of God intended to do.

Many of those looking to Jesus would become permanently disappointed as a result, any interest they had almost certain to die soon thereafter, the old notion that He was a Roman stooge gaining new life as it spread through the populace, making it easier for the Sanhedrin to foment a backlash.

Freedom was exactly what Jesus came to give those who would accept Him, Darien thought as He stood, alone, atop the Mount of Olives, *freedom from enslavement to sin . . . from the damnation brought in by sin on leaden feet. What the crowds wanted was only temporal, but what He offered would last through time and eternity.*

There had seemed to be a great deal of hope in the beginning, a flood of enthusiasm, of zest for the cause to which they were devoting themselves.

They all were caught up in the joyous mood of healing.

None had ever experienced the emotions they felt as a myriad of illnesses and disabilities disappeared . . . as those made whole were taken from hopelessness to monumental rebirth.

It was almost as though Satan had been bound once again and could not harm them or deter them from any goal.

Peter was among those caught up in the stirring moments of obvious triumph over the forces of evil.

"You told us to resist the arch deceiver and he would flee from us," Peter remarked repeatedly. "We have done just that, Lord, and Satan leaves each time."

Even Thomas, normally so taciturn and always the one with endless questions in nearly every instance, was given to wild moments of abandon, jumping around with great exuberance, and shouting heartily.

Only John, the youngest, seemed at all subdued, which he had been ever since that encounter with the man possessed by multiple demons. Darien continued to worry about him, missing the energy this youngest of the men had shown at the beginning.

What goes on in your soul? the angel wondered sympathetically. *What visions enter your mind that you cannot discuss with anyone because you have to understand them yourself before you can tell anybody else what they are like?*

That Jesus felt especially close to John seemed obvious, but it was also clear that He cherished the relationship He had with each of the others. It was just that John, of all of them, was in the process of being groomed for a special responsibility that God Himself had planned, and Jesus seemed to be preparing him for that.

No jealousy over this surfaced among the others. Each man except Judas had come to realize that he had a separate destiny and that it was not in anyone's power to control what that would be.

. . . each man except Judas.

For most of the months of Jesus' ministry, Judas Iscariot seemed as happy as the other men in that little band. It was true that Peter, Andrew, and the rest were more outwardly jubilant, but none proved to be more dedicated. Among his assignments, Judas did special work with those poor who had no physical ailments but were close to starvation. At the end of the day, He took any food the apostles had left over and distributed it among the needy. This consistent work garnered for Judas a sizable following of his own, groups of people who would seek him out as the group traveled to various places throughout the land. There were occasions when beggars seemed reluctant to go to any other apostle.

Judas had not been given any power to heal, but he became associated with the dispensing of food as well as clothing that had been donated, and such essentials made him a magnet for the needy. As a result, sometimes the crowd waiting for Judas was a bit larger than the one that had gathered to hear the Son of God or be touched by Him.

The man has seemed happy, devoted, as eager to sacrifice for the good news as anyone, Darien thought as that final week was beginning. *And yet, now, Jesus is acting so very differently toward Judas. I must go to the Lord soon and find out what is wrong so I can be prepared for what is ahead.*

But Jesus indicated He was unwilling to talk about the matter, so Darien chose not to raise it again, thinking he had misread everything, which was not unusual for him. Instead, the angel contented himself with enjoying those many good moments, moments he hoped would continue on for a long time to come.

Pockets of opposition did arise.

The Pharisees and Sadducees along with most of the veteran scribes became aroused, since they saw their once unimpeachable status being threatened by someone they thought of as mere riffraff, though He was proving clever enough to deceive a growing percentage of the masses. After a long period of not knowing exactly what to think about the Nazarene, these self-centered leaders stumbled into a kind of collective antagonism that grew like a dangerous plague, warping their every action so that no rationality or fairness—and certainly no open-mindedness—could possibly survive.

Despite this backdrop, mighty spiritual victories flowed daily for the members of that first small group of Christians as they continued in their mission, and these victories were so invigorating that even the sporadic but often venomous public censure they endured had the effect not of discouraging them but of spurring them onward, propelled as though by a patriotic call to arms, with the enemy of their souls to be faced without hesitation, falsehood retreating before the onrush of divinely inspired truth.

Upon Me will be heaped the sins of the whole world. That is what you feel. The voices of millions upon millions of sinners crying out.

From the moment Jesus uttered those words, Darien knew nothing would continue as it had been.

I never saw You quite so sad before, the angel realized. *You had a crusade that You knew was a direct command from almighty God, and You were determined to carry it to wherever legs or donkeys or ships would take You. There was no sense of despair. You seemed only to feel excitement, as did the apostles, as did—*

Darien realized then that this melancholy he sensed within the Son of God was becoming his own as well, except that he did not know the reason for it.

CHAPTER 48

NOW WHEN they drew near Jerusalem, to Bethphage and Bethany, at the mount of Olives, He sent two of His disciples; and He said to them, "Go into the village opposite you; and as soon as you have entered it you will find a colt tied, on which no one has sat. Loose it and bring it. And if any man says to you, 'Why are you doing this?' say, 'The Lord hath need of it.'"

Darien was directed to accompany John and Thomas in the task Jesus had assigned them. The angel noticed that every man, woman, and child he passed seemed to know that something remarkable was going to happen that day.

Excitement . . .

He could see their excited expressions, hear their emotional whispers, all of which showed that God already must have sent other heaven-based messengers to stir the hearts and the souls of the people.

On the way, Darien met fellow angel Stedfast. A long time had passed since their last meeting.

"How has it been for you?" Darien asked.

"I have spent much time with Mary and Joseph," Stedfast acknowledged, *"and can say that they miss Jesus very much. But, then, they also know that He must be about His inspired mission, and they must learn to sacrifice the physical closeness with Him they once enjoyed so completely.*

"But it has been good that Jesus' several brothers continue to stay with their parents. They are a source of companionship that helps to alleviate some of the apprehension and loneliness."

Darien would have liked to spend far more time with the earthly parents of Jesus, especially since Joseph had become quite ill over the past several weeks and there was some real uncertainty whether he would make it to Jerusalem. But Darien's assignment was not with them.

"I sense something cold and dark ahead," Stedfast spoke suddenly.

The chill of a howling winter wind across the bleakness of a pauper's graveyard, kicking up suddenly, fiercely.

"*As I do,*" Darien agreed. "*Something Jesus said seems to suggest this.*"

"'*The voices of millions of sinners crying out. . . .' Is that what you mean?*" asked Stedfast intuitively.

"*Yes! How did you know?*"

"*Jesus' agony at that moment came from the very center of Himself.*"

Stedfast's entire countenance shook.

"*It was heard in heaven, Darien!*" he said again with great emotion. "*We, like you, cannot simply cast aside such words, for what the Lord said continues to hang like a funeral shroud over us, though we have been completely successful in keeping how we feel from the numbers of precious human souls who have been ascending to heaven since the days Noah and his family found solid ground again.*

"*After all, they were promised freedom from that which nevertheless continues to assault you and me and our unfallen comrades, and we could not disappoint them, no matter how badly we ourselves have felt!*"

"*Has God said anything about what lies ahead?*" inquired Darien, torn between his commitment to be at the side of Jesus during the period of incarnation and his yearning to return to heaven more often.

I hunger to be with Him, and I hunger for my home, he thought. *Earth can never be home for me. It is only a temporary place for both of us.*

"*Nothing, my comrade,*" Stedfast assured him. "*But there are some hints in the many parchments.*"

"*I know.*"

Truly Darien did know.

He would slip away now and then to the huge temple at Jerusalem and watch the cadre of scribes conduct their daily examinations of the many different scrolls stored away from centuries before. Much of the time, they read the prophesies of Ezekiel, Daniel, Isaiah, and others that were lesser known.

What are you searching for? What drives you there each day in a quest that seems to have gone on for most of your daily lives? Darien asked himself as he remembered the last of those visits, and then instantly he answered his own question. *The Messiah, of course. That is what you crave, is it not? Some new understanding of any ancient clues, buried in the temple's archives, that will point you more clearly to the moment of His coming.*

The scribes had no other reason for living. The seeking of knowledge, the finding of it, was what sustained them all, from the younger ones bursting with expectation to those who were the oldest.

Most of the men had chosen to remain unmarried and celibate, and they lived as near to the temple as they could, so they could get to it quickly whenever bursts of insight would hit them, which sometimes happened in the middle of the night as words gleamed from the parchments stayed deep within their minds, acting very much like mental signposts on a theological road.

The scribes always walked as fast as they could since this was part of a longstanding custom that publicly expressed their eagerness to get to the temple and start whatever they intended, which was always of a religious nature, be it meditation, study, debate, or whatever else. Devout Sabbath worshipers approached the religious part of their lives with much the same seriousness, entire families scurrying from their homes to the temple at Jerusalem or to a synagogue in the village where they lived.

So close to the truth, Darien thought about the dedicated scribes. *What the prophets wrote so long ago was inspired by your heavenly Father. It is waiting there for you. But once you have found it, will you know what you have at your fingertips, or will you have searched so long and hard that it will pass right by you and be lost as you keep on, more and more aimlessly, not realizing what that truth is?*

The angel recalled that extraordinary time when he had overheard two temple scribes talking.

"He will surely come soon," the shorter, older one had mused.

"But how can you say that?" the younger, stockier scribe countered. "How often in the past have we hoped for exactly the same answer to our questions, only to be disappointed? Many times, Aaron. You know that as well as I do!"

With a touch of resentment, the scribe named Aaron had replied, "Some say the Nazarene is really—"

The other man shot him an expression of icy anger mixed with contempt.

"Surely you have not fallen for common gossip?" he snorted, interrupting.

"There are some similarities," Aaron told him. "I would be stupid if I did not admit this."

"Name one."

"His ability to perform miracles."

"Charades, clever little frauds perpetrated—"

It was Aaron's turn to interrupt.

"Not so!" he declared with equal anger. "Benjamin, I have seen some of the healings myself. I am not as easily deluded as you seem to think. Here is an example: Hopeless and twisted lepers, their wretched bodies transformed in an instant. There is no delusion in these instances with what I saw. I did not succumb to the hysteria of a crowd. You know me to be far more level-headed than that."

Benjamin was prepared to fling back a retort when he hesitated.

"Lepers, Aaron?" he asked instead.

"The sores disappeared even as I watched. The missing fingers were restored—crippled, misshapen toes made normal. There was no imagination involved. What took place was visible and quite real, dear friend."

Benjamin blushed.

"You anticipated me," he said, smiling slightly.

"I have known you long enough to be able to do that. But what about the blind? It is quite easy, you know, for some to fake something like blindness or deafness or anything of that order."

"Under ordinary circumstances, I would agree with you completely, my dear Benjamin, but I must tell you that two of those healed and given back their sight happen to be long-time acquaintances of mine. I *know* them to have been blind for many, many years . . . and yet, now they see.

"Furthermore, I have recently sat with them both as they were overwhelmed by the beauty of seeing a meadow filled from edge to edge with the most colorful of flowers. Can you imagine how these men reacted to a sunrise, a sunset, to seeing stars in a night sky? Neither could find words, Benjamin."

Aaron smiled reassuringly.

"Besides, these are men of principle," he added, "men who would not have allowed themselves to be drawn into anything like what you are suggesting."

Benjamin hesitated, still torn between his respect for the other man and his own cynicism.

"If you are so certain about this Jesus of Nazareth, what is it you continue to search for here, in this old place?" asked Benjamin as he indicated their surroundings with a nod of his head. "If you have found so much, as you have claimed, what more could there possibly be to unearth?"

"What I see with my eyes is not the entire answer," Aaron answered. "What I *know* with my very soul is what I need."

"So you are still skeptical, I gather. After all your protestations just now, that is what it boils down to, correct?"

"I want to be sure."

"And then what will you do?"

"Approach Caiaphas and the others. Tell him what I think. Tell him that if the Nazarene is our Messiah, finally come to us, then there is no choice but to offer the fullest protection. The Romans cannot be permitted to get their hands on Jesus. To step aside and let this happen would be an offense flung in the face of Jehovah Himself!"

CHAPTER 49

THERE ARE some hints in the old parchments.

Darien's thoughts returned to the present, for much time had passed since he had overheard the two men.

He told Stedfast about his recollection.

"I know the two you mean," he said. *"Soon the one who was open to divine truth will no longer serve as a scribe. The other will continue to be."*

Darien found that disturbing, though he was not particularly surprised in view of what he knew about the other men who must have been involved, men so enslaved by the manmade rules of previous generations of their kind that they could not avoid adding yet more of their own to an already burdensome stack.

"Why?"

"His departure will come because he has urged the others to recognize Jesus for what He is."

Darien was pleased to learn of this. He had been hoping that Aaron's search was not a fruitless one.

"So his search led him to the truth."

Stedfast nodded.

"That it did," he announced. *"The Sanhedrin could not tolerate this."*

"How long does he have before they banish him forever from the temple library and vaults again?" Darien asked.

"Perhaps only a week or two, possibly less. His detractors are still conducting meetings to decide. There is a split. Some, including Nicodaemus, have been against any action and are trying to get Caiaphas to relent and let Aaron stay on."

"Where is Aaron now? Is he at the temple?"

"No, he is on his usual midday break," Stedfast replied. *"When this occurs, he usually returns to his home to meditate, or else he walks to the Garden of Gethsemane and kneels in prayer."*

"Why that particular place?"

"Aaron has never told anyone. It is apparently something so private he can do nothing but keep it to himself."

"The Lord wants me to stay with John and Thomas, but I admit I would like to go to Aaron for a little while. What am I to do?"

"You should not delay," encouraged Stedfast. *"Go ahead."*

"But—"

"It is fine. That is why He sent you with them, Darien."

"Because He knew I would come upon you here, and Gethsemane is only a short distance ahead? Is that it?"

Stedfast smiled.

"That is why," the angel confirmed. *"It must be something our dear heavenly Father feels you* should do."

"But what is of such great importance about Gethsemane?"

"Find out, Darien . . . find out for yourself but without so many questions."

Darien knew he deserved this gentle rebuke.

"My comrade?" Stedfast asked.

"Yes . . . ," Darien answered.

"I love you in the Lord."

After Stedfast had left and Darien was headed toward Gethsemane, he thought of that sudden expression of love by his comrade, a love of purity and spirituality and eternity.

If I, as an angel, could die, Darien thought, *I would die for you, for the others. If I could die for my Lord, I would do that gladly. But I cannot. I must go on for eternity unable to sacrifice what others have done for their faith.*

He was at the entrance to tiny Gethsemane now, at the base of the Mount of Olives. Already he could hear a plaintive voice crying out from within.

"Oh, God!" it said. "Please help me out of this misery!"

Darien hurried inside. He saw Aaron prostrate on the ground.

"Father, Father! I tried to tell the others, to warn them; but they would not listen," he was saying. "They pay no heed to the holy Word of God they have guarded for so long. They tell me to leave."

Aaron stood and glanced sadly at the garden.

"Your Son will come here, will He not?" Aaron asked, looking up at the midday sky, which was clear of clouds that day. "Perhaps it will not be now or tomorrow, but sometime soon, I suspect. He will be much like I was a moment ago, torn with deep sorrow while in humble prayer with You. I felt

His Spirit for a moment, and then it was gone. And there was also the sudden rush of evil."

The scribe stood.

. . . the sudden rush of evil.

"What did you mean by that?" Darien asked, though the man could not hear him. *"What did you discover those past few days before the others forced you out of that tight little group of theirs?"*

The angel saw Aaron wrap his robe more tightly around himself though there was no wind or cold that bright, warm day; still, he looked pale as the flesh of his well-protected body nevertheless shivered with an unnerving suddenness.

Then he headed straight for the center of Jerusalem, which had far fewer customers than usual because everyone had headed toward the main gate to see Jesus come through it and declare His messiahship.

He saw a merchant who was complaining about the dropoff in business, and though he was slighter than the burly leather craftsman, Aaron was intimidating in his rage.

"Do you not *care?*" he shouted. "The Messiah is coming! He may even now be among us. How can you go on as though things are the way they always have been?"

"You sound like one of those fanatics who have created such a stir that even reasonable people have joined them in this business this afternoon."

"What business?" Aaron demanded.

"Oh, that Nazarene!" the other man told him.

"I still do not know what you are saying."

"That carpenter's son, you know, who claims to be the Son of God. Maybe He's the one you ramble on about."

He had heard about the Nazarene over the past three years but paid little notice, too busy with his work to let his concentration be distracted by such seemingly inconsequential matters, though several of the other scribes were more attuned to the "Jesus matter," as some of them spoke of it.

"Where is He supposed to be?" he asked.

"Coming in from the countryside, I hear," the merchant grumbled. "This is bad, I am afraid. It may provoke the Romans. And it certainly gets under the skin of those priests with the Sanhedrin."

"The main gate? Is that where He will enter?" Aaron pressed. "Do you have any idea if that is it?"

"I think you have guessed right. Now let me be. One of my few customers today is heading in this direction."

Aaron apologized and hurried up one of the streets that led in the direction of the main gate. The closer he got, the greater the number of people he saw waiting and talking with elaborate gestures.

"It must be soon!" One of the men exclaimed. "I think this Nazarene is the One we have been seeking."

Aaron thought he would not come upon any people he knew for he had few friends since his intense pursuit of truth tended to isolate him and erode any social skills he might have had

But he saw one individual who made him stop in puzzlement.

He seems familiar, Aaron thought. *But I do not know where or*

Then it hit him.

Just the week before . . . quickly glimpsed . . . furtively meeting with Caiaphas and the others.

There had been some kind of transaction going on between them, money being offered then rejected, and then Caiaphas called sarcastically after the man, "Where are your principles now, Judas? We know you held out only for more than twenty pieces of silver. Is not twenty enough to buy your loyalty away from the Nazarene? *You say you want thirty?*"

Judas was standing with a large, burly man who was several inches taller than he and nearly as much wider. And with them were others, all conversing among themselves as they waited.

The street! It had been overlain with the branches of palm trees. And several men and women were on their knees, praying.

Then the man on a donkey came into view.

Aaron had been surveying the throng, trying to see what types of people would join together to make such a commotion, the noise of it multiplied a hundred times the moment the Nazarene came into view.

The scribe's gaze settled on the Man's eyes.

So peaceful! he thought. *In the midst of all this din, the Nazarene seems utterly calm. How can that be?*

"Hosanna!" people cried. "Blessed is He who comes in the name of the Lord. Blessed be the kingdom of our father David. . . . Hosanna to almighty God in the highest."

Aaron also noticed certain members of the Sanhedrin standing to one side, looking angry and disgusted. One of them glanced over at Judas, who reacted in an embarrassed manner and turned away.

The Son of God shall be wounded for our transgressions. He shall take upon Himself our iniquities . . .

Those ancient words came to the scribe's mind along with others that spoke of betrayal and death.

Jesus turned in his direction.

Those eyes!

Aaron tried to look away but could not.

The Nazarene, on the back of the donkey, passed directly in front of where he was standing.

"I want to come and sit at Your feet and listen to whatever You might say," Aaron shouted to Him, not expecting to be heard despite that instant of close proximity, but wanting desperately to try.

And yet the Nazarene seemed to understand because He nodded, not to the crowd, nor to anyone on either side of the scribe, but at *him!*

His short, thin body shuddering from head to foot, Aaron fell to his knees, banging both of them painfully on the uneven surface of Jerusalem's ancient cobblestone street while scores of men, women, and children abruptly scrambled away from him. They did not have the slightest idea what had caused such strange and alarming behavior to overtake this stranger; he had the look of a scribe, perhaps, but none of those present had seen him before that moment, for he had been accustomed to inhabiting a narrow and confined world of his own making, seldom venturing beyond it. He had been content instead to stay within its boundaries and search, sleep, and eat, search, sleep, and eat, with no more to his existence than that regimen. A substantial bond of sorts had developed over the many years of his service, a bond between him and the oldest of writings on the oldest of parchments. Other scribes before him had read the very same words and yet had not fully comprehended their meaning, a certain intellectual and spiritual denseness suffocating them, but he was not deterred by such a history of failure. He got up in the morning as always, hurrying to the temple a short distance away, reading hour by hour, analyzing every word, line, verse, and book until well past sunset many of those days, even through to the midnight hour on occasion, hoping to discover what had eluded other men like himself, causing them simply to give up, and leave, forsaking their self-imposed mission. But he remained, determined not to have the truth run through his fingers like fine white sand at the edge of the Mediterranean, to be gathered up by its persistent tides and taken away, claimed forever by its depths.

This truth, this glorious truth, cannot have that same fate, Aaron declared to himself. *It must not be seen only by men too blind to its reality to understand what it was that they have had in their possession for so long.*

He stood, reaching out to the Nazarene who was nearly past.

"I know who You are!" he shouted. "I know You are not what others expect. Oh, Lord, Lord, I know that You are God-in-the-flesh!"

Jesus stopped the donkey and sat still, looking at Aaron, then reached out His right hand toward the scribe.

Suddenly the crowd was hushed as though struck dumb in an instant, wondering what there was about this little man that seemed to be capturing the attention of the Nazarene.

Aaron walked forward slowly, his heart beating so rapidly he seemed on the verge of an attack, perspiration all over his body; he stood beside the donkey, looking up into the Son of God's face.

"I know so much more now," the scribe gasped, "and yet I feel so very unworthy of You, Lord."

Bending over, Jesus whispered to the scribe, "Blessed are you this day because of your faith."

"I know what is going to happen," Aaron went on, his own voice low as well, unheard by anyone else. "I weep for You, Jesus."

"Read further through the prophecies and other writings, good scribe. Pray more fervently. Rejoice at what is to come after."

Aaron nodded, a sad, wistful smile creasing his pale, drawn cheeks that had become wet with tears.

"Good-bye . . . ," he said. "Good-bye, my Savior."

Then the donkey moved on, the throng resumed its clamor, and the scribe returned to the temple as quickly as the mass of bodies would allow to look with special eagerness for the last fragments of what was "to come after."

CHAPTER 50

Later *in the week, after the majesty of that Sunday and the adulation of the crowd . . .*

Darien could not predict the future, for he did not know what was in the mind of Christ. And yet because of his extraordinary closeness to both the human self and the divine self of Jesus, he was being blessed with a sensitivity that mere men and women did not have. Interestingly, though, children possessed some of sensitivity until it was squeezed out of them later in life, and so did animals.

You have a bond with both, Darien thought as he went with Jesus and the apostles to a room above a merchant's shop in the center of Jerusalem. *No creature has ever run from you. No child has ever turned away.*

But how many adult men and women had done so? How many had allowed their maturity to dissuade them from following Him?

The wisdom of God is as foolishness to men, the angel repeated to himself. *But for the little ones and the beasts, that makes no difference. They come to Him with such—*

As the group walked up a narrow street, four of the many scraggly dogs that roamed the city approached Jesus, then abruptly stopped and sat down, looking at Him.

"Again!" Matthew exclaimed, though he was no longer as astonished as when such encounters had first occurred. "The animals!"

The Son of God walked up to the dogs and knelt in front of them, patting each one with gentle love on the head; then He called over His shoulder to the apostles, "Have we any food to spare?"

Peter replied, "We might have a little left after setting aside what we will need for supper."

"Then please feed these poor creatures," Jesus told him.

Peter got some bread and approached the dogs cautiously. At first the four snarled at him; then Jesus spoke reassuringly, and they calmed down. The bread was spread out before them, and as Jesus and the fisherman stepped back, the dogs started frantically consuming the few pieces, little enough food but badly needed even so.

"Why do You feel as strongly as You do about such mere animals?" Andrew asked, deeply curious.

Jesus pointed to the four dogs.

"Look at them, Andrew. How much like unsaved mankind these creatures are, wandering from place to place, with nothing to anchor their lives. They grab what they can, then go on to another spot. They are lost and lonely. They experience little or no genuine love. And they are without hope."

Jesus closed His eyes and frowned, a throbbing in His temple strong enough to make the veins show.

"There is more, is there not?" inquired John, knowing the Lord's ways so well.

"Oh, yes, yes, there will be more, John, but many years from now. Then terrible tortures will be inflicted on dogs and cats and other animals."

None of the apostles pursued this matter because they saw how saddened Jesus was, His foreknowledge giving Him visions of a future that not one of them could guess; but they could gleam from His mannerisms the wrenching sorrow He felt.

How You hold Your head, Lord, the tone of Your voice, the way You walk now, Darien thought. *These loyal ones can tell a great deal even if there had been no words.*

The Son of God spoke to him then: *"Loyal, yes, eleven of them will remain loyal in the long run, though Simon Peter will soon deny Me thrice."*

Darien knew that Jesus was never capable of exaggeration or any kind of falsehood or deception, that these acts were of darkness, and He was Light and had no fellowship with any of that. So it was obvious that what He had just said could be nothing other than true.

. . . Peter will soon deny Me thrice.

Then the angel realized that something else had been revealed by Jesus.

"You said eleven will remain loyal. One will not, Lord?" Darien asked.

Jesus paused, seeing bitter images.

"Judas is going to betray Me this very night . . ."

Judas!

Darien was hardly able to cope with that revelation. Judas, who had always seemed capable of so much that was kindhearted and generous—devout-seeming Judas was set *to betray the Son of God!*

Finally the thirteen of them walked up a few steps to a room over the merchant's leather business and gathered around a long table. The apostles laid out bread and wineskins and brought out a silver, hand-tooled chalice that had been given to them by a wealthy benefactor from Caesara.

"We should sell this," Thomas suggested as he held it in both hands. "The proceeds could be given to the poor."

"That can come later," Jesus admonished him. "The poor you will always have with you, but I shall not tarry here much longer. And we have need of the chalice now."

Darien shot a glance at Judas, whose forehead and cheeks were covered with beads of perspiration.

"What are you about?" the angel asked. *"What has driven you to—?*

Then he turned and looked at the other men around.

None of them seemed to notice the serious expression on the Master's handsome face, or the slow, deliberate way He talked, as though He were overseeing a funeral instead of some evening fellowship with comrades, men who had devoted every moment of their lives to Him for more than three years.

The Passover meal began with its usual solemnity but also with a sense of community because it was a traditional event followed by Jewish family members and friends for many centuries. Judas became increasingly restless as the time passed, though his behavior seemed to go unnoticed by all present except Jesus Himself.

The Son of God glanced at the apostle knowingly, and Judas had to avert his own gaze, unable to look intently at the One whom he was soon to betray.

Perhaps an hour later, the main part of the meal having been consumed, Jesus rose from the table and laid aside His garments; then He took a towel and wrapped it around Himself. He found an earthen basin and filled it with water from a nearby jug, and silently He began to wash the apostles' feet.

Judas became so restless he could no longer control himself, and he left. The others were not certain why he left, but Jesus knew, and so did Darien.

When He came to Peter, the fisherman immediately spoke in a quarrelsome tone. "Lord, why do You kneel before us as You do and wash our feet? This is the act of a servant and not You, our Master."

Jesus looked up at him and said, "What I do now, you cannot fully know, Simon. But there will be a day when it is all very clear, and you will weep because you questioned this very act."

Peter replied, "You shall never wash my feet, Lord."

To which Jesus answered, "If I do not wash you, you have no part with Me."

Peter, seeing the expression on His face, was struck with embarrassment and wanted very much to make amends; so he added, "Then, Lord, not my feet only, but also my hands and my head."

"He who is bathed all over needs only to wash his feet to be entirely clean," Jesus told him. "Now, Peter, you are clean. But that is not the truth regarding everyone here in this room this night.

After He had finished washing the feet of the apostles, He had sat again at the table and started to address them all. "Know you what I have done just now? You call Me Master and Lord: and you say well; for so I am.

"If I, then, your Lord and Teacher, have washed your feet, you also ought to wash one another's feet. For I have given you an example, that you should do as I have done to you. Most assuredly, I say to you, a servant is not greater than his master; nor is he who is sent greater than he who sent him."

Jesus looked at them with such love that Peter and Andrew and John and others were moved to tears. Then He concluded the supper by taking the unleavened bread, blessing it, breaking it into pieces, and in a short while, giving each of the men a portion.

"Take, eat: for this is My body," He told them.

When they finished eating the bread, Jesus took the cup, which had been filled with wine, and after He had given thanks for it, passed it to each man, and they all drank from the chalice. This itself was a break in the normal custom of those days since cups of any kind usually were not shared. But Jesus was doing it this way to signify all that they would be partaking of during the rest of their lives.

"This is My blood of the new covenant," He said solemnly, "blood that is to be shed for the redemption of many."

His blood shed for the redemption of many!

Darien shuddered at the dark and terrible feeling that assaulted him after Jesus had spoken those words, but he recognized this as part of the developing pattern of the past few weeks, hints of what was to come given to men and angels alike.

Jesus looked at each of the men and He sighed deeply.

"All of you will desert Me this night," He started to say.

A clamor arose from them all, but Jesus, His expression stern, held up His hand to silence them.

"For it is written," He continued, "God will strike the Shepherd, and the sheep of the flock will be scattered. But after I have been raised, I will go before you to Galilee."

As the next few minutes passed, they all sensed that something profoundly climactic was about to happen, and they began to argue among themselves as to which of them should be accounted the greatest when Jesus established His kingdom.

"In this world the kings and great men order their slaves around," He told them, "and the slaves have no choice but to endure it. But, among you, the one who serves you best will be your leader. Out in the world the master sits at the table and is served by his servants. But not here, My beloved! For I am He who is your servant. I, here and now, grant you the right to eat and drink at My table in My Father's kingdom, and you will sit on thrones judging the twelve tribes of Israel."

Then He added, "Verily, I say unto you, 'He who receives you receives Me, and he who receives Me receives Him who sent Me.'"

A few minutes passed as they all sat quietly, contemplating those profound words.

Finally Jesus spoke again, telling them, "The glorification of the Son of Man is at hand. Little children, I shall be with you a little while longer. You will seek Me; and as I said to the Jews, 'Where I am going, you cannot come,' so now I say to you. A new commandment I give to you, that you love one another; as I have loved you, that you also love one another."

He paused, closing His eyes briefly, and then opened them wide.

"By this all will know that you are My disciples," He added, "if you have love for one another,"

He spoke to them all about many other matters during the short time remaining. As He was apparently concluding, several of the apostles wondered among themselves what Jesus had meant earlier when He told them He would not be with them much longer.

Overhearing this murmuring, He said, "Are you inquiring among yourselves about what I said? . . . Most assuredly, I say to you that you will weep and lament, but the world will rejoice; and you will be sorrowful, but your sorrow will be turned into joy.

"A woman, when she is in labor, has sorrow because her hour has come; but as soon as she has given birth to the child, she no longer remembers the anguish, for joy that a human being has been born into the world.

"You now have sorrow; but I will see you again and your heart will rejoice, and your joy no one will take from you. . . .

"These things I have spoken unto you in figurative language; but the time is coming when I will no longer speak to you in figurative language, but I will tell you plainly about the Father."

He smiled, and they felt the beauty of His presence more than ever.

"The Father Himself loves you, because you have loved Me, and have believed that I came forth from God. Yes, I came forth from the Father, and have come into the world. Again, I leave the world and go to the Father.

"Behold the hour is coming, yes, has now come, that you will be scattered, every to his own, and will leave Me alone. And yet I am not alone, because the Father and His angels are with Me.

"These things I have spoken to you, that in Me you may have peace. In the world you will have tribulation: but be of good cheer, for I have overcome the world."

After He had prayed fervently, lifting up His eyes toward heaven, they all sang a hymn, then left that upper room to head first east, then north out of Jerusalem to the Mount of Olives and to Gethsemane at its base.

It was a journey Darien had taken before with them. The Garden of Gethsemane was a quiet place Jesus favored, where He could be alone if He wished and give Himself over to whatever contemplation He needed at the time.

But now it is so different, Darien thought. *This night's darkness seems so much deeper, and I hear—*

Demons.

He knew they were not *always* present. They did not *have* to be everywhere, for human nature was capable of much evil on its own.

"Lord . . ." Darien spoke directly to the incarnate Deity. *"Do You hear—?"*

"Yes, I hear them," Jesus replied.

He saw men huddling furtively in dark corners, thinking they were alone, thinking no one could overhear them talking about clandestine meetings with high priest Caiaphas and other members of the Sanhedrin, talking about a plot, talking about—

The death of the Nazarene!

Darien left the side of Jesus just long enough to listen with great intentness to the common men being deluded by religious leaders who should have been steering them toward the shining truth of almighty God, but instead were detouring them along a path constructed entirely by their own vanity and an overpowering fear of being toppled from the pedestals of respect and power they had been clinging to for a long time.

"We are supposed to show support for Caiaphas and the Sanhedrin when the time comes for the mob to react," one man was saying.

"And what do we get in return?" another asked.

"A day's wage. Judas received more, but I can understand why."

"Judas? One of those men so devoted to the Nazarene? They got to him?"

"And he will be giving this Jesus a kiss tonight, a kiss of death."

"How could you know this?"

"Some of my wife's family members are related to Caiaphas. He can hardly wait to bury Jesus."

"Do you realize what you are saying?" Darien instinctively cried out to them, but the veil between the finite and the infinite continued to be in place, and they heard nothing from him, continuing on with their shameful talk.

Another truth grabbed the angel.

If I am aware of this, then Jesus Himself must be as well. How much my holy Lord needs me! This is surely why God, through His foreknowledge, asked me to be at the side of His only begotten Son.

Darien hurried on to Gethsemane.

By the time the angel arrived, Jesus had separated Himself from the apostles, eight of them asleep some distance away, and three—Peter, James, and John—much closer but also asleep. He was on His knees, sobbing, not from weakness but from sorrow over how badly mankind needed a Savior.

"My eyes have seen the sins of the world, Father," He was saying when Darien came upon Him, "so I know there is no other way."

He was aware that Darien was present.

"You have heard them say what is to be?" Jesus asked through His spirit so no one could overhear them.

"I have, Lord," Darien confirmed.

"This body of flesh feels so cold now."

Darien had no ability to feel sensations produced by natural sources, the heat of hell—yes, but not the chill of that evening in Gethsemane.

"What can I do to help, precious One?" the angel asked.

The physical Jesus shook His head.

"Nothing, dear guardian . . . ," He replied.

"But I have a shining sword with me, Lord," Darien reminded Him. *"I can do what must be done, and if there is too much for one angel, I can have many others come to this place and stand with me."*

Shoulders slumping, Jesus sighed, though not with exasperation.

"I feel the despair of the damned," Jesus added. *"I feel the punishment of their sins. And it will become worse, Darien, My body bearing all this as—"*

He looked up at the angel through His spiritual sight.

"You know it all?" He asked, understanding the answer before it was spoken.

"That men want you dead, Lord. I do know that."

"But you know so little then, my dear, dear friend."

At that, Jesus fell prostrate.

"Abba, Father!" He cried out through His physical form, *"all things are possible for You; I beg You, take away this awful cup from Me. Nevertheless, not as I will, but as You will, Father."*

Despite the cold, Jesus was beginning to sweat what looked like drops of blood from His forehead.

"Lord, you are—!" Darien said, panicking.

"It is more than what it looks, more than blood," Jesus said. *"My body is suddenly contaminated, Darien. What you see is filth, all those poisons I have not had until now, that My physical form was able to avoid because of the Father's protection but are now rushing in and cannot be stopped."*

"Sin is the basis of all disease, Lord? Is that what You mean?"

"No, but some diseases, yes, some illnesses are the result of sin. If I were not to give up My life tomorrow, I still would die soon after, with pain in every muscle, every nerve."

"Lord, You will surely not die as You have said. The Father sent Me to act as Your guardian. Nor am I alone in this. Gabriel, Michael, Stedfast,

and ten thousand others are waiting, I know this, as You must also. All that needs be done is for me to call out for them, and they will rend the veil, Lord. They—"

Jesus stood abruptly, not responding to the angel. He walked the short distance to where He had left the three apostles.

Asleep.

With a sad tone showing His disappointment, but with no harshness on His part, Jesus awakened them by addressing Peter. "What! Could you not watch with Me just one hour?"

Peter, James, and John were embarrassed by this, and all three meekly promised to stay awake.

"Watch and pray, lest you enter into temptation," Jesus told them. "The spirit indeed is willing, but the flesh is weak."

The Son of God went away a little distance for a second time and prayed as He had done before, begging the Father to take the coming cup of suffering away so He would not have to sip from it.

"I taste it," He said, *"and know that the bitterness on My tongue comes from the blood of Your many saints through the end of time, those who died because of the sins of men who strove against them."*

Jesus prayed for a number of minutes longer, His body convulsing on the ground.

Lord, if I could only reach out and touch Your body, Darien thought, *and heal it as You have done with so many.*

As Darien realized he could do nothing for Jesus physically, a feeling of helplessness started growing rapidly within him.

Then Jesus stood, slowly, as though even this modest movement were accomplished with difficulty, and went back to Peter, James, and John.

"My friends, my dear friends," He lamented, not awakening them this time. "The hour is at hand, and the Son of Man is being betrayed into the hands of sinners, and yet you cannot do for Me as I have asked."

Again Jesus returned to His previous spot and continued to pray, this time doubled over, moans escaping His lips.

"I see before Me the mottled faces of men crying out for relief, Father, for salvation, and I know that I must do what You have decreed to be the course laid out now, or there is henceforth no hope for sinners.

"I act as I do, filled with anguish, with pain throughout this human shell, because men have chosen to act as they have done, from Eden onward to the

flood . . . and beyond. Rather, it is My assumption of their depravity that sends its poison throughout this now ravaged body."

Darien knew Jesus was not saying that He had become as these others, ready to commit any of their own individual sins, but that the *penalty* of those sins was being poured into His finite self.

"I take it all upon Myself, heavenly Father," the Son of God continued, *"so that when I hang from that dreadful tree, You will have to look down upon Me with disgust and turn away because You have seen in this one body of mine all the sins of which mankind has ever been guilty."*

Then He returned to the three apostles for the final time.

Such pain in Your humanness, Lord, Darien thought. *You give deeply of Yourself, and yet they return so little now before the storm breaks.*

The angel spoke to the Son of God, not in His physical incarnation but in the form that was His divine Spirit.

"Let me act now!" Darien begged. *"They can be stopped. Not all the might of Rome can prevail against You if You allow me to do what the Father wanted from the beginning."*

"*Sleep on,*" Jesus whispered with a tenderness that, in that circumstance, would not have been possible through His humanity alone, "*and take your rest: the hour is come; behold, the Son of man is to be betrayed into the hands of sinners.*"

"Lord, listen! Noises!" Darien exclaimed urgently. *"People talking, swords clanging against metal shields . . . just beyond Gethsemane's entrance! Something must be done!"*

"I hear it," the Son replied. *"I have heard it since the beginning of time."*

A short while later, a great multitude arrived.

CHAPTER 51

While Jesus was speaking, Judas came, and with him a restive throng, with swords and staves, from the chief priests and the scribes and others. And he who would betray the Son of God had given them a token, saying, "Whomever I kiss, He is the One; seize Him, and lead Him away . . ."

Judas quickly approached Jesus, saying, "Master, master," before kissing Him on the right cheek.

The soldiers were obviously ready to move that very instant.

Peter saw what was transpiring.

"This will *not* happen!" he screamed, his rage making even the hardened Roman soldiers jump back.

Taking a sword he had brought with him, contrary to normal, a gift from a centurion whose child had been healed of some disease, he cut off the ear of the high priest's servant. But Jesus was not pleased by this impetuous and violent act, and He replaced the ear, healing it at the same time. Everyone witnessed this extraordinary miracle but refused to say anything, trying to keep their astonishment from showing, aware that if they validated it, they would have to acknowledge the One who imposed it.

"Put up your sword, Peter!" Jesus demanded sternly, "for all who take the sword will perish by the sword. Or do you think that I cannot now pray to My Father and He will provide Me with more than twelve legions of angels? How then could the Scriptures be fulfilled, that it must happen thus?"

Peter started to protest, but Jesus cut him off by pointedly turning away and facing the impatient throng, some of them common people enlisted by the religious leaders as lying "witnesses" against Jesus.

Some of the intruders had come for healing in days past, Darien ascertained, recognizing a few. *But when they did not receive it, for whatever reason, they went away with bitterness in their hearts.*

"I am going blind," the angel overheard one of them mumbling. "The Nazarene could have helped me, if He is to be believed, but since He did not, I am unable to think He is anything but a charlatan or a cruel beast!"

The man standing next to him whispered, "I brought my teenage son, who was dying, but the Nazarene turned His back on that poor boy's desperate need. I put him in the ground last week."

"*Lord?*" Darien asked of the incarnate Deity, reaching beyond the flesh-and-blood shell wrapped around Him.

"*It is not what they say,*" came Divinity's immediate reply. "*The man is going blind because of a disease he received while involved in perverse acts with his daughter. She is now a prostitute who will soon lose her mind from guilt and shame.*"

"*The other one?*"

"*His son died from a wound to his chest.*"

"*What was the cause, Lord?*"

"*Trying to beat another boy to death. The one he was attacking was able to strike back with a knife.*"

"*But why chastise his parents with such sorrow, Lord?*"

"*Because he is their child, and they have taught him that such violence is acceptable. For this boy to go on in their care and become an adult would mean more victims later in life when he is stronger and can do even greater harm.*"

Darien accepted the wisdom of what he had been told and turned away from the crowd.

Jesus surveyed the faces of those present.

"Have you come out, as against a robber, with swords and clubs to take Me?" He asked of them. "I sat daily with you, teaching in the temple. You listened to Me as I taught, but did not seek to imprison Me until now. But I know that you come tonight to this place only in order that the holy Scriptures be fulfilled."

Two Roman legionnaires, grabbing hold of Jesus, started to take Him from that place. For an instant, He looked back over His shoulder for the eleven apostles, but all had forsaken Him out of fear and fled from Gethsemane to hiding places in Jerusalem and elsewhere.

"*Surely I can call the legions into action now!*" Darien shouted. "*They cannot be allowed to do this to You.*"

Jesus smiled knowingly and said, "*Good Darien, the soldiers must do what they do because the Father has decreed it.*"

"Evil men dragging You off to face those who are so spiritually blind they are unable to recognize who it is they treat so roughly?"

"It has been written thus, and it will come to pass. There is nothing else to be done, Darien, nothing under the sun."

And then He was gone, but Darien remained, as Jesus had asked him to do just before He disappeared into the night.

"You must not follow," He had said. It was a command that was exceedingly hard to obey as the angel watched Jesus being given over to a band of sinners. *"Go with the eleven. They will need you, Darien."*

Those who had deserted their Master were now the ones the angel was to be concerned with while anxiously wondering where the soldiers had taken his beloved Lord.

Judas turned for a second or two and looked back toward where Darien stood, a traitor soon to die by his own hand.

"Is someone there?" he asked.

He waited but received no answer, only the mournful cry of a nearby animal, then, after that, a silence that could not have been more complete if it had been inside a sealed and quite ancient tomb.

"Is someone—?" Judas Iscariot started to repeat his question, then he stopped, a certain terror in his eyes as he hurried away, a horde of scampering demons at his feet, anxious for the coming moment of seizure.

CHAPTER 52

*O*R DO YOU *think that I cannot now pray to My Father and He will provide Me with more than twelve legions of angels . . .?*

Darien had been prepared to do just that without the precious Son of God having to say anything.

But You would not let me, Lord! the angel thought, deeply grieved. *It was as though You have known that moment would come for a long time.*

Barred from the presence of the holy Lamb of God, his mission now was to hunt for those weak men whose concern for their own safety transcended any desire to stand beside their Lord, sending them to flee before the face of the enemy.

Anger . . .

Angels, fallen and unfallen alike, were not devoid of such feelings, any more than God Himself was.

Satan, as well as those who followed him, was filled with anger rooted in pride and jealousy. Every evil act, every corrupt thought, stemmed from the rage that motivated them throughout the course of infinite and finite history.

But, for unfallen angels, there was only great anger toward sin, anger for what Satan had done to corrupt a virgin planet.

Every time they saw someone murdered, Darien and the rest of his kind had to deal with their rage.

Every time blasphemy was spoken or practiced, they were filled with fury. Robbery, rape, adultery, homosexual acts—all filled these spirit beings with the desire to express their wrath, to reach out and do something quite awful to those who were embracing the ways of Satan rather than almighty God.

But it was a wrath that set them apart from His human creations. It was purely *righteous,* never expressed over any act or circumstance but that which would cause the rage of the holy Creator as well. In contrast, men, women, and children could become angry about inconsequential, even petty matters.

Thus, for angels, the *only* causes were those that violated Jehovah's standard of righteousness. Lies did it; covetousness did it; lustful thoughts did as well, and much else. Nothing else mattered. Angels were no less than extensions of God Himself. Their anger was His; His joy was theirs.

Yet Darien, Gabriel, Michael, and ten thousand upon ten thousand others were not divine in the sense that the members of the Trinity were. They shared the Godhead's eternality, but that was the end of it. They had to *deal* with anger, had to fight to keep it from taking them over and making them its slaves.

Darien was beginning to sense some light in his darkened spirit, for he realized they *always* succeeded in this goal. Not to do so would be to fail their Creator, and that was something they could never allow. They had chosen to remain true to the Trinity at the time of the casting out and had not departed as they saw one-third of their kind forsake goodness and follow evil.

He bowed down in the midst of Gethsemane.

I give my rage to You, Father God, he prayed earnestly. *It is rage over the monstrous act that has just been committed, and I know You feel it Yourself. But I am not You. I cannot handle it by myself.*

If I were to keep it within me, I would become like so many of those flesh-and-blood ones who let their emotions control them until they are no longer wholly rational, and out of this flows the sin that You despise.

Sobbing.

He heard the sound of sobbing, and looked about. It seemed to be coming from the far end of the garden, and he hurried in that direction.

Behind a large boulder.

John . . .

On his knees, tears flowing down his cheeks and soaking the front of his tunic.

Go with the eleven. They will need you, Darien . . .

Darien knelt next to the young apostle, remembering . . .

Sometimes, the more sensitive of them, especially John, caught hints, one of the reasons God had chosen him to record the graphic series of revelations of future events that were to be given to him several decades later on the Isle of Patmos.

But that night it would prove far deeper. It would be a time of rare and sublime communication between humankind and an angel, this time in beautiful little Gethsemane on the outskirts of the holy city of Jerusalem, a spot so unlike the crude barrenness where John's final years of life would be spent.

"I have been sent to help," Darien whispered to the apostle.

John snapped his head up, eyes wide, then, as understanding came to him, he just as abruptly began to steady himself.

"From Jehovah you come?" he asked.

"Yes, it is because of the heavenly Father," the angel replied, *"that I am able to be with you now."*

"They have taken my precious Lord away. What can we do to stop them, to thwart this madness?"

"It is madness, John, but it must yet be a part of the Creator's Plan, though we are not aware of the details. We cannot stand in the way. We must allow it, all of it."

For Darien, saying those words was one of the most awkward and troublesome acts of his existence. He felt more than passing empathy with the emotions John was experiencing but knew he could not betray any of his feelings, for the apostle needed his strength, not his weakness. He hoped he did not slip over into hypocrisy in the process.

Am I lying to this man, Lord? he thought. *Am I misleading him?*

No reply.

The separation had begun, and he knew this, but that cold silence seemed so sterile, so dark, that he felt as though he were actually on the threshold of hell, and that he, too, had been cast adrift by all that was holy.

That was when Darien drew closer to John, when this almost unfathomable bond between spirit and flesh seemed suddenly so precious.

"Let us pour out our anguish together, young John," he said.

The apostle nodded with relief as, during the next few minutes, he poured out words of guilt and shame.

"Jesus talked about loving us so completely," he said. "And all twelve of us swore our devotion to Him for the rest of our lives."

Pain gripped John's stomach, and he started to fall forward.

"Yet we ran! We turned, and we ran. What must He think of us now when He needs us more than ever?"

John reached out to the seeming emptiness in front of him.

"Where . . . where have they taken Him?" he cried. "What are they going to do to the Son of God?"

John staggered to his feet.

"Are we truly any better than the ones who have taken Him away? Our cowardly actions accuse us!"

Darien touched his shoulder.

"*You know that I am here.*" He spoke into the apostle's mind. "*You have had a sensitivity toward my kind since before you met Jesus.*"

John held his breath for a moment.

"Yes . . . ," he said out loud. "Even as a child, I . . . I felt the presence of angels. When I spoke about this, my mother and father hushed me up. They said I was being too imaginative, that I should not waste time with meaningless fantasies."

"*What you felt was real then,*" Darien assured him, "*and it is real now!*"

John could scarcely form any words. He just stood there, listening to what the angel was telling him.

"*But there is more,*" Darien went on. "*You have a greater bond with Jesus than any of the others. You can do what I cannot. You can put your arms around each one of the disciples, and comfort them. I yearn to do that, John. I yearn to take the pain on myself that is coming to them so they do not have to experience it. But—*"

"That is not possible, is it?" John finished the sentence for him. "What is to happen cannot be changed. We all have to go through some portion of the troubles ahead."

Curiously, the apostle's tears ceased. His body straightened.

"*You have a clearer picture than any of my kind,*" Darien said, understanding rushing in on him. "*You have had this for a long time.*"

John nodded as he replied, "It has not been that way from the beginning. It was just little impressions at first, and often I would ignore them, remembering what my parents said, but in time I could look at Jesus and feel only the greatest sorrow. I could find myself thinking, 'Your days will not be long, Lord. Sometime soon, I will weep at the entrance to a cold, awful tomb into which the sins of men will have put You.'"

Darien saw how much John's outlook mirrored his own.

"And then I see something else," the apostle continued, "the loneliness that will be mine during the last days of my life. The only other human beings I shall see are those pledged to keeping me a prisoner.

And they will stay at a distance, choosing not to be involved with me in any way."

The angel was amazed at the clarity of John's foresight.

"Not true loneliness," he hastened to tell the apostle. *"You will be surrounded by many like me, come from the hosts of heaven itself. But they will be by your side long before then. You will never know loneliness again."*

"Thank you," John said, smiling a bit. "I have lain awake at night, looking into the darkness, and wondering."

Darien was about to tell the apostle to be at peace and feel no fear when he stopped himself.

No one will be able to experience peace over the next few days, he reminded himself, responding to what seemed to be a growing, ever sharper awareness that God was granting him moment by moment.

John decided to return to that upper room where he thought at least some of the others would be gathering, and Darien accompanied him.

In the distance, they both could see the faint outline of a hill named Golgotha caught in the pale Judean moonlight.

PART XII

Go with me, like good angels, to my end;
Make of your prayers one sweet sacrifice.
And lift my soul to heaven.

WILLIAM SHAKESPEARE
Henry VIII

Everyone was there except Judas and Peter.

"I am worried about Peter," Andrew told the others. "It seemed almost as though the devil himself was chasing him."

The others murmured agreement, for they, too, were concerned, seeing in Peter their own weakness and wondering what extremes they would go to over the coming hours and what guilt would overwhelm them.

"I heard that Jesus would be crucified if Pilatus decides to side with Caiaphas and the others," Thomas remarked.

Everyone gasped at the very thought.

"But what for?" John asked. "He has urged no violence, condemned no one except the hypocrisy of the priests and others belonging to the Sanhedrin."

"Sedition," Thomas added. "They will try to claim that He urged the overthrow of Rome's rule."

Matthew had an idea.

"Suppose we make contact with Barabbas somehow," he offered. "These people must be stopped. Surely the insurrectionist understands that and will want to help us."

Thomas bowed his head, his shoulders sinking.

"From what I hear, Barabbas has been taken into custody as well," he whispered. "Caiaphas seems to have persuaded the proconsul that Rome's grip will be more completely assured, with no embarrassing uprisings, if both Barabbas and Jesus are removed from the scene."

That speculation only deepened the melancholy of the eleven remaining apostles.

"Heavenly Father?" Darien asked God.

The angel was getting ready to ask Him about helping Jesus break free from those who had led him away, captive.

"Be patient," God told him.

"But He is with evil and brutal men! They will try to harm Him, I am sure."

"As My Son knew would be the case before you were ever created."

Darien fell into silence for a moment.

"I would like to help Him," the angel said. "So would Gabriel, Michael, Stedfast, and the others. Demons are gloating even now, Father."

"Only because they do not know that their defeat is about to be sealed for time and eternity, Darien."

"But if anything happens to Jesus, what then?"

"It is because of what will transpire in a few hours that you will ultimately have reason to rejoice, Darien. But in the meantime, be prepared for the valley of the shadow of death at its most fearsome."

Contact was broken then. Heaven's gates were shut.

"Death?" Darien repeated, feeling a devastating panic. "Is that what will befall my beloved Lord?"

He waited, hoping to hear the Creator speak again.

"Please, I beg You, Father God," the angel pleaded most earnestly, "let my kind and me stop this madness."

Only silence from heaven at that hour greeted his entreaty, yet in the distance the sounds of hell seemed all too close.

CHAPTER 53

JESUS was taken before Caiaphas and the other members of the Sanhedrin.

"Lord, Lord," Darien begged. *"The Father will not allow me to do anything. Give me Your permission to do whatever I can on my own."*

The angel could sense the presence of demons, more gathered together at one spot than he had ever before known to be the case, demons who had quietly possessed the souls of countless numbers of men, including Caiaphas himself, manipulating the aging high priest as though he were merely a hapless puppet.

More and more demons poured forth from hell until it must have been that almost none were left there to continue tormenting the damned.

"Lord!" Darien screamed to the Son. *"There are too many! I cannot stop this ghastly crime alone."*

Jesus broke His silence but just that once, and only briefly.

"It is to be as My Father wills." He spoke spirit-to-spirit.

"I cannot abide this, Lord," Darien protested. *"I shall have to act on my own."*

And then a voice from heaven, unheard by men, stung the angel with its force . . . *"Are you to tread* Angelwalk *yet again?"*

Darien froze.

"Are you to tread Angelwalk *yet again?"* God repeated.

Though he tried, the angel could not ignore that reminder, one that caused old memories to return with great pain.

He bowed before his Creator.

"Forgive me, Father, for what I thought to do," Darien prayed humbly.

"What you thought to do was out of love, though love can go astray. Be patient, even as marauding creatures gather in the darkness. In time, you will know what you should do, not what you want to do."

And so Darien stood, and watched, and cried his angel tears.
He was not alone in that.

After Caiaphas and the others had tried and failed to force their version of the truth from Jesus, He was taken to the palace of the proconsul-governor.
"Are You the King of the Jews?" Pontius Pilatus demanded, though not in a harsh tone, in fact, more gently than might have been expected.
Jesus' answer was a simple one, without subterfuge.
"You have said it," He answered, His own voice not disdainful but curiously pitying as He looked straight into the other man's eyes.
Dear Procula, Pilatus thought. *You have warned me about this gentle soul, and I must agree with you, mad creature that you are.*
Caiaphas, seeing this strange and unanticipated empathy between Jesus and the proconsul-governor, attempted to harden the latter's attitude by accusing the Nazarene of many and various crimes, but he was so vociferous, he and the "witnesses" brought along for that purpose, that Pilatus was, if anything, less inclined to grant the demands of what he deemed raving and wholly insincere Jews.
Jesus had not spoken since the tirades began. Now that Pilatus had ordered everyone to be silent, he turned to Him and said, "Do You not hear how many things they claim against You?"
But, still, Jesus uttered not a word of rebuttal.
"Be gone until I summon you again," Pilatus told Caiaphas and the others. "I must be alone with the Nazarene."
The high priest objected, worried that the proconsul-governor might be brought under some spell that Jesus might cast over him, as surely must have happened with those who followed in His steps day after day.
And so it was that Pontius Pilatus was in the banquet room of his palace, sitting at a table piled with food as Jesus stood to one side, with no one else around.
"You must be very hungry," the Roman said.
"I have that which sustains Me, which You know not," replied Jesus with no disrespect in His voice.
"Do you mean some private garden, Nazarene? Your group has planted a garden, and You all draw from it as there is need. Is that it?"
Jesus did not answer him.
Pilatus graciously offered to have Him sit down and partake of some ex-

quisite karl soup made of black beets that had been cleaned and cooked in *mulsum* with a bit of salt and olive oil.

"It is excellent!" he proclaimed. "I have heard that, a long time ago, Varronis claimed that it is even better if pieces of chicken are added to the broth. He was quite right, you know. Very nourishing, to be sure. Will You not join me?"

"I will not eat again of anything in this world until the prophecy has been fulfilled," Jesus said in response, His voice at nearly a whisper.

"Such riddles!" Pilatus exclaimed as he pushed away the bowl of thick, dark liquid and turned sharply toward the Nazarene.

"Have You no fear?" he demanded.

"Fear is for those who know not their eternal destiny," Jesus told him. "Pain is but for a moment, and then it is gone. True fear comes when the door to this life is closed and another is opened. That which lies beyond the second door is either to be feared or embraced with the greatest joy, for it leads either to heaven or hell."

"My wife . . . ," Pilatus started to say.

"She dreamed of the two of you standing before the judgment seat of My Father in heaven," Jesus said.

Pilatus's eyes widened.

"How could You know that, Nazarene?" he asked, startled. "How could You ever know that?"

Once again, Jesus chose not to reply.

Pilatus stood and paced back and forth in front of Him.

"How could they want You crucified if they see in You what I am seeing this very moment?" he puzzled out loud.

"Their hearts are hardened, but yours is not," Jesus said.

"Is it as simple as that? I am, after all, a Gentile according to Jewish law and, worse yet, because of the gods I worship and the nation I serve, the worst of pagans."

"Those gods no longer seem to you as they did before. They are little more than cold works of clay and marble."

Pilatus felt sudden hot anger surging through him, and instinctively he raised his hand to slap Jesus across the cheek.

"You *mock* my faith!" he declared. "How can You be so foolish when I have the power of life or death over You?"

"Am I the one who mocks a dead religion? Or is it the gods of men turned to dust that mock you when you reach out to them for solace?"

Pilatus's hand hovered inches from Jesus' face.

"I have knelt before the gods You mention for however long, often until my knees are sore, and worshiped their images as the aging temple priests have told us Romans to do with each generation over the centuries."

He trembled visibly, regretting that his state of mind was so obvious, particularly before Someone whose death was being demanded by the masses outside.

"Always it is a cold time, an empty time, a time that has seemed increasingly futile as the years have passed, and my faith, such as it was, ceaselessly withers and dies, and in its final throes, calls out, 'There is nothing out there. There is no hope. We live, we die, and the grave is the awful end of even the grand caesars as well as those of less esteem such as proconsul-governors of backward nations.'"

He lowered his hand, sighing.

"I know not the truth of Your various and sundry claims," he said, "but there is something else of which I *am* persuaded—that You do not deserve to die on a Roman cross while the people of this land gawk at Your agony. I, Pontius Pilatus, am more worthy of an early grave than one Jesus of Nazareth!"

He was ready to call for a guard when Jesus spoke again. "You *will* surely send Me to Golgotha."

"I have decided to release You and crucify Barabbas instead," Pilatus told Him. "You would be wise to say nothing more."

He saw Jesus' expression then and thought it to be bordering on pity.

"How could You feel now as You do?" he asked, perplexed. "How could—?"

Abruptly, the proconsul-governor turned away, trying to ignore the sad, shrill siren sounds of despair and dread that called like grotesquely insinuating phantoms amidst the corridors of his long-weary and disillusioned mind.

CHAPTER 54

CAIAPHAS was unaccustomed to being refused anything by the other members of the Sanhedrin, or by anybody else for that matter, and he was not about to be denied the death of the Nazarene.

Hands on his hips, legs spread apart, anger glaring across his face, he stood before Pontius Pilatus and reiterated his demand, adding a threat just in case the proconsul-governor doubted his resoluteness.

"If we must appeal directly to Caesar, then we will not hesitate to do so." Caiaphas's very direct words stung Pilatus's ears, backed up by emotions that alternated between almost fire-breathing rage and loathing.

"You can certainly do as you say, but he will not pay attention," the proconsul-governor shot back while reluctantly admitting to himself that the high priest had every chance of being successful. "Nor, I must warn you, is he accustomed to having the decisions of one of Rome's officers contradicted."

"But I am not a Jew of the masses," Caiaphas said at nearly a shout. "I do not stand here begging for some crumbs from the imperial table!"

He realized he was letting his emotions control him and that this would only be to his disadvantage, so he paused for a moment, consciously forcing his feelings back as much as possible.

But, still, Caiaphas, confident that he was on the most solid ground, would not retreat.

"Are you prepared to put your career on the line to back up that assumption?" he countered. "What is this Man to you that you would risk everything that has been so important in your life?"

Pilatus was sweating, annoyed that this miserable Jew was being so successful in ferreting out the one argument that could have any impact upon him.

To his right was Jesus, to his left Barabbas.

The Roman proconsul-governor pointed first to the insurrectionist and then to the Nazarene, offering the mob a choice, thinking surely they would come to their senses and see the contrast between an honorable Man such as Jesus and an unruly and vulgar criminal such as Barabbas.

But they cried out instead for the release of Barabbas.

"But this other one," Pilatus said, "the one who is called king of the Jews—what is it that you would have me do with Him?"

"Crucify Him!" they cried out repeatedly, the loudest members of the mob having been paid silver coins from the temple treasury by high priest Caiaphas to make sure the rest were swayed to join their cries in the terrible emotion of that moment.

Nevertheless, Pilatus would not consent to this immediately, seeing out of the corner of his eye his wife, the look on her face.

"Why?" he asked. "What evil has He done? It is Barabbas who has incurred Rome's ire, not this simple carpenter."

But the mob would not be dissuaded; they all shouted in a single voice comprised of many, "To Golgotha! Crucify Jesus now!"

Pilatus did not want to go so far as to risk any kind of bloody confrontation, especially if the emperor were to discern the reason behind it.

I was sent to quell rebellion, he thought, *not provoke it!*

So he summoned Barabbas, one of the worst criminals in all of that region, and promptly released the insurrectionist. Then, in a symbolic gesture before the crowd, the proconsul-governor washed his hands in a bowl a servant held in front of him.

"See this now, you who want the Nazarene dead, see truly that, by this act, I am innocent of the blood of this just Man," he declared to them all, his contempt for what he considered human swine not at all hidden.

In response, scores of voices arose from the mob, shouting in unison, "His blood be on us and on our children."

Pilatus then delivered Jesus to his personal band of soldiers, who scourged Him, then clothed Him with purple and platted a crown of thorns and put it about His head. Mockingly they began to salute Him, saying, "Hail, king of the Jews!"

And they spat on Him and struck Him on the head with a reed. Then, bowing their knees, mockingly pretended to worship Him.

"Hail indeed to the king of the Jews," they all shouted blasphemously. "Glory to His holy name!"

As they arose, they spat again in His face and slapped Him on the cheek, one after the other, laughing all the while.

When they were finished, they took off the expensive purple robe made of fine, handwoven silk and put back on Jesus His own clothes and started Him along the Via Dolorosa toward Golgotha where His crucifixion was to take place . . .

Darkness . . .

Darien saw that it seemed to be everywhere, not only in the sky, indicating a storm seemingly about to burst forth, but also in the hearts and souls of men, women, and children as well, a darkness of the soul.

Throughout Jerusalem, those who had not allowed themselves to be drawn to the crazed mob scene a short while earlier were huddling in their homes, except for a few strong-hearted men who chanced standing just outside and watching as long as they could endure the pathetic sight of Jesus carrying His cross, stumbling, being forced to stand, little droplets of blood trickling down His brow, perspiration stinging His eyes.

A man approached Him and hastily reached out with a sponge that had been soaked in water, quickly squeezing the contents into His mouth.

"You have grown up . . . ," Jesus said to the man, His voice strained and hoarse, any utterance painful to Him.

"My mother lived for many years, Lord," the thirty-year-old man told him. "And I no longer wander through this city as a street beggar. Joseph of Arimathea took us in soon after You saw me, and I now run his business for him."

A Roman soldier stepped between them.

"When You see my mother in heaven, tell her how much I miss her, Lord, how very much I love her," the man shouted before he was pushed back into the crowd along the Via Dolorosa.

Jesus continued on, His strength ebbing by the minute.

"Father, Father," Darien begged, *"have mercy, my Creator, my God. Behold Your Son. Whatever it is that You plan, whatever act of sacrifice is to come, help Jesus now, Holy One. I ask this of You with all the love of which I am capable now and ever shall be. Let me do something to ease His burden."*

"Do as you say," He spoke. *"You will be blessed for this, My remarkable friend."*

Friend . . .

No name could have meant more to Darien.

If he were human, all the wealth of every earthly king could not have equaled the value of that name, no amount of finite or infinite power, no degree of knowledge, could have come close to comparing with being called *friend* by the God of creation.

"I wish I were more of a friend," the angel lamented. *"I wish* Angelwalk *had never entered my life. I wish I had never doubted anything. I wish—"*

"Nothing could separate you from My love," God said. *"Just trust Me, Darien. Trust Me, and obey, dear friend. Then it shall become clear to you, so wondrously clear."*

"Thank You, Father," Darien replied.

"Go, and help your Lord."

That he did.

One of the legionnaires took pity on Jesus, who had fallen again and was having difficulty getting up.

A black man named Simon, tall and strong, a Cyrenian by birth, who had been standing beside the road with his sons Alexander and Rufus, was pressed into service, the soldier demanding that he take up the cross and carry it the rest of the way for Jesus.

Far stronger than the Roman soldier, and a veteran of brutal warfare, Simon was on the verge of objecting to any treatment that made him behave like a common slave.

"Please, do this kind act . . .

Simon "felt" those words rather than heard them.

The Son of your heavenly Creator needs your help in His humanity.

For a second or two, Simon, frowning, stood there, listening to the silent thought swirling through his mind.

"Turn toward heaven. Let its light shine on your face. Look past it in a glimpse of the magnificence of heaven. Feel the very touch of God, and remember this until the end of your days."

The big man glanced up at the dark sky and gasped.

For an instant, Simon saw what the voice had promised, then he turned away, unable to endure the sight any longer.

He and Jesus looked at one another, the pain on that wise face tearing at the Cyrenian's very soul.

"I *shall* help, Nazarene . . . ," he said simply, and not because of the legionnaire's intimidating manner.

"My Father will bless you, Simon," responded Jesus.

"My name, you know it, you—!"

Then two legionnaires thrust the heavy beams of the cross upon the black man's broad shoulders as the Son of God was cruelly jerked to His feet by another soldier and pushed along that narrow street. The two of them, condemned "criminal" and unexpected benefactor, now struggled together toward the dreaded Place of the Skull while distant thunder heralded a coming storm.

A dozen women in black garments descended upon Jesus as soon as He was past the main gate and almost to Golgotha.

Weeping . . .

They were weeping and wailing at Him, coming to that spot because it was expected of them, and also, because they wanted to be seen by their fellow Jews as they zealously performed a kind of official duty that suited well the purposes of public image ordained by Caiaphas and his cohorts.

The Roman soldiers were about to push them aside when abruptly, a dozen more women, dressed similarly, swelled the original number. And just behind them, more still appeared, until even the burly legionnaires could do nothing with them all.

"Jesus, Jesus!" they cried out to Him. "Our hearts are breaking for you!"

These were the wives and mothers of people whose lives Jesus had touched to cast out demons or give sight to blinded eyes or hearing to ears long held captive to silence or were even raised from the dead.

Jesus straightened Himself as much as His wounds and bruises and wrenched muscles would allow.

"Daughters of Jerusalem, do not weep for Me," He told them all as best as He could with a voice that was strained. "But weep for yourselves and for your children. For indeed, the days are coming in which they will say, 'Blessed are the barren, wombs that never bore, and the breasts which never nursed!' Then they will begin to say to the mountains, 'Fall on us!' and to the hills, 'Cover us!' For if they do these things to Me, the Living Tree, what will they do to you?"

"We would die for You now," one of them told Him, "if that is what is necessary to get Pilatus to stand with us and stop this atrocity."

It was unusual for women of that time to step out of what had been a matter of long-held custom and take such a forthright stand.

Jesus smiled weakly as He replied, "Dear woman, if you were to interfere with My Father's Plan, you would be committing a sin greater than what Pilatus and these soldiers have set as their course."

She looked up at Him, for He was considerably taller than she, and said, "Remember my friends and myself when You stand before the great and glorious Yahweh."

Jesus reached out and started to place a hand on her thin little shoulder, but one of the legionnaires brushed it aside. The woman's anger flashed across her face but she relented and told the others to step back.

And so it was that, at last, Jesus, with Simon of Cyrene before Him, approached the edge of Golgotha and started up the winding pathway to the top.

"You must stop this now!" a voice demanded, one so commanding that even the legionnaires froze where they stood.

Everyone turned as a tall, broad-shouldered, white-haired Egyptian jumped off a large chariot that, seconds earlier, had been stopped a few feet away.

Jesus recognized him instantly.

"My name is Baktar," he said as a nearby slave stepped behind him holding a rolled parchment in his hands.

Age had added lines to his face and a greater weariness to his step but he also had increased in stature in his native country, becoming a power in the Egyptian government and even wealthier than before, his business requiring him to trade in a number of countries, Israel being one of these.

"What is it you want?" snapped the veteran centurion who commanded the other legionnaires.

"This execution must be stopped," Baktar demanded.

"It *cannot* bc stopped," lhe centurion replied.

"This man is under the protection of the government of Egypt. He has been given immunity."

The centurion blanched, some of his authoritarian manner dissolving.

Waiting atop Golgotha had been Caiaphas. Seeing what had arisen, he hurried down the winding pathway to the hill's base.

"This crucifixion will go on as planned," he insisted.

"You cannot condemn anyone who is being protected under the auspices of my government," Baktar said.

"You are quite wrong, Egyptian," Caiaphas rebutted him. "There are clearly exceptions to the treaty between Rome and Egypt. One of them is sedition. The Nazarene is guilty of traitorous acts."

"Against Judea or against Rome?"

"Against both."

Baktar hesitated, in part because he was surprised that the high priest was so well versed in matters of secular law.

"How did you find out about these matters?" Caiaphas asked. "We are a long way from Egypt."

"I was in Joppa on business."

"Then I recommend that you get back on your boat and return to Alexandria or wherever you are based. Leave this day's events to those who are familiar with the details."

Caiaphas was turning his back on the Egyptian when Baktar snapped his fingers and the slave unrolled the parchment.

"The conviction of Jesus has been based on distorted and perjured testimony," he said, raising his voice to a shout.

Baktar held out the parchment to emphasize that he had come very much prepared.

"I have written down statements from several of your so-called witnesses who have now decided to recant their earlier lies," he went on. "Look at their signatures. All are genuine, I can assure you."

Baktar ordered the slave to take the parchment to the high priest and point out what he had just stated.

"Yes, I see what you are saying," Caiaphas acknowledged. "But these are not all the names of everyone who gave testimony. Where are the rest?"

Baktar was perspiring.

"My men and I could not reach *all* of them in time," he said, some frustration showing in his voice.

Caiaphas narrowed his eyes.

"Is it truly as you say or was it that a few refused to give in to your pressure and, as you say, *recant?* Therefore they remain as accusers? It matters not whether one or a dozen are right. If just three verify that the Nazarene is guilty because He spoke of such things in their presence, then He *is* guilty. Neither I nor the *Roman* proconsul-governor need to be convinced by yet more statements of similar content."

He handed the parchment back to the slave.

"Leave this place now, you and your lackey here, or suffer the consequences of interfering in the internal affairs of *my* nation and of imperial Rome since this execution is being carried out by order of a Roman official."

Baktar had no recourse. Knowing this infuriated him, but since he had not brought an army with him he could not simply wrest the Nazarene from the grasp of His captors.

He walked up to Jesus.

"Because of You," he said, "we will one day walk streets of gold together."

And then he stepped back, and the dreadful procession continued.

CHAPTER 55

THE APOSTLE John was already there, standing to one side, his head bowed. With him was Mary Magdalene, her knees pressed against the uneven, rocky surface, her hands folded together, words of prayer escaping her lips.

But no one else who had been so close to Jesus during His earthly life showed up. Instead they huddled in that upper room, held hostage to their miserable fears. As he was leaving, John had tried to shame them into admitting their pathetic behavior and showing the kind of courage they had evidenced in the past with only their words. But none of the others listened; they turned away from him and pretended not to pay him any heed

Two thieves . . .

These criminals already were hanging from other crosses. Caiaphas had insisted that their crucifixions be done this way in order to allow Jesus some extra moments to view His own fate, something Pilatus regarded as unnecessarily cruel and sought to change, but once again, he gave in to political pressure and ordered the sequence of monstrous events the high priest wished.

As though in response to the pitiable anguish of those who knew and loved Jesus, the sky darkened ever more dramatically and thunder sounded again, but still no storm burst forth.

One of the Roman legionnaires present was Decimus Paetus, who had been serving Rome for many years. Darien had noticed him on another occasion that involved a group of rowdy soldiers speaking blasphemously about Jehovah, the God of the Jews, as they were sitting around a campfire near Jericho.

"You should not do to the religion of the Jews what you would not want them to do to our beliefs," he told the others sternly.

"But *our* gods are far finer," one of the other men had said. "Many come to us from the Greeks, and who can argue that the Jews, at their best, are far more uncouth than the worst of the Greeks?"

"When you give a beggar some food, is it because you loathe him? Or is it rather that you feel some compassion?"

"What is your point, Decimus?"

"If the Jews are so underprivileged, if they lack so much of what the rest of the civilized world possesses in abundance, should we not pity them rather than fling our ridicule in their faces or, worse yet, behind their backs?"

The others were silent.

Decimus had started to turn his back and walk away in disgust.

"Wait, Decimus, you are right," came one reply. "We respect you for standing up for righteousness."

Darien, now at Golgotha, could tell that this legionnaire was becoming more and more uncomfortable as the Man he heard someone refer to as the supposed Messiah of the Jews was being pushed down onto the cross.

Paetus stood back, turning his head away, as the first spike was hammered into the yielding flesh.

His body being ripped and torn!

Darien felt the shock of hard metal enter Jesus' feet, sensed a measure of His pain as the Roman legionnaires impaled Him.

Then nails were hammered into His hands.

Each blow brought a cry of anguish from Jesus, for in His humanity He did not have His divinity's freedom from pain.

"Lord, I cannot . . . I cannot stand here . . . and . . . and . . . ," the angel started to say but found the words smothered by his emotions.

The Son's eyes closed for a moment, and His head tilted to one side.

"The Nazarene is dying already!" some bystanders shouted harshly, disappointment coloring their voices. These were the same ones who would come to enjoy gladiatorial games where blood was shed for so-called sport, and crowds would decide who would live and who would be murdered for their perverse sense of pleasure.

Even the Roman soldiers hesitated, thinking He had succumbed to some premature death swoon.

"Darien . . ." God the Father spoke finally. *"My Son is dying. Nothing can be done."*

Darien could feel the blackest despair of his existence reaching out and gripping him, a sensation quite unlike any he had known before, utterly devoid of hope and peace and joy, a reminder of damnation itself.

"But He is an eternal member of the Godhead," the angel protested to his Lord. *"He cannot die."*

"Yes, Darien, truly I know that," God told the angel. *"But it is His incarnated body that will die."*

"But His spirit, Father, what of His spirit?"

A new spasm of pain tore through Jesus' body, diverting the angel's attention.

Many women from Jerusalem and elsewhere had come to Golgotha, but not yet the mother of Jesus nor anyone else from His earthly family.

The angel sighed as he thought, *She must face this nightmare with only John and another son at her side.*

Joseph was dead.

He had died after his Son had been taken prisoner at Gethsemane.

The announcement had come to the old man without warning, surely the most startling of his long life, and there had been no way for Joseph to steel himself, to somehow anticipate it in any way.

He had been in Nazareth at the time, and when a neighbor told him what was happening, he had immediately made haste for the journey to Jerusalem. But he was now so much older and had retired from being a carpenter because he was too frail to continue; the stress of the news overloaded him, his old heart giving out.

He died in Mary's arms in their modest home on a dusty street in Nazareth.

"Leave me," he begged her. "Go to our Son."

She knew that he was right, that Jesus could not be allowed to—

"Father God, help us!" she cried out.

Joseph reached up one hand and gently touched her cheek with it.

"My precious wife . . . ," he whispered. "Tell me you understand who our blessed Jesus is. Let me go to His real Father knowing that, dear, dear Mary."

Mary did not want to cope with that at the same time as she was holding her dying husband, but there was no way she could ignore any longer what she had tried to do all those years, to avoid the realization the truth would force on her.

. . . *His real Father.*

She felt a surge of renewed love for this kind man, so devoted as he had been to a Son he had always known could not possibly be his own.

Mary put her arms around Joseph, feeling his beating heart against her chest. It was pounding hard and fast, as though any moment it would burst.

"I cannot live without you, my beloved," she said. "Soon, if what we have heard this day is true, Jesus will be gone too. I pray to God that He takes my life now so I do not have to face the pain of losing both of you."

"Mary, you must not talk as you do," Joseph managed to say, though his strength was rapidly becoming depleted. "Jesus will need you; He will need your strength, your comfort. Do not deprive Him of that! Please do this for—"

Noise behind them interrupted him.

Jude, the younger brother, who had never taken Jesus seriously and was, in fact, markedly antagonistic to Him, had finally arrived home after hearing the awful news about what was going on in Jerusalem.

He saw his parents outside.

"Father!" he said, tears starting to fall as he bent down beside them.

Joseph turned slowly, with great pain, in his direction.

"My son, my son," he said.

"Father, I love you so much," Jude told him, taking one hand in his own while Mary held the other.

"Son . . . I ask only this."

"What is it, Father? Anything you want."

"Love Jesus, my son . . . my son. Do that for your father, please. Go to Jesus before it is too late, and tell your brother how much you care. Let me die hearing the promise I seek from your lips."

Jude could not stop the rush of tears that commenced while his father spoke, could not stem the words that poured out along with them when it was time for him to reply.

"May God forgive me for the way I have treated my brother," he said, deeply under conviction but not telling Joseph that he remained unconvinced about Jesus' incarnate nature. "Father, I will leave now and hurry on to—"

Weary, his body unable to carry on any longer, the old man shuddered briefly as his eyes closed, his lips parting slightly. His breathing became erratic. Wife and son heard a faint sigh come from him, and then his body was completely still.

By then James had arrived. But Mary would not listen to either of her sons when they begged her to stay home.

"I will not!" she declared.

"Then we both will go with you," Jude told her.

"Stay with your father. Wait until your brothers are here."

"But, Mother, I loved Jesus too," James said.

"And your father less?" she countered tellingly. "Is that what you are saying? That he can be left here in the middle of this dirty street until—?"

James placed the fingers of his right hand gently on his mother's lips.

"I will stay, then," he assured her. "Jude will go with you."

And so Mary and Jude left for the holy city of Jerusalem, which was hours of hard travel away, not knowing whether they would get there in time to be of any help to the One they had known only as son and brother.

Finally, the two of them arrived in the morning . . . just as the last spike was being pounded into Jesus' right hand.

Mary! Mary!

Darien saw the mother of Jesus and His brother slowly walking up the pathway to the top of Golgotha.

She stopped short, a shudder tearing through her frail body as she heard the sounds of Jesus' suffering.

Then, hurrying the rest of the way, she tripped in her haste. Stumbling to her feet, she reached the plateau just as the cross was being hoisted up and placed in the ground.

Jesus did not fling words of anger upon any of His executioners, did not rail against Caiaphas and the others who had sought His crucifixion.

He said only, while He was still able, "*Father, forgive them, for they know not what they do.*"

Immediately Mary threw her arms out in front of her in a wild gesture of revulsion and horror.

"My Son! My Son!" she cried as she ran up to the cross, reaching forward and touching her Son's blood-and-sweat-covered feet. Then, mindlessly, she tried to pull out the nails but was pushed back by a legionnaire.

Jesus' blood-streaked head moved slowly, the burden of His agony increasing as He saw His blessed mother.

"Behold your Son!" He murmured to her, His words raspy, faint.

Impulsively, his emotions controlling him, Jude stepped forward too until the soldiers stopped him.

"I love You, my brother," he shouted, crying. "I shall go on loving You until my last breath of life."

Jesus saw him and seemed to nod with understanding, His lips moving but no words heard.

One of the crucified thieves jeered at Jesus, daring Him to save Himself and come down off the cross.

But the other thief was respectful and rebuked the first.

"Do you not even fear God?" he said, "seeing you are under the same condemnation as I and other sinners this day?"

The other man groaned, his body growing ever weaker.

"And we indeed receive justly for we receive the due reward of our many awful deeds," He went on. "But this Man has done nothing to deserve a similar death as imposed on you and me.

The second thief spoke directly to Jesus now.

"Lord, remember me when you come into Your kingdom."

Darien was astonished by such wisdom, coming as it did from a common thief, a man whose robberies must have been many and severe to warrant death, as opposed to imprisonment or flogging in public.

Slowly, seized by almost incomprehensible pain, Jesus turned toward the dying thief.

"Verily, I say to you," He said with great effort, "today you shall be with Me in paradise."

The time was noon, but a mournful darkness descended over the land, completely blocking out the sun and causing those present at Golgotha and elsewhere to wonder if the end of the world was about to occur.

Three hours.

It lasted until about midafternoon, and people rejoiced in the streets of Jerusalem when the darkness waned.

More minutes passed, the strain on Jesus' abused body mounting.

Every so often, Jesus would gasp, His lungs increasingly deprived of oxygen, each attempted breath sending searing tendrils of pain straight through His chest and into His stomach, causing it to tighten.

As light appeared again and the darkness was banished, the Son of God spoke out in agony. "*My God, My God, why have You forsaken Me?*"

Everyone present felt the hopelessness of those words. Jesus the Incarnate One's cry pierced even the heart of high priest Caiaphas and his cronies.

"We must leave now," he told them.

"But you wanted to be here to see the Nazarene die," another priest replied. "And He still lives!"

Caiaphas hesitated, his gaze turned toward Jesus.

Eloi, Eloi, lama sabachthani . . .

Words became phantoms in his mind, racing along its corridors then down into his heart and through to his soul where they lodged, little demons incessantly accusing him of a crime that would haunt him until his own wretched death years later, when his tortured soul escaped from a body riddled with disease. The illness, undiagnosed in those days, would mercilessly shrink him into a pile of bones with yellow-tinged flesh stretched tautly over it and take his sanity as well as his health—at least, what there was left of it.

Demons standing at the red-hot entrance to hell, eagerly awaiting the torment of the man who had caused an incarnated member of the Godhead to be put to death . . .

"We go now!" Caiaphas now said with difficulty, turning away from the cross.

"But, sir . . . ," the other priest persisted.

"*We go now!*" Caiaphas said, barely managing to control himself in front of so many witnesses when his rage threatened to spill over into physical violence.

Darien looked up at the trembling body of his Lord.

"*Is it not to end now?*" he asked. "*Whatever the Father's goal, has it not been accomplished with this?*"

Jesus did not reply, and the angel felt Him slipping away by the moment.

"*I cannot let you go!*" Darien cried out. "*Even if it means damnation for myself, I must disobey the Father and save You without His permission.*"

Jesus raised His head briefly, no strength remaining for any more movement save that one simple act.

"*No, My beloved Darien, you shall not, for you would be acting alone,*" the Son of God said. "*Not a single other angel will help you. If you do this, you will be as Satan himself, and you will have cast yourself out.*"

Darien pleaded with Michael, Gabriel, Stedfast, Virtue, and others to stand with him. Perhaps if they did so, the heavenly Father might relent after all, might allow this horror to be stopped before—

"I thirst . . . ," Jesus the Man managed to say.

Standing so close by, Jude was able to hear him.

"Let me provide my brother something, please!" he begged of the legionnaire named Decimus Paetus.

"Here," the Roman said, nodding. "Give Him some of this. It's all that we have."

He dipped a sponge into a vessel filled with vinegar, then crushed some mint-tasting hyssop leaves over it.

"Here," Paetus said. "Do it quickly."

"My arms are short," Jude told him. "I can't lift the sponge up to my brother's lips."

"He is your brother?" the Roman asked.

"Yes, and this is His mother."

With that, Paetus turned away and found a long stick, then handed it to Jude.

"Thank you," the brother of Jesus replied.

Jude stuck the sponge on the tip of the stick and raised it up to Jesus' mouth. The Son of God partook of its bitter-tasting liquid, then shook His head.

A spasm shook through Him. When it had passed, His eyelids half-closed, His head leaning back against the cross, He said, "It is finished." Then He fell forward, His body straining against the spikes.

Darien shouted, *"No! I will act. Please, my Lord, my precious, precious Lord, forgive me for what I am about to do contrary to your wishes, but I can do nothing else. I cannot be idle while infamy rules."*

Demons came to help.

One by one, they issued forth from hell. Doubt came. Rebellion followed him, along with Distrust and Impatience and a vast army of others.

Doubt approached Darien.

"We, too, think this is horrible," he said. *"It is odd, but you and I and the others of my kind seem to be on the same side this day."*

The countenance of Doubt was so horrible that Darien had to turn away.

"You want Jesus to live?" he asked.

"Oh, yes, yes, Darien," the fallen angel said. *"It would be no fun if He died. He must live, to continue the battle. If He goes like this, we reign supreme. Surely you, of all angels, would not want that!"*

Darien's instincts were beginning to react now.

"But it is God who has ordered this today," Darien retorted. *"If it is of God and you oppose it, then—"*

He swung around, facing the horde of creatures that descended upon Golgotha, ready to drive unredeemed men mad.

"If it is of God, Darien, then why have you responded as you are doing now?" Doubt assailed him, snorting the most venomous contempt. *"Could it be that you, like so many of us, have at last stumbled upon a greater wisdom than Jehovah's, however reluctant you might be to acknowledge that this is so?"*

As Jesus neared death, Darien felt ill, not in the way human beings did, but far more profoundly, far more completely.

Jesus was gasping for air now.

"Wait no longer," Doubt screeched, *"or it will be too late! We cannot do what you seek by ourselves but must act in concert with you, fallen with unfallen, to avoid upsetting the divine Plan. Do not delay. The fate of this cursed world is yours to decide!"*

. . . to avoid upsetting the divine Plan.

As soon as Doubt said those six words, he wished he had not, for he realized what they would trigger in Darien.

And he was right.

"It is not my lot to do what you say," Darien declared, reminders of *Angelwalk* rising from the past. *"I have been your way. I have been in hell, remember. I know where everything Satan plans will end up."*

He faced Jesus at the foot of the cross.

"Lord, there shall never be another Angelwalk *for me,"* he said with dignity and resoluteness. *"It is over now. I stand in front of You without knowledge of what lies ahead but no longer with doubt about the course of any events, for if this is all part of the heavenly Father's Plan, then who can abide against it? Not I, my Lord, not I!"*

Behind him, demons pulled back into their abode of damnation to face the fury of the master they had failed.

Thunder sounded again, and lightning streaked across the sky, causing everyone atop Golgotha to start to run, before the full fury of the coming storm engulfed them.

The anguish was too strong for Him at last, and the battered heart of the Savior of mankind stopped beating, but not before words issued from His lips that would live for the rest of history and beyond.

"O heavenly Father, into Your hands I commit My spirit," He said, His voice suddenly strong and clear, astonishing those who heard Him.

And then Jesus the Christ was gone from that place.

CHAPTER 56

WITHIN SECONDS, it seemed, after the bodily death of Jesus by crucifixion, God no longer chose to hold back the elements, and the storm that had been threatening for some time was allowed to smash down with maniacal fury upon that entire region, from the north at Giscala and Ramah on to Gerar and Goshen in the far south. But its greatest destructive force was felt in and around Jerusalem as well as along the coastal area where the Mediterranean shoreline was dramatically altered by the relentless fury of giant waves of near-tidal proportions that had been stirred up by what amounted to a Middle Eastern hurricane. Seagoing vessels of great size were tossed about as though they were tiny playthings, and the port city of Caesarea was smashed so severely that it would be a very long time before the wreckage could be cleared away, docks as well as other structures could be rebuilt, and essential commerce anywhere could return to anything near normal. This presented a devastating blow to the already tenuous economy of that region, a circumstance destined to stir up substantial outrage throughout the columned halls of power in Rome, especially from the emperor, who could not help but notice the unpleasant impact upon the imperial treasury—and anytime the treasury was strapped, his ability to do as he wanted was also hampered.

. . . the greatest force of it was felt in and around Jerusalem.

No one could remember a storm of anywhere near that magnitude. Some families would never recover from the loss of life and the appalling economic nightmare.

People were being flung off the flat pinnacle of Golgotha, and the mount itself seemed to be sway from the driving wind.

The three crosses . . .

Only the three crosses held steady since they had been sunk so deeply into the hard rock.

Everything and everyone else was endangered, from hardy Roman soldiers to religious leaders to common Israelites—shepherds and farmers and beggars and others—including the mother of Jesus, His brother, and the apostle He loved.

Then the very ground beneath them moved, a sensation Mary had known all too well.

An earthquake!

It was so strong it rent asunder the veil of the holy temple at Jerusalem from top to bottom. Parchments were flung from their cubicles, and worshipers were tossed from one end of the main sanctuary to the other.

Mary became terrified, not wanting to leave her son but knowing He would want her to be safe.

Egypt, nearly thirty years earlier . . .

Her mind recalled the widespread devastation that had occurred in that country so long ago.

"*John, John,*" Darien said, hoping the apostle could sense his words, could be a bridge between finite and infinite so that Mary was comforted. "*Put your arm around her. Tell her the Father is looking after her and will not desert her.*"

But John was too distraught to be sensitive even to an angel's prodding as he was knocked over by the earthquake's devastating force.

Baktar also had been sent tumbling to the ground and was now getting uncertainly to his feet.

He stumbled over to Mary, James, and John.

"Come with me!" he told them urgently. "We shall flee this place!"

Mary no longer resisted leaving Golgotha.

"You are right," she agreed. "Nothing more can be done. I have lost my beloved son the same day his father died in my arms."

"Do not give up, Mary," Baktar told her as he helped her up into the chariot, with Jude and John following behind her.

As the mother of Jesus was getting onto the awaiting Egyptian chariot, she glanced back at the three crosses being eerily illuminated by lightning that flashed across the sky with unusual rapidity. One bolt hit a member of the Sanhedrin, who had made it to the base of the mount and was starting to head toward Jerusalem; he died in a split second.

"All of nature is rebelling this day," Baktar shouted loudly, his powerful, well-trained stentorian voice barely audible above the din of people screaming amidst the crackling of lightning, the roaring wind, and the general sounds of chaos.

Toward Nazareth.

That was where Darien saw them heading, though the severity of the storm might force that small party to settle momentarily in Sichem, if room were available, or even closer, in Bethel, at least until the weather cleared.

Darien noticed that only one soldier remained at the mount, a centurion who had not left Golgotha as yet, but was clinging to the bottom of the middle cross.

Mumbling . . .

The man mumbled incoherently at first; then his words came more slowly. Suddenly, he stood back, looking at the lifeless form hanging above him, lightning flashes sending bursts of illumination across his hardened military face.

"Truly, this was the Son of God," he shouted, with no one except Darien to hear him.

A fierce gust of wind carrying cold, stinging needles of rain lashed at him, and he fell backward, tried to stay on his feet, but failed, his head banging against a large rock a few yards away from the crosses.

His death came instantly.

And instantly he saw Darien.

"Are you sent from the God of the Jews?" he asked with surging hope as his spirit began to rise from his body.

"I am as you say, centurion," the angel told him.

"Was I correct? Was the Nazarene from the God of the Jews also?" the man asked, glancing behind him at that one cross.

"He was the Christ, the Son of the living God," Darien answered, anticipating this one's final leap of faith.

Now the Roman stood before him.

"Am I to be condemned to the punishment the Jews have called eternal damnation?"

Darien answered him the only way he could.

"Have you recognized Jesus as God-in-the-flesh?"

The man's spirit brightened perceptibly.

"Yes, I do!"

"Is He your Savior, your Lord?"

"As much as I can understand what this means, yes, yes; He is what you say as far as I am concerned."

Heaven took him then.

Darien returned to Jerusalem and found turmoil throughout the city. The earthquake had caused damage everywhere, and debris littered every winding, narrow, ancient street, making passage even more Sisyphean than usual.

Many people died, either immediately when they were crushed to death or later, as a result of multiple injuries. Wailing could be heard from every direction.

"Is this the judgment of God?" someone screamed. "Is this the judgment of God for the death of His Son? The Nazarene should have lived!" The mob asked that His blood be upon *their* hands. But now we all are suffering as a result!"

Another voice followed.

"What did we do to try and stop the slaughter? We did nothing. We sat back and comfortably bemoaned such an atrocity."

And so it went as Darien moved through Jerusalem. Right along the Via Dolorosa, as it turned out, the bodies were piled the highest, dying agonies frozen on contorted faces of dozens of men and women.

Darien considered the irony.

How many of you shouted for my Lord's death? he asked silently.

Groaning.

He detected the sound faintly, muffed as it was.

Under a small mound of building stones!

Only the eyes, nose, and mouth were showing through. The rest of the man's body was completely covered.

"I see someone!" the injured man exclaimed. "Please, help me!"

"I have no substance. I cannot do what you ask."

"I will die if you do not pull me out."

"Did you demand the death of the Son of God?"

"Who?"

"The Nazarene, as you probably called him."

"Jesus, you mean?"

"Yes . . ."

"He was a faker, a pretender. What kind of god could He have been if He dies on a simple cross like an ordinary man?"

"That part of Him is dead, yes."

The man grunted disdainfully.

"Send someone to help me," he begged. *"You must do that, whoever you are. In the name of God you must!"*

Darien felt the sensation of heat.

And those odors!

Fetid odors that smelled like innumerable centuries of death.

He also heard the slithering approach of those who once walked side by side with him in heaven.

"It is not God who is nearby now," the man said with no change in his manner. He had been deluged for most of his life with all the religious teachings and phrases of that era. But his familiarity with the monsters of hell became something else, essentially contempt, whether he admitted this or not.

"I care little if it is the devil himself. Waste no more time, stranger. Do not forbid whoever it is."

"As you say," Darien assured him, *"as you say."*

CHAPTER 57

THE CENTER of Jerusalem, with its many merchants and their wares, could not have looked worse if a tornado had ripped through it. Leather goods were strewn about, bottles of expensive perfume were smashed and spilled. Pottery goods were in shards. Exotic gems had been tossed side by side with the remains of humble storefronts and living quarters in that area. Ostrich and other feathers fluttered gently among the debris.

A young man, tall and thin-faced, stood in the middle of what was left of his wine stall where he had offered different vintages from a variety of countries.

"I have nothing, I have nothing, I have nothing," he kept repeating in a dead monotone, shock having addled his mind until he could do nothing else, "I have nothing, I have nothing, I have nothing."

You had the Messiah in your midst, Darien thought, *and you cast Him out. You murdered Jesus the Christ! What you say now is truer than you know. Once you have rejected Him, there is truly nothing left for you.*

Righteous rage had replaced Darien's despondency.

He was filled with it, with seething rage that the eternal Godhead purity had been condemned by the blackest sin instigated by the most evil of creatures. Held in their exigent sway, religious leaders, men supposedly in their positions of influence solely to help the members of their flock but given over instead to safeguarding their own power, were the human culprits. They had bribed one of the followers of Jesus to betray Him, threatened the Roman proconsul-governor, and pushed a mob to vent its lust for death, a mindless savagery that should have grabbed hold of Barabbas and driven him instead to Golgotha. After all, Barabbas was a true criminal by the laws of any land, given to an endless succession of crimes including murder, robbery, and rape, each committed under the pretense of a heady patriotism. But it was not to be Barabbas after all, for they preferred to murder an innocent Man without sin.

. . . a Man without sin.

The angel was seized by a compulsion to return to Golgotha, to see what was being done with that blessed, battered, lifeless body.

I was with Him as He was growing in His mother's womb, Darien thought. *I talked with God as a human child!*

The angel felt as though he were made of lead; he could scarcely move. He pushed *through* people and buildings, hurrying as fast as his propelling will would take him.

Finally, at the main gate, Golgotha stood in the near-distance like an oversized gravestone framed against the star-filled nighttime sky, the storm at last spent, the wind barely more than a breeze.

Darien reached out toward that mount as though he had a mystical artist's brush and could paint over that part of the wretched scene and cause it to cease to exist.

"I would do anything to change all this, Lord," he whispered.

None of the three bodies had been touched since a practical matter—concern for the living—had superseded any thought of the condemned dead, especially in view of the multitude of tragedies spawned by first the storm and then the quake.

My beloved Lord, my dear, dear Jesus . . .

In an instant, Darien was standing before the cold, hardening body hanging from the center cross.

"*My God, my God,*" he cried out. "*Let it be me instead! Take my spirit and not this precious One's! Bring Him back, oh heavenly Father, and let His good work continue throughout this needful land.*"

And then other words came, words that cut to the very center of Darien's misery.

"I have failed You! Your charge for me was to protect Your Son. I did not do that. I have changed the course of history through my abysmal failure. How can I go on, Father, knowing what I do?"

The veil between heaven and hell was parted for an instant, and Darien saw what his mind had refused even to contemplate.

Mourning . . .

All the angels of heaven were mourning.

Darien realized he had not had contact with any of his kind for some time. They had retreated to heaven and then looked down on the hanging body of their Lord, wondering how they could go on without Him.

Consequently, their once-luminescent brilliance had dimmed until the whole lot of them could scarcely be seen, their majestic wings drooping, their hymns of joy stifled, their silence a kind of funeral dirge.

And at the throne of almighty God was an empty spot where the Son had once stood, where once the holy Lamb had provided so much joy for all those angels who came to worship Him or to ask for tender reassurance as only He could provide when they had returned from their travels around the ravaged planet named Earth.

Without Him . . .

The very idea would have been anathema days before.

Without Him, heaven no longer can be a place of . . .

Darien turned away, unable to look any longer into heaven, but as he was doing that, he caught a glimpse of Stedfast, gentle Stedfast, a sweet and fine comrade, not a fierce warrior angel like Michael and Gabriel and others who had been stationed on the supernatural battlefield of spiritual warfare. Instead, Stedfast was an angel empowered by the Holy Spirit to provide solace, but he himself was not comforted just then. It was a sad Stedfast Darien glimpsed, with a bleak mask of despair pulled over his dismal countenance.

"*I want to return, to be with you, with the others,*" Darien shouted, angel-to-angel. "*There is nothing for me here now, for any of us. The world is lost, claimed by Satan for time and eternity.*"

He was alone atop Golgotha, alone at the center of that place of an infamy so severe that, literally, the earth beneath him had moved in protest.

Stedfast stepped out from the rest and seemed to want to speak, but the words were either not spoken after all or lost somehow between heaven and earth.

"*We have only each other,*" Darien called up to his friend. "*Jesus is gone. I have no reason to stay in this crude and ugly world a single moment longer.*"

He prepared himself for the departure.

"*I am now going to return,*" he said, his tone one of inexpressible defeat, "*so that I can be with you again to share this grief that seems so obvious among you, for it is mine as well.*"

As he was about to do just that, God spoke suddenly.

"*No,*" the Creator declared. "*You must remain. Something special has been set aside for you, and no other.*"

Darien started to protest.

"Think of this," God interrupted. *"You are the only unfallen angel anywhere in the world, the one link that is left with divinity. If you were to leave, Satan and his slaves would have full and unimpaired sway."*

He paused, waiting for the angel to absorb every word.

"Is that what you wish the consequences to be," God continued, *"hordes of malevolent entities running from end to end throughout what I once intended as Eden forever, returning to the very pit of a foul and dreadful hell with the lost souls they regularly capture in this rapacious onslaught of theirs? Return to heaven if you can abide that outcome. I forbid you not, Darien."*

Men and women snatched from their death beds, screaming their horror, as the hideous creatures spawned by Satan's rebellion prowl the earth, their blood-red lips and sick-green eyes—

"*No!*" the angel proclaimed with a desperation born of experiences with those same repulsive beings, three hanging bodies in silent witness of his trauma.

There but for the grace of God . . .

He shivered as that truth came from Yahweh Himself.

"You had a strength," said the Almighty. *"You shared it with those others who, like you, were not swayed by Lucifer's deceptions. That strength is still within you, Darien. Let it take hold. Force out the despair you feel. Give it back to those responsible, and tell evil itself that there shall be no more entry."*

He indicated those comrades who had been born, like Darien himself, in the mind of supreme holiness, and then spoken into being.

"They mourn what you mourn," the Father went on. *"They feel what you feel because they are of the same spirit. Where you end, the next of them begins. Lucifer was the first, but it was you who followed before any of the others. You are a direct link with Me."*

A direct link with Me . . .

Never before had God revealed to him what had just been said.

"That is why you must stay. That is why Satan will dominate if you do not. You represent goodness, Darien. My Son represents salvation."

"But Your Son in this incarnation is dead," Darien muttered, some shreds of Angelwalk still clinging to him. *"You will have to go through it all again, pick another young woman, give to her of Yourself and—"*

The next words came from the angel like a self-inflicted knife thrust again and again into a helpless human heart.

"But if the Son is gone then, as now," he reasoned, *"who will You send to be born of a virgin the next time?"*

It was for an instant only, but he felt the disappointment of God, the hurt of God, the pathos within the omniscient Creator of every living thing.

"You trust as you love and where you love," He addressed this angel solemnly. *"If you love Me much, surely you shall trust Me much."*

The angel was overcome and began to sob, speaking no more in opposition to his Creator's pronouncement.

"Yes, Father, I will stay," Darien assured the almighty One. *"It should be enough that You want me to do this. Otherwise I am little different from the swarm of demons that will follow my every step."*

God smiled then with the joy that this angel was responsible for giving Him.

"Have faith," urged Divinity, *"and never feel that evil is stronger."*

Darien had fallen to the ground, his countenance bowed. Now he looked up, toward the sparkling sky of that Middle Eastern night.

Then the veil fell back into place as it had been since the beginning of time, witnessed by the last angel on the face of the earth.

PART XIII

A dungeon horrible on all sides round
As one great furnace flam'd, yet from those flames
No light, but rather darkness visible,
Serv'd only to discover sights of woe,
Regions of sorrow, doleful shades, where peace
And rest never dwell, hope never comes
That comes to all, but torture without end.

JOHN MILTON
Paradise Lost

NOW IT SHALL BE!

Long-withheld triumph so close it could almost be touched and held or tasted and savored!!

Satan was not able to restrain his delight. He jumped about gleefully, surprising those other demons near him.

All unfallen angels save one, confined to heaven!

Satan was jubilant, and those fallen ones who had followed him out of heaven eons ago were getting ready to fling open the gates of heaven wider than ever before.

"We have it all now," Corruption shouted. "We can go after anyone we please. Only their natural instincts are left to resist us."

"And that means victory every time," agreed Satan, banging his talons together with such glee that an echo of the resulting sound ricocheted through part of hell, and souls cowered for fear of what he was planning.

Only Darien stood in the way.

"While he is there, he is hardly omnipresent," Corruption persisted. "Still, we are partially restrained, as you must know. If he can protect one soul, then another perhaps, this victory is not as sweet as it must be before we are fully satisfied, before we can shake our fists at the Godhead, the now shrunken and ineffective Godhead, and proclaim triumphantly our intention to wrest heaven away from Jehovah Himself."

CHAPTER 58

JUDAS . . .

Darien found the pasty-gray, hardening body of Judas Iscariot hanging from a twisted, long-dead tree at a location officially named the Valley of Hinnom but also known as Gehenna, just outside Jerusalem. It was both an area maintained for the dumping of garbage but also as a plentiful source of Judean clay, a beacon for sculptors and potters of all kinds.

The malicious irony fell most heavily upon the dead poor, those who could not in life afford bread to eat nor decide where they would be buried, although buried was not precisely the word to describe the scene that Darien found disturbing in ways he could not begin to articulate to God, to other angels, or to himself.

Gehenna . . . where human garbage was sent.

Deep pits had been dug in an area where no plants or other life could be sustained because of the toxic clay deposits.

The Jews, eager to let nothing go to waste, had long before converted that square mile of barren land to its present use.

But while all seemed to be dead, one was not, having swooned in an appearance of death, fooling those who were given the task of disposal . . .

One of the half-dozen emaciated male bodies was beginning to move, nudged out of a deathly stupor by the heat below.

The man was trying to climb up the side of the pit, digging into the red clay surface to keep himself steady as, inch by inch, he made his torturous way upward to the edge where a laborer was standing, aghast.

He screamed for mercy, begging, "Do not send me back! Do not send me back!" His cries reached the observing angel as the laborer took a long, heavy wooden pole and jabbed it into the man just below the chin, his blow so strong that it raised the victim up nearly to his feet and then sent him tumbling to the bottom.

"One less piece of beggar filth!" the jaded and embittered man muttered. "I do us all a favor by giving you the fate that was intended."

"*You mad beast!*" Darien screamed at the one whose action was manifestly devoid of even the vaguest humanity.

But what the angel experienced next was nothing that could be sensed by this cruel, remorseless laborer, jaded and unfeeling after so long at a well-nigh intolerable task, a horrid spectacle only for the sight of angels or demons.

Suddenly, a dying human being glimpsed Darien and started reaching out to him from that red-hot pit.

"Take me from this place!" he begged. "Beyond these flames I see other flames, and amidst those, I see ghastly creatures smiling!"

But Darien could do nothing.

Finally he could not stay so close to that awful pit any longer after such a grisly encounter, the vivid images of that spot too strongly reminding him of another, not altogether dissimilar visit he had made, that also involved souls in torment.

But he had to pass by other pits like it, each the same as that first one, each reminding him of suddenly open doors to Satan's massive domain. A heavy sulphuric odor was carried by breezes that whipped the flames across helpless flesh.

Dear Lord, my blessed, blessed Lord, Darien prayed, *where are You? This is not a world where there is any longer the fair touch of righteousness. It is a black and unholy place. Come, Jesus, I beg of You, come quickly, and take me where You have gone.*

That was when he came upon what was left of Judas, the thick rope around his neck, squeezing it, tiny bones had broken, blood vessels had been constricted, muscles were unable to perform the simple act of swallowing, lungs starved for air until the heart stopped beating and the brain seemed to explode.

The eyes were gone, attacked by hungry predator birds, several kinds of which seemed to hover continually over Gehenna, undoubtedly hoping to find scraps of food. Some were so desperate that they flew into one or more of the pits, as close to the flames as they dared, to grab chunks of flesh from bodies that had not slid down all the way.

Darien looked up into the blood-stained empty sockets.

You were with the holy and precious Son of God, he thought. *You touched the very hand of incarnated Deity. You broke bread with a member of the Trinity. You heard the greatest outpouring of truth and wisdom in the history of the world. How could you have committed so malevolent and dastardly an act?*

There was no answer from the corpse.

Only in hell was it to be found, grasped in an eternal, flame-shrouded embrace. Thirty pieces of silver had proved to be the price of Judas's soul, but damnation's home was giving up no secrets that day.

CHAPTER 59

It was worse than during Angelwalk . . .

Two unholy days, literally unholy.

Darien spent the greater part of that period after the crucifixion, according to finite time, not only traveling throughout the land of Israel but in Rome as well, since no angel was bound by normal conventions of distance and speed. He could will himself to be anywhere he wanted, and this was accomplished in an instant.

The religious leaders the angel came upon seemed no better to him than the commonest thugs, men who daily demanded so much of others but seemed only to wallow in their own criminal behavior.

Except Nicodaemus.

He found all the members of the Sanhedrin, except for that one man, joining together in celebration in a far room of the temple.

Though preaching a stringent standard of sobriety to those who looked to them for spiritual guidance, they relished their victory so much they had allowed themselves one night of drunkenness.

Not even the storm and the earthquake had opened their eyes!

"We invite the scorn of the world," Caiaphas admitted to the rest, "but it was necessary to remove this threat from our midst."

Others nodded in agreement and murmured approvingly among themselves, expressing their satisfaction with this man's leadership.

"I overheard one of the Roman legionnaires saying this may mark the beginning of the end for us Jews," another priest told him. "What do you think this foreigner could have meant by that?"

The question was not anticipated and seemed for a moment like cold water splashed across Caiaphas's face.

The high priest became silent, carefully pondering the other's words, at least as much as the wine would allow, while thinking of that crowd of Jews screaming so deafeningly. They had done so only because he had bribed enough of them to stir up the others in the frenzied demand, "Let the Nazarene's blood be upon us and upon our children, and upon the children of many generations to come. *He must die this day!*"

Cold.

Where did that cold come from? he asked himself, feeling through his body from head to foot a deeper cold than he could have imagined. *I had not noticed it before.*

Caiaphas shivered involuntarily, then shrugged as he put another glass of wine to his lips and drank the numbing contents quickly; other priests took his lead and continued consuming their own supply until none of them was able to stand without wobbling and all, including their leader, spent the night in that temple room, not daring to venture outside and risk being seen by a common Jew, for they had no satisfactory explanation for their behavior after the tragedies of that day.

On another street at the opposite end of Jerusalem, Nicodaemus had gone to be with a businessman named Joseph of Arimathea, who maintained one of his residences near the Via Dolorosa.

"I watched Him go by from this very window," Joseph confessed as he stood before it, gazing outside. "For a moment He seemed to look up in my direction while that black man was picking up the cross. I wanted to turn away but could not. He seemed to see beyond my physical body and into my soul."

"I believe you," Nicodaemus told him. "I felt the same way when He saw me one day some months ago."

He stood beside Joseph, and pointed outside.

"I should have done more yesterday," he went on. "I should have hired someone to carry the cross the entire way. I could have gotten Pilatus to let me do it by promising more money in the royal treasury."

Nicodaemus turned from the window.

"The suffering He endured because I did nothing,"

"You put your position on the line by arguing in His defense," Joseph said. "Do not let unjustified guilt weigh you down, my friend."

"We have to get His body taken down and then decide where to bury Him. I think Caiaphas would be happy if it stayed there until it rotted and the wind carried the smell of it over the entire city, but this is the Sabbath so the body cannot be left there."

"I have to agree with you, Nicodaemus. There is some great irony in the solution I can offer."

"What is it?"

"I maintain a tomb right down the slope from the top of Golgotha. It was dug many years ago, not more than a hundred feet away from where Jesus died!"

The two men determined to approach Pilatus immediately, not waiting until morning to do so.

May you be granted your request for His precious body, Darien whispered to himself.

Darien left them, hoping they were successful, that Pilatus would ignore politics for once and give in to any decent instincts he had left.

Briefly, Darien left the holy lands and traveled elsewhere, throughout Europe, on up to Britain, and always he sensed the same impression, whatever the nationality.

Fear . . .

There was a universal fear abundant wherever he went, the ancient cultures suffering from it for reasons not known to them. Nevertheless it fell upon their societies without warning during that short period, with men and women feeling a bleakness that almost drove them to end their lives in whatever way they could fashion.

It happened in the cultures that gave birth to the Mayans, Aztecs, and Incas in another hemisphere. Each would later record the phenomenon on stone tablets and by other means, generally calling that time by the unembellished name of the Dark Days, describing long hours of a sudden melancholy taking hold within their very spirits, causing many to commit suicide out of their ignorance of the truth. Sacrifices of animals and babies increased, for they assumed that the gods were angry for some reason, and all means available to placate these deities had to be utilized or, these people thought, they were doomed.

Elsewhere, in the "civilized" population centers of Europe and Asia Minor, great orators succumbed overnight to morose and often pretentious musings as they stood on polished temple steps in Rome before gathered listeners, decrying the world around them while surrounded by great opulence and unmatched power.

"We are at the bottom of an abyss," the angel heard someone cry. "Below us is darkness and above is darkness. It begins and it ends, not outside, in this place of towering columns and marbled majesty, but within, my listeners, where what we are rises up and mocks what we want to be."

Nobody knew what was happening, but they all *felt* it. Not a single human being was immune to this plague-like fear, clutching as it did at their throats and causing their hearts to beat faster in dread.

They sense the approach of evil, Darien realized. *It is black and clammy and unseen. They can neither smell it nor hear it, but they know it is there.*

He quickly went on from Rome to Athens, another center of culture, the two cities representing the very center of Greco-Roman achievement. As he walked the streets, Darien came upon a quotation engraved over the entrance to a building where public meetings were customarily held.

Fear is pain arising from the anticipation of evil.

That one sentence had been written by Aristotle, whom the Greeks would never stop revering, in that age or any other.

. . . from the anticipation of evil.

Darien read it again, for he knew he was close to the cause of what he had encountered everywhere in his travels, and he knew his initial suspicions had hit the mark.

With the Son of God gone, fear was taking His place, and men and women were no longer confident in themselves or their devices or their institutions, not a new circumstance but the acceleration of an existing one. They would pray to other gods and be given no solace in return. They would stand on the shores of the Mediterranean or the Aegean and find no answers from Neptune or any other god of their imagination, just the endless tides and waves. And all was as it had been and would ever be. So they sought escape through debased conduct and vulgar imaginings.

With the Son of God gone . . .

Like captive beasts abruptly freed from their cages, men and women felt the freedom to come out with lies that set the stage for the destruction of others, usually rivals in business or government, and felt no shame from this.

And they seemed far less constrained by the limits of perversion and other sexual transgressions, while not having to suffer from remorse.

Some felt as though they had become children again and were being given a whole new set of toys!

"What has happened?" one Roman senator asked wonderingly of a colleague. "I have never indulged my sexual fantasies with so many people as

I have over the past two days. Even you would blush if you knew *everything!*"

The other man was shocked by this and became obviously uncomfortable, but the senator merely snorted, expressing his contempt for values more rigid than his own, and he went on to provide him with some disturbing details.

Twice before such a period of debauchery had happened, at Sodom and Gomorrah, and just prior to the Great Flood in the time of Noah.

Once again . . .

After years of relative restraint because of the incarnated presence of a member of the Godhead, Satan now could move about freely.

With one exception.

A single angel.

Darien . . .

The only source of pure divine goodness that remained.

I cannot let this little angel spoil everything, Satan told himself with a curious mixture of apprehension as well as gloating. *I must somehow invalidate his testimony and, in doing so, destroy him in the process, perhaps even get him to come and acknowledge me as his new master. Doubt once before lodged within him as he embarked upon that* Angelwalk *odyssey, and I shall make sure it takes up residence one more time.*

The arch deceiver snickered to himself.

There shall be no escape, he declared, *for Darien is alone, alone against a full array of my most capable demons . . .*

He knew he had to defeat this last remaining angel, a defeat that should be as vicious and ignoble as possible, before mankind *en toto* could be plunged into that reign of evil that he had been waiting to foster since God had cast him out of heaven.

And next, ah, yes, yes, next, Your throne! Satan added, looking up toward heaven's gates through the brimstone mists while absent-mindedly feasting on the cries of Absalom.

CHAPTER 60

DARIEN returned to Jerusalem and sought out Nicodaemus and Joseph of Arimathea, finding them worshiping in the temple. After they had finished, they walked outside, heading toward the main gate.

"Caiaphas seems more peculiar than ever," Joseph observed.

"I hear he is drunk half the time," Nicodaemus remarked.

"How could that be? Is he not concerned that the general populace will find out? I never thought the man was a complete fool before this."

"He seems to have lost the power to control himself, Joseph."

The other man stopped walking and stared at his friend.

"What did you just say?"

Nicodaemus repeated himself.

"What is it that startles you?" he asked, puzzled and a bit alarmed. "It is as though I have slapped you hard across the cheek."

"I have heard other stories within the past few hours," Joseph acknowledged, "in addition to what you have told me now."

"About what?"

"The actions of ordinary men and some women as well," Joseph told him.

Nicodaemus shook his head.

"It is not like you to be so cryptic," he observed. "Tell me more clearly what is on your mind."

Joseph was frowning, given to momentary contemplation.

"If Jesus were truly the Son of God . . . ," he mused.

Upon hearing his friend say this, Nicodaemus sighed knowingly.

"I have been wondering about that myself, Joseph," he said.

"If that is truly the case, then it means God has given up on us, Nicodaemus, that we as a people, perhaps as an entire world, have been cast adrift because in rejecting the Nazarene, we have rejected Yahweh Himself."

Nicodaemus was nodding in agreement.

"No one should know better than the two of us how cold, how hard, how deathly gray His poor body became."

"If I could," Joseph remarked, "I would go there right now and kneel in front of that tomb and cry out to Him with all my heart, with all my soul, hoping that the grave somehow would not be a barrier to his hearing me, though I know how futile this is."

Nicodaemus's eyes widened.

"Everyone is forbidden!" he exclaimed. "There was some talk that a band of insurrectionists or a group of His followers intended to steal the body away and claim a resurrection for the Nazarene."

"Futile or not, dangerous or not, I *need* to do this," Joseph persisted. "I need to go there and beg Him to forgive me for not doing more."

"I, too, need forgiveness, dear friend," Nicodaemus said, trying somehow to reassure the other man.

"Friend, friend, you spoke out! You stood up before the other members of the Sanhedrin and tried to stop this shamefulness."

"But I failed," Nicodaemus murmured as he threw up his wrinkled old hands in a gesture of futility.

"Does God love you less?" Joseph spoke softly.

The two long-time friends turned disconsolately toward Golgotha and stood there, just inside the main gate of Jerusalem, quietly sobbing out their pain.

Darien saw the direction in which Nicodaemus and Joseph of Arimathea had been facing before they decided to go to their separate homes.

It must be near where Jesus was buried, where His body is now, he started to tell himself.

The angel wondered if he would ever be able to finish that sentence, for every time it invaded his mind he found his spirit drenched in darkness and heard again the death sounds of the One he loved.

Slowly he walked forward, easing down into the small ravine separating that end of the wall around Jerusalem from Golgotha.

Sunrise was beginning, and with it came the early-morning sounds of wildlife stirring as well as the sound of a cock crowing.

Peter, Peter, Darien thought sympathetically. *How will you ever deal with your guilt?*

He saw movement in the semi-darkness.

And he detected a familiar stench, odors only an angel could notice.

Legion!

Darien stopped, looking about himself.

Others.

More *things* appearing out of nothingness!

Legion was not alone, though he was surely powerful enough to handle any assignment given to him by Satan without the help of other demons.

This time, Legion's master was not permitting any possibility of error. Darien could not be destroyed, nor could any eternal spirit, but he could be stopped, yes, Satan reasoned, or, better still since it meant the same thing, he could be corrupted.

"*Back in Egypt,*" Legion leered, "*you had help. At other times, Gabriel or any of the rest of them were available to you. That is no longer the case, my former comrade. The Trinity has ceased to exist.*"

So quickly he taps into my worst fears, Darien thought. *So expert they have become! How easy it is for him to find the most promising weakness of a man or an angel.*

He stood quietly, not responding.

"*This world will become worse, with or without divinity among its weak little creatures,*" Legion continued. "*There are so many other worlds. Worry about them. Let this pathetic one go. It is lost anyway. Adam and Eve saw to that. Risk nothing further. Leave now before it is too late.*"

Ten thousand demons now filled that *wadi.*

Darien recognized them all, could call each by name.

"*Behind you . . . ,*" he said, looking past Legion.

Startled, the creature spun around, wondering what it was that had drawn Darien's attention.

"*What is it?*" he asked. Then realizing he had overreacted, he added, "*I see. You are not above playing games. You succeeded with that once. It will not happen again. You are too transparent, if you will pardon the expression.*"

Demons from hell chuckled.

"*Behind you . . . ,*" Darien repeated.

"*See!*" Legion exclaimed defiantly. "*Your trick, once revealed, has lost its power. I thought you were smarter than that.*"

"*You do not know what I intended to say,*" Darien continued. "*For I was simply going to remind you where lies the body of One you once loved,*" Darien continued.

Legion sneered.

"You speak properly when you say once. *That no longer is the case. Once a great many things were different."*

Darien caught something in Legion's voice.

. . . once a great many things were different.

It was fleeting but pronounced at the same time.

"What do you mean by that?" Darien probed carefully.

"We were enslaved to the wrong master. Why have me repeat the obvious?"

"Enslaved, Legion?"

"I spoke clearly. Did you not understand me?"

"Enslaved—or devoted?"

Legion wavered, not rejoining him.

"And why *were you devoted?"* Darien went on. *"Was it out of fear? You cannot say so. Was it out of some kind of perverse addiction, once begun, hard to break?"*

The demon started to speak but ended up sputtering unintelligibly.

"Or was it out of love?" spoke Darien slowly.

Murmuring broke out among the others.

"We have no love for God," one of them shouted with near-deafening vehemence. *"How could we be expected to? He abandoned us."*

Darien faced that one.

"Is what you say true, Shame?" he said. *"Is that how your present master has rewritten history?"*

He saw Observer, the journalist-demon assigned to write the history of the world from Satan's perspective.

"Answer that, Observer," Darien demanded, *"remind him of the truth. Remove the umbrella of lies under which he hides to avoid the tears of God."*

Getting no answer, Darien faced Shame again.

"Remember your name in heaven?" he asked.

"No!" the demon demanded. *"You shall not speak that word!"*

"Oh, but I shall. I shall speak the name you once had."

Shame turned away.

"Face him!" Legion demanded. *"Do not let this one last shred of truly divine goodness in the world intimidate you."*

Darien stepped between Legion and Shame.

"It was Glory," he said with a voice louder than he thought he possessed. *"And now there is only Shame. You left Glory behind you, Shame.* You *turned*

your back on Father, Son, and Holy Spirit. You took Shame upon yourself. God did not force it upon you. You bespoiled the Glory that was once beautiful, embodying what you had been before the Casting Out. As your name now reflects what you are today!"

That demon had stepped out from the others. He was like the rest, bloated of shape and foul of countenance, with blackened, ragged wings misshapen by the ravages of hell, a face constantly erupting in what looked like gangrenous poisons, eyes red, glowing in the semi-darkness that the morning sun had not altogether abolished for the day.

"*Damn you to hell!*" Shame spat out as he faced Darien again.

"*You speak of what you know all too well!*" Darien confronted this tragic figure. "*I have no shame in my spirit nor sin that would earn me damnation. There is regret, yes, regret truly, but even that has been washed away by the shed blood of the One before whom you once fell in adoration.*"

Legion ordered Shame back into the crowd of evil ones.

"*Strong words, Darien,*" he scoffed. "*Eloquent speech, to be sure, worthy of applause, but of no use. We are as we are, and that is as it shall be until the end of time.*"

"*I offer no argument to that. You have dug your pit of damnation, and you shall always return to it. But as for me, Legion, I will go this moment to* my *Master's—*"

That opportunity was not lost on the demon before him.

"*—grave?*" Legion shouted immediately, not letting it slip by. "*Is that not what you were going to say? Yonder lies the tomb of Divinity. A very large stone has been rolled across the opening. Four of Rome's finest wait as guards to stop any Jews who might want to feign a resurrection. The battle is over. The war is being won. The victor sits not on a pure white throne in heaven but on a seat of lost souls crying out for mercy they shall never receive!*"

While speaking words of great triumph, Legion seemed given to an abrupt shivering then, as though saying what he did had drained him badly.

"*You spat the word* grave *at me!*" Darien rebutted this former comrade. "*But why are you not celebrating with great abandon even as you speak it?*"

He pointed toward Golgotha.

"*A place of sorrow and despair, as you have made it,*" Darien said, his voice breaking. "*But something has apparently escaped your grasp of reality: You see, I must take my sorrow back with me into the presence of my loving heavenly*

Father, and so must you carry yours every last step of the way ahead, but the one before whom you will stand has no love in him."

"*Why should we share anything of the sort with you?*" Legion protested feebly. "*These demons and I will walk the streets of gold once again while what is left of the Trinity cowers before the new ruler of that kingdom. We* rejoice *over this, Darien. Do not allow yourself to foolishly think otherwise.*"

"*So intelligent, and yet so deluded,*" Darien responded, pity in his voice. "*Listen well, my former comrade: For me, it will be to heaven that I go henceforth. For you, Legion, hell and only hell is where you belong. The crucifixion has not changed anything as far as your eternal destiny is concerned.*"

Legion was glowering, green spittle foaming over his thin, red lips.

"*Nonsense, Darien,*" the fallen angel said, his cloven feet shuffling nervously. "*That cross was a defeat, but not for us. We walk the world and snatch souls as it pleasures us.* Your *kind can be seen nowhere. Now tell me again who meets the rising sun victorious this day?*"

"*Poor, poor Legion. You see, but you are blind.*"

"*And you are not making sense, good Darien. Which one of us clings to delusion now, I ask?*"

Darien stood straight, a certain dignity in his stance.

"*I have within this spirit sorrow so profound that often it threatens to crush me, but then so must you, admit this or not, and yet it* is *of a truth different for you, Legion, and every last one of you here, different because not only sorrow must be your burden, but with it guilt, guilt over what you have done. You have destroyed the One you once loved. That cannot be denied, no matter how much you have learned about deceit from the master of it.*

"*You say that you* once *loved the One your master* now hates with such *venom. Not so, I say again, not so! The truth, the precious, wondrous truth you hoped would be buried with Jesus, is but this, Legion . . . that, as you stand before the Place of the Skull, you have one more reason to hate your hellish master. Turn and look behind you, Legion and Despair and Mifult and the ten thousand others sent forth by the raving beast who now sits in hell, awaiting your return. Think of what you have become, and what he has made you do in the hearts and the souls of men. Think of that dead, cold body in its bare tomb. There lies sweet Jesus, not He whom you* once loved *eons ago in another place but the One you* still *love and, mark this well,* will go on loving forever!"

Darien half-smiled, not cruelly, but rather a bit wistfully, aware of what they all had lost as a result of their choices.

"Do not forbid my passage," he demanded but with no ire or impatience. *"You can never have me nor any like me. You know that; truly you* do *know that, Legion. Yes, the earth is yours, but that is where dominion ends for you. Whatever your grandiose plans to the contrary, you* will *be stopped at the gates of heaven because evil* is *doomed along with your master, the father of it, and you its demon children."*

Darien gazed over the lot of them.

"Did any *of you feel like victors when last you stood before that cross,"* he asked, *"or more like criminals who should be hanging from it yourself?"*

Wings slumping, head bowed ashamedly, Legion stepped aside, whispering, *"Do not hate us. Hate our master, but spare some pity for us. You go back to God this day or another. We return to that which damnation ordains."*

Nodding sadly, Darien approached Golgotha.

Behind him, a strong wind kicked up along the length of the ravine, its howling sound like the mournful cries of desperate anguish that had descended suddenly upon those so accustomed to inflicting it.

"Dear Jesus." Darien spoke softly. *"Dear Jesus, I come now."*

Darien reached the top and approached the tomb's entrance. Four Roman legionnaires lay prostrate, asleep and unmoving.

The angel walked past them and stood before that humble burial spot. Since he was spirit, unlike those of flesh and muscle and bone nearby, he was not held back by physical properties and entered *through* the giant round stone blocking the entrance.

The body was there, on a slab to his right, wrapped in a gauze-like grave cloth.

Darien walked the few steps to it and knelt with simple solemnity.

"Jesus, Jesus . . . ," he sobbed. *"It* is *true what they are saying, demon and human alike. You* are *dead, and I know not what has happened to Your spirit, Lord. Is that also gone, for it is not in heaven, or else I would not have seen so much sorrow?"*

He reached out, probing the body, foolishly trying to uncover some spark of life that would surely respond to him, but there was nothing.

"Oh, if I myself could but die," he cried, *"and not have to face this separation. Without You, my Lord, I am nothing. Without You, all of heaven shall remain in mourning."*

He heard an unfamiliar voice then, a soothing voice, a sweet and tender voice.

Coming from outside! Just beyond the stone!

In his desperation, Darien started back through it and saw immediately what awaited him outside.

Another angel of light, like himself!

He fell to the ground.

"*You have returned!*" Darien exclaimed. "*Praise God, you have come back. Does that mean Jesus has been found, that He survives?*"

Laughter then.

"*Fooled you!*" A voice spoke, harsh and cackling.

A familiar voice . . . the voice of Satan!

Darien backed away instantly.

"*Do not be so surprised!*" Satan exclaimed. "*You* must *have known that I and the others can transform ourselves and become like angels of light.*"

Darien stood, intending to return to the tomb.

"*Please, my former friend, you must not go back there,*" Satan pleaded. "*Only death reigns inside. You have seen this for yourself . . . just a poor lifeless body, a pale, hardening corpse rests on that slab. Out here I offer* life! *When will you come to realize the truth? When are your blind eyes going to have the only sight that counts? If you join* me, *you will be* in charge *of all demons! Only I will be greater.*"

He walked toward Darien, suddenly shorn of light or anything else from his former pretense. Now only his normal grotesque countenance was visible.

"*Feel the energy!*" Satan exclaimed. "*It is here, not in heaven. Heaven is dead this day. That is where the sorrow is. I offer you real joy, the joy of power, the joy of freedom from restraint of any kind.*"

Darien stumbled back through the stone and into the tomb. But Satan, though also spirit, stayed outside.

Why do you not come inside? Darien thought to himself. *If only limp flesh can be found here, what is there to stop you?*

Moments later, *shrieking* filled the area, so loud that the ground seemed to vibrate from the sound of it. Massed demonic *things* poised beyond the heavy round stone, shouting the worst of blasphemies at Darien.

"*Yea, though I walk through the valley of the shadow of death,*" Darien repeated to himself, "*I shall fear no evil.*"

Some were speaking with chilling coherence, recalling for him every moment of his previous journey along *Angelwalk* and the reasons it had occurred in the first place, that thread of doubt, doubt about his Creator's wisdom, doubt about the mercy of Satan's condemnation, and the shame he finally felt until God's forgiveness had washed it away.

For a very long time they continued, throwing everything in their vicious arsenal at him, every trick they had learned, with *Angelwalk* always at the center, a looming reminder of the worst of times for him.

And none of it worked.

Darien held strong, not allowing melancholy or guilt or any of their other weapons to wound him.

Then the unholy chorus ceased, and he could hear nothing outside.

Darien understood the deadly technique behind what they had done. They surely had sensed that he would be impervious to their mere words, even the unnerving images they flung at him one after the other.

. . . but perhaps not the cruel reality that confronted him as soon as their hue and cry was over!

He was still in a tomb, and next to him was the corpse of God's incarnated Son. That was far, far more torturous to endure and remain faithful!

Words that would not be written for more than a thousand years but were known long before by their eternal author were released by the Father to be grasped in that moment by Darien's mind as the specter of defeat seemed so close, so ready to overwhelm him.

Beyond the shining and the shading
I shall be soon.
Beyond the hoping and the dreading
I shall be soon.
Love, rest and home—
Lord! tarry not, but come.

"*If only it were so . . .*" Darien spoke, knowing that no one human or divine could hear him, his pain unnoticed, it seemed, buried like the One he loved.

Lord! tarry not, but come.

Some hidden resource of strength refused to be squandered or ignored in the midst of that moment's weakness and propelled him to a prostrate position, almost forcing him to speak in supplication.

"*Satan, you are truly a losing foe,*" he said deliberately in a somber tone, trying to convince himself that what he was saying was true and not just a foredoomed hope, trying to push past the sense of futility that had wrapped around him much like the burial shroud around that body of flesh so near, *"a vanquished—"*

Darien felt the ground slipping out from under him, not the physical earth but another kind, symbolic as opposed to literal, the ground that formed his once-unshakable trust, trust in God's handling of the affairs of men and angels alike. Nothing could destroy his faith . . . but that trust was another matter.

He slowly stood and walked over to the bier.

It was real, not something of idle whimsy. Unmovable, it seemed to pronounce irrevocably the end of an ages-long drama, the final dismal chapter in a book that once promised blessed redemption but now was lost in a dreary cave cut into the side of a blood-soaked mount.

And then sounded another voice, so different from Satan's counterfeit one, speaking simply.

"Remove the stone . . ."

As Darien stared at that stone in helpless dread, that same voice repeated, from heaven above or earth below he could not be certain, *"Remove the stone, Darien,"* it told him. *"Remove it for all time."*

"But I am not of flesh and blood," the angel replied. *"How can I do as you say?"*

"You shall, as I speak this very moment, have a new body for a little while, My dear guardian," the voice added, *"just as I will, just as I will."*

From behind him now, familiar-sounding, the words coming from lips that had spoken to him often over the past thirty-three years!

Darien looked at his own form, his own hands, in wonderment. Then he reached out and touched the cold, flat side of the gravestone.

He could *feel* it!

"If I tell you to do something, Darien," the voice admonished him, *"do not doubt that I will give you the means."*

The angel spun around and saw Jesus standing in front of him, smiling, that ravaged body now washed clean of the touch of the grave, the shroud in a neat little pile on the slab where He had lain, the gray pallor of His skin gone, replaced by a vibrant sheen, glistening and pure, a body alive and strong, transformed from the old, like a moth from a cocoon, triumphant.

Awkward in his physical form, Darien fell to his knees and looked up into the face of Jesus the Christ.

"Hosanna to God in the highest!" Darien shouted. *"This day sin has lost its power forever. Salvation now comes to man. Behold the risen King of Kings and Lord of Lords!"*

Darien stood after a few moments, hesitating, his emotions now nearly uncontrollable.

"Shall I roll the stone aside now, Lord?" Darien asked.

"Yes, friend," Jesus replied. *"Do as you say, and we shall stand together in the morning sun."*

As he pushed, the massive stone slid easily to one side.

Darien fell to his knees again before the Son of God.

"My dear Jesus! My blessed Friend! My holy Lord!" Darien cried as sudden light that would have been blinding to human eyes encircled them both.

"Rise now, faithful one," Jesus told him patiently. *"There is a final task you are to perform."*

"I am not worthy to stand before You here or in Your Father's kingdom," the angel cried in shame. *"When You were gone, my weakness rose up like a demon itself."*

The smile crossing the Son of God's face was that of a million stars twinkling in unison.

"In forty days, you shall ascend with Me," He said. *"Nothing else matters. The rest has been washed away by My shed blood."*

"It should be Gabriel, who has been so loyal," Darien persisted. *"Or Michael who has fought so valiantly in battles of spiritual warfare since Eden."*

Jesus spoke then with so much kindness in His voice that the angel could say no more in protest, *"They stepped aside to let you be here."*

Darien reached out to touch that face.

"The thorn wounds are still in Your forehead, Lord," he gasped, and he saw that the Lord's hands and feet were likewise wounded as they had been on the cross.

"It is not yet time for me to go to the Father," Jesus told him, *"to be as I was, before this incarnation. I will bear these marks until then."*

With that came the magnificent sound of a multitude of trumpets from inside and outside the tomb.

Darien stepped through the tomb's open entrance and looked up toward heaven, seeing what he had thought would be denied him forever.

The veil had been cast aside! And eternal glory shone forth once again!

He saw Stedfast, Gabriel, and Michael standing on either side of the

Father and the Holy Spirit. Their despair was gone. Golden points of light issued from around the great white throne.

Jesus was now outside with Darien. The Roman soldiers had fallen into a deep coma and were aware of nothing.

"I will go with You, Lord," Darien said pleadingly, *"wherever Your journey should next take You."*

"You must stay here for a little while. There is a reason."

Darien nodded without protest.

"Then let me embrace You, please, before You go."

Jesus stood there as Darien's form touched His own.

"I thought You were dead and gone," the angel mumbled in awe.

"And the angels in heaven joined with you in believing that."

Darien glanced toward the *wadi,* which was only a step or two away.

"There are demons in the ravine, Lord," he warned.

"I know."

Jesus left him for a while, slipping over the edge and into the *wadi* and standing in the midst of those wretched beings.

"We have lost, have we not?" Legion said quietly as he watched what was happening. *"It may not happen by sunset tonight or before a thousand sunsets after that. But it* will *come."*

"You have *lost,"* Jesus told him.

"Could we not join with you again? Could everything be forgotten?"

"Can you join Me? Can *you do that?"*

Legion thought of the snarling monster who was waiting in hell for them all, and from whom neither he or any of his kind could ever turn away.

Jesus, Jesus, he thought, *what could have been, oh, what could have been.*

Legion could not look upon that holy face any longer.

Above them, heaven was still open, the veil not yet fallen back into place.

"I have never forgotten how beautiful it is," Legion said. *"That is part of my torment, You know, remembering."*

The demon reached out toward Jesus, toward His side, where a lance had been thrust, his talon passing through that extraordinary light, touching the deep wound with dried blood around its edges, then quickly withdrawing.

"How we abused You . . . ," Legion whispered, his shame like a physical entity, strong, squeezing him hard, *"how much pain You faced because of us."*

Then the entrance to heaven shut again, and ten thousand doomed creatures of darkness returned to their abode as a single unfallen angel waited at the empty tomb . . . because the Son of God had asked him to do so.

When the sabbath was past, Mary Magdalene and Mary, the mother of James, and Salome had brought sweet spices, that they might come and anoint Him. . . . And as they looked, they saw that the stone was rolled away. . . . And they entered into the sepulcher, and saw a young man sitting on the right side, clothed in a long white garment; and they were afraid.

But he said to them, "You need not be afraid of me. I have been sent by the One you seek, to tell you that Jesus of Nazareth, who was crucified, is now risen. He is not here. Behold the place where they laid Him. Go your way now, tell those who followed Him, including Peter, that he goes before you in Galilee. There you will see Him . . .

It was not often that angels were allowed by the Father to take human form. But this was one of those times, a rare privilege.

As Darien watched those dear women leave, he prayed with great fervor, "*O heavenly Father, thank You for letting me be here, to announce the glorious resurrection of my Lord Jesus.*"

He smiled as memories came back briefly and then were gone with a finality that he had never before sensed.

"At last," Darien said out loud, so very happy that peace had settled upon him, "at last I will finally leave it all behind."

All the pain, the searing doubt, all the temptation of *Angelwalk* were gone now, he knew, gone forever.

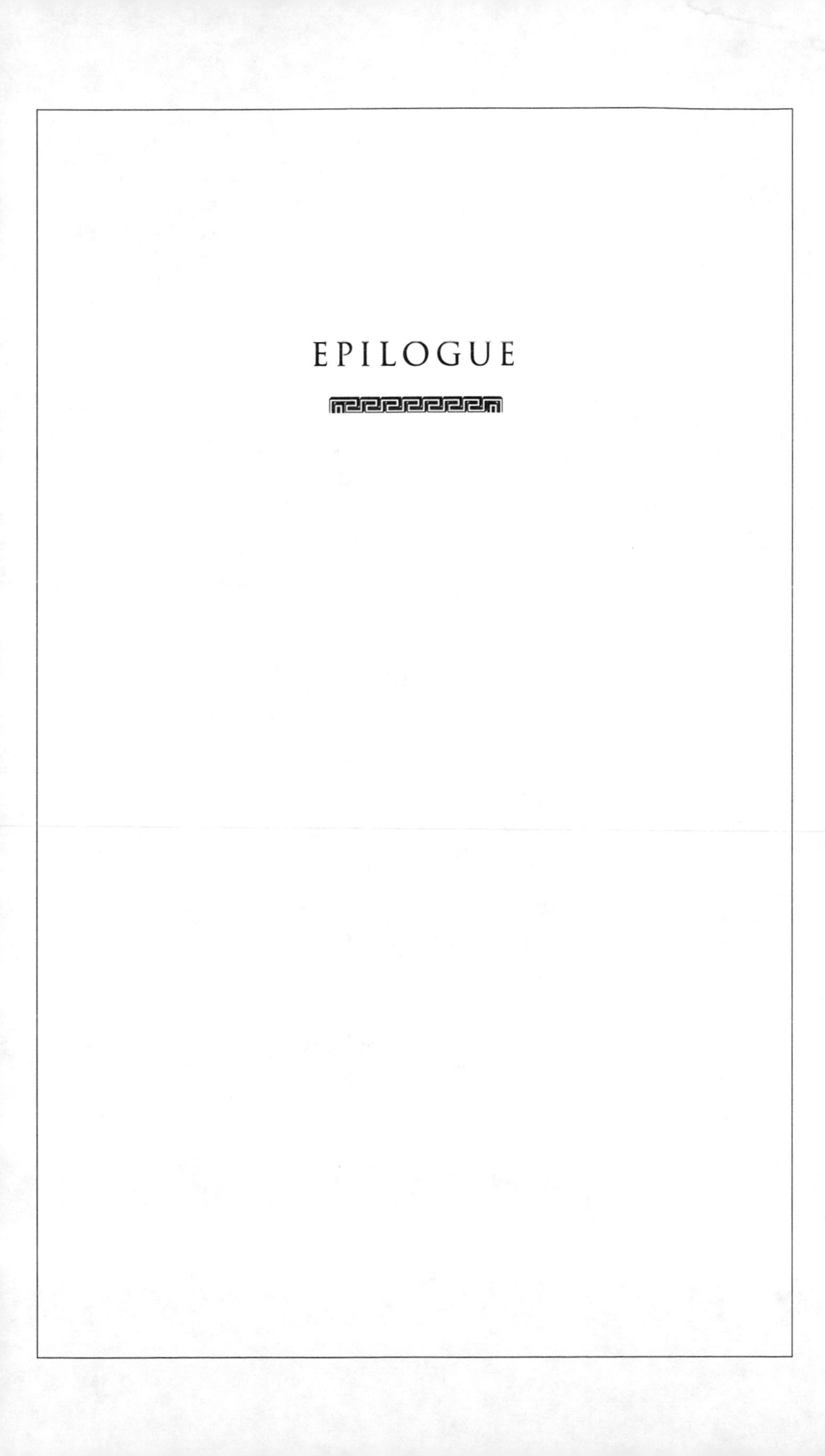

EPILOGUE

FOR SOME forty days after the resurrection, Jesus the Christ remained on earth. He ate fish with the apostles on the western shore of the Sea of Galilee. He was seen by other friends and strangers alike.

But then the time predetermined by the Father for the Son's ascension and return to heaven came upon Him, and He knew He had to tell the remaining apostles a truth they would find both sad and beautiful.

"It is My time to return from where I came," He told them as they stood on the slope of the Mount of Olives, their backs to Jerusalem, their heads turned upward toward the familiar figure who would continue to affect their lives for decades after His departure that day.

"Go into all the world and preach the gospel to every creature," He said, His arms stretched outward. "He who believes and is baptized will be saved; but he who does not believe will be condemned.

"And these signs will follow those who believe: In My name they will cast out demons; they will speak with new tongues; they will take up serpents; and if they drink anything deadly, it will by no means hurt them; they will lay hands on the sick, and they will recover."

He saw that they were troubled, uncertain, and He reminded them all of what He had said some time before.

"Do not be as you are." He spoke with great compassion. "As I had told you, My peace I leave with you. Soon, you shall be visited by a Comforter that the Father shall send to you. Be well, be strong, be faithful, My blessed ones."

Each of the eleven men spoke of their love for Him, love that would continue on until the very end of their mortal days and stay with them through eternity itself. Peter's cheeks were the first to be wet with tears, and then John's, but before long, this was true of the others as well, even Thomas.

"*Darien, are you ready?*

"*Yes, I am truly ready.*"

"*The Father is pleased with you, dear friend.*"

"*I need know nothing more, precious Lord, truly nothing more.*"

Finally, the Son of God was taken up out of their presence, and a certain angel with Him, no longer having to act as His guardian, yet who would never leave His side again.